WITHDRAWN

Slow Bleed

Slow Bleed

Trey R. Barker

FIVE STAR
A part of Gale, Cengage Learning

Farmington Hills, Mich • San Francisco • New York • Waterville, Maine
Meriden, Conn • Mason, Ohio • Chicago

Copyright © 2014 by Trey R. Barker.
Five Star™ Publishing, a part of Gale, Cengage Learning.

ALL RIGHTS RESERVED.
This novel is a work of fiction. Names, characters, places and incidents are either the product of the author's imagination, or, if real, used fictitiously.

No part of this work covered by the copyright herein may be reproduced, transmitted, stored, or used in any form or by any means graphic, electronic, or mechanical, including but not limited to photocopying, recording, scanning, digitizing, taping, Web distribution, information networks, or information storage and retrieval systems, except as permitted under Section 107 or 108 of the 1976 United States Copyright Act, without the prior written permission of the publisher.

The publisher bears no responsibility for the quality of information provided through author or third-party Web sites and does not have any control over, nor assume any responsibility for, information contained in these sites. Providing these sites should not be construed as an endorsement or approval by the publisher of these organizations or of the positions they may take on various issues.

LIBRARY OF CONGRESS CATALOGING-IN-PUBLICATION DATA

Barker, Trey R., author.
Slow bleed / Trey R. Barker.–First edition.
pages cm
ISBN 978-1-4328-2912-4 (hardcover) — ISBN 1-4328-2912-2 (hardcover) — ISBN 978-1-4328-2910-0 (ebook)
1. Correctional personnel—Fiction. 2. Policewomen—Fiction. 3. Police—Texas—Fiction. I. Title.
PS3602.A77555S58 2014
813'.6—dc23 2014018582

First Edition. First Printing: September 2014
Find us on Facebook– https://www.facebook.com/FiveStarCengage
Visit our website– http://www.gale.cengage.com/fivestar/
Contact Five Star™ Publishing at FiveStar@cengage.com

Printed in the United States of America
1 2 3 4 5 6 7 18 17 16 15 14

Slow Bleed

Chapter One

She was in the tree again.

Sitting with Gramma in the here and now, nerves as tight as a garrote, Jace Salome was also in that tree so many years ago.

There had been a new tenant in 2-F. He'd come into the office, smelling of pecans, eyes blazing like the tip of his lit cigar, and demanded a room. He'd dropped some money on the counter and Gramma's smile never faltered. She'd had him sign the registry, gave him two keys, and slipped his money into the ancient cash register.

Gramma's smile had stayed in place until the man was gone, but it hadn't been Gramma's regular smile. Not the one that sometimes asked—with no words—did Jace want some ice cream or did she want to go to the zoo or maybe Dennis the Menace Park? It was a hard, plastic thing that had scared Jace.

When they were alone, Jace had asked, "Why's that man angry?"

Gramma had traded the ugly smile for her real one and shooed Jace outside. "Go get some sun and don't worry about that old coot."

"His money's as good as anyone's."

Gramma had laughed. It had been Grapa's saying.

Rather than going outside, Jace had sulked in the lobby. "I miss Nancy."

"I know you do, but she couldn't stay here anymore."

"You could have let her stay without paying."

"I did, Jace, for six months. Nancy's problems were bigger than not being able to pay her rent."

"You think she still has Sophie?"

Sophie was a yellow Lab, Nancy's closest friend and getting to be Jace's closest friend until Nancy had quietly slipped away beneath a full moon two nights before the new tenant showed up.

"Of course she does."

"You think Sophie's hungry?"

For a split second, Gramma had been grim-faced. "Yeah, she might be. They might both be. Now get outta here."

Forced outside, Jace had sat near the Sea Spray's pool and hummed along with the gospel music coming from Preacher's apartment. It was then she had heard the new tenant.

"What the—? Hah." His voice, as brittle as old paper, had still somehow boomed through the U-shaped hotel. "Somebody left their damned dogs and ain't that too bad."

The old man had found a box of seven puppies left in the ceiling tiles. Six were already dead, the last near death. Carrying the puppy, he strode to the second-floor balcony and tossed it over the side.

The puppy had fallen toward Grapa's ash trees, its paws scratching the empty air. It crashed through the leaves and came to rest in a branch.

"Gramma! He killed the dog." Jace had bolted from the pool and heaved herself into the tree. A hot breath later, she'd held the puppy tightly against her chest. When it peed on her, she hadn't cared. She'd been scared enough to pee, too. When the puppy let fly again, the urine was so strong Jace smelled it years later in memories.

"Come on, I'll get you down."

But she hadn't been able to. She'd needed both hands to climb down, but had refused to let go of the dog.

Even when it began to rain dead puppies.

"Call the garbage man," the old man had said gleefully, tossing the dead puppies over the railing one by one.

Their bodies had tumbled over her as Gramma came from the office, her face pale. Then the firemen arrived and a big man had climbed up, grabbed her by the hand and the dog by the scruff, and taken them down.

"Don't worry, sweetie," the fireman said. "You'll be fine."

Gramma said the same thing now, to a twenty-five-year-old granddaughter rather than an eleven-year-old girl, as wisps of steam rose from dinner. "You'll be fine, Jace." But her smile was the ugly one.

"Who are you trying to convince?" Sighing, Jace pushed her dinner plate away while the daylight disappeared as slowly as a lumbering old man.

"You don't like?"

"I always like, Gramma. You're the best cook in town."

"Well . . . the best within earshot."

Brisket, slathered in a rich, tangy sauce, along with homemade macaroni and cheese, some store-bought coleslaw, ditto the peach cobbler. The sauce's aroma lingered just over the smell of the desert: dry, a thin layer of greasy oil and earthy cattle. Those smells were comforting. The safety of home could be found in the spice of barbeque, the chemical bite of drilling rigs and the burn-off at the wellheads, the meaty and musky aroma of cattle, and the odor of desert dirt, which was as dry as the smell of an old, protective cowboy.

"Thank you, Gramma. I appreciate it."

Gramma flashed a grin. Her fork played idly in the remains of her coleslaw. "Pish, it wasn't any effort. Cooking is about the last thing this old woman has left."

"What about the Hot Five?"

She chuckled. "Anyway, I thought you might need a good

meal, being your first night and all."

"I've worked there now for nearly two months."

"Training and going to the Academy and more training. This is your first night by yourself. I thought you might have some jitters."

Freight trucks roared past on Interstate 20, headed deep into the desert. Under their thunder, the wooden deck shook. Old and weathered, stained gray from the rare west Texas rainstorms, the deck was perched on the roof of the hotel's lobby and office. When they sat there, the ladies felt the rumble of every truck and every freight train through their feet and behinds.

Jace slid her arms around her middle. "Man, I hate that."

"The ground shaking beneath your feet?" Gramma laughed. "Maybe that's because you've had too much ground shaking in your life."

"Gramma, don't."

Gramma piled another helping of brisket onto Jace's plate. "You know, brisket hath charms to soothe the savage blah blah blah."

Ignoring the food, Jace put her hands under her thighs.

The Zachary County Jail housed more than three hundred prisoners and now it—and they—were Jace Salome's job. Murderers, rapists, thieves. It was Jace's job to keep men and women warehoused until someone else made a decision about them. Her dreams the last two months had been filled with angry inmates or inmates with HIV or hepatitis C spitting at her, or inmates facing life with no possibility of parole slicing her open with a sharpened toothbrush.

"You talked in your sleep this afternoon." A chunk of corn bread disappeared into Gramma's mouth.

"Did not."

"Sure did."

"I'm not that worried."

"Sure are."

"Did it scare you . . . me sleep-talking again?"

Gramma set her fork down. "You bet it did. Doesn't it you?"

"Nah." She couldn't hold Gramma's eyes and she knew the woman heard the lie. "Maybe a little."

Jace picked at her food while they stared at the highway. The traffic never stopped. People headed to or from work, or to the airport between here and Midland–Odessa or the bars strung along the highway like burned-out bulbs on a Christmas string. Or maybe, Jace thought, they were headed down the road deeper into something unknown.

Right now, as her brisket cooled and drew flies, the cloudless blue sky became pale pink and striking purple, festooned with orange and blood red and slashes of mint green. The street lights winked on and cast blue-white circles every thirty feet that marched, soldier-like, past the hotel and the Denny's just across the highway. The light-circles ignored the people headed to the nearby bowling alley and the passing cars and trucks and the dogs howling plaintively.

"They sound like that," Jace said.

"Who sounds like what?"

"The inmates."

That sound had been one of the early, harsh lessons at the Academy. Locked down for the night, most inmates slept, but a handful were awake all night and some of those who were awake cried.

"Want me to sing?"

Jace laughed, embarrassed, as she dished up peach cobbler. "I'll be okay."

"Don't be ashamed of that song."

"I'm not." She shoved the cobbler away, her taste for it gone.

"Do you regret it?"

"Man, Gramma, our dinner talk have to be so heavy?" Jace

wiped her lips, stuffed some of the brisket into a Tupperware for her dinner break, and dumped on a ton of sauce. "Remember the puppy?"

"I do. Think one of those dogs is him?"

A metaphorical question. Even eleven-year-old Jace had understood she couldn't keep the dog. It would have been unfair to keep a Lab without a yard so Jace had given the dog to her second-grade best friend. At the end of the school year, the girl's family had moved to Dallas and taken the dog with them.

"Regret the new job?"

"No." She paused. "I don't think so." She paused again. "Maybe. I don't know."

"You can always quit."

"I know, Gramma."

"It's a bad job."

"I know, Gramma."

Gramma sighed. "I guess I just miss my friend."

"I'm right here."

"Yeah, but now you're a big girl. Got yourself a job and responsibilities and all the rest and that's fine. If that's what you want, it's what I want for you. But you listen to me, big girl. I don't care how old you get or how well you do at the Sheriff's Office. Hell, even if you get yourself elected sheriff, you will always be my little girl."

Heat flooded Jace's cheeks. She took Gramma's hand.

"Little girls can always come home, turn down that air conditioner, and climb their rear ends under a pile of comforters."

Jace laughed. "And get some of your tea?"

"With tequila . . . if you're not on duty." Gramma winked and slurped up the last of her peach cobbler. "I'd better get this cleaned up."

"I'll help."

"Pish. Get your uniform on, let me take some embarrassing pictures, then get out. You've got work and I've got poker."

Chapter Two

Two hours later, Jace stood at the back of the jail.

She'd seen a building once, in Washington, D.C. Ten, maybe twelve stories, not a single window, and built entirely of black stone like a black hole in the middle of the city. The Zachary County Jail made her just as uneasy as the building in Washington had. This was beige stone rather than black, and three stories rather than ten or twelve. The front of the building was the political face of the Zachary County Sheriff's Office, the side with "Sheriff's Office" written in large, comfortable letters just above a huge five-pointed star. Beneath that, signs welcomed the public and directed them to various places. That side was decoratively lit with colored floodlights on the landscaping and spotlights on the sheriff's name and the badge. But back here, in a parking lot that was never empty, there was no pretense. Around front was where the sheriff's politics were done but back here was where the sheriff's business was done. This was where people surrendered their freedom—sometimes voluntarily, usually not.

Jace clamped her hands around the steering wheel of her tired, old Acura. *I've been through orientation and field training. I graduated third in my class at the Academy. Why is my head pounding? Why is my uniform shirt so much tighter than I remember?*

At the secured door, she pushed the buzzer and a gruff voice answered. "What?"

"Uh . . . Deputy Salome."

There was a second of silence, then an impossibly loud, metallic click. Jace startled.

"You coming or what?"

Take a breath, Jace, and go do your new job.

"In or out," the voice said.

"Yes, sir."

"It's a secure facility, *Deputy* Salome," the disembodied voice said. Though she heard it through a speaker mounted above the door, she knew it came from the control room deep in the jail. "Stay or go, I don't give a shit long as that door's secure, you got me?"

"Yes, sir."

With a tug, Jace made sure the door was secure behind her and then stepped into her first night.

Ten minutes later, conversation flowed around her like a summer sandstorm. Some conversations were as harsh as those sandstorms while others were as easy and comfortable as an occasional spring rain.

At orientation two months ago, no one had said much of anything. It had been a room full of scared recruits, some wondering if law enforcement was right for them, others absolutely convinced of it, but all of them fingering their new badges.

When Sergeant Alan Dillon slipped into the room—peacefully as befit his five-foot frame and lack of body heft—everyone quieted. "Evening, all, good to see you. Most of you."

The room oozed laughter, with everyone making a guess as to whom Dillon meant.

This was what Jace had expected; this kind of laughter and camaraderie. Through her two weeks at the Academy, she'd heard about the brotherhood. And yeah, it sounded like bullshit—bunches of people pinning a badge to their chests and suddenly deciding they were kindred spirits—but with the correctional officers heading out on the 11 p.m. to 7 a.m. dead shift, Jace enjoyed a small taste of that brotherhood.

Dillon chuckled. "You know who you are."

Another round of laughter and then Dillon handed out assignments. There was no quick hit of special problems—moving inmates to and from the courthouse across the street, inmates going to meetings with lawyers, dealing with state inspections or medical call or the myriad of other things that clog the day shift—because so few of those particular problems touched the dead shift.

Jace was glad of it. Though she wasn't sure she'd like working overnights, she wanted to start on dead shift. Other than a few surprise shakedowns at the Academy, she hadn't yet spent any real time with any prisoners. Working this shift would give her time to get some grit under her nails and get over her anxiety about the prisoners. On the dead shift, most of the inmates would be locked down and asleep in their cells; locked doors would give her a chance to find her feet before she had to deal with any serious problems.

Standing behind the battered podium, Dillon finished the assignments and ground his teeth together. "Sonny Lee Brook has popped back up on our radar." Dillon waved off the chorus of shock. "Listen up, people. He made a snatch in Austin. But this time it was a thirty-two-year-old woman."

"What?" a jailer said. "An adult?"

"Son of a bitch shouldn't have been out," said an angry middle-aged jailer on the far side of the room.

The entire room was angry, Jace realized, and that anger had come suddenly, as though someone had hit everyone with 100,000 volts.

"Should have fried his ass in Huntsville when he was there."

Dillon said, "The State does what the State does. Keep your

ears open, boys and girls, for conversation on the pods. His closest family is Ector County but he plays in our sandbox, too." The sergeant grimaced. "Sorry, bad choice of words. I'm sure he knows some of our frequent flyers so pay attention, you might hear something from the inmates that helps find the woman. Or, barring that, helps put Brook away."

"Again."

Taking a breath, Dillon wiped his face. "This is a bad transition, I know, but for those of you who haven't noticed yet, for our first shift of the month, there is a newbie in our midst . . . a little fresh meat."

"Newbie newbie," someone said.

"Rookie playa," another one said.

"Got ourselves a worm."

The vets glanced at her and Jace staggered beneath their inspection.

"Jace Salome, lately graduated from the Academy," Dillon said. "Ladies and gentlemen, do remember what it was like on your first day, okay? No practical jokes, no false fire alarms, no reports of a mass escape or a riot in the discipline pod."

Jace's hands trembled. Yeah, she was scared to death, but law enforcement was completely alien. No one in her family had ever worn a badge and being a police officer was not something she had ever really thought about. But some of her fear came from the size of the job. She'd worked at a pizza place, at a miniature golf course, and a music store. Pleasant little jobs all, paying just enough to cover rent and a handful of new jazz CDs every month. But wearing a badge was the biggest thing she'd ever jumped into in her life.

"Salome," Dillon said. "A Pod."

"That's the red stripe," someone called. "You know, the stripes on the floor?"

"Stop it," Dillon said. "A Pod is the blue stripe."

"Right," she said. "Red stripe is medical."

"Well . . . she knows her colors anyway."

"What about the floor?" someone asked.

"You know where the floor is, right?" Dillon asked with an easy smile.

A chuckle ran through the room. Jace said, "I'm sure I can find it."

"Don't worry about it, you'll be fine. And A Pod should be nice and quiet."

Somewhere near the back of the room, someone snorted. "Come on, Sarge, give her something challenging."

"Gonna be a challenge tonight," a youngish jailer said. "Mister Tate came in last night."

Jace's stomach tightened.

"Don't sweat it, sister," said a female correctional officer sitting next to Jace. "Tate's not a big deal."

"Who is he?"

"Frequent flyer. Here once a month or so, usually for misdemeanoring."

"Misdemeanoring?"

"Minor crap," the woman said. She brushed a lock of dark hair from her face. That hair framed her light-colored eyes and made them seem as though they were floating. "Disorderly conduct, stuff like that."

"We bring people to jail for dis con?"

"Not most people, but Mister Tate isn't most people. Most people like to leave their clothes on." The woman offered her hand. "Rory Bogan."

She was a thin woman, probably weighing no more than 110 or 115, with a slim build and a face that ran almost sallow. But something hinted at toughness.

"I'm Jace Salome."

"Don't sweat Tate. By the time we get done here, everyone in

A Pod'll be locked down for the night."

"Urrea. You've got medical," Dillon said.

A Hispanic man, maybe late thirties, groaned. "Great. Just what I wanna do tonight: listen to everyone complain."

"They complain in medical?" Jace asked Bogan.

Bogan grinned. "Every inmate thinks they're getting screwed on medical. They all come down with something as soon as they get here. Suddenly they want treatment for whatever they ignored on the outside. Dr. Cruz doesn't work that way. So most inmates are pissed off about medical pretty much all the time."

"Bogan?" Dillon called.

"Yo?"

"Booking."

"I hate booking."

"Such is the burden of life, deputy. Do it anyway."

"Long as you put it that way."

Booking meant newly arrived prisoners and newly arrived frequently meant angry. Many of the fights in a jail happened in booking, when people got processed and photographed and fingerprinted, when they got strip-searched and cavity searched and showered and were handed a uniform worn by a thousand other inmates, and suddenly understood jail was real.

"Salome?" Dillon said in a voice much bigger than his frame. "You hear me?"

"Uh . . . yes, sir. I . . . uh—"

"He ain't no sir," one of the older guys said. "He's a sergeant."

The room laughed. Bogan winked. "Don't worry about him, he's an idiot."

"Sergeant Dillon or the jailer?"

Bogan frowned thoughtfully. "I'll get back to you. You'll be fine, Salome. These guys give you any guff, just shoot 'em. They gave you a gun, right?"

"Shoot them?" She blinked. "Uh . . . yeah, they gave me a weapon, but—"

"Joke. Lighten up or you'll have a heart attack before your first hanging."

Jace paused. "Hanging? That the best you guys can do for fun?"

For a long moment, Bogan stared, surprise ripe on her face. "Keep that sense of humor because sometimes it gets ugly around here."

"Like always with a newbie," Dillon said. "Answer her questions."

He said the right things, Jace realized, but there was a bit of mischief in his tone as though he expected them to lead her astray. Jace took a deep breath. *They'll harass you for a few nights, then it'll be over. Or it won't be and you'll run screaming into the night, crying like that little girl who helped the firemen gather up the dead puppies.*

"All right, that's it," Dillon said. "Hit the bricks. Salome, a word?"

As the room cleared out, Dillon pulled her aside. "I know you're scared, but—"

"Not at all, sir."

"You had any brains, you'd be scared. But you can do this. You did pretty well at the Academy—"

"Not as well as I wanted."

"Well enough. But this is the gig, your career starts now. Don't be stupid, don't be dangerous, don't be gullible. Those inmates will tell you anything and everything, whatever they think you want to hear as long as it gets them on sick call or extra food or privileges or whatever."

"You're saying it'll all be crap?"

"Not all of it, there will be things you need to listen to,

information you need to remember, but most of it will be Grade A crap."

"But what if I think it's crap and they end up dying or something?" A medical condition she didn't recognize or someone edging toward suicide were two of her biggest fears.

Dillon shook his head. "You'll learn to sort the crap from the real. And don't sweat the dying. You know how long it's been since an inmate died in custody here?"

Jace snorted. "Means we're about due, doesn't it?"

Dillon laughed. "No one ever dies on an officer's first night." His laugh faded. "If you're not sure, ask someone. Ask everyone. These officers will screw with you, but when it gets serious, they will be there for you."

Jace nodded.

Dillon locked eyes with her. "As you will be for them. If the shit hits the fan, you jump your ass in and help protect your fellow officers, right?"

"Yes, sir." God, was he trying to ratchet up her fear? Was he trying to convince her to hand over her badge even before she'd worked a shift?

He turned his radio up. A jumble of voices exploded. There were so many that a single one was nearly impossible to distinguish.

—hah, get him out here—

—456 . . . you sign on yet—

—don't give me that, get me—

—prisoner in booking—

—401 . . . medical to D Pod—

—498 . . . where—

—405 . . . sarge you on air?—

Dillon keyed the mic clipped at his shoulder. "Stand by."

—10-4—

It was chaotic chatter. She'd heard that clearly enough when she'd been working with a training officer. But that had been different; there had always been someone with her, listening and relaying anything that had to do with her. This was her, now. She was expected to hear through this riot of noise; translate it and understand it and act on it.

"Keep your ear glued." He tapped her radio. "Lotta people talking, they'll be doing it all night. Most of it won't have anything to do with you. You listen for your badge number, listen for me, listen for calls for help."

"If I hear a call, what should I do?"

His eyes narrowed. "What do you think you should do?"

Jace licked her lips. "Stay in my assignment unless I am specifically called."

"Good, solid, Academy answer."

But not, she thought, the answer her sergeant wanted. She hesitated.

"You will," he said, his voice soft in the empty room. "Stay in your assignment. Unless you hear someone call you."

Coming from him, those words had a different texture but his deep-set eyes gave nothing away. "Ask questions. Again, don't be stupid, don't be gullible, don't be dangerous. Make sure you go home at the end of the shift. Now get outta here."

Breathing deeply, trying not to show how scared and nervous and exhilarated and anxious and alive she was, Jace picked up the blue strip amid the mass of colored stripes snaking along the concrete floor. She followed it down the short hallway and around a corner into the main hallway. Branching from this corridor were all the support and supply offices. Further down, near the end, the hallway broke off into booking and the five housing pods.

Back the other direction was the main outer doorway to this part of the facility. Two thick, metal doors with tempered glass at the top, giving deputies a visual on anyone who might want in. Hard to tell who it might be, though, Jace thought, with the lightbulb burned out.

Just now a man knocked at that door. He was shrouded in darkness. His head tilted slightly and its oval shape caught a bit of orange light from the parking lot light almost directly behind him.

"Hey, how'ya doing?" the man said, slamming the door behind him. He emerged into the hallway light, a badge on a chain swinging from his neck.

"Good."

"Newbie?"

Jace ground her teeth together, wondering at the scarlet letter that must be on her forehead.

He pointed to her radio. "The old hands always turn theirs on as soon they leave roll call. Worms never do."

Jace clicked the radio on. A buzz filled the air. She understood exactly none of it.

—giddy up and open that door, control—

—giddy up and bite me—

—all call from 405: a bit of professionalism here, can we please?—

—yes, sir—

—booking from control got two coming, separate sides of a bar fight—

—control 10-4—

—Doc Wrubel to medical, please—

—415 medical outer—

She closed her eyes. How was she ever going to learn to listen through that? Listen for 479 and 405, she told herself. Ignore everything else right now except for your and Dillon's badge numbers.

The man winked. "Plus, I've been teaching here a lot of years and I know all the jailers." He extended a hand. "Will Badgett. I teach control tactics. Ground fighting, baton usage, edged weapon defense, that kind of thing."

She shook his hand. "Jace Salome. This is my first night."

"First night?" He grinned. "Man, to be back on my first night. I worked outta San Antonio PD. About ten years. Had to take a medical leave. This a great job, Deputy Salome, a great job. Not to sound too corny, but we are society's first line of defense against everything." He clapped his hands together and licked his lips. "I'd give anything to be back on the first shift, looking ahead to thirty years of taking care of people. You're going to have a ton of fun, but—" His face lost the grin and went dead serious. "Be careful. See everything and hear even more. Everything you hear in that pod means something, get me? Every sound has a reason. Know the sound, know the reason. After all, it doesn't take long to get stabbed, does it? Blink of an eye and you've got a shiv sticking outta your throat."

Almost unconsciously, she ran a hand along the tattoo at the base of her neck.

"I can help with all that, though. Come take a class. Or better yet, come join us."

"What?"

His chest swelled and he stood an inch or so taller. "Total Force. My group of guys—guys being both men and women. A support group for officers. We have a newsletter and do classes and seminars together. Our focus is self-defense . . . ground fighting, that kind of thing. Sometimes we go to defense expos or tournaments. It's great fun and it might save your life someday." He winked. "We have a banquet once a year, too."

Christ, she thought, *enough with the "might get hurt on duty" stuff.*

"Pretty soon we're going to build a brand new facility. I just bought a beautiful piece of land." He winked. "Got a couple sites, but the main one is right up the road from some good fishing, if that's your bag."

"So . . . beat each other's brains out, then go fish."

He chuckled. "Something like that. But we got all kinds of stuff going on. Got a couple members who have a band and one guy does woodworking. There's one guy here in Zachary County—Sacco—who brews his own beer. Godawful stuff but he keeps trying." Badgett laughed. "So it's not all fighting, we like to have fun, too. You should check us out."

An older man, wearing the green pants of the Zachary County Sheriff's Office but a white shirt, came around the corner. The white shirt denoted him as administration, though Jace had no idea who he was.

"Badgett," the man said, his voice tight.

"Chief Cornutt, how'ya doing tonight?" Badgett looked at his watch. "Working late, huh? Getting the files cleaned up for the vacation? A month in Mexico." Badgett sighed as though he could already smell the beaches and ocean.

"Listen, I want that advanced CT class next month. Got it approved so get it scheduled."

Badgett nodded. "I've got a couple of dates already open for it."

The Chief nodded. "Good. I've got a list of possible students. I'll email 'em over."

"You're the boss."

Chief Cornutt smiled but shook his head. "Absolutely not. Couldn't pay me enough for that." He nodded at Jace. "Deputy, you coming on or going off?"

"Coming on, sir."

"Have a good shift and be careful."

"Yes, sir."

With a brisk nod, Cornutt disappeared back down the main hallway.

Badgett smiled and clapped Jace on the shoulder as he headed toward Dillon's office. "Have a great shift, Deputy, and welcome to law enforcement."

Two minutes later, in front of A Pod, she waited for a break in radio traffic.

—control from 410. Looking to get into medical—

—10-4—

—inmate in main hallway—

—405 . . . on air?—

—go ahead for 405—

Dillon's voice. She tried to fix that in her brain. Dillon, if she needed him, was 405.

—445 . . . medical to B Pod—

—all call . . . tomorrow's court docket is up. Check for your inmates—

—453 from 498—

—498, go ahead—

—Mexican?—

—again? How often can you eat that stuff? Gotta be Italian tonight—

When the conversation lessened, Jace keyed the mic clipped at her left shoulder. "A outer. Uh . . . sorry, Pod A . . . uh . . . A as in Adam, outer door. Uh . . . this is 479."

"Yeah, yeah." The control room voice was tinny and thin over her radio, but the man's exasperation was all too clear.

Half a heartbeat later, the lock on the thick metal door popped, the snap deep and metallic and jarring. She stepped inside, let the door close behind her, then checked to ensure it had closed.

"A-adam . . . uh . . . inner."

This time, it took a few seconds for the inner door—the one leading directly into A Pod—to pop open. With a deep breath, Jace Salome stepped into her jail.

Chapter Three

Immediately, the eyes were on her.

All those eyes put sandpaper in her throat. At the Academy, she'd seen some prisoners and dealt with a few during exercises but this was different. This wasn't a student learning how to do things. This was her jail, these were her prisoners, and so their anger was directed specifically at her as the one in uniform.

—429 . . . 10-88 line three—

—434 . . . 10-19 the squad room—

—419 . . . 10-59 to booking—

Her nose twitched with the jail smell. Stale, sweaty, enclosed. Unwashed clothes and bodies, a tinge of food—Ramen Noodles, bologna, chips and soda—traces of blood and urine and shit. It wasn't the smell of despair, that was too melodramatic, but it certainly was the odor of the lesser part of humanity.

"Officer?" an inmate asked. He stood against the wall a few feet from the pod's main door. Sweat dotted his forehead and his face.

What are you still doing out, she wondered. *Why are any of you guys still out? Lights out lockdown should have been an hour ago.*

"I'm Officer Salome. And you are?"

When his darting eyes came to hers, she flinched. "You've got to help me. I didn't do anything, I shouldn't be here."

"Ain't none of us should be here." A second inmate's laughter dissipated into a game of dominoes.

"Been trying to get my money back from my lawyer," said another.

Jace shrugged at the sweating man, unsure what to do.

"I know you think it's bullshit, but it's true. Yeah, I drove without a license. Whatever. Get me a fine or community service. But I swear to God if you don't let me out, I'll die."

"You're not going to die," Jace said.

"Don't let them murder me."

"Whoa. Them, who?" Jace caught herself moving toward the guy, a calming hand out to steady him.

"Get away from me." He batted her hand away and bared his teeth.

Shocked, she backed away, one hand on her radio, the other resting on her baton.

He snorted. "Yeah, better call 'em 'cause I'll jump on you."

"Them, who?" she asked again, trying to keep her voice calm.

"Any of them. All of them. He wants them to kill me."

"Hey, I've got an idea, how about we go to M Pod and see if maybe there's someone there you can talk to."

"You fucking bitch." He spat the words. "Don't patronize me. I'm not some psycho who needs medical. I'm telling you, they will kill me."

She nodded. "Fine. Let's talk about it, then. I just got here, I have no idea what's going on. Explain it to me. Why are they going to kill you?"

"Because he thinks I—because he told them to. He hates me."

"He, who? And why does he hate you?"

"Because he knows. Because he thinks he knows, anyway."

"Knows what?" She frowned in frustration. "Who?"

"Back up, Thomas," a commanding voice ordered.

Jace spun. One hand played at her radio, ready to call the emergency response team in.

"Easy, I'm one of you." The jailer glared at the inmate. "Thomas, back the hell up or we'll go 'round right here."

—control room to 410 you guys good?—

The jailer keyed his mic. "We're fine." He waved at the camera. "Get outta here, Thomas. No one's going to kill you. No one talked about you."

The officer jabbed a finger into Thomas' chest, backing the inmate up until he bumped against the wall. "Hell, no one thinks about you at all."

The man straightened his spine. "My family does."

"Your family?" The officer crowded Thomas. "Your daughter can't stand you. Same as your wife. None of your family ever wants to see you again."

"That's not—"

"Your wife called me, you know that? Asked me to let her know if you managed to bail outta here."

The man looked stricken. "No, she didn't, she—"

"Ain't gonna be there when you get home." Another step, another finger jab. "If you get home."

Jace's heart pounded. Her skin was hot. The officer's body language reeked of violence. "Deputy." She tried to slip between the two men but the deputy pushed her back.

"You don't like hearing this?" the jailer asked the inmate. "Yeah, raise those hands to me, boy, get 'em up. I'll tear you apart, you won't even know what hit you and I'd have to call the coroner."

Thomas jammed his hands behind him. It made him look even more vulnerable.

A smile slipped across the jailer's face. "Just telling the truth, boy. Something you ain't done since you got here."

"Officer." Jace put a hand on the deputy's arm.

He shook it off. "Tell the truth." He got louder, drawing gazes from the other inmates. "Tell us why you're here."

"I don't know—"

"Tell us what you did." The officer's voice boomed. His hands clenched.

A stain of piss spread down the inmate's legs. "I didn't—"

"Tell me or—"

"Deputy." She tried to pull him away from Thomas.

He spun, his eyes like burning acid. "Get your hands off me." He looked at Thomas. "You get shook down today?"

"Jesus Christ, ain't three times a day enough?" Thomas said.

Instead of answering, the officer stalked back to the jailer's desk. "It'll come out. Yeah, baby, it'll damn sure come out."

Keeping her hand on her radio, Jace stepped away while Thomas stayed against the wall, his face both angry and scared.

At the jailer's desk, the officer whistled a few bars, stood with his hands locked behind his back, bouncing back and forth on the balls of his feet. "Yeah?" he called to Thomas. "Got something to say?"

Silence fell over the entire pod and time drew out like a blade from a chest. Jace kept her eyes on the inmate, her hand on her baton.

"Didn't think so," the jailer said.

Thomas moved to the bottom of the stairs. Once there, he put his back to those stairs, his eyes constantly on the mass of men. *He doesn't want anyone behind him,* Jace realized, *just like when he stood back against the wall. That way, he can see everyone in the room.*

"Holy crap," she said, heading to the jailer's desk.

"Scared you pretty good," the jailer said. He chuckled. "Sorry 'bout that."

"I wasn't scared."

"Okay."

Jace frowned. "What's the deal?"

"With?"

"With Thomas. Guy's scared to death."

"He's a newbie. Doesn't have any hard yet."

"Uh . . . okay. I'm Salome. I'm—"

"A newbie, too," the jailer said. His voice hardened. "Listen up, worm. Don't ever get in my face again. I'll punch a shitty officer as quickly as I'd punch a shitbag criminal."

She bristled. "I did my FTO before the Academy. I've got a few hours in."

"Yeah . . . okay." Reynolds, his nameplate said.

—410 from 453—

Reynolds keyed his shoulder mic. "Go ahead, 453."

Over the radio, 453's voice crackled like fire.

—so, these three rabbis walk into a titty bar—

Reynolds laughed, a loud braying sound. "Don't even say it," he answered. "Man, that's evil. You're going to hell for that."

—am not—

—are, too, so shut up—

—you shut up—

—both of you shut up—

Dillon's voice.

—if you can't be professional, sign out and go home—

Reynolds smirked. "Dillon's own little power trip."

Jace surveyed the pod, trying to fix every face in her memory. "Why are they still out?" When her eyes passed over an older man playing cards, the man nodded a greeting. "I thought lights out was ten o'clock."

"Evening, rookie CO," the older man said, his tone playful. He slapped a card down on the table. Another inmate snatched the card, threw his entire hand down.

"Gentlemen," Jace said.

"Gentlemen?" Reynolds said. "I don't think so."

"Oh, now, CO," a younger man said from near the TV. "We got all kinds'a gentlemens in here. 'Course I ain't one of 'em,

I'm a stone cold killer."

"No one's talking to you, Billy." To Jace, Reynolds said, "Figured I'd let you lock down top tier tonight, being your first night and all."

"Gee, thanks."

After glancing at the computer that controlled the individual cell doors, Reynolds grabbed a small newsletter. When he saw her looking at it, he gave it a shake. The logo was an intertwined and stylized T and F. "Total Force. It's a professional group I belong to."

"Hmm."

"By the way, it'd been me? I'd'a thumped his skull." Reynolds nodded toward Thomas. "Put his hands on me like that, thump thump."

"He barely touched me."

"Shouldn't have touched you at all."

—all call . . . Doc's 10-6 dinner break—

Jace frowned. Like with 95 percent of the 10 codes, she had no idea what 10-6 was. "Wasn't a big deal."

"Yeah, but maybe next time he throws a punch. Maybe him and some other guy drag you to the rec room when I'm not looking." Reynolds shook his head adamantly. "Nobody touches me. Thump thump."

"Thump thump, huh?"

"You betcha." He rattled the newsletter again. "I made the newsletter three times. I've won a few tournaments." A well-thumbed white sheet slipped out from the bottom of the newsletter. Reynolds stuck it in his pocket and flexed a bicep. "First in my class in ground fighting. Mr. Badgett taught me well."

"Badgett? I met him earlier."

"He's putting together another advanced class. You should take it. He teaches control tactics all over the state. I can fight anyone in this entire jail." He gave her a long, sideways look. "Inmate or copper."

Jace nodded toward one of the cameras hanging like spiders in a corner of the pod. "Wouldn't look too good in court."

His nose twitched, a man sniffing something offensive. "Court, huh?"

"Make sure you're not on camera when you beat somebody." She'd meant it as a joke, just a way to cover the unease his hard face hammered through her. "First lesson in the Academy."

"First lesson is go home alive."

"Fair point."

"Wouldn't go to court anyway. An officer's got the right to defend himself. DA would never charge."

"Lucky there's no tape, though, huh?"

Now he grinned, his teeth clean and white. "You betcha."

Few areas were videotaped constantly. A watch commander could record any area if needed, but only problem areas got taped twenty-four hours a day. Booking. Medical. The discipline pod. Where the fights happened, where inmates or officers were most likely to find themselves at the bloody end of a shank.

"Have to defend yourself often?" Jace asked, trying for conversational.

—456 10-25 squad—

—10-4—

—. . . ah . . . 10-22 I found it—

Without answering, Reynolds strolled the pod. His fingers, long as snakes, touched everything. Tables and chairs, the dominoes game, inmates' cards. He stopped near the TV and changed the channel a few times, oblivious to the annoyance on the face of the inmate watching TV. Then he walked past all the cells on the lower tier, tugging every door to make sure it was locked. Eventually he came back to the control desk.

"This is my pod, Salome. I own it, and I have to defend

myself all the time." He stood behind the desk and surveyed his kingdom. "This ain't no panty-waist job. Sooner you figure that out, better off you'll be. That guy right there? Billy?"

"The stone cold killer?"

Reynolds nodded. "Mother. Father. Sister. Tore 'em up with a machete."

Right now, the stone cold killer sat at an empty card table, head back, eyes closed, a string of drool leaking down the side of his face.

"What about him?" Jace indicated Thomas.

"Idiot thinks someone is out to get him."

"Thinks someone has told the inmates about him. Is he a stone cold killer, too?"

Reynolds laughed. "Ain't nothing but a troublemaker. Got picked up on a failure to appear for driving revoked."

—479 from 456—

Troublemaker? Jace found that hard to believe. The man had been cowering and now stood quivering and ready to get locked into his cell for the night. *Watch him,* Jace thought. *When they're scared is when they'll do something crazy.*

—479 . . . 456—

"Hey," Reynolds said. "She's calling you. You deef?"

—479. Salome? You there? Meet me in the go-between—

"Ten-four," Jace said. "456 . . . that's Bogan."

"This ain't my first rodeo, I know who's who. Get back quick, past time for lockdown."

She headed for the inner door, trying to keep her eyes on the inmates as she walked away from them. She felt obvious and foolish. At the door, she keyed her mic. "A Pod . . . A-adam. Inner door."

When the door popped, she stepped in, then closed it behind her. Bogan was already waiting.

"Hey. How's it going?"

Jace took a deep breath. "Fine so far. Except the pine cone smell is driving me crazy."

Bogan laughed. "That's the cleaner. Trusties clean every day. Can't stand the smell of pine cones anymore."

"And what about everybody calling me worm?"

The woman shrugged. "It's what we call newbies."

"Sort of denigrating, isn't it?"

"Wildly denigrating, but what'choo gonna do?" Bogan eyed the pod through the slim window set in the middle of the inner door. "He going to let you put them to bed?" She glanced at her watch. "Should have been done before you got here."

"He's testing me. He's been doing it since I got here."

"Boys will be boys, and that boy doesn't particularly cotton to chicks with a badge."

"I would have thought chicks with badges and guns were just the kind of red meat that'd get him going."

For a second, Bogan looked surprised. "Oooh, I knew I'd like you."

"What's this?" a voice boomed through wall speakers rather than their radios. "Two babes in the go-between . . . it's like a dream come true."

"Bite my ass, Bibb," Rory said, staring at the camera. She flipped a quick bird to the camera, then pointedly turned her back on it.

"Who's that?" Jace eyed the camera and shivered at the thought of someone watching her and Bogan.

"Segeant Bibb. Dead-shift control room. Runs all the cameras, pops all the locks, stares at all the women."

"I heard that," he said, his voice elongated by the speaker.

Rory put a hand innocently to her chest, as though she had honestly misspoken. "Excuse me? What I meant to say was that Sergeant Bibb is in control of everything and carefully watches our backs to ensure our safety and that we go home at night and we love him for it."

"I heard that, too," he said.

"Now turn it off."

"Sorry, Rory, you ain't my sergeant."

"Yeah, but I know where the sexual harassment forms are, don't I?"

Silence answered her.

"He's still listening. He will be until he knows we're talking about dinner, then he'll find someone else to watch."

Jace kept her face away from the camera. "He watches everything?"

"Pretty much and in spite of him being a fourteen-year-old pubescent boy, he's damn good at what he does. No officer, at least as long as I've been on this shift, has ever spent more than about twenty seconds in a fight with an inmate in the go-between. Some of those other controllers, especially during day shift? They get to talking and reading the newspaper or whatever. There've been fights where the jailers were by themselves for two or even three minutes before anyone noticed."

The hair on Jace's scalp crawled backward. "Two or three minutes?"

"Eternity when you're fighting for your life, lemme tell you."

"You've done it?"

"We've all done it." She nodded at the camera. "That's why it's good he watches. Creepy or not, it's always better to have someone watching out for you. But there are places in this building that don't have cameras. Make damn sure you don't end up there alone with an inmate. Bad thing to be on your own. Never know what'll happen."

"Damn straight, rookie," Bibb said.

"Damn it, Bibb, get outta—"

"I'm gone."

This time, the women heard the two-way mic click off. Rory chuckled, then said, "Wanna take dinner together?"

"Sure."

"Call me when he decides you can eat."

"I will. Thanks, I appre—"

The emergency buzzer exploded and for a second, Jace thought Rory had done it by putting her hand on the outer door handle. It filled the go-between with a bone bruising thrum.

—ERTs Pod D—

—10-10 Pod D—

"Shit." Bogan keyed her mic. "A-adam outer."

"What is it?" Adrenaline dumped into Jace's system. Her heart felt like it had blasted through her chest and banged off her badge. Her skin burned and her teeth clamped together.

"ERT call. Ten-ten is a fight." Bogan pointed to A Pod as the outer door popped open. "Get in there, get them locked down right now, no screwing around. Don't leave the pod until you hear the clear."

Then she was gone, her body language dead calm.

"A-adam inner," Jace said to the distant control room as she pulled on the locked door. "A-adam inner."

She pulled again. Still locked.

—10-10 . . . possibly eight subjects—

—ERTs responding—

"Damn it, A Pod—as in Adam. Adam adam adam—inner door. Now."

Still the door didn't open and she realized the other door wasn't completely closed. She raced across the go-between and slammed the slow-closing outer door shut, then radioed again.

As though mocking her, the door remained locked.

—recount four subjects on 10-10—

Calm down, Jace, she thought. *They're busy popping doors for the ERTs and punching up monitors to account for every inmate in D Pod. You're not the priority so take it easy until they get to you.*

—all call: full lock . . . lock down the entire facility immediately—

—all call: priority radio traffic only . . . priority only—

Inside A, Reynolds moved the inmates toward their cells. All of them, prisoners and guard, seemed relaxed. Making jokes with the inmates—she assumed he was making jokes because some laughed—herding them easily. In other words, he was calm and cool while she stood trapped in the go-between, freaking out, yelling into her radio and yanking the door.

"Damn it." Her voice bounced off the go-between walls.

—ERTs ten-twenty-three—

Inside A Pod, the upper-tier cell doors closed one by one and locked automatically by the computer. Five doors, ten. Fifteen doors. Twenty. Twenty-one. Twenty-two. Twenty-three.

And then silence.

No twenty-fourth door. No twenty-fourth lock.

"Son of a bitch." Jace jammed her face against the inner door, eyeing every cell. "A Pod, inner door. Now. Now."

Still the door remained locked. And still there was no twenty-fourth locked cell door. Then she saw it. At the last cell on the upper tier, almost out of her vision.

"Oh, my God."

—10-10 recount only two subjects—

Thomas and Reynolds were in a heap of fists and legs, of punches and kicks. Thomas' thin hands clamped around Reynolds' throat, shoved him backward to the rail.

—medical get moving to D pod—

"No, no. Stop it. Uh . . . freeze." She banged her hand against the door. "Stop it, that's an order."

A useless order, though she couldn't stop herself from giving it. Thomas couldn't hear her and wouldn't stop if he could. Reynolds fumbled his pepper spray over the handrail and tried to jam his thumbs into the soft pressure points on either side of Thomas' neck.

This can't be happening. No, no, I can't be stuck out here. "Stop it. That's an order. Thomas! Stop it. Damn it, open the door. A Pod. Violent inmate. Open the door. Open the damn door."

The two men twisted, banged arms and legs against the cell door, leaving a dark, bloody smear. Thomas managed to shove Reynolds against the handrail. The officer's head and shoulders, his upper back, leaned out into space.

"Damn it," Jace yelled into the radio mic. "Officer going down. Officer going down."

—what the fuck? where? where?—

"A Pod."

Immediately, the door lock popped.

Jace dashed across the day room toward the stairs. Thomas yelled but Reynolds was absolutely silent.

"ERTs A Pod. Officer needs assistance."

Thomas landed a heavy punch against Reynolds' face and the officer fell sideways against the rail. Thomas drew his hand back, preparing to toss a monster punch at Reynolds, who lolled, seemingly punch drunk, half on his knees against the rail. But as Thomas' fist flew at him, Reynolds dodged the punch. He came to his feet as Thomas stumbled forward with the momentum of the missed punch.

Jace heard a solid slap, flesh against flesh, and a terrified howl.

"Shit."

She raced up the stairs. Thomas' howl clawed the air as he fell over the railing.

"Hah," Reynolds shouted. "Call the coroner-man, get the meat wagon down here, we got some garbage."

Thomas fell past her. She reached out, stretching as far as she could, as though she could catch him. Instead, his harsh slam against the concrete floor snapped his howl off.

But the emergency alarm never stopped shrieking, and somehow, in her ears, it sounded like the yap of a tiny, terrified puppy.

Chapter Four

—all call: ERTs are 10-23—

—all call: the fight is secure—

—405 from 410—

—410 go ahead—

—we'll need Adam 1—

—Adam 2 is enroute—

—10-4 Adam 2 . . . we'll need 10-79, too—

—understood. 405 to all call: stay in lockdown until further notice . . . priority radio traffic only—

The knee jammed her hard.

"I'm a jailer," Jace said.

"Good for you," the cop above her said. "Be quiet."

"But I'm—"

"What'd I say?" His knee pressed harder.

Pain shattering her head, Jace Salome clamped her mouth shut while the ERT's plastic shield jammed her face immobile into the floor. The Emergency Response Team members had come in fast, six officers in full gear bursting through the heavy steel doors called the War Doors. When the ERTs exploded into the pod, they shoved her to the floor and pinned her. On the upper floor, an ERT had pinned Reynolds the same way.

Now the remaining four ERTs tugged on every cell door and accounted for every prisoner.

I've peed myself. I've seen a man killed, an officer attacked, and all I could do was piss on myself. Jace, you screwed this up in a huge way.

Humiliation was thick on her tongue.

I'll bet you know what that tastes like, she thought, staring at a bottom-tier inmate. Jail degradation sat heavy in every line of his face. The man's eyes were melancholy, like the eyes of an old man who's realized all his friends have passed.

The inmate placed his hand over his heart and nodded. As best she could, Jace returned the nod.

This place should be chaotic. A man was dead, an officer battered while other officers, geared in black uniforms and faces hidden behind protective masks, methodically worked the pod one end to the other. It should be loud and in total disarray. Everyone should be upset. The inmates should be banging their doors, upset at the death of one of their own. The officers in charge should be yelling at Reynolds, at her, at anyone who was anywhere near it when it happened. Yet the pod was silent save for the bang of feet marching from cell door to cell door. Even the alarm had fallen quiet.

Finally, Jace heard a voice full of the clipped cadence of authority. "Let 'em up."

"Sorry about that," the officer pinning her said.

"Get the hell away from me." Jace knocked the officer's hand away and hated the way his eyes caught the stain at her crotch.

"Get used to it, Deputy, that's how we roll."

" 'Roll?' Even when I'm wearing a damned uniform?" She pulled at the badge on her chest with one hand while trying to hide the wet spot on her trousers with the other. "Those high-powered observational skills make you miss this big, ol' shiny badge?"

"Calm down. That's how it's done. I don't care if you're wearing a uniform. If you're standing, I'll take you down."

"Probably love that part, don't you?"

The contempt in his snort, coupled with his last glance at the wet stain, made her grind her teeth. *Am I the only one falling apart?*

"Salome," Dillon said. "You okay?"

She straightened her uniform shirt. "Yes, sir."

"You need to go home?"

On the first floor, Thomas lay directly beneath his cell, his head cocked sideways like a dog hearing a strange sound. His yell had snapped quiet when he hit the ground, though his mouth was still open. His eyes were open, too. One stared straight out. The other was disconnected and stared sideways.

"Uh . . . no. Thanks." One arm around her stomach, she tried to slow her breathing. "I'll be fine."

Face stony, Dillon took her measure. "It's not a problem to go home. Reynolds is going. No one will think any less of you."

They already do, she wanted to say. She was the newbie and she'd been in the go-between. It was only going to get worse when word spread that she'd pissed herself, too.

"Go home, come back tomorrow, we'll put you in E Pod."

E Pod was filled with the elderly and infirm, also sometimes those with nonviolent mental problems. Most of those inmates were too fragile with age and medication to fight.

"I'm fine."

"Jace, you saw a man die."

"So much for no one dies on an officer's first night, huh?"

"Yeah, guess I jinxed that one." His words were light, but his tone was heavy.

Jace's stomach lurched, tightened, and then heaved. Hot vomitus spattered Dillon's boots.

"Saw that coming."

"I'm—God, I'm sorry . . . sir." Tears burned her cheeks.

"Not the worst thing I've had on my boots."

As she wiped her mouth, the pod flooded with detectives and

supervisors and an army of crime scene techs. They all gathered around Chief Deputy Cornutt. He looked from them to his clipboard and gave each one of them a set of orders. He spoke quickly and certainly, his voice calm.

"He seems to know what he's doing," Jace said.

"Chief Deputy David Cornutt has been here . . . twenty years? Twenty-two years? He's Adam 2 on the radio."

At his orders, the techs taped off the scene and began evidence collection. The flash from their digital cameras spotlighted the ERTs gathering their gear and heading out. One officer started a log of who had been on the scene and why.

"I can't believe this."

"I know," Dillon said. "Tough night. Well, nowhere to go but up, I guess."

"Not funny."

Dillon indicated the cut on her cheek. "Inmate or ERT?"

Jace wiped the blood away. "ERT. When he threw me down."

"Yeah."

"I didn't get in—well, whatever. Now what, Sarge?"

"Didn't get in on the fight, huh?"

"It was—I was—no, sir, I wasn't able to help Reynolds."

"Don't worry about Reynolds. He can handle himself."

In fact, as they spoke, Reynolds was near the control desk with three ERTs. To their laughter, Reynolds described the fight punch by punch. He whistled like a falling bomb when he described how Thomas fell over the rail.

Dillon clapped her on the shoulder. "Your hands bloody?"

"Sir?"

"Way you were beating on that door, trying to get in. Might not have been able to help, but you surely tried."

Wiping her cheek again, the sting still on her face, she absently cleaned her hands on her uniform. "If that officer hadn't hit me so hard. Why'd he pin me like that? I work here."

Dillon shook his head. "It's a bitch getting old, Salome. Forget lots of stuff, you know? I used to have a fantastic memory. I could remember crap from when I was a little kid. Now I can barely remember my own kids' names."

Picking at her uniform, pulling her trousers away from her hips and crotch, she said, "I'm not following, sir."

"But I do remember the dead jailer. Good man. Wife used to make cookies for everyone on the shift. An inmate caught him in a hallway—this is back in the old part of the jail downstairs—and clipped him with a metal fork from the chow hall."

"Metal?"

"Way we used to do it."

Jace couldn't imagine giving an inmate a metal utensil. The Zachary County Jail only handed out sporks—half spoon, half fork—made of a plastic that couldn't be sharpened.

"After this guy killed a cop, he put on that cop's uniform and took his keys. He was one door from freedom before anyone realized it. Until that last door, everyone thought the inmate was a guard."

"What about his radio?"

"Crappy radios, hardly ever worked."

"If the guard was carrying keys, then I guess there was no control room, either."

"Not like there is now." Gently, Dillon wiped a bit of blood from her face. "The point is, Salome, there's a reason for everything. Sporks because they can't be sharpened."

"ERTs tossing everyone because an inmate looked like a guard."

"Because of that policy, you got hurt. Now you've got piss and blood on your uniform and that's the way the job goes."

With a deep sigh, she said, "This is going to get ugly, isn't it?"

Dillon stroked his beard. "I don't know. Maybe. An officer

got attacked and a man died. Tough situation all the way around, but this isn't the first time someone has died in custody, Salome."

"Well, that makes me feel better."

"No, it doesn't."

"No, it doesn't, but that's not what I meant."

"What, then?"

How could she tell her sergeant that she'd fouled this thing up? She had left her partner alone and a man died. If she'd been there, maybe everything would have worked out.

"Jace?"

She shook her head. "Nothing."

He paused. "When are you going upstairs?"

Upstairs. Administration, detectives. What she assumed would be hours of questions.

"Take your time. Take a few minutes, anyway. Get yourself together. They'll wait."

"They're detectives, sir, they—"

"First off, don't call me sir, I told you already. Second, they're detectives, not gods. They'll wait and if they don't, piss on them." He glanced at her pants. "Sorry."

Jace headed for the pod's inner door. The lock popped before she got there. *Of course,* she thought. *This time it opens before you need it.* It closed behind her with a heavy thud and the outer door opened, spilling her into the main hallway.

Chapter Five

Twenty minutes later, as the sweaty Monday night slipped into Tuesday morning, Jace stepped into the detectives' room. The air conditioner wheezed like an old man. Clearing her throat, she caught the attention of a detective on the phone and took a step. The man's eyes flashed and she froze.

"Sorry." She slipped back into the hallway.

—Control Adam 1 is 10-23—

—10-4—

"Yeah, yeah." The detective's voice was a harsh bark.

His desk was disorganized and his face was filled with the same bottomless tension she saw on many of the road deputies. "I got it, I got it. Lee Street Apartments. Christ, that place is a pisshole, isn't it? Yeah, yeah, I got it. Sexual assault. What? Well, I'm not there yet, am I? Can't figure who done it when I'm sitting here, can I? What? Well, of course the boyfriend did it; stupid until proven smart, I say." With a laugh, the detective banged the phone against his desk four or five times. "Damn, James, you are just about as dumb as a box of used condoms. How'd you ever make it out of traffic?"

Through the phone, as the detective hung up, the patrolman's response was loud and clear.

The detective looked at Jace. "Who're you?"

"Uh . . . sir, I'm Officer Salome."

"Salome? Like from the Bible? Looking for someone's head?" He leaned back and played with his tie. "Never heard of you."

After a quick scratch of his ankle, he said, "Road duty?"

"No, sir, corrections."

He picked his teeth with a finger. "Corrections. What a load. You're a jailer, Salome. We don't correct, we jail. The State corrects. The Feds correct. Rehab programs and college degrees. All we do is jail."

"Yes, sir."

"Why are you in my office?"

"I was told to see a detective."

"Why?"

Jace licked her lips. "I . . . uh . . . I—"

"For crap's sake, spit it out."

"Mr. Thomas."

Sorting files, shoving them from pile to pile, he said, "Who?"

"The inmate. Died in A Pod. Half hour ago."

His hands stopped. His head swiveled, like a Gila monster's, toward her. "You mean killed?" He motioned her into the room but didn't offer her a seat. "You do it?"

"Absolutely not, sir. I wasn't even—"

"In the pod."

He'd known. He probably knew everything about the case before she got here. His reveling in the knowledge made her cringe like an elementary school student suddenly thrust into Harvard.

"What a mess." The detective motioned her to a chair. "Might be a while before someone gets to you."

"Yes, sir. Busy night?" She sat in a beat-up desk chair with most of its padding worn out. They were easy words, spoken to fill the tense space.

"One dead inmate isn't busy enough for you? You want what . . . three? Five, maybe? How long you been on, rookie?"

"This is my first night on shift."

"Uh-huh . . . and this is what you get. Maybe next time you'll be where you're supposed to be."

"But, sir, I was—"

His glare shut her up. "When I worked the jail, couldn't have pried me from my partner's side." He stood. "Welcome to the big leagues."

Grabbing a couple of file folders, he slipped out the door and she took a deep breath. He was one of the veterans she'd been warned about. During a particularly honest moment at the Academy, an instructor told her that there were more than a few veteran cops who didn't care for rookies. Next to useless, they thought, because those rookies want the glory but don't want to pay the dues.

Maybe that was unfair. It was entirely possible this guy was having a terrible day. Look at how many open files were on his desk. She bit back a laugh. *Maybe there are so many files because he sucks as a detective.*

"Officer Salome?"

A man stood at the door. He wore a tidy straw cowboy hat and in spite of the heat, his shirt and jeans were both crisp and neatly pressed. "Just a while longer. Sorry about the delay. Things are a little . . . well, you know."

"Yes, sir."

"Damn, it's cold in here. Can you shut off that air for me, please? Thank you."

The detectives called this room The Pulpit. It was overstuffed with desks and file cabinets and the detritus of too many detectives with not enough space. Every desk was piled with case files and notepads, uncapped pens, handcuffs, stray magazines. An entire wall was covered by memos and wanted posters and seemingly random mug shots, handwritten notes announcing birthday parties, a funeral notice of an officer from Howard County killed on duty by a drunk driver, and a five-dollar bill with a note asking if anyone could identify the bill. Just beneath that was another note stating the bill was "green, approximately six inches long, with a picture in the middle. It's probably mine." In the far corner, five pictures were taped up alongside each other. Three were mug shots, one looked like a high school picture, and the last was from a surveillance camera. Beneath those pictures were pictures of clubs and beneath that, what looked like quick informational hits.

She'd been to most of those joints. Luigi's. Johnny's Barbeque. Tamales by Gomez. She and Gramma went to the 007 Room at least once a week and Gramma danced with whoever she could get on the floor while a big band ripped through 1940's hits. So what was the story, Jace wondered, clamping her forearms against her breasts to wipe the sweat into her bra. Burglaries at those places? Or dealers working the back rooms? Sweat dripped into her eyes. She wiped it away as it ran down her shirt.

Nearly an hour after she'd arrived, the cowboy-hatted man came in. "Sorry about the wait."

Where the other detective had been dressed in a suit, jacket off and tie undone, this man was in jeans, pressed with a knife-edge crease down the front of each leg. His gray boots were shined until the entire room was visible in them. The hat was perfectly clean and had, in the hatband, a miniature plastic sword like what Jace sometimes saw in mixed drinks at the 007 Room.

Cowboy through and through, she thought. Except for the simple silver belt buckle.

He saw her looking. "I love the big ones. Big silver monstrosities fit for rodeo champions and big egos. My grandpa had one with the Texas flag on it. Grandma had one, too."

"Rodeo? Didn't get the big buckle 'cause the bull threw you?" She wanted the words back as soon as she said them. She was hot and tired and annoyed that he made her wait but she probably shouldn't get mouthy her first night in.

With an amused snort, he sat and rifled through the desk until he found a pen. He wheeled away from the desk and stopped when there was nothing between them.

"The bull throws us all eventually." A finger wound up to a faint scar under his chin. "Bull's name was Danny Krevitz. I arrested him for murdering a guy in a bar over who got to pay for the next game on a fifty-cent pool table. I kept him away from my weapon but not my grandpa's belt buckle. Tore that thing off me, slung it around, opened my chin right up." It was an old scar, gone shiny and thin by time, and it didn't fit the rest of his compassionate face. "I don't wear that buckle much anymore."

"I'd imagine not."

His voice softened. "Sounds like maybe the bull threw you tonight, Officer."

"Sir, I—" She took a deep breath. "Sir, I never got close enough to get thrown."

He frowned in surprise. "Hanging out in the go-between?"

"Stuck."

"Fair enough. What were you doing? Shouldn't you have been with your partner?"

She bristled. "I guess my partner handled it just fine, didn't he?"

His right eyebrow rose. "Think so?" His eyes lingered on her for a few seconds, then he made some notes. "Well, either way, the deed is done and the man is dead."

What was he writing down? Had she somehow advocated killing an inmate? Or maybe she had rationalized it.

"Where do you stand on self-defense, Officer Salome?"

The chair, with its worn padding and slight lean to the right, was too small, as though its arms were reaching in for her. When she got up, she didn't quite jump, but close. At the window, she tried to lick the sweat off her upper lip without the detective seeing it.

"Officer?"

She turned to him, but stayed near the window. "All the offices in this complex have central air."

"Yeah?"

"Why doesn't this office use it?"

"This office doesn't have it."

She glanced at a ceiling vent. "Why the window unit? So you can sweat me. Literally."

He nodded. "Not you specifically. One of the oldest tricks in the book. Let them get hot and uncomfortable."

"Like putting me in that chair? It's off balance, makes it hard to get comfortable."

"I didn't put you in that chair."

"The other detective did. You sweat me and then make sure there isn't any furniture between us when we talk? Open communication?"

"Pretty much, Officer."

She nodded. "Why not just treat me with respect and ask the question."

"I did, if you'll remember."

"Self-defense."

"Yes." His eyes were bright. "But nicely done, trying to turn the conversation back on me, make me uncomfortable and defensive."

Jace took a breath. "If it's self-defense, it's self-defense. Better than letting a man attack you. I'd bet there was some self-defense when that bull threw you."

"Officer, calm down, okay? I'm not the enemy here and I'm not trying to trap you into admitting anything."

"There's nothing to admit."

His grin reminded her of a desert coyote. "There is always something to admit, Officer. Good, bad, or ugly, there is always more to know."

"If that's an accusation, I want my union rep."

"Union rep? Whoa . . . back up, Officer." He raised his hands, palms out. It was the same move the Academy instructors had taught her in control tactics. On the street, they'd said, showing those palms can calm whoever you're dealing with. *My hands are out, they're empty, I'm no threat.*

The detective's eyes stayed on hers.

But hands raised was also tactically defensive; up and ready to go if the situation called for it.

"Salome, I'm just trying to write a report. Tell me what happened, okay? What did you see and what did you hear? Let me worry about everything else."

With an embarrassed nod, she sat and wiped her hands on her thighs. "Sorry, Detective, I'm nervous. First night and this happens."

This time, his predator's face disappeared into something friendlier. She knew it might well be just another face, but right now, with her hands shaking and her bowels hot, she accepted that softer face.

"No problem. And by the way, I'm not a detective."

"Huh?"

"Texas Ranger."

Chapter Six

His words sank deep into the hot night. His hands played over his shirt and jeans, smoothing them of wrinkles Jace didn't see. "Deputy?"

Gramma had been right. Jace could not do this job and now a man was dead and a Texas Ranger was going to question her about it. He'd want to know why she'd been out of the pod, and then he'd write his report and Jace would lose this job.

"Deputy? You okay? Take a breath for me, okay? Everything's fine. The Rangers investigate custodial deaths. Not by law, but by common sense. I'm just a formality."

Jace breathed deeply. "Because if someone dies in custody, it should be a separate agency investigating. Transparency and conflict of interest . . . in case charges need to be filed."

With a nod, he offered his hand. "Exactly right. I'm Captain Barry Ezrin, Commander, Company E, Texas Rangers."

So not just a Ranger, but the commander of the largest company in the state. Swallowing was like sucking down a pound of nails. "Yes, sir."

"You okay, Deputy? You got a little pale on me."

"Bet that always happens when you drop that bit of information."

He grinned and licked a lip. "That's why I do it that way. Look, it's been a hard night, just tell me what happened."

"A man died."

"Yeah, I got that much. I saw the body."

She chose her words as carefully as she had shined her boots and badge that afternoon. She started with roll call and the talk with Sergeant Dillon and then finding lights still on in the pod.

"Reynolds wanted me to handle lockdown. Thought it would be good for my first night."

"Why didn't you?"

"I was about to, sir, I just—"

He waved his hands in front of him. "I'm not a sir, Deputy, I'm just a cop."

"Excuse me, sir, but just a cop wears the same badge I do, not a Ranger's star."

"Just means I've had more time to kiss ass and get the good job."

His easy banter did not lower the temperature on her nerves. *What do I say? How careful should I be? Damn it, this isn't what I wanted.*

"So you were handling lockdown and heard the alarm for the fight—"

"No, si—no. I hadn't started lockdown yet. I was actually in the go-between."

"Doing?"

"Planning dinner."

His eyebrows rose. "Really?"

"What?"

"You always this honest?"

She frowned.

"My company investigates maybe fifteen custodial deaths every year, and every time, the cops on duty fudge the embarrassing details. If they were in the bathroom, stroking the dolphin, they tell me they were in the hallway talking. If they were out back smoking when they shouldn't have been, they tell me they were engaged with an inmate. But you tell me you were planning dinner."

"I'm getting grief for being honest?"

"So you're in the go-between, planning dinner—" His body language beginning to relax, he scribbled in his pad. "And then what?"

"We heard an emergency call for the ERTs. D Pod had a fight."

" 'We?' "

"Deputy Bogan and myself."

"What kind of fight?"

"I wasn't there, I have no idea. But Deputy Bogan ran toward D and I tried to get into A to help with the lockdown."

"Couldn't get inside the pod?"

"No. The control room was too busy getting the ERTs into D, I guess."

He brought his chair closer to Jace. "Tell me about the fight."

"I don't know . . . they were on the top tier. Thomas was punching Deputy Reynolds and Reynolds was fighting back."

"So Reynolds was on the defensive."

"Yes."

"Okay, so the inmate attacked him. Did he try to get to his OC spray or his baton?"

Jace hesitated. She did remember Reynolds grabbing at his pepper spray, but she wasn't sure he was going for it or if his arm was just banging around in the fight.

"Deputy?"

"I don't remember."

His gaze never left her. "What happened . . . exactly? Thomas threw the first punch and hit Reynolds where? Or did he kick at the officer?" He stood, held his hands up in a boxer's pose. He motioned her to stand.

Hesitantly, she did and raised her hands like she'd been taught at the Academy.

"You're Reynolds, I'm Thomas."

He telegraphed every move. "Face punch, maybe?"

Regardless of how slowly Ezrin punched, it jarred Jace. She backed up. "Sir, I didn't see the first punch. I didn't realize there was a problem until I heard the shouting."

Ezrin looked surprised. "So they were both bloody by the time you saw them."

"Yes."

"So even though we both know Thomas struck first—obviously Thomas struck first—could it have been Reynolds? If you didn't see it, who knows who commenced the hitting."

From the go-between, when she'd looked through the inner door's slim window, she'd wondered the same thing. Why was Reynolds beating the prisoner? But it was only a wisp of a thought and it evaporated quickly.

"Got something to say, Deputy?"

"That's not what happened."

"Tell me what you would have done. If I come at you, what do you do?"

"Depends on what you're doing."

"I throw a punch."

He tossed a soft punch at her head. She leaned back and let it pass, then grabbed the punching arm and wrenched it backward. Ezrin spun until he faced away and his arm was tightly pinned to his back. If it'd been real, she would have snapped her knee into his thigh and taken him hard to the ground.

At least, that's what her control tactics instructor had taught her.

"We going to stand here all night?"

She released him. "Sorry."

"No problem." His face alive, he sat. "You know the moves pretty well. Where'd you academy at?"

"Lubbock Law Enforcement Academy."

"Good academy. Let's see, your control tactics guy would have been Schlosser, right? Good guy. Norworth still teaching human behavior and use of force?"

"For my class."

He snapped his fingers. "What about Dave Sneed? Or Lionel Stimson? Joe Paul Hewson ring a bell?"

While he reeled off those names, Ezrin played with the pen, twirled it, dropped it to the floor twice. "I loved touring the other jails when I was in the Academy. You guys do that?"

"A couple."

"Ector, maybe? Sterling or Randall counties? Take a look at how they do things in Amarillo? What about Gaines? Hell, there are only about 14,000 people in that whole county. Be interesting to see how small jails do it, wouldn't it?" Still the pen twirled between his fingers, but his gaze stayed on her. "You know any of those jails?"

"No."

"Did Reynolds say anything about Thomas?"

"Said he was a troublemaker."

Ezrin's right eyebrow rose and he did some quick scribbling. "What kind of troublemaker?"

"Reynolds said Thomas was a newbie, that he hadn't yet adjusted to being in jail."

"Thomas strike you that way?"

Jace shrugged. "I'm new."

He eyed her. "A bit disingenuous, Deputy. Graduated third in your class. Had a 97+ average in human behavior." He indicated the chair and the air conditioner. "You figured those little tricks out pretty quick, too, didn't you?"

Jace kept her face empty.

"I don't come into a room empty-handed, Deputy. Was inmate Gene Thomas having trouble adjusting to being incarcerated?"

"I'd say yes, he was. He told me he was scared."

"Of jail? Or Reynolds?"

Thomas' eyes had darted to and from Reynolds quite a bit, hadn't they? "You think Reynolds did it on purpose, don't you?"

Ezrin shook his head. "Deputy, I don't think any—"

"Yeah. It's why you keep circling around to Reynolds."

"No, I keep circling around to Reynolds because he was involved in a fight and a man died. I circle around to him because I want to know why Thomas died and more than that, why Thomas attacked a law enforcement officer."

"But you—"

"Damn it." His voice boomed around the room, its volume looking for an outlet. With a violent twist, he capped the pen and threw it at the desk. "I circle around because I know there will be lawsuits, Deputy Salome. They'll come from everywhere and someone will get swept away, whether laws were broken or not."

Jace backpedaled. "Sorry, sir, I just—I've never been through this before."

"And I have, so let me do my job without your bullshit."

He strode to the window. It was after two o'clock in the morning and still the night was full. Most of the neon business signs were still on, like they didn't want to miss an opportunity to advertise to either the nighttime road guys or the insomniac inmates.

Chastened, Jace didn't know if she and Ezrin were finished or not. While she waited for him, she looked again at the photos adorning the far wall. While staring at the surveillance photo, a grainy black and white with the subject at an odd angle, she frowned. Part of his ear was gone. Just a slice, a tiny bit from the top, flattening the ear out, giving him a slightly off-kilter look.

"Thanks for your time, Deputy. Sorry about being an ass.

I'm tired." After he rubbed his neck, he said, "I'll be talking to all the inmates in that pod. And whatever guards dealt with Thomas from his first day. Going to pull records, too: booking and medical and whatever."

"Yes, sir." Then she nodded toward a single photo hanging above a lonely desk in the corner. "Might talk to that detective, too."

He eyed her and under his gaze, she was uncomfortable. "Why?"

"Because the guy in the surveillance picture is that guy." She pointed from the surveillance picture to the booking photo on the opposite wall. "The ear."

Ezrin took a closer look and she knew he saw it. In both pictures, regardless of the shadows and graininess and odd angles, Jace knew the Ranger saw the bit of missing ear. He grinned. "Well done, Deputy. Next time I ask you a question, don't give me that rookie crap."

Chapter Seven

At the end of her first solo shift, as the morning sun gave bright light to the plunging darkness within her, Jace stood in her gramma's doorway, watching the trio play dominoes. Though there were only three of them left, she'd named Gramma and her friends after five members of one of Louis Armstrong's first jazz groups. They hadn't been five since Grapa died and Galena Brown, an old woman who had been a stripper in the 1950s, had left without a word.

"Throw down, mofo," Hassan demanded of Preacher.

Jace didn't know much about the original Hot Five, but she was pretty sure they hadn't used language like that.

"Shut up, towelhead, I'll throw down—" Preacher's fake teeth chattered.

"Towelhead? Did you just call me—"

"Keep calling yourself 'Hassan' and what do you expect," Preacher said.

"Play the hand, Preacher," Gramma said.

"I ain't no towelhead."

"Preacher, play the hand," Gramma said again.

Hassan sniffed. "I'm Jewish."

"Play the hand."

"Or what?" asked Preacher.

Gramma's face constricted. "Or I'll go home, you goody-two-shoes-son-of-a-bitch, that's or what." Gramma stood and reached for the pile of unsmoked cigars in the table's middle.

"I'll take my cigars and—"

"If you're taking the cigars," Hassan said, "I'm taking the women." He stood and his knees popped like small caliber gunshots. "Where the white women?"

Preacher put his eyes back on his dominoes. "First, there ain't no women except Gramma. Second, you ain't in no Mel Brooks movie. Third, even if you were, you couldn't play Cleavon Little's part 'cause you ain't black. And you ain't going anywhere," he said to Gramma.

"Why won't I?"

" 'S your place." Preacher concentrated on his dominoes.

"Christ, what a burnout," Hassan said.

"I thought you were Jewish," Gramma said. "Or Arab or something."

"So?"

"You can't say Christ . . . he's my Savior. If you have to say something, say . . . I don't know . . . something like—"

"Abraham, what a burnout," Preacher said. With that, the man slammed down a domino. The rest of the dominoes bounced and warm beer, poured hours earlier, sloshed.

"You bounce that cigar and catch my money on fire," Gramma warned as she sat, "and I'll show you burnout."

Preacher looked at Gramma, but poked an exasperated finger toward Hassan. "I didn't call you a burnout. He did. Besides, don't you threaten me, you dried-up old slumlord."

"Slumlord? What about you? Wearing the same damn suit every day. What, your church can't front you enough for a new suit? You preached for them . . . I don't know . . . for 500 years or something. Make them get you a new suit."

Hassan shook his head. "Man, we always get to the slumlord and the new suit, don't we? Why do we always end up at the same damn place?"

Back and forth it went, insults as thick as the cigar smoke

and as stale as the beer. Nearly every morning, left over from just about every night before, it was like this.

Jace, standing at the doorway to Gramma's apartment, laughed. "You end up in the same place because as a group, the Hot Five has Alzheimer's. Keeps you too stupid to think of anything new."

"Jace," Preacher said in what had once been a beautiful Sunday sermon voice, but was now ragged from too many years and too much tobacco. He stood, smoothed his black suit, and smiled his soft, delicate grin at her.

"Morning, sunshine," Gramma said.

"There she is," Hassan said. "Done beating down inmates like they do in my home country?"

"Your home country is Houston," Gramma said.

"I rest my case." Hassan crossed his arms.

"Officer Salome," Preacher said. "Care for a drink?"

She sat. "I'll pass on the warm beer, thanks."

"Warm beer and cold pizza," Hassan said. "Breakfast of champions. That's what got me through college. Back before I found my street name."

Gramma rolled her eyes. "Ten pounds of ganja a day is what got you through college, and you only stole your street name because your dealer was an Arab named Hassan."

"Call it an homage," Hassan said.

"Crap, shut up," Preacher said.

"No, you shut up."

Jace raised her hands. "Children, chill out."

"What'choo doing here?" Preacher asked. "Ain't you should be in bed? Working all night like that. Girl's gotta get some beauty rest."

Jace grabbed a few dominoes from the facedown pile. "Saying I'm ugly?"

"No, ma'am." Preacher spluttered, his black face gone dark

with embarrassment. "I ain't saying . . . uh . . . no . . . you already beautiful enough and—"

Hassan hooted and banged his hands against the table. The domino game, a black snake curling around most of the table, bounced out of shape until it became several snakes.

"You screwed up the game," Preacher said.

Jace slammed down a game piece, a one and four up against a one and six. "Game was probably already screwed up the way Preacher plays." She grabbed at Preacher's left arm as he put a piece down. She shoved the sleeve of his suit jacket up, then did the same with his right. "Nothing there."

"Today, anyway," Hassan said. "Yesterday? Bastard had dominoes strapped everywhere. Arms, legs, chest. Probably on his—"

"Whoa." Jace scrunched up her nose. "Don't need to hear it."

"Me, either," Gramma said, putting down her own piece.

"So? How'd it go last night?" Preacher asked.

"Uh . . . fine. Yeah, I guess. Fine." Jace put down a piece and broke the snake into a new direction.

"Well . . . that's . . . certainly . . . acceptable," Hassan said.

"That's all you got to say?" Preacher asked.

"Jace?" Concern wormed through Gramma.

"Yeah, I'm fine. But just . . . It was a night. It's a job. Leave it."

"Sure, Jace," Hassan said. "Whatever you say." He snarled at Preacher. "This ain't twenty questions, Preacher-boy."

"Twenty questions?" Preacher asked. "Wouldn't'a thought you could count that high."

"You'll see it when I get my old service M-16 outta the closet and count bullet by bullet every time I shoot your ass."

"First of all," Gramma said. "He's right, you can't count that high. Secondly, you sold that thing ten years ago."

Hassan frowned. "Whatever."

They settled in for a few hands of dominoes. Jace tried to concentrate on the pieces, but knew everyone was watching her. She squeezed her temples between her fingers and tried to not think about how she'd made a career-crippling mistake, and how her first night would probably be her last.

Eventually Hassan bowed out. " 'Bout time to be getting home. Gotta get some sleep and then go to work."

"Yeah," Jace said. "Because selling dope is so taxing."

"Dope?" Hassan said, his face one of theatrical innocence. "I have no idea what you're talking about, Officer."

"Deputy."

"Officer . . . deputy . . . whatever. A cop is a cop."

"You have a problem with my job?"

"Jace," Gramma said. "He wasn't saying anything."

Jace forced a wink. "I'm sorry, Hassan. Tough night."

"Gonna have those," he said. "You need a pick-me-up, come see me."

Jace smiled in spite of her exhaustion. "I think I'll pass. Random drug tests."

Hassan nodded, put a finger next to his nose. "Hush-hush. But you need help passing those tests, you let me know, 'cause I know a guy—"

"Here we go," Gramma said. "Hassan, my granddaughter doesn't need to know anybody you know."

"She gonna get to know them soon enough anyway," Preacher said. "All of 'em gets arrested about every twenty minutes."

"Hah." Hassan grinned. "Tha'ss true. Tell Tate hello."

Jace frowned. "Tate? Guy who likes to take his clothes off?"

"Met him, didja?"

"Didn't get the pleasure, but he's there."

"He's always there." Hassan nodded. "Good enough. Good night then, you old windbags."

When he was gone, Preacher, Gramma, and Jace stood awkwardly around her table. Preacher finally pulled a battered old pipe from his coat. "I think I'll get some fresh air."

"Hey, old man," Gramma said. "You need this?"

Gramma handed Preacher his briefcase and he took it outside to Gramma's balcony. Gramma's apartment, like Jace's, was carved from the remains of two hotel rooms, one atop the other. Grapa had hired some of the unemployed roustabouts and tool pushers to gut and redo the four rooms into two studio-style rooms. Gramma's door was downstairs with an upstairs balcony. Jace's room had a second-story door and patio downstairs.

Preacher lit up and Jace breathed deep. She loved the rich odor of Preacher's spicy tobacco with its hint of orange and mint. The three watched some of the hotel tenants head to work and others just sit and stare out their windows. It was an everyday ritual that always left Jace melancholy.

"How's Robinson's homework going?" Jace asked.

Preacher shrugged. "Ain't bad. I don't understand some of it, but I do what I can."

"Is he going to graduate this year?"

The man smiled around the pipe. "I'm thinking so."

"You're a good father, Preacher."

The man's face flamed beneath Gramma's compliment. "I'm'a guessing things didn't go great last night."

"Am I that transparent?" Jace asked.

Gramma laughed. "Those who love you know you, little girl. You want to tell us about it?"

"It was a bad night. A real bad night." Jace clenched her fists. "An inmate died."

"Mmmmm." A blue smoke ring left Preacher's mouth and floated over the railing.

"Oh, my." Gramma's eyes closed as she turned away. "Died?"

"Well . . . killed."

Preacher toyed with his pipe. "That's a little different than died, ain't it?"

Jace told them the entire story and while she talked, Preacher put a hand on her shoulder. It was a gentle, wonderful touch and she found herself pressing against it.

"Puts some tarnish on that badge, don't it?"

"What?"

"I told him how long you spent polishing that thing." Gramma tapped Jace's toe with hers. "I told him about those boots, too."

"Shining and shining and shining," Preacher said.

She pulled out her badge wallet and handed it to Preacher. When he opened it, the sun glinted brilliantly off the brass, and a surge of pride worked through her. It always did when she looked at it. It was a beautiful five-pointed star, the county seal dropped delicately in the middle, "Deputy" curled above the seal and "Sheriff's Office" curled around the bottom.

Now Preacher dragged his long fingers over the badge. "You do it?"

"What? No. He attacked a guard and fell off the second-floor tier."

"That's awful," Gramma said.

"I . . ." Jace felt as though she were still trapped behind that locked door. "I wasn't there. I was—I was in the go-between. It's an area between the main hallway and the cells. It's a secured area and I was talking to a jailer. I got stuck, okay? I got stuck and I couldn't help my partner."

Her face flamed and she wiped ineffectually at her eyes. "I couldn't help him. Damn it." She smashed a fist against the balcony railing. "I couldn't do anything."

Gramma wrapped her arms around Jace. "Shhhh, Jace, it's fine. Everything'll be okay."

"It won't be okay, Gramma. I left a deputy alone and now a

man is dead. It's not like I forgot some paperwork. A man is dead because of me."

"Could you have stopped it?" Preacher asked, the pipe smoke a blue halo.

"Yes, I could have."

"You sure about that?"

"Yes, Preacher. If I'd been there, the inmate wouldn't have attacked Reynolds. If there had been two of us."

Preacher's thick voice sat heavy on the air. "Guard got attacked, huh?"

"What? Well . . . yeah. Policemen have to protect themselves." Jace disentangled herself from Gramma.

"Too right about that. Good thing they got all them detectives to figure it out, huh?" He drew the word out, "deteeeeectives."

"A Texas Ranger is investigating."

"I guess they couldn't get Wonder Woman," Gramma said.

Jace cracked an embarrassed grin. "She'd know what to do."

Preacher frowned. "Ain't nothing to do, babygirl. A bad guy attacked a good guy, got hisself killed."

In that moment, she almost told them of her uncertainty and suspicion and the coincidence of Thomas' words with Ezrin's questions. How was it that Thomas could get in an argument with Reynolds, tell Jace "they're" going to kill him, and end up dead fifteen minutes later? On the other hand, she was a brand-new jailer. What did she know about anything?

"That everything?" Preacher asked.

"Yeah."

Preacher chuckled. "You funny, babygirl. I been knowing you most of your life, and long as that's been, I can always see it."

Jace frowned, uncomfortable at being under Preacher's gaze. "Meaning?"

"Babydoll, you a mile smarter than anyone at this flop. You

know what you want outta life and you pretty certain you know how to get it. You know what it means to know life, which shouldn't surprise anybody considering how much life you've seen."

"Preacher, I have no idea what I want out of life or how to get it if and when I do figure it out. The reason I don't tell you everything is because the rest is police business." Under his eyes, she withered. "Really. I had to sign a confidentiality statement and everything."

Preacher nodded. "Ain't no doubt. But signing a paper ain't what keeps you quiet."

"Yeah?"

"Your mama does," Gramma said. "You have too much of her in you."

"Too right," Preacher said.

"Meaning?"

"Jace, I know you loved your mother, but she was terribly confused about herself. Sometimes, you are, too." Gramma tried to smile but failed.

The old man handed the badge wallet back. "If there's something to be done, then do it. If there ain't, then get some sleep and get back to it tonight."

"Or quit," Gramma said.

"Gramma, stop. I'm not going to quit. That was Mama's thing."

Her mother had lived job to job, with no next paycheck in sight. Jace was damned if she was going to repeat Mama's mistakes. She wasn't sure what her thing was, but it was going to be better than Mama's thing.

"I'm staying." Jace stood up as tall as her 5' 6″ frame would allow. "Besides, after what I did tonight, things can only go up, right?"

Preacher raised his eyebrows. "Just about tempting fate, ain't you?"

Regardless, it wasn't going to be her decision. It was Dillon's and the sheriff's, but it was also going to be the decision of every other deputy. They would decide it for her in how much trust they would give her from here on out.

Around them, a breeze blew up and caught the pool water. Tiny ripples slid gracefully across.

"Wrong direction," Jace said.

"What?"

"Breeze is coming out of the south."

"So?"

"Usually comes west."

"Ain't you Miss Observant."

"Deputy Observant," Gramma said.

"Hah. Too right." Preacher cleaned out his pipe and shoved it back in his pocket.

With a sigh, she said to Preacher, "Have you been around lately?"

He shook his head. "In fact, I ain't, babygirl. You wanna stroll? Ask around a little bit?"

"I do."

Gramma put a hand on Jace's chest and kissed her on the cheek. "I'm sorry this happened, honey, I really am. If I could do anything—"

"I know, Gramma. Thank you."

The woman hesitated, as though there were one last thing on her tongue. Instead, she nodded. "I'd better get to bed."

"Get changed, babygirl. Maybe along the way, we'll find some breakfast."

After changing, Jace met Preacher at the swimming pool. Arm in arm, they headed toward the bowling alley west of the hotel. From there, they'd head north, into the thicket of strip malls and tattoo parlors and DVD rental shops and corner bodegas.

And still the breeze came out of the south.

Chapter Eight

Long before cancer had stooped and withered Grapa, a small boy had drowned in the hotel pool. No one had seen him go swimming or heard him splashing. As far as Jace knew no one had heard him drown. There had been silence and then a body floating in the water. But once discovered, everyone had come out: tenants, employees of nearby businesses, even some of the area's meth whores.

But no one helped. No one cried or gasped in shock. An indifference, a piercing casualness, blanketed everyone. It was a tragedy, but it was also an opportunity to see old friends or drum up new clients.

Jace arrived at the jail early Tuesday, too anxious to stay home and it all reminded her of the dead boy.

In A Pod, visitors and inmates sat on opposite sides of a thick sheet of shatterproof glass with a simple phone the only connection between them. Jace watched some visits and never saw an inmate or visitor look to where Thomas had died. *It's their world,* Jace thought, *and there isn't time to worry about a drowned boy.* It's tough and bad, she could imagine them saying, but my life is tough already, what with rent and food and medicine for the baby and court fines and possible prison time.

They didn't have enough spirit left to expend on some dead prisoner.

In booking, a thin officer said to her, "You hear about the croaker?"

The man's partner, a middle-aged man with a wide, defensive stance, fingerprinted a Hispanic gangbanger. "Attack a cop, get your ass beat."

Jace stood near an open area where prisoners were held while waiting to be booked. Sometimes they were there only a few minutes, sometimes it was hours. One man, she'd been told, had been in holding for two full days, forgotten by the arresting officer.

"Left hand," the printing officer said to the prisoner. "*Izquierda.*"

"Maybe." The booking officer's nameplate said Smit. "Something like that, you wonder if Reynolds could have talked the guy down."

"Hell, no. Guy attacks, there's nothing to talk about."

The booking hallway ran a hundred feet long, a metal bench against the wall most of that length. Every three feet, a D-ring was bolted to the bench where new arrestees were handcuffed. At one end was a bank of computers, two Livescan fingerprint computers, and two digital cameras. After being booked, inmates were strip-searched, showered, and given a uniform. Then a temporary housing unit until the jailers decided which pod was best for them.

But booking was more than just the welcome mat. It was also the jail's muscle. Most of the booking officers were members of the Emergency Response Team and near the booking desk were the ERT doors, the War Doors.

"We go through those," she'd been told during her training schedule, "it's war. Means some inmate got stupid. Or maybe a few inmates. We go through the War Doors, we're full on, baby, full speed."

Smit said, "I'm with you. Attack me and I'll kick your ass. But now you've got the investigation and Reynolds? Who knows when he'll be back."

"Back?" Jace asked.

Smit's partner's fleshy face turned toward her as he continued to print his prisoner. "Who're you?"

"Deputy Salome."

The man's eyes lit up. "The worm. You were there."

"In the go-between."

"I heard that." He directed the prisoner toward an officer at the showers. "Heard you damn near beat the door down."

Not quite. "They wouldn't let me in."

Smit nodded. "Not until that outer door is closed. Got a fight going on and both those doors are open? You got a huge problem. I saw it once, too. I was working B Pod and these two mopes got twisted up over some Oreos, and I called ERTs and—"

The heavier officer shook his head. "You're full of crap."

"I'm telling a story," Smit said.

"Someone else's." His partner chuckled. "I'm Warner; 472 on the radio." He offered his hand. "You done good from what I heard."

"Then why couldn't I sleep?"

He frowned as though he'd never been sleepless in his life. "I'd'a slept like a baby."

"I'm not you, I guess."

His frown deepened, as though he got a whiff of some foul odor. "Don't much sound like you are." To Smit, he said, "Two weeks."

Smit shook his head. "A month."

A satisfied smile spread over Warner's face. "Can you imagine? A month off? Paid, no less. Give my left nut to get that time off. Maybe both nuts."

"What are you talking about?"

Warner stuffed the arrestee's inventoried personal belongings into a nylon bag, numbered the bag, then hung it on a conveyer belt attached to the ceiling. A flick of a button and the bag was gone, now hidden amongst hundreds of other bags, each hanging from the conveyer like sides of beef.

"Administrative leave until the investigation is over," Smit said.

"For self-defense?"

"Have to make sure that's what happened."

"Didn't play out no other way," Warner said. "But you know there's gonna be a lawsuit. 'You violated his civil rights!' "

Smit nodded. "Violations of the civil rights of a person in custody." He waggled his eyebrows at Jace. "Second degree felony."

Warner snorted. "The Sheriff's Office has to have it all down on paper. Can't stand those assholes."

"The Sheriff's Office assholes?" Jace asked.

Smit grinned.

"What? The bleeding hearts who don't understand how it is down here." Warner turned toward her, his eyes now the orange of a furious sun. "Worm. You ain't been attacked, ain't been in no fight. Hell, the skells probably ain't even been in your face yet." He blew out his breath. It was stale, laced with dinnertime onions. "Some mope is gonna get mouthy. You'll tell him to shut up and he'll keep getting mouthy. Back and forth. Shut up. Mouthy mouthy. Shut up. Mouthy mouthy."

"There's nothing wrong with talking," Jace said.

"Except the entire block is watching. You let one of 'em walk on you, they all will. They all walk on you and you got no cellblock control." He winked at Smit. "She'll be calling ERTs every damn time, won't she?"

"I don't know, she looks like she might have some tough."

"Got no tough."

Jace stepped up to Warner, let her chest bump him. "I've got plenty of tough."

"No, you don't," he said with a chuckle, easily pushing her backward with his own chest.

"Test that whenever you want."

"Not too smart, either," Warner said. "Talking to a senior officer like that? While you're still on probation?"

Jace swallowed, eventually took a couple steps back, disgusted at herself.

"Reynolds had some tough and now he's suspended."

"He did the right thing, then, killing the guy?" Jace asked.

"Damn straight, Miss Bleeding Heart," Warner said. "If there's any justice at all, he'll be back within a couple weeks."

"Won't happen," Smit said. "Remember Sterling. It'll be a month minimum."

"Load of crap," Warner said.

"Who?" Jace glanced at her watch. Fifteen more minutes until dead-shift roll call.

"Sterling County," Warner said. "Deputy was on leave for eight or ten weeks, something like that." He plunked a finger against her badge and she shrank back a step. " 'Cause Captain Ezrin had some doubts about it all."

"Hey," the Hispanic man said. He stood, dripping wet, under the shower head. *"Toalla?"*

"So let him investigate, if he has doubts." When she glanced at the naked man, Jace flushed and turned away. "That's what we all want, right? No doubt? Self-defense all the way?"

"Listen to me, Miss Bleeding Heart," Warner said. "A cop should never question another cop in that situation. Reynolds or this other guy, this Sterling County guy—"

"Vasquez," Smit said. "Deputy Eduardo Vasquez."

"Reynolds or Vasquez says it was self-defense, that's damn well what it was."

"As much as I want to." Jace tried, and failed, to make her voice as low and intimidating as his. So she jammed her finger into his badge as he'd done to her. "And it's not Miss Bleeding Heart . . . it's Deputy Bleeding Heart."

Instead of getting red-faced, he grinned. "Stepped up quick, didn't she?"

Smit nodded. "Impressive." Smit smiled at Jace's confusion. "He's like this with everybody. Gets on everybody's nerves."

"He's acting like an asshole," Jace said.

"No, he actually is an asshole. Likes cranking people up. Frontal lobotomy."

With a warm smile, Warner wiped the corners of his mouth, and winked.

"Gringo," the man called. *"Ropaje?"*

"Calm down, Pedro," Warner said. "Or you ain't getting no clothes at all."

Chapter Nine

That second night, Dillon gave her transport duty.

"Interviews," Dillon said. "Get them to Captain Ezrin."

"Uh . . ." Jace glanced around roll call. "What do I . . ."

"Shackles and cuffs," Dillon said. "Take them to Interview Three, stand outside the door until he's done, then take them back and hook up the next one."

Bogan, sitting next to Jace, sucking on candies from a bag of Skittles, said, "Interviews at night?"

"Whenever he wants, Deputy."

"Man's a Ranger," someone said.

"Calm down," Dillon said. "Ezrin's doing his job."

"Yeah." It was the voice from the back of the room again. Jace looked over, saw a heavy woman, a fifteen-year pin on her uniform and the whisper of a mustache on her upper lip.

"How long is it going to take?" Jace asked.

The list of names Dillon fluttered at her was nearly a page long. "As long as it takes."

"Roger that," the heavy woman said. "Whatever they want, whenever they want, as many times as they want."

"I'd be a Ranger in a second," another jailer said. He glared at the woman and she rolled her eyes in dismissal.

Dillon's jaw set. "Those of you who hate the Rangers, shut up. Those of you who want to be Rangers, shut up."

"So," Bogan said, munching the candy. "Are we assuming everyone is a security prisoner right now?"

"Until further notice."

Jace ground her teeth. She didn't want to spend her night roving the halls with shackled men. Even though she was scared, she wanted to get back to the pod. She wanted to prove to the other deputies she was ready for this job. At roll call, some had been fine and given her a nod and a smile, some had told her she'd done well. But others wore their distrust like a gunbelt, holster unsnapped.

"All right," Dillon said. "Anything else?"

The fifteen-year female jailer with the mustache looked like she wanted to speak, but didn't. Instead, she set her jaw and slammed her notebook closed.

"Fine. Get to work and for God's sake be careful, tempers are probably running a little hot."

"Gee, Sarge, you think?" Mustache Woman said.

"What was your assignment?" Dillon asked.

"A Pod."

"Yeah, change that to medical."

Her face fell. "Come on. I don't want to deal with whiners all night."

"Me either, but we all have our crosses to bear, don't we? Dismissed."

Ten minutes later, Jace was in A Pod while two older guards watched her carefully from behind the jailer's desk. With the exception of a lone white man near the TV, the pod was empty.

"Already locked down?" Jace asked.

"Never unlocked," the female jailer said. "Had a death . . . or don't you remember."

Jace ignored the comment, nodded toward the inmate near the TV.

"Waiting on you," the woman said.

The male jailer handed her a pair of leg shackles and handcuffs while the inmate came toward her, hands behind his back, his eyes on hers. His body language was slow and deliberate. He didn't want anyone to mistake his intentions.

"Kneel, face the wall, and don't move your hands off that wall." Jace hated the strain in her voice.

The man knelt. "Ain't moving, CO." From the ends of his pants, two skinny white legs poked out.

"Deputy? You okay?"

Jace blinked at the two jailers. "Huh?"

"Got a little pale, honey," the female said.

"What? No, I'm fine. Just a little—I'm fine. Thanks."

Licking her lips, Jace hooked the inmate up, feet first, then hands. Before he stood, the male guard said again, "Tight."

"Aw, CO, come on, ain't running nowhere."

The jailer shook his head. "Tight. No chances, not tonight." He pulled Jace aside. "Little tense around the old homestead today, Deputy. Especially in here."

Jace had felt it the moment she cracked A Pod's inner door. Tension ran as thick as sewage; on every face in the pod, both inmate and guard. Last night the tension, until the fight, had been hers. Now it was everyone's. God knew how long it would last. Maybe it would never go away. Maybe for her entire career she'd have to breathe this tainted air.

"Okay," she said. "Thanks."

Before she could radio for the door, the inner door opened. She glanced at the camera behind the jailer's desk.

The woman said, "They watch close when you're moving inmates around."

With a nod, Jace took the inmate into the go-between. The inner door closed and some part of her waited for the alarm to shriek just as it had last night.

"A-adam outer door, please," she radioed.

And again, like last night, nothing happened.

"Control? A-adam outer."

—who are you and where you going—

"Deputy Salome . . . 479. I'm going to Interview Three for Captain Ezrin."

—tell him you were coming?—

"He knows."

—no. Did you tell him you're coming right now? You're not going to wander my halls with an inmate, waiting for Ezrin to get back from the john—

"Uh . . . no."

—yeah, lemme do your job for you—

The radio fell silent while the control room officer called Ezrin. Jace and the inmate waited, the inmate shackled, Jace sweating, for two full minutes before the outer door opened.

—he's waiting—

"Ten-four."

In the empty hallway, the inmate stopped.

Jace tensed, kept her left hand on the inmate's elbow, her right hand near her pepper spray.

"Calm down, Deputy," the man, his name was Bobby, said. "I just wanna ask can'cha loosen these things?" He rattled the cuffs and shackles. "They too damned tight." His face looked like that of a sad dog. "Come on, where I'm gonna go, even if I do get free?"

After a moment's hesitation, Jace knelt in front of him and loosened the shackles. When she stood, his eyes were tight on hers, a tiny smirk at the edge of his lips.

"Ever'body's gotta be a rookie for a while."

—405 to medical—

—10-4—

Kneeling in front of an inmate. Could you be any stupider, she wondered? Bobby could have split her skull open with his cuffs or kicked her in the face. Swallowing, her hands clenched, she stepped away from him.

"Ain't gonna do nothing stupid, Deputy."

"Damn straight." The words were more for her than him.

At the far end of the hallway, a camera stared at them. "Hah, they watching, Deputy, don't think they ain't. Newbie like you? And the night after you murdered one of us? They all watching."

"I didn't kill him."

"Y'all all together. One badge, don't matter the face." He rattled his shackles. "They saw you loosen these. Gonna getcha a yelling." He winked. "Ain't no worries, Deputy. You done me a favor. You have any trouble, it ain't gonna be from Inmate Bobby."

"Uh . . . thanks. I appreciate that."

The shackles forced them into a slow walk. The metallic rattling bounced off the wall and the concrete floor. *They didn't need to call Ezrin,* Jace thought, *he could hear us a mile away.*

—control room to 419—

—go ahead control—

—one male 10-95 ETA five—

—10-4—

"You know that fight wasn't what it looked like, right, CO?"

"Thomas attacked my partner."

The inmate never stopped moving, never raised his hands or turned his head. "Yeah? Didn't look like it from where I was."

"You were on the first tier. On the other side of the pod."

"I seen it all, CO."

"Don't think you did."

"Then why that Ranger wanna talk to me?"

"Talking to everyone."

"Everyone?" Inmate Bobby asked. "Ain't everyone, jailer ma'am. That list you got is thirty names long. Thereabouts."

Crossing from the main hallway into a smaller one, she said,

"How do you know that?"

He shrugged. "Thirty names on that paper and how many inmates you got overstuffed in that pod right now?"

They both knew the answer. It was 97 last night, 102 tonight. By tomorrow it might be 105. Or it could be 95. There was never any predicting how many people would get arrested, how many would get transferred to prison, or how many would make bail or finish their time.

The inmate slowed, forcing Jace to slow. She glanced at the camera.

"Take it easy, CO," Inmate Bobby said. "We just having a talk, tha'ss all. And I'm going to tell you this because you're a decent cop."

She frowned. "You don't know me."

He laughed. "Bullshit. That was me in the lower cell. When you were on the ground, under that plastic shield? That was me you was looking at. I know last night bothered you. Bother you even more when you understand what's what."

"Uh-huh." *Don't listen. They'll say anything, do anything, to get extra food or extra phone time or whatever. Don't listen to anything he says.*

"You keep your ass away from Deputy Reynolds," the inmate said.

The end of the hallway, Interview Three, was about fifty feet away.

"He's bad news." The inmate whistled.

"Meaning what?"

The man grinned as they passed Interview One. "Some guards don't like some jailbirds. Knowwhadda mean? Sometimes those guards go to getting in an inmate's face. Or go to taking away privileges for no reason."

"There is always a reason."

"Think so? Wait 'til you been here a while. Look, I saw how

you handled that guy."

"What guy?"

"The dead guy. He wasn't a bad man. Wasn't no piece of shit. We got some here, but not him. I saw how you talked to him before the beating. He was scared. You calmed him down."

They stopped at the door to Interview Three. "So what?"

The man swallowed. "I been that scared. I been as scared as he was and it'd'a been nice if someone gave me the kind of respect you gave him."

"When were you that scared?"

"When I spent the rest of my life looking up the barrel of a gun. See, I ain't got no family left, Deputy. We was all sitting one night, watching them Cowboys beat up on the Raiders and then they was gone."

"Who was gone?"

"My family. My brother came in, flying on meth or I don't even know what. Waving his gun around, screaming about how it was too hard."

"What was too hard?"

"Life, I guess, I don't know. He wasn't making no sense, just talking and talking and all I saw? The shadow of the sweat on his lip, swear to God. Kept thinking, hey, he'd look all right with a mustache but there ain't no way he's gonna get old enough for a mustache and it ain't gonna grow in no coffin. I kept thinking, he's gonna be dead in a little while. Maybe a cop will shoot him or maybe he'll shoot himself. Either way, we all gonna be dead."

The man took a deep breath. "Then he started shooting. Kept saying it wasn't worth it. Nothing was worth all the shit."

"What happened to you?"

"Took two bullets to the abdomen," Captain Ezrin said. He stood at the door. Tonight he wore a suit and the same boots. "Spent weeks in the hospital."

"Captain," Jace said. "I was just about to bring him in."

"The problem with the story—" Ezrin said.

"Captain," Inmate Bobby said. "Come on, now, don't do me this way."

"The problem with the story is that his brother wasn't the shooter." With a chuckle, Ezrin motioned them to follow him inside.

"Who was?" Jace asked.

Ezrin put Bobby in a chair. "The other problem is that Bobby's night wasn't that sexy. No one died."

"No, but they all went away, didn't they, Captain?"

"What?"

"Bobby likes his candy. When his family was gone one night, he robbed the house, looking for candy money. Then he shot the house up. When he came out of his stupor a week later, the family was gone. Left almost everything behind and beat feet outta town."

"Yeah," Bobby said. "I'm pretty sure they living in Odessa now."

Ezrin grinned. "Nice try, Bobby. I can't tell you what I don't know."

Bobby winked. "I'm just serving out some county time, tha'ss all."

Jace ground her teeth. "No trouble from you, huh? Guess that favor didn't get me much, did it?"

The inmate grinned. "Didn't give you no trouble in that hallway, did I?" He got somber in a hurry when he saw her face. "I come through on my promises, CO. Ain't gonna give you no trouble at all. I was just having some fun."

Ezrin laughed and nodded Jace toward the door. "Close it behind you, Deputy. I'll let you know when I'm done."

"I should go?"

"Absolutely not. You wait by that door. I'll call you."

"Yes, sir."

"I guess we're done." Ezrin shook his head. "You ought to talk to me, Bobby."

"Been telling you for a half hour, Captain, I got nothing to say."

"Five bucks on your commissary account."

The inmate snorted. "Five bucks? Tha'ss pretty funny, Captain."

Ezrin's face went a deep scarlet that crawled from beneath his collar and disappeared beneath his thick head of dark hair. "How about ten? That do it for you?"

"Can we go, CO?" Inmate Bobby asked Jace.

"Uh . . . sure," Jace said.

"They find anything in Thomas' cell, Deputy?"

Inmate Bobby answered. "When they shake three or four times a day, a man ain't got much time to get himself some contraband, does he?"

Without another word, Ezrin closed the door. She took three or four steps before her radio buzzed.

—479 where are you going—

"A Pod."

—told you already, don't wander my halls with an inmate unless I know what's what—

"Boy ought to chill out," the inmate said.

"Yes . . . uh, sir. Yes, sir."

—i'll have A Pod hook up the next one—

"Ten-four."

Then it was quiet and they were alone, two people in a hallway, separated by nothing more than metal. Bobby's was hardened steel, tightened and locked around his ankles and wrists. Steel that kept him from moving much; that kept him exactly where the officers wanted him.

"Why didn't you talk to him?"

"He ain't done me no favors."

"Ten dollars is pretty good. Our commissary isn't that big, not all that much you can buy. Ramen noodles, maybe."

Bobby cocked his head. "That supposed to be funny? Noodles? I'm gonna buy something, I'm gonna get me about a hundred packs of those little chocolate donuts." He smacked his lips and the sound echoed in the hallway. "Take a crapload of punches for some'a those donuts. Couple weeks in lockdown wouldn't be nothing 'cause when I got out, I'd have those mofos all to myself."

Jace laughed.

"Fifty bucks they get and little Ranger man offered me ten. He wants the word, he gotta fork over the juice."

"Fifty bucks? Those donuts aren't that expensive."

Bobby smacked his lips again. "Take a lot of punches for fifty bucks. Buy a lot of donuts. You ever need anything from me, CO, get me some donuts and my world is yours."

She keyed her mic, "A-adam outer," then said to him, "I have no idea what that means."

He laughed. "Don't mean nothing. Nothing from nothing don't mean nothing."

They entered and Jace waited for the door to close. "A-adam inner."

When it popped, she handed Bobby over to the jailers.

"When do you start as trusty?" the female asked as she held tightly to Inmate Bobby's arm.

"Tomorrow, ma'am." He smacked his lips again. "Few extra privileges, maybe get me some chocolate donuts without having to take them punches."

Another inmate, shackled and cuffed, stood with his face to

the wall near the TV.

"Can you call Captain Ezrin," Jace asked the jailer. "See if he's ready for this guy?"

The male jailer, his face heavy with boredom, made the call. "Yep."

"Thanks." Jace took hold of the inmate's arm. "A-adam inner."

—Ezrin know you're coming—

"Yes, sir. I already told him."

—I'm not a sir. But you're learning, I guess—

They moved into the hallway and again, the only sound was them rattling along the corridor. Once again, Jace realized each of them had their own metal. The inmates had the hard steel of the shackles and cuffs.

And hers, pinned to her chest, was nothing more than soft brass.

Chapter Ten

When she got to work Wednesday night, the lifting had begun.

At roll call, Dillon announced that lockdown was partially over, by order of Chief Deputy Cornutt. "Trusties can get back to their jobs."

"Good," Mustache Woman said. "I'm tired of doing their mopping."

"You ain't never mopped in your life," said a younger jailer.

With a flick of a finger, Mustache Woman continued filing her nails.

"Calm down, people." Dillon made a few announcements about vacations and overtime, as well as two federal prisoners coming through for housing. "They'll be here a couple of weeks, then move on down the road."

"Dealers?" a jailer asked.

"Coyotes. Going district to district, ratting out smugglers."

"Any news on Sonny Lee?" someone asked.

"Austin PD's still looking for him and the woman." Dillon shrugged. "Anything else? Get to it, then. And people, please, a little more professionalism on the radio. You guys know the sheriff pops up at odd hours. Let's not let him think of C Team as the least professional one."

When the room was empty, Jace breathed. Last night and so far tonight, the jailers had been too casual with their glances. Their comments dwindled when she came into a room and the war stories they told when she was around were told with psychic ice picks. This deputy helped his partner take down a jail gang. That deputy—and his partner—thwarted a drug smuggling ring inside D Pod. Some other deputy, and his partner, stopped an inmate from shanking a guard. It wasn't even the tacky glory covering every story that Jace hated. It was that every story had a partner. They were all reminders that she'd left her partner alone.

"Where you off to?" Bogan asked.

Jace glanced at her list of names. "Guy in D Pod. Apparently he was in A that night."

"Been a bad boy since then, I guess. Wanna do dinner?"

"I brought some of my gramma's barbeque."

"What if I'm a vegetarian?"

"There are no such creatures in Texas, goes against our DNA."

"Too right, sister." Bogan offered a closed fist and patiently waited for a surprised Jace to touch hers to it. When she did, Bogan nodded. "Catch you in a few hours."

"Later."

A few minutes later, Jace stood in D Pod, her senses alive and only a notch or two dialed down from the previous night. Everyone, save a single trusty, was locked down and—judging by the empty windows in each of the 48 cell doors—already in bed.

"They're down," the jailer said. He offered a hand. "I'm Royce. 459 on the air."

"Nice to meet you. Are you dead shift?"

He shook his head. "Second. My relief is in the can. I'll always give a man a few minutes for the bathroom."

She chuckled. "Collect those IOUs, I guess. I'm looking for—" She looked at the list. "Reid. That him in the corner?"

"Shackled and ready to go. But I got something, first, if you don't mind." Royce pointed toward an upper-tier cell. "Massie.

He needs to come downstairs. He's got some kind of heights thing, can't stand being up there." Royce shrugged. "Normally, I wouldn't give a shit. I mean, they're bad guys, right? But I figure I've got an empty cell so what's the harm."

"Sure."

Jace headed up the stairs to the cell Royce popped open via computer. Inside, an older man sat on his bunk. None of his belongings were packed. He frowned when she came in.

"You ready to go, Mr. Massie?"

"What? Go where?"

"Downstairs. The CO said you wanted a downstairs cell."

"It's your world, boss."

Massie packed quickly and walked in front of her downstairs. From the control desk, Royce popped open a cell and Massie went in. Jace closed the door, checked to make sure it was locked, then went back to the jailer's desk.

"Thanks," Royce said.

"No sweat." Jace nodded toward the shackled inmate. "Can you call Captain Ezrin for me, please? See if he's ready."

As Royce called the Ranger, a familiar voice reached out from behind Jace. "Hey, Sheriff Salome."

"Bobby. How are you?"

Inmate Bobby took a deep breath. "Glad to be outta that cell." He swung his mop a few times. "Got me some mopping to do."

"Mopping for donuts."

He smacked his lips. "Food of the gods."

"Mr. Reid. Are you ready?" When he looked up, Jace motioned him over.

"Yo, CO," an inmate called through the chuckhole in his first-tier cell. When he had Jace's attention, he stood back from the window and flexed his biceps. Then he pressed his face back against the door.

"Got tickets to the gun show?"

An electric shock blasted through her. *Is that a threat? Because of Thomas? Or just because of the badge?* With a hard swallow, Jace let her right hand hover near her pepper spray.

"Phillips," Royce called. "Shut up. Go to sleep. No one wants to hear it."

The inmate turned away with a sly grin that left a herd of horses pounding in Jace's gut. When she looked at Royce, he shook his head.

"Anyways," Inmate Bobby said, following Jace toward the inner-door entryway. "I love being trusty. Get outta the cell, get some freedom? Ain't nothing better." He lowered his voice. "Captain Ezrin getting anywhere?"

"Might be, if you'd help him out."

Inmate Bobby laughed. "Ain't gonna happen, Sheriff Salome. I already helped who I'm gonna help."

"Yeah? Who's that?"

He aimed a finger gun at her and dropped his thumb as though firing it.

"I'm ready, CO," Reid said.

With his head low and shoulders hunched, Reid reminded her of one of Preacher's penitents. Or of Thomas. The way he looked when Reynolds was jabbing his finger in the man's chest. Uncomfortable with the picture, she grabbed Reid by the shoulder and forced him to stand taller. Then clicked on her radio and keyed the mic.

"Control from 479 . . . D-david inner." She eyed Royce and he gave her a thumbs-up. "Headed to Interview Three for Captain Ezrin. He knows we're coming."

—479 from control . . . you are figuring it out, aren't you—

A heartbeat later, the inner door popped.

Chapter Eleven

It didn't end Wednesday night.

Escort duty stretched into Thursday. That night's shift passed in a monotonous smear of badges and inmates, and ultimately, Inmate Bobby had been just about right. Ezrin had interviewed thirty-four inmates, all of whom had been in A Pod the night of Thomas' death. Jace escorted most of them—including eleven who had since been moved to other pods—in the three nights after the death, and none spoke to her the way Inmate Bobby had. He seemed to have no problem talking to her.

His only problem, she believed, was his insistence that Reynolds' fight with Thomas was other than what it seemed. That insistence was what had kept her awake most of the day between shifts. She'd slept maybe four hours each day and that had been mostly tossing around her bed.

"Deputy?" The civilian records manager eyed her as she paced back and forth in front of the elevator.

Other than a set of restrooms, there was nothing in the Sheriff's Office basement except the sprawling records room and a stairwell down to a sub-basement hallway that led to the courthouse. This area had once been the section for violent inmates and the records manager still locked his kingdom behind a heavy iron door dotted with five separate deadbolt locks.

"Can I help you?" The counter behind which he stood ran the entire width of the room.

"Uh . . . no."

One of his eyebrows rose. "Either you came for records or you're lost. Are you lost, Deputy?"

"Uh . . . no. I just—I just needed someplace quiet."

"Well, certainly." He frowned. "By all means, do come in, take all the time you need. Don't let us interrupt you. After all, we're just working here."

Emphasizing his point, the man waded into reams of folders and loose pages. Behind him, a single staff member pulled files from a wall of shelves, wrote, then shoved those folders back into their slots.

"I . . . uh . . . I'm sorry." Jace's mouth went dry. "I didn't mean to cause any problems."

"The moment you stepped off the lift."

"The what?"

"The elevator," said the file clerk. A cigarette sat cocked behind her ear. "In England they call it a lift. Friggin' Anglophile. America isn't good enough, I guess. Wants to be in England."

"Deputy, this area is restricted to—"

"Hey, Queen Victoria," the file clerk said. "It is not. Quit giving her crap."

"That is not my name."

"Whatever." The clerk disappeared into her stack of red folders.

Whether he meant to or not, Inmate Bobby had sent her down here. *Fifty dollars is what I could've gotten.* His comments were both too random and too specific. *Take a lot of punches . . .* His three nights of gentle yapping had brought her down here.

"Deputy, you look lost. Perhaps you'd like to take the lift back to your part of the world."

"Actually, sir, I need to see the current commissary accounts, please."

"Absolutely not."

Jace blinked. "What?"

The man shook his head. "Rookie deputies don't ask for records." He paused. "Why do you want them . . . worm?"

Because I think a fight that killed a man wasn't as much of a fight as we'd like to believe and because my sergeant's words about why we're cops won't get out of my head.

"Uh . . . blackmail. A couple of inmates have threatened to attack other inmates."

"Unless?"

"Unless the families of the guys they threaten put some money on their accounts."

His steel gaze sat heavily on her. "An investigation? Quite good duty for a probationary officer. You are probationary, are you not?"

"Yeah. Uh . . . yes, sir. Sergeant Dillon asked me to look into it."

His eyebrow rose again. "Which inmates?"

"Uh . . . names?"

"Holy crap, Queen," Deputy Bogan said. She stood in the elevator doorway. "Can't'cha see she's trying to make her bones? Chill out."

His face was still harsh and angry around the edges, but every time his eyes fell on Bogan, he melted a little. "Trying to make bones, is she?"

Bogan didn't quite bat her eyelashes. Smiling, she leaned chest first over the counter. "Like every other newbie cop in this place. Gotta get some attention, get some attaboys, don't want to be in the jail forever. Like me, Queen. I've been inside the crossbar hotel how long?"

"Three years."

"Three long years. Can't climb that ladder out if I don't build some rungs. Same thing with Deputy Salome. She's building her rungs."

"Ambition," he said. "Nobody wants to do what they're hired for. Everybody wants to get to the next thing. Fine." He held up a finger. "Next time you come here in and lie to me about Sergeant Dillon, I will turn you over to him. Understand me?"

"Yes, sir."

"Lighten up, Queen," Bogan said.

His face reddened. "Balsamo. Albert Balsamo. Take care not to forget it."

When Bogan winked at him, Jace felt the last bit of his edge disappear, along with the last touch of his faux-Britishness. "I swear to God, Rory, you're going to get me in trouble. One day I'm going to look up and see eight or ten detectives standing in my elevator, search warrants in hand, evidence bags full of everything I do and—"

"My God, James," Bogan said. "When did you get to be such a drama—" she paused for a beat "—queen?"

A disarming grin played at his lips. "This queen stuff has got to stop."

"No chance," Bogan said.

"You know I won't hesitate to give them your name, right?" he asked.

"Because you'll need to save yourself?"

"Because he'll need a cellmate," Jace said.

Bogan laughed and the sound startled Jace. It was high and sweet like a summer rainstorm.

"You are, I think, using sex as a tool," James said. "I'll file suit, don't think I won't."

"I'm not using it as a tool, I'm using it as a promise."

With a shake of his head, he punched up a file. "Who?"

He stared at Bogan, who in turn stared at Jace.

Jace shrugged. "Anybody get fifty dollars on their accounts in the last couple of weeks?"

Without a word, James clicked through a few files. A second later, a printer spit out four pages. Rows and rows of dollar amounts, alongside listings of what the inmate had bought. Not that many inmates, but lots of activity.

Jace took the pages. "Thank you."

The man gave a quick bow. "Anytime, Deputy."

"Oh, yeah," Bogan said. "Now you've got a new girl toy. What, I'm a used condom so you toss me in the garbage?" She winked at Jace. "An Anglophile or not, he's a dirty old man, sister, and now he's looking at you."

With a casual shrug, Jace headed for the elevator. "As well he should be."

"Ouch," Bogan said with a chuckle.

"So," Bogan said. "What'cha doing?"

They stood outside the jail and although the sun wasn't particularly high yet, the air was already hot. By noon the air would be heavy with the stink of heat and traffic.

Jace took a deep breath. "Something Inmate Bobby told me."

"The trusty?"

"When I took him to Ezrin, he said the fight wasn't what it looked like."

Bogan put her hand on Jace's arm to quiet her. In front of them, a van pulled up and spilled out two members of the extradition team.

"Got a good one today, boys?" Bogan asked.

"Same old shit, different day." The older man shrugged. "Ector County, Lubbock County. Swisher. Be back before dinner."

"Bad guys?"

The driver nodded. "Two tweakers, cooking meth in a garage next to a day care. One guy on a felony failure to appear."

When they were alone again, Bogan cocked her head toward them. "Everybody's got open ears and runny mouths. If you learn anything quick, learn that. Anyway, which fight? There were two."

"He could be talking about both of them, for all I know."

"You believe an inmate?"

Jace shrugged. "He seemed sincere. I talk to him a little every night. He keeps saying the same thing."

"Look, they all know how to play the game."

"Isn't that a little cynical? Are you saying they're never sincere?"

"Nope. I'm saying they all seem sincere the first time. When you get grown-up, your radar will start working."

Jace tried to read Bogan's face, but it was stone empty as though she had no thoughts about any of this. "I think this is real."

Bogan stared hard at Jace. "Inmate's word over a deputy's?"

"Don't you think it's at least worth a look? If he's lying to me, I'll see that pretty quickly, right? I mean, the records are all here." She waved the pages.

With a tired sigh, Bogan nodded. "So let's give a look-see. But you're wrong. This was nothing but an inmate attacking a guard."

"So why are you looking with me?"

"I got nothing better to do. Plus, I love seeing trains fly off the tracks and crash into people's careers."

"Gee, thanks. And what if the Amtrak doesn't go off the tracks?"

For a split second, no longer than a flash of lightning, Bogan's face opened and Jace thought Bogan considered the possibility. But almost immediately, the woman's face closed back down. "It will."

" 'No such thing as just a fight.' You told me that last night."

It had been during a break in the middle of a hot night. The two of them had stood in a far corner of the parking lot, watching the newspaper delivery trucks pass, the yellow reflective stripe that speared the side of the truck snapping the arc-sodium streetlamp light back at them. Prisoners don't fight, the veteran had said, because they're bored. They fight for a reason, regardless of how stupid that reason might be.

"Yeah, well." Bogan shrugged. "First of all, don't use my words against me. And second of all, what do you think is going on? What's the big conspiracy?"

"I don't know. I'm the worm, remember?"

"You're new and new cops see everything everywhere."

"I just want to know what they're fighting about. I'm only asking a question."

The pages fluttered in the vague breeze. Eventually, Jace looked and pointed to two names. Each had fifty dollars deposited in their accounts a few days before the ERTs exploded into D Pod. "Fifty bucks a reason to fight?"

"I'll bet there are a bunch of inmates with fifty bucks on their accounts."

"Yeah, but not all of those inmates got in a fight Monday night. Those are the two who did and Inmate Bobby implied they were paid to fight."

Bogan looked at Jace. "Brother gangbangers, too. But is fifty bucks enough to get two South Side boys to beat each other bloody and get some segregation time?" Rory held Jace's gaze.

"You know what else strikes me about that fight?"

"What?"

Jace licked her lips and watched the squad cars coming and going, back seats sometimes filled with the newly arrested, sometimes empty. The extradition team came out carrying a handful of files. They hopped in their van, waved to Rory and Jace, and slipped into traffic. "The timing. They were fighting just before Reynolds and Thomas had their little set-to."

Bogan shook her head. "Everybody knows what that alarm is.

Thomas heard it and figured if the ERTs were busy, he'd take his shot."

"Maybe." Jace stared at the two inmates' accounts until something caught her eye. On the far right side of the page, in a column filled with the names of who put money in the accounts, sat a number: 410.

"That's Reynolds," Bogan said.

"Bobby was right. He paid them to fight."

Chapter Twelve

The night after Thomas died, Bogan said, "Those nerves will be better when you getcha some jail balls."

Jace had bitten the last of a fingernail off and stared at the woman. "What?"

"I ain't scared of nothing, sister. Jail balls." Bogan had banged a fist against the steering wheel as they drove to a twenty-four-hour McDonald's on a 2:30 a.m. dinner break.

"Whereas I'm scared of everything." Jace had avoided Bogan's gaze.

"You're not scared of everything, you're scared of the big thing."

"The big thing happened to Thomas."

"Might happen to someone else, too. Inmate. Guard. Maybe a road deputy. That's the job. But Thomas' death isn't the worst thing you'll see in your time in the jail."

"You make it sound like a sentence."

"Well . . . sometimes it is."

"I guess . . . I don't know." Jace sighed. She and Bogan had fallen fairly quickly into a vague comfort zone but maybe some things were best left by the side of the road. "I'm not sure I can do this job."

Rummaging in the glove box, Bogan had come up with an unopened bag of Skittles. After ripping the top off, she sorted out the yellow. One by one, they had disappeared. "My favorite. You might be right, you might not be a jailer. I think you are, but what do I know from nothing? We're all scared, if we have half a brain. Look, my first few weeks, I was terrified some idiot was going to get me alone and beat me to death."

"What happened?"

"*It* did. I got my butt handed to me. I was so worried about not getting hurt that I guaranteed I'd get hurt. I was tentative and cautious and jumpy. And I'll tell you what, you'll see it soon enough, those inmates can smell fear. Don't worry about getting hurt, Jace, because you absolutely will. You are going to be in fights and you are going to get hurt and yeah, you will see dead inmates. A guy staring down twenty years in prison with no parole will hang himself or a kiddie-diddler realizes he'll be locked down in protective custody twenty-three hours a day for the rest of his life and he'll slash his throat or whatever. There's no way you can work a job like this and not get hurt."

"That kind of fatalism is okay with you?"

"Strangely liberating," Bogan had said, munching contentedly. "But all the other bullshit aside: bullies are pussies."

A strained laugh had bubbled out of Jace. "What?"

"If they get in your face, get back in theirs. Ninety-nine times out of a hundred, they'll back down."

"It's that one time they don't that scares me."

"It ought to. But remember: every copper in that jail is as close as that radio. Doesn't matter if we like you or not, someone wearing a badge will come busting through that door when you do get in that fight."

"And if I'm alone?"

"If you're alone, then the bad guy has already killed me."

"More fatalism. You're freaking me out."

"Yeah, well, whatever." With a laugh, Bogan had run them through the drive-thru and they'd eaten hamburgers at the park.

This morning, after getting records from Balsamo, and instead of going home, Jace went to breakfast with Bogan. Once again Jace marveled at how quickly they'd found a groove. Bogan was intelligent and quick but with a sarcastic, funny edge. And that Jace had yet to see her back down from anything made her the ballsiest person Jace had ever met.

"You don't make friends quick, do you?" Bogan asked as they arrived at a café.

"Why do you say that?"

"Haven't used my first name. Ain't any too gabby, either."

"Well . . . I guess I don't have much to say."

"Everyone else can't tell their same old stories fast enough and there you are—" Bogan closed her mouth and let her eyes go wide in a caricature of silence.

The café was called Alley B's. A bar and grill on the northeastern edge of the city, sandwiched between what had once been a rich man's cemetery and a baseball field where the AA team played.

"Ever go to a game?" Bogan asked.

"I'm not much of a baseball fan."

"Goofy game. And unfair. I mean, nine guys against one guy with a stick? Come on."

Alley B's was full of customers but in spite of them, heavy desolation was always near. Dark walls, no music, no pay phone jangling. The front wall, which faced Big Spring Street as it became a state route headed for Lamesa, was a giant plate-glass window. Alley B kept it covered with thick, heavy blinds that were only opened during the ball field's July fireworks.

"So," Jace asked after they were seated. "Do you think Reynolds bought that fight?"

"Yep. Seems obvious, given who we're talking about. All I was trying to say is, don't automatically take the word of an inmate over that of a cop. No one tells you everything exactly how it is. Get used to it. We are the poh-poh, everyone lies to us to some degree."

"Why buy a fight?"

"Blood sport. Every time there's a fight in the jail, Reynolds goes straight to Bibb and finagles a copy of the vid to watch at home."

A waiter came. "Ladies. What can I get you?"

Jace randomly pointed to a numbered breakfast. "That'll be fine."

When she shook her head, as she did now, Bogan's board-straight brown hair shook like tall grass in a heavy breeze. "No breakfast. One banana split each. Fudge, nuts, whipped cream. Bag the cherries."

The kid, probably no more than twenty-five years old, frowned. "What?"

"Bag the cherries. Give 'em to the next guy. Put 'em on some huevos rancheros."

"No . . . I mean . . . banana splits?"

"Not just for breakfast anymore." Bogan winked.

With an amused grunt, the man wandered back to the kitchen.

"He looks confused," Jace said.

"Lots of confused people walking around these days."

"Banana splits?"

"Eggs and bacon and toast and coffee? Blah. Plus, they've got bananas, right? So that's breakfasty." Bogan leaned toward Jace. "Kind of girly, though, isn't it? 'I'm stressed so bring me ice cream.' "

Jace laughed. A few old men glared at her and she resisted the urge to snarl at them. "So are you stressed?"

"I'm always stressed. Standard operating procedure."

That was a surprise. Bogan seemed so easygoing and relaxed. "About?"

Bogan waved her hand dismissively. "Wish I had me some Skittles. Wouldn't that be great? Skittles over a split?"

"A delicacy of the modern world."

After an awkward moment, Jace touched the pages she'd gotten from Records. "So a guard puts money on someone's books. How does that work? The jailer gives the money to whom?"

"Jail shift commander or maybe the sergeant. They write a receipt and deposit the money in a safe in the office. Once a week, Lieutenant Traylor goes to the bank, gets working cash for the jail, and deposits inmates' money."

"So Reynolds didn't think anyone would notice."

Bogan laughed. "Getting some money to an inmate isn't a big deal. Happens all the time. It's supposed to be for information only, and sometimes you can get reimbursed, but guards do it for all kinds of reasons. There was a guy once fell in love with one of the female inmates. Put a crapload of money on her account."

"That seems like a problem."

Bogan nodded. "Quit his job over it. They got married and had a couple of kids. Happily ever after and all that crap."

Alley B's was noisy, silverware and glasses clattering, the rumble of indistinguishable conversation, the impatient pad of shoes and boots around the tiled floor. Yet in spite of the noise, it was quiet in their little bubble.

No radio, Jace realized, blaring incomprehensibly in her ear. No string of endless ten codes and badge numbers, and that made everything seem quiet.

"Thanks for the help with Balsamo, I don't think he was going to give me anything."

"He wasn't. It's against regs and Queen is crazed for regulations."

"He gave them to you."

"What can I say? He loves me."

Jace swallowed hard. "Against regs?"

"Only way you can see that stuff is with brass on your

uniform: lieutenant, captain, chief deputy, sheriff, whatever. The tall end of the food chain."

It made sense, Jace supposed, keeping inmate records out of the hands of as many officers as possible. Lessen the chances of tampering or of an officer using the records against an inmate.

Or buying off an inmate or two.

"Then why—"

The waiter interrupted them, depositing a split in front of each woman. Bogan dove into hers, the spoon making quick work.

"Then why did you help me? What if he turns us in?"

Bogan stopped mid-bite. "Queen? Never happen."

"Because he's mentally doing you every time he sees you? What about the file clerk?"

"Rosalie's a gamer."

Jace leaned back. "So answer my question. Why are you helping me?"

"I'm not helping anything. I came downstairs. I happened to find you. We left together to get some breakfast." She slurped. A melty puff of vanilla ice cream disappeared between her lips.

"You helped me get those records. You're helping me prove it wasn't just a fight." Jace leaned in close. "You're helping me prove Reynolds had something else going on."

Bogan shook her head. "First, I didn't help you. Second, even if I had, all I've shown you is that deputies put money on inmates' accounts all the time."

"Have you?"

A bit of ice cream clung to Bogan's bottom lip. Slowly, she raised a napkin and wiped it away. "I have."

"Why?"

Bogan wiped her face. In her hand, she held the napkin so tightly her knuckles were white. *Son of a bitch,* Jace thought. *I just dumped a white-hot load of tension right on this damned table.*

"Bogan?"

"Yeah, my name's Rory, by the way." She paused. "You don't even know what it is you're trying to prove." She banged down her spoon. "This is because of that goddamned inmate. He told you some crap and now it's gospel."

"No, but that guy told me something that made me ask some questions. Isn't that what we're supposed to do?"

"We're supposed to support our fellow officers."

"Even if they've killed someone?"

Disgusted, Bogan slumped against the booth seat. "Christ'a'mighty, Salome, get over it. Reynolds bought a fight because he likes to watch. During that fight, he got attacked. He defended himself. The guy who attacked him died. Did you see anything else?"

Jace let her spoon play idly around the sliced bananas. "Sometimes I can feel his fingers. Thomas'. I reached for him. When he was falling." It had felt as though Thomas touched her and that she'd never be able to wash away the stain of his skin.

What about Reynolds' fingers? What about how they had jabbed into Thomas' chest? Reynolds was a few inches taller than Thomas, but that finger made a difference. Thomas had not only backed away, he'd seemed to shrink when Reynolds towered over him.

"He grew. When he was getting in Thomas' face, Reynolds grew."

"Puffed up."

"Like a chicken," Jace said.

"Like a co—like a rooster. Yeah."

The ice cream was cool going down, counterpoint to the heat outside and deep in Jace's heart. It was all getting to her; not just the death, but the aftermath, too. Interviews and administrative suspensions and tension in the jail where every inmate's eyes pinned every guard to the wall with a terrible ferocity.

But also it was Reynolds. The way his breathing sped up when he dealt with Thomas, the way his body language grew harder. The man wanted to fight. As he talked to Thomas, he wanted Thomas to swing on him.

"He likes to fight, doesn't he?"

Bogan nodded, scooped a bit of fudge over a chunk of banana and pineapple. "He's all about blood sport. Best in his class at control tactics."

He had told her that, hadn't he? He'd told her—and Thomas—that he could kill both of them without breaking a sweat.

"He pushes, too. Pushes the inmates."

"I'll give you that, but that doesn't mean anything, Jace."

"It does, too. You didn't see him, you don't understand. When he was talking to Thomas, before the fight, he was just about out of control."

"This is the job. Better get used to it. Sometimes it looks rough; like someone is out of control, but what they're trying to do is get control."

"That's not what I saw."

Bogan pointed her spoon like an extension of her finger. "You don't know what you saw. It was your first night, how could you even begin to know what you saw? You think you saw one thing when everyone else knows it was something else. Hell, even the inmates know it was legit. You think they'd be this docile if they thought Reynolds had actually murdered an inmate?"

"They have to be docile, they're on lockdown."

"And they can't tear the hell outta their cells on lockdown? They can't bang their cups against their cell doors on lockdown? They can't throw their food out the chuckhole on lockdown? There's a ton of crap they can do on lockdown." Her eyes narrowed. "They know it was legit."

"But don't you find it interesting that there was a fight requiring the ERTs at the very moment Reynolds and Thomas had their fight? Reynolds paid those D Pod guys to fight because he knew the ERTs would crash the pod. He wanted the ERTs to be busy when he went after Thomas."

"Jesus God." Bogan leaned back, banged her head hard into the top of the vinyl booth. "Did he kill Kennedy, too?"

"Sure as shit did," Reynolds said, appearing as suddenly as a West Texas coyote. "Lennon, too." When he slid into the booth, he crowded Jace into the wall, pressing her until their thighs touched. "Why would I go after that slimebag?"

"Which one? Kennedy or Lennon?" Jace asked. The heat from his leg bled through her pants and she shoved back at him. He didn't move.

"What the hell, Reynolds?" Bogan's gaze hardened.

Reynolds ripped Jace's spoon from her grip and shoved it into the split, cutting the remaining banana neatly in two.

"Man, scoot your ass over, you're crowding her." Bogan's face flared.

"We all get a little crowded from time to time, don't we?"

"Two-dollar psychology all you can afford?" Jace asked. Under the table, her hands curled into fists.

"Oooh, pretty good." Reynolds glanced at Bogan. "You must have told her about jail balls. Get back in their face, don't let 'em see you're scared." He leaned close to Jace, his aftershave too sweet in her nose. "I *can* see it, Deputy Salome." He sniffed toward her breasts, then her crotch. "Smell it, too." His eyes dropped to her neck, then back. "Nice tat. Couldn't afford to have it finished?"

At the base of her neck was half of a heart, a tattooed version of the necklaces teenagers bought each other. "Back the hell off'a me, asshole, or we're gonna have a big problem."

With a grin, Reynolds pushed forward.

"Goddamn it." Jace made a grab for his hand, thinking to force it and him backward. But he saw it coming and caught her fingers in his, bending them backward painfully. She yelped.

"Don't ever touch me, bitch, or you'll regret it."

"And you let her go or you'll regret it." Bogan's face blazed.

Smiling, Reynolds let go and put some distance between himself and Jace. "Heard you guys spent a few minutes in Records."

Jace's hand moved to cover the pages sitting on the table.

"Nice try, Deputy Salome. Better try a little harder next time. Rory, so sweet of you to visit Queen."

"That's not his name, jerkwad. It's Albert Balsamo. Sir, to you. And my, oh my, didn't you get that bit of information quick." She looked at Jace. "Guess Rosalie's not as much of a player as I thought."

"You have to put out to get the files?" Reynolds asked.

Bogan licked her spoon. "I was going to, but he mentioned you. Dried me right up."

"Sir," the waiter said. "Can I get you anything?"

"Yeah—"

"No," Bogan said.

"Actually," Jace said. "He's bothering us."

The young man straightened and indicated the door. "Sir, if you could please leave, I would appreciate it."

Reynolds stood and faced the waiter straight on. "Tell you what, why don't you take your faggoty ass back to the kitchen and get some of those wetback cooks. Then all of you can decide exactly who's going to make me leave."

The waiter smiled and, without another word, left.

Reynolds leaned heavily on the table. "I'm not sure what you think you're going to find, worm bitch, but stay the hell out of my business and out of my face. Otherwise—" He grabbed her hair and yanked her head backward until her eyes were directly on him looming over her.

"Whoa. Hey, asshole, let her go." Bogan's voice boomed in the tiny café. When she tried to stand, Reynolds shoved her easily back down in the seat. "Damn it, let—"

"Stay away from us or—" Using two of his fingers, he imitated Thomas falling over the railing. "You'll end up as dead as Thomas." When he let go of Jace, her head snapped forward and bounced off the table. Warm blood cascaded over her lips.

Jace grabbed her nose, tried not to wince at the pain that hit her like an incoming tide, and stared directly at Reynolds.

"Jace, you okay?" Bogan asked.

"You wanna square up on me?" Reynolds said to Jace. "I'll kill you right here and be done with it."

"Are you kidding me?" Bogan asked. "You did not just threaten her like some cheap-ass Tony Montana, did you?"

His face, red-eyed and jaw-clenched, swiveled to Bogan. "I threatened both of you."

"How 'bout this for a threat?" Alley B stood behind Reynolds. When he turned, she showed him a foot-long carving knife stained with sausage, ham, and steak remains. "Get out or we'll have special of heart today. We'll serve it with a nice Romaine salad, some spicy corn, and a Lone Star beer. It'll be a big seller." She flicked the blade toward his chest. "Too bad you won't be able to join us."

The four of them had become everyone's focal point. Cell phones sat forgotten on tables and newspapers fluttered in the stifling breeze. Some customers clearly wanted to see Alley B get to the bloodletting. Others seemed to want something more nuanced.

"Terroristic threat, ma'am," Reynolds said. "Threatening a peace officer. Class A misdemeanor."

"Damn, and here I was hoping I could gin up a felony before breakfast was over." Alley B yanked a cell from her apron. "Why don't we call Sheriff Bukowski and tell him about it. Punch three and you'll get him at home."

Reynolds turned the phone over and over in his hand while he stared at Alley B. Eventually, he set the phone down and headed for the door. At the threshold, he turned back to a bloody Jace and again imitated Thomas going over the railing.

"Sell it on the street," Jace said, spraying blood on the booth and floor. "I'm not buying."

When the door closed, Alley B disappeared. A busboy efficiently cleaned up Jace's blood, as though blood were no surprise. The customers went back to their own worlds, as defined by their tables and booths, and Bogan stifled a laugh.

" 'Sell it on the street'?"

"Leave me alone," Jace said, leaning her head back and pressing a napkin against her nose. "It's the best I could do on short notice."

"No problem, I like seeing a woman sprout some jail balls."

"Just what I always wanted."

Bogan jabbed her spoon into the ice cream. "Man, this would be so much better with some Skittles. Maybe orange."

"Shut up, freak."

And for a few ice cream–slathered moments, the sudden fissure between them closed a bit.

Chapter Thirteen

The worst memories always came by train.

"Can we ride the train, Mama?" As though this time, Mama would say, "Why, yes, Jace, that sounds great. Let's do that. Twice around?" "Three times," Jace would say. "Three times, then." Mama would buy tickets and they'd ride it around the edges of the county's tiny zoo. The smell of the animals, thick and gamey, would stick in their clothes while the sound of their bleating and roaring would lay as heavy as a heat wave on the air.

"Deputy?" Sergeant Bibb said.

In reality, it had always gone like this:

"Mama don't feel like riding." Her eyes were sad, tired things, and always came up from her secondhand book. "But you go. Have fun." Then Mama would give her a pile of wadded-up single dollar bills.

"Salome? You with me?"

The memory dissolved into the control room. It was as dark as Jace's bedroom when she'd shut the lights off and close her curtains. There were no windows here and Sergeant Bibb kept all the overhead fluorescent lights, as well as the two desk lamps, off. A black and white portable TV sat in the corner, blaring with a western movie with a train whistle and a shootout. The Zachary County Zoo's train never had a whistle, though there was a sad and lonely bell.

Jumpy light came not just from the TV, but from fifteen other screens hanging five across and three tall along the wall just beyond the controller's desk. They blasted out a violent glow of blacks and whites and dull grays.

"Salome," Bibb said. He gave her a soft whack on the shoulder.

She startled. "Sorry."

—D-david inner—

—A-adam is down for the night—

—lights out in discipline—

—goodnight, boys—

Red and green lights on the touch screen embedded in the main desk flickered and changed colors in response to Bibb's fingers on the screen. From somewhere deep in the bowels of the jail, Jace heard corresponding doors open and close. The lights were the status of every secured entry in the jail. Bibb opened and closed them all, responding to deputies' calls or sometimes just to seeing a deputy head for a door. The din, overlaid with the constant radio squawk, set a small throb in the back of Jace's head.

—445 from 405 gimme a 25—

—10-4—

"From here," Bibb said as he spread his hands across the computer screens. "I am in charge."

Bibb was a big man and under the glow of the screens, his blotched face shone somehow. His boots were dirty and scuffed and who knew when they'd last seen polish. His uniform was generally clean but worn. The fronts of his thighs were shiny where the polyester pants had worn down under the constant rubbing of the bottom side of the desk top.

"Why am I here, Sergeant?" Jace asked. He'd opened the outer door for her when she arrived at work, but then directed her to see him before roll call. She tapped her watch. "I've got to get to roll."

"Dillon knows where you are."

—D-david outer—

Bibb never even looked. His fingers hit a button, the light changed from green to red as the door opened, then back to green as it closed and locked. As soon as he saw the light change, he popped another door. Again the change from green to red and back again.

"D Pod inner?" she asked.

"Inner comes after outer."

"I guess so," she said. "Fifty percent of the time."

He grinned. "I told Dillon you needed to see the Pen in action so you'd understand what was what."

"I understand—"

"Absolutely nothing." His face stone empty, Bibb pulled a CD from a drawer and dropped it into a machine. A second later, recorded radio traffic filled the small room, muscling aside the current traffic.

"ERT call." Bogan's voice. "Probably a fight." A second of silence, then one of the doors popped open. Bogan said, "Get in there, get them locked down right now, no screwing around. Don't leave the pod until you hear the clear."

"A-adam inner," the recorded Jace said. Her voice was mostly calm and it surprised Jace to hear it. All she remembered was full-throated hysteria. "A-adam inner."

Then a few muffled thumps, probably her pulling on the locked door.

"Damn it, Pod A—as in Adam. Adam adam adam—inner door. Now."

Then a loud bang as she closed the outer door and radioed again for access to the pod.

"You didn't let me in," Jace said to Bibb.

"Nope."

A few seconds passed.

"Son of a bitch," the recording said. "A Pod, inner door. Now. Now."

Her voice boomed with panic. Hearing it again, she ground her teeth.

The speakers spit out, "Oh, my God." This time, the panic was gone. Instead, her voice was almost church quiet before it exploded back to white-hot panic. "Hey. Stop it. Uh . . . freeze."

When she banged the door to get in, Jace lowered her head, somehow embarrassed at her performance.

"Stop it, that's an order." Her voice howled on the recording. "Stop it. That's an order. Thomas! Stop it. Damn it, open the door. A Pod. Violent inmate. Open the door. Open the damn door. Damn it. Officer going down. Officer going down."

Then, as though that had been the magic phrase, Bibb had popped the door lock.

Bibb shut the CD off, stared hard at Jace. "You get what I'm telling you?"

"You haven't told—Sir, excuse me, you haven't told me anything."

"Do the inmates pester you all the time? Asking for aspirin or clean clothes or extra this or that? Asking about mail or toilet paper or whatever?"

—main hall gate—

This time, the light went green to red, indicating the gate had been open and was now closed. Moving a prisoner, Jace thought. Or maybe prisoners. This time, Bibb didn't automatically reopen the gate.

"Do they pester you?"

"Yes, sir."

"I swear to God I'm not a 'sir.' " With a snort, Bibb sat heavily at the desk and cast a quick eye around all the cameras and lights. "They treat you like they're the only person in the world, right? You gotta not treat me the same way, okay? On any given shift, I've got maybe seventy or eighty people moving through this facility. Jailers. Roadies. Detectives. Police from other agencies. Sometimes administration. Medical staff. The public."

"In other words, don't pester you."

"Damn straight. Don't worry, I'll know you're there. I won't forget about you, I'll get you where you need to go." He smirked. "I see all."

As though to prove his point, he popped a door open while his gaze stayed on her.

—thanks, Bibb—

She swallowed. "Sorry, sir. Uh, sorry, Bibb. I just was scared, I guess."

"I know you were, first fight and all. And you done good, Salome, but believe in the support system. I know how to do my job." He pulled the CD from the player. "Like this, for instance. You weren't keyed up, Salome. It wasn't your radio."

She thought about it. "You recorded off the audio you used to talk to us."

"Yep. If an inmate gets you in the go-between, he might kill you if you try to call for help, so all betweens are wired. Don't have to key up but still get some help coming. They are not automatically recorded, but whenever I have an ERT alarm, I flip a switch and put all the betweens into record mode. Not all the control officers do. Never needed it, but you never know. Nothing's ever a problem until it's a problem."

Officer safety. Damn near always the first thing on everyone's mind. Keeping themselves and every other officer safe, get them home after a shift.

"I know how to do my job," Bibb said.

"Yeah, you do," Jace said. "I apologize for pestering you."

He laughed. "Don't worry about that so much, you'll pester me a lot more before you retire."

"Or quit."

"Well . . . whichever . . . but don't worry about officer safety, I've got my eye on you."

Jace cocked her head. "Which means what, exactly?"

For the first time since she'd come into the Pig Pen, Bibb looked flustered. He made an obvious show of studying each and every camera. He popped doors all over the place.

Opening and closing just to cover his embarrassment? Were you a high school AV guy? One of those guys always playing with the latest gear? Computers and recorders and filtering programs. Did you secretly record people and replay them later, all washed and changed and filtered?

"It's not just audio, is it?"

She thought he probably didn't want to say anything, but she also knew this kind of guy. A larger part of him was supremely proud of this little kingdom. He wanted to show it off.

Bibb grabbed a joystick controller and tapped one of the screens. "See that? Deputy Timmy. Pissed that he bid for days but got nights. Got screwed on seniority. Pissed that his trampy girlfriend recently found another friend . . . one with ti—uh—like you. Pissed about pretty much everything right now."

On the screen, the deputy walked the main hallway. Then he turned and slipped away from the camera. Except Bibb punched something and the screen changed to a smaller hallway, and there was Deputy Timmy's face, rather than his behind. Bibb and Jace watched his entire trip into the squad room, which Bibb punched up on yet another screen. Deputy Timmy popped his head into the watch commander's office and then headed for the garage. With Bibb's hands flying over a touch-screen computer monitor, punching up camera after camera, they watched the deputy cross the garage, get into his squad car, drive out the sally port door, and hit the street.

"Watch this."

On the screen, the squad car headed away from the jail,

toward Interstate 20 and Deputy Timmy's assigned area. Bibb played with the joystick and the car got bigger, not smaller. Even the plate was clear as the squad disappeared nearly a half mile down the road.

"How'ya doing, Mr. Blair," Jace said.

"Who?"

"Eric Blair."

"Who?"

"George Orwell's real name."

Bibb frowned. "Orwell a frequent flyer?"

"Frequent fly . . . ? No, no. What I mean is—" Jace nodded toward the screen. "A little Big Brother, don't you think?"

"Nope. Gotta see everything to be on top of everything."

Jace let her laugh taper off. "Man, you are out of control, sitting here watching everything like that. You're like some kind of voyeur."

Still grinning, but his embarrassment replaced by pride, Bibb shook his head. "I'm not *like* a voyeur. I *am* a voyeur." His fingers flew across the keyboard. A few seconds later a file opened on the main screen. "Lemme show you outta control. Hah."

At first it was just A Pod's inner door, from inside the pod. And then there she was. Even in the baggy polyester pants, ugly green with the black stripe down the side, she knew it was her, walking out of A Pod into the go-between. The back of her head, her back and shoulders, her rear end, her legs. Embarrassment flooded through her. Why in hell was this guy recording her walking *away* from the camera? Was he that desperate to see some female behind? Even when it wasn't particularly sexy? "What . . . what the hell is this?"

"What?"

"Why'd you record this?"

The man colored instantly, like a twelve-year-old boy caught with his father's porno mags. "I . . . uh . . . well, I watch . . . uh . . . all the rookies. Gotta make sure you don't do anything stupid."

She said nothing.

"Like with Captain Ezrin. Hell, you were headed right out the door. Nobody knew where you were going. That's an officer safety and facility security problem." He'd found his authority now and laid heavily into her. "My job is the security of this facility and if I have to watch a rookie to make sure she doesn't get herself killed, that's what I'll do. You have a problem? File a complaint."

She nodded.

"Besides, it's all digital. Brand new tech and it rocks my world. I don't have a lot yet, but I've got more coming. D Pod was first, obviously, because of the discipline problems. But this—" He indicated the picture. "Sharp as a tack."

The camera focused on her—closing the distance and making her butt grow—as she walked through the inner door to the go-between.

"Sorry about that," Bibb said. "Uh . . . just getting used to the new joystick."

"I'll bet."

Bibb smirked and a second later, Bogan's face popped into view through the door window.

"But man, look at that definition. God, I love these cameras."

Up close and personal, her face filled the entire screen. Then Bogan's again, as though she and Bogan were dancing back and forth. The view pulled back enough to see both women through the inner door's window. It all seemed so innocuous, so workaday; two employees talking about dinner. But something deep in her gut closed, like flood doors around a town that sat below river level. She hadn't expected this. She'd known there were cameras in the jail and that nearly everything was watched, but she hadn't known someone would watch her like some back-alley old man staring through an open window.

When the camera pulled back, dizzyingly fast, Jace fought a wave of vertigo. The camera view reset on a long, wide shot across most of the pod. This camera, she realized now, was the one hanging over the upper tier in the far northwest corner of the pod.

Concerned, Bogan disappeared and her own face, panicked and terrified, became clear in the window. Her scared eyes, clear even on this recording, put a hot ball of fear in her throat.

"Pretty freaky, ain't it?" Bibb had a self-satisfied grin on his face. "As soon as I heard you screaming—"

Jace bristled.

"—and saw the look on your face, I banged that baby into a hard drive continual save and let it rip."

"And then what?"

"What?" He frowned.

"Then what did you do?"

"Turned my attention back to D Pod, where the real fight was."

On the recording, she saw a face in every cell window, riveted on the dead man.

Then everything else: the ERT team, her on the ground, the command staff, detectives and forensics.

Frowning, she leaned forward and tried to bring the picture to a better focus. "Can you run that back? So I can see it again?"

His gaze came to her and held hers for a long moment. Without a word, his fingers danced once again. The picture started again from when she entered the go-between. "Do you see something?"

"It's the—uh . . . I just want to see my reaction again. Maybe I can see how to do it better next time. Because there will be a next time, right?"

He nodded. "Sun gonna rise in the west?"

I hope to hell not, she thought. "If I watch it again, maybe I can figure out how to handle it better when that ol' sun does indeed rise in the west."

The truth was the sun didn't rise in the west and she wasn't looking at her reaction. She knew it intimately and had even dreamed about it just about every time she managed to find some sleep. She was looking for something else.

As the angle pulled back again—before the fight actually started—she saw it.

Reynolds and Thomas. Stick figures at the far end of second tier, just outside cell number 24. Everyone else was inside their cells, behind self-locking doors. Reynolds and Thomas talked. Then yelled. With his back to the railing, Reynolds backed Thomas up and crowded the man into the wall.

Then she watched, fearfully, when Thomas' mouth burst in a shower of blood while Reynolds remained untouched.

Again, Bibb's gaze came to her and there was something in it, some satisfied flash of light. "See what you need to see?"

"Uh . . . yeah, I think so."

"Make sure, rookie." He spoke deliberately. "If you think you see something on that tape, then make sure you see something on that tape." He ran it back again, then watched her as she watched it. "You got it now?"

"Can I get a copy?"

Without a word and without taking his eyes off her, he opened a desk drawer and pulled out a DVD. When he handed it to her, she unzipped her uniform shirt and popped it inside between her puncture-resistant vest and her shirt, and zipped up.

"Okay." Bibb nodded. "Get to your shift. Trust me, okay? I know what I'm doing. I hear everything and I see everything. More to the point, I hear you and I see you. I'll keep you safe."

With a nod, she tried to open the Pig Pen's heavy door. It didn't move.

"Gotta wait for me."

"Sarge," she said as he popped the lock. "You said you had to get back to D Pod, where the real fight was."

"Yeah?"

"A man died in my pod. That was a real fight."

His face clouded, and the door closed heavily behind her, the click of the automatic lock banging through the main hallway.

Chapter Fourteen

The next afternoon, Preacher left the warmth of a soft kiss on Jace's cheek as someone banged on her door. "Just tell her," the old man said, his dark skin shining in the early afternoon light. "Say it out."

"I can't."

"Better get to can, babydoll. Just yank that Band-Aid off."

"It's a little more serious than a Band-Aid, Preacher."

"Principle's the same."

Jace snapped the two locks and swung the door open. Bogan stood on the threshold, a grin ripe on her face. It slipped a little when she saw Preacher.

"Oh . . . sorry." She backed out of the doorway to let him pass. "Like a whorehouse, I guess, people coming and going." She grinned mischievously. "How much you charging today, sister?"

"Uh . . . yeah, this is—"

"They call me Preacher . . . on account'a I used to do some gospelin'."

Bright red flooded Bogan's face. "Well, doesn't that shoe taste good." She offered a hand. "Sorry about that. I'm Rory Bogan."

Preacher shook. "Jace likes you pretty good. Said you've helped her out a whole bunch."

Jace shifted from one foot to another. "He's a crazy old man, don't listen to him."

"What I'm doing, see, is training her. If we're partners and she can do it all, then I don't have to do anything. All the lazy and none of the guilt."

"Ever'body's got to have a plan." Preacher stepped onto the landing and looked out over ash trees. "Had a dog in those trees once . . . long time ago."

"What?" Bogan followed Preacher's gaze to the trees.

"Crazy old man." Jace gave Preacher a gentle shove.

"Might have to help her again," he said.

Bogan plopped herself on the small couch. "Nice place."

It was a carbon copy of Gramma's except that Grapa had put Gramma's front door on the ground floor and he'd put this apartment's front door on the second floor. So rather than go up, Jace's apartment opened beneath her. The two bedrooms, along with a full bath, were downstairs. Up here was the kitchen and living room, along with a smaller room she used as a den. Though she vaguely remembered a house over on Crockett Street from when she was young, this—or Gramma's apartment—had been home pretty much as long as she could remember.

"So what's the deal?" Bogan asked.

"With what?"

"You've got . . . like . . . a ten-foot poster of Wonder Woman on your living room wall."

It dominated the living room. White costume, gold belt, hair flowing in a breeze. The American flag fluttered behind her, the barest outline of the invisible plane behind that. Her face was stone-set. There was no question in her eyes; everything, no matter what, would come out okay.

"The poster a little weird, you think?"

"Uh . . . yeah." Bogan held her fingers a hair apart. "Maybe just a little."

Jace picked at a fingernail that had cracked. "Okay, well, first of all, it's only a three-foot poster . . . maybe four. Second of all, I don't think it's weird. I think it's . . . well . . . okay, maybe it is. But I don't care. In fact, I like weird, I like it a lot. I like weird people, too. I mean, not weird, but people willing to walk the wrong way on an escalator."

Bogan frowned. "Okay."

"I mean, if you have a conviction—"

A deep worry line creased Bogan's forehead. "Whoa. You have a conviction? Must be a misdemeanor, otherwise you wouldn't have been hired."

"No, no, that's not—that's not what I meant." Jace sucked her cheeks in. "I'm not saying this very well. What I meant was that I like people who stick with what they believe, what the evidence shows them, regardless of what other people think."

"Evidence? What the hell is . . ." Bogan's voice dipped. "Jace, you okay? What are you talking about? Stop staring at Wonder Woman."

Jace took a deep breath, left her fingernail alone, and plunged ahead. "Reynolds did it."

Bogan's eyes rolled but her jaw tightened. "Again with this? He didn't do anything. You have got to let this go." Bogan strode the apartment. "Man, I had no idea you had OCD."

"OCD?"

"Obsessive compulsive disorder? You've got it in spades when it comes to Reynolds. He didn't do anything. If he had done something, he'd have been arrested."

Jace stood beneath Wonder Woman's gaze as her friend circled the place. "Not if they can't prove it."

Bogan's voice split the air. "There's nothing to prove. Goddamn it, Jace, what's the matter with you? Why are you so hot for Reynolds? What'd he do to you?"

"Not to me, to Thomas."

"He didn't do anything."

"He killed Thomas."

"Yes, he defended himself and an inmate died. But that's not what you mean. You mean murder."

Jace didn't shift her weight or look down to pick at her nail. She stood tall, ignored the pounding in her head, and stared straight into Bogan's eyes.

Bogan's brown hair moved, side to side in that strange hula dance it did when Bogan shook her head. Bogan prowled the apartment, a tiger stalking the ringmaster. On her fifth or sixth pass, she noticed Jace's phalanx of CDs on a medium-sized TV stand. She stopped short, her head cocked sideways as though reading the titles.

"Music, huh? Not much else. So, what do you do? Crank up some tunes, read some dirty novels?"

Jace said nothing.

"What kind of music do you like?"

"Everything, pretty much."

"Right, but what's your thing? The music you know better than anyone."

"Jazz."

"Hmmm." Bogan's fingers trailed over the discs, past the Brubeck and Davis and Hampton reissues, the box sets of Basie and Ellington and Getz. "Don't understand jazz, never did. Too free-form." She pulled a Marcus Roberts disc off the shelf. "These guys . . . they play whatever they want."

Not strictly true, though it certainly had been for some of the experiments of the '60s, but Jace kept her own counsel, let Bogan take her wherever she wanted.

"I'm not much into music, really. Used to like classical a little, but only because I wanted to be a ballerina—like every other little girl in the world—when I was seven." She turned to Jace. "No free-form there. You knew exactly what was going on. This flute or that trumpet or violin or whatever. Always exactly the same. Boom boom boom." The knife edge of her right hand pounded her left palm. "Boom boom boom. They played the song the same way and you danced the same way."

With a frown, Bogan shoved the Roberts disc back on the shelf, but not in the same slot. Instead, in the heavy and oppressive silence, she quickly rearranged all the Roberts CDs. Her fingers strayed to the music on either side of Roberts, but then quickly fell to her sides. Embarrassed, she looked back at Jace. "Jazz? Everybody doing their own thing? No, thanks."

"No one walking on escalators, huh?"

"Whatever that means." Bogan rubbed her hands together and glanced toward the kitchen. "I don't suppose you have any Skittles, do you?"

"Preacher ate the last ones."

The joke fell flat and the silence made Jace sweat. It crawled along the backs of her legs and between her buttocks, dripped from her upper lip.

"Bibb called me in."

Bogan's eyebrows shot up. "Into the Pig Pen? Doesn't do that to many people. Doesn't like anyone in his space."

"He made it sound like he calls in all the rookies."

"Hardly."

"Anyway, he yelled at me for yelling into the radio that night."

"Only need to call him once." Bogan's jaws tightened and the muscles flexed while her eyes caught everything in the apartment except Jace, as though she couldn't look at her anymore.

That fissure's back, isn't it, Jace wanted to ask. *The one we discovered at Alley B's. It's back and growing. You're on one side and I'm on the other, like a bad TV movie of the week. And both of us can see it growing but we have no idea what to do.*

"That's what he said."

"He's right. Trust him. He's a creepy son of a bitch, but he's good at what he does." Stiffly, Bogan sat and put her feet on

Jace's small coffee table. She managed to look at her friend again, though there was still ice in her eyes. "For that matter, trust all of us." With a dismissive shake of her head, she asked, "What'd he really call you in for?"

Jace pointed to a disc. It sat near Bogan's feet on the table. Jace hadn't watched it again. She'd tried to sleep it out of her vision, but it had spent all day with her, like an unwelcome visitor.

"Jazz?" Bogan said.

"No."

Disgust smeared Bogan's face. "He watching you?"

Jace nodded. "But that's not really what—"

"Son of a bitch." Her feet came down hard on the floor. "He was told about that."

"What?"

"Got a seven-day vacation because he was watching people." Bogan held her hands in front of her chest, as though cupping a large set of breasts. "Get me?"

The DVD player whirred to life as Jace snapped the disc into the machine. A second later, Jace's ass popped up on the screen.

"Yep. Just like that."

Jace froze the image. "Bogan . . . Rory, listen."

The woman's eyebrows rose. "Rory?"

"Rory, please."

A silence, probably only a moment long, but something that felt like years, slipped between them.

"What's on that disc?"

"Just watch it." Jace clicked the remote and they watched her head for the go-between.

"It's the fight, isn't it?"

"Yeah."

"Stop it."

"What?"

"Stop the disc. Turn it off. Now."

The picture of the go-between went black. "Why?"

"Bibb gave you that? He shouldn't have. Pod footage is never given out to just anyone."

"Why?"

"Why?" Bogan's face went battle-red, her eyes as hard as the bars around which she worked. "Policies. Procedures. Because that's the rule. Because—because it's prison porn. There are cops and cop groupies and cop wannabes and whoever who pay money for that shit. They sit and watch the inmates and the fights and the lowdown between two men and whatever else the camera catches. It's like war porn. People sitting around watching soldiers' video of people getting killed."

"All right, Rory. I didn't realize."

"You could get suspended for having that. Plus, if there is a lawsuit from Thomas' death, and you know there will be, you could get subpoenaed."

"I was there, I will get subpoenaed."

Bogan's thin finger shook when she pointed at the TV. "And if I watch it, I could get called, too."

Jace sat on the couch and lowered her voice. "You won't get called, Rory. No one will ever know you saw it."

"Bullshit. Everything always comes out."

"You know what's on it, don't you? Down in your gut, you know what's on this thing. You know what happened."

Bogan stared at Wonder Woman. "You told me what happened. The rest of them told me, too."

"But you *know.* It wasn't that an inmate attacked him. It was that he attacked an inmate."

"Damn it, Jace, I don't know any such thing. I don't know it, I don't believe it. I can't believe you're going after this thing. What's the deal? You a cop hater? Are you a plant from the fucking ACLU? Reynolds killed the guy, we all know it. He got suspended for it. Doesn't matter what the footage shows."

"It absolutely matters what the footage shows because we're supposed to be the good guys."

Rory barked out a grunt. "Nice answer, rookie, but you have no idea. We aren't any of us good guys. Just like none of them are bad guys. All of us are a fuckup of good and bad."

"Rory, listen."

"I thought we were friends . . . getting to be friends, anyway."

"Aren't we?"

"Not if you keep going after a fellow officer."

"But this officer did something wrong."

"You don't know—" Rory bit down her yell, shook her head. "You think something happened, get your ass to the press. Get some TV cameras in here. Get a little flashbulb going for yourself."

"I don't care about the flashbulb. I care about the fact that Reynolds murdered a man."

"So what?" Rory turned away, her face red and angry, her shoulders back and defiant. "Thomas was a piece of crap . . . they all are. If they weren't, they wouldn't be in the system. Maybe Reynolds was doing humanity a favor, getting Thomas out of the gene pool."

Jace took a deep, steadying breath. "I don't think you believe that. But look at it this way: what if he did murder Thomas and we don't care? Do the inmates? As soon as we take them off lockdown, what are the chances there will be fights and maybe a few staff assaults?"

Rory's silence told Jace she'd gotten it right.

"So for our own safety, shouldn't we do something about Reynolds?"

Rory paced the apartment slowly. "How come you don't have any family pictures?"

"What?"

"No pictures. Anywhere in this apartment. How come?"

"That's what you want to talk about?"

"Don't want to talk about any of this. And how come you don't have any Skittles? You call me over, dump this bullshit on me, and don't have any comfort food?" She stomped toward the door. "Man, this sucks."

"Rory, please—"

But the veteran deputy shook her head. "I'm sorry, but I won't be part of this. I don't want to be in the jail my entire career. I want a squad car, and there's no way in hell I'll get there by ratting out other officers."

"But—"

"Even if I believed it. Which I don't." She popped the door open. "Lose that disc, don't talk to anyone about this."

When Rory crossed the threshold, Jace stood in the middle of the apartment. "What about dinner when we get back on Tuesday night? I can bring some of Gramma's barbeque."

Rory let her gaze wander out across the swimming pool and parking lot. Finally, she pulled a set of car keys from her pocket. "I'll pass. Thanks anyway."

"Rory, don't do—"

"Yeah, it's Bogan. I'll see you around."

The door snapped hard and it left Jace standing in the middle of her apartment, Wonder Woman looking down on her.

Chapter Fifteen

"What would she do?"

That evening, they were in Gramma's apartment, Gramma on her couch, her latest knitting project in her lap while Jace was on the floor with her head tilted backward against the couch cushions.

"Wonder Woman?" Gramma shrugged. "Whatever's right. Might be painful, but she'd do what was right."

Jace cast an eye toward her grandmother.

"I know you like this job—or think you do—but it might not be the job for you. Maybe you're not built for police work. Cops looking the other way while a man is murdered? That's not you and it's not Wonder Woman. You both know what the right thing is and right now, only one of you is having any trouble seeing it."

Jace had come to Gramma's apartment after Rory had stormed out of hers. She'd been looking for comfort but the fridge had been empty.

"You and the boys eat all the barbeque?" she'd asked.

Gramma had grinned out of one side of her mouth but said nothing.

So she hadn't drowned her confusion and restless anger in spicy sauce or warm corn bread. Instead, she'd sat on the floor and leaned her head back against the overstuffed couch cushions like she had since she was little.

Jace curled her legs under her. "I was talking about Mama,

by the way."

Gramma stopped knitting. "What?"

"When I asked what would she do. I was talking about Mama."

Gramma set her knitting aside and wrapped her arms around Jace from above. Jace strained up into the woman's familiar scent.

"Your mama never slept very well."

Like mother, like daughter, Jace thought. "Hard to sleep when you're moving that fast."

Gramma blew a hot sigh against Jace's neck. "She never moved a step. All the jobs and friends and plans and everything? She never moved a step. Jace, you have to do whatever lets you sleep at night." She squeezed. "Please please please don't be your mama, Jace. Whatever that means to you, please don't be your mother. I saw that once, I don't want to see it again."

"Keep moving, in other words."

"However you define that."

"In other words, move on past the Sheriff's Office."

Gramma would have been just as happy if Jace had stayed at the music store, selling sheet music and karaoke tapes. Gramma had come to Jace's academy graduation but her smile had been the hard, plastic thing Jace detested.

But that heartbeat, the one you're feeling right now against your back, has made an immense journey for you, Jace. Don't forget that.

At least four times Jace knew of, Gramma had ordered tenants to leave the Sea Spray because she'd discovered they had guns on her property. But when Jace took the job, she had made a kind of peace with Jace's being armed. Gramma knew the gun was in Jace's apartment or slung like a gunslinger on her granddaughter's hip, but she never said a word. *Because she believes you know that gun, Jace. She believes you know how to handle it and how to be safe with it and how to make sure no one gets hurt with it.*

In other words, Gramma moved past her unease. She kept moving and found a way to trust Jace absolutely with something she hated completely.

"You don't like my job."

"No."

"Why?" Once again, like every other time Jace had asked this question, she expected no answer.

Gramma took a deep breath but in the end, just shook her head. "It's all dirty water under the bridge."

For a few more minutes they'd stayed that way, wrapped up in each other. Eventually, Jace untangled herself and stood.

"I'm going to bed."

"Think you'll sleep?"

Jace shrugged.

"Think you'll sleep-talk?"

"Probably."

Gramma nodded thoughtfully. "You want to sleep here tonight?"

"Yeah, I think I do."

"You want me to sing?"

Jace craned her head toward the open window. She wanted to hear a storm, but it wasn't there. There was nothing but the black yaw of a West Texas night, with only an occasional coyote or truck on the highway.

One moved constantly but never left the desert. The other never stopped leaving it all behind.

"Yeah, I think I do."

Chapter Sixteen

More than twenty-four hours later, at nearly two a.m., Captain Barry Ezrin whistled. "You look pretty bad."

"I'm having a little trouble sleeping."

He blew out a long breath. "You and me, both."

"Because of this?"

He shook his head. "Just in general, I don't sleep well. Never have. That's one of the reasons I work at night so much."

He sat expectantly, leaning forward in the booth with his hands light on the table. His straw cowboy hat was off to the side and his thumb continually ran over the tiny, plastic sword stuck in the thin, black slip of a hatband. The sword was the same kind this place served in mixed drinks.

Music filtered through the bar's smoky air from a jukebox in the corner. Thumping bass lines, pounding drums, guitars screeching while a singer screamed himself hoarse. A frantic tempo, as though the band were somehow afraid of slowing down.

"You guys cool?" a waitress asked.

"Yes, thanks," Ezrin said.

Jace drank from a sweating Corona bottle. She'd offered to buy him one, an apology for dragging him down here, but he'd declined.

"What do you think happened?"

He seemed to think his answer over carefully. "I think there was an altercation between an inmate who was scared and a correctional officer who likes to fight."

"That's not an answer."

"What do you want me to say? That I believe an officer killed an inmate for no apparent reason? There is no proof of that."

"You've talked to everybody? Staff and inmates and everyone?"

Though his face softened as he leaned forward, she got the feeling he was explaining something obvious to a child. "Deputy Salome, even if I spoke to everyone in the facility at the time, and even if staff or inmate saw it happen, no one—absolutely no one—would tell me."

"Why?"

"For the same reason you danced around me so badly last Monday night: because everyone believes I'm out to get cops."

There were few other people in the bar. It was one of the reasons why Jace had chosen it. A few years ago, this bar had been something. Four nights a week live jazz and a drink menu that ran deeper than Budweiser, Coors Light, and Lone Star. Jace came out two or three times a week, almost always by herself. She'd sit in the back corner, buried by darkness, nurse a drink or two for four or five hours, and let the music wash over her.

The owner hadn't been able to make it on jazz and exotic drinks. The customers had run out, the money had run out and, eventually, the owner had run out on a mountain of debt. The place closed and within a month, had reopened as just another bar on the stretch of highway between Zack City and Odessa. But this completely undistinguished bar, along this barren stretch of roadway, did just fine and it didn't seem to bother the new owners that Jace never came back.

"You're not out to get cops?"

"I'm out to get the truth, good or bad."

"What about Sterling County, then?"

His eyes snapped to hers. "What about Sterling County?"

"You have an investigation there?"

"Had an investigation. Just like Zachary County and Howard County and everywhere else in my jurisdiction. They had an in-custody death. I investigated. I forwarded my findings to the District Attorney."

"Did they prosecute?"

"Not to my knowledge."

"But the deputy was suspended for two months? That seems like a long time."

He nodded slowly. "I had some doubts. I wanted to make certain. It took a while."

"Zachary County going to take that long?"

"Zachary County is done, Deputy."

"After only a week?"

"If no one will talk to me, then no one will talk to me."

"I thought maybe . . . I don't know." She lowered her head into her hands. "This is a disaster."

"Naw, this place ain't so bad," he said with forced levity. "Jace, why'd you call?"

Her dry lips cracked. She rubbed at them. "You know why. You just want me to say it. Like that'll make it more real?"

Stevie Ray Vaughan came on the jukebox and she shook her head. The bluesman had done the right thing—getting clean and sober—and the cosmos paid him back with a fatal helicopter crash.

Grinding her teeth, she retrieved the disk from her purse, placed it on the table.

Ezrin didn't touch it. "What is it?"

"It's what you've been asking for. What you asked me and all the rest of the deputies for, and what you asked every one of those inmates for. It's your evidence."

"Of?"

"Come on, Captain, don't screw with me."

Slowly, his eyes tangoing between the disk and her, he nodded. "Where'd you get it?"

"Does that really matter?"

"If you obtained it illegally, yeah, it does matter. Don't hand me a plate full of rotten apples."

"Fruit of the poisonous tree."

"Damn straight," he said.

"I don't like fruit." She laughed.

"What's funny?"

"Sitting here throwing my job away and twenty minutes ago I was flashing my badge like Sergeant Friday."

"Yo, baby," the man had said. He'd spilled from one of the sleazier bars along the road as she had passed. "You looking to play?"

Behind him, another man had come out of the same doorway and watched them carefully. She yanked her badge wallet and flashed it so both men could see. With a half-nod, the man in the doorway had split.

"I'm the police," she had said to the player. "Go roll somebody else."

"Dig you," the man had said. He had never stopped walking but when she flashed the badge, he had altered his path to avoid her. He had passed to her right and glanced into the ragged nothingness behind her as though he'd been looking for a friend the whole time, then had gone back into the bar.

Ezrin grinned. "Flashed it bright as day, huh?"

Jace cracked a smile. "Maybe not the smartest thing I've ever done."

Ezrin shrugged. "Maybe they were impressed with your balls."

"Jail balls."

A yip of a laugh slipped from Ezrin. "That's funny."

"Why?"

"I always hear jailers talking about jail balls. There ain't any such thing."

"Rory Bogan thinks so."

"And she is?"

"A friend."

"Look, either you have balls or you don't. And I don't think they come out of the jail, I think they come out of the heart."

"Heart balls? This more of your cornpone? Like how cops should act?"

He shrugged. "I am King Corn. Problem is, I actually believe the crap I spout. You either have the guts to be a cop or you don't. You don't suddenly find the courage because you've been in a pod for a week."

Jace finished her Corona. "Then I guess I don't have it."

"Why do you say that?"

"Because I'm scared shitless." She indicated the disk. "My first night, I made the kind of mistake cops don't recover from."

"Leaving your partner alone?"

"I thought that was the end of the world. I thought the other deputies would toss me in the garbage for that."

"They didn't."

"Not at all. Most of them told me I'd done well. Can't you imagine? I'm stuck in the wrong place and a man dies and they tell me I did a good job. But no, I'm throwing it away because I don't have the faith to stand up for what's right."

"You don't think you're standing up?"

"Captain, after I hand you this disk, I'll sweat it and worry it and probably throw up. And then, tomorrow, when I'm nothing but nerves and shakes and God knows what else, I'll start thinking about how to word my resignation. How stand-up is that?"

"You won't quit."

"Not just a Ranger, but a mind reader as well. You don't know me or anything about me, buddy."

"Hah. Jace, I *am* you, said King Corn. You are stand-up, you just don't realize it yet. And you'll be a good cop someday. I believe that. I mean, I'm not going to predict an entire career from a few days, but—I got a feel for you."

"When everyone realizes I dimed Reynolds, I'll be lucky not to get killed. I'll damn sure get hounded out of that jail. I won't get any backup, I won't get any help, I'll be left on my own."

He shook his head. "You believe each and every cop in that jail is dirty? You think all of them'll leave you hanging?"

Jace blinked. "Yeah, right now, I do."

"Well, that's crap. The vast majority of those people are good cops—"

"Shows how much you know. It's already started. When I tried to show Rory the di—"

His head cocked. "What?"

"Nothing. I meant—nothing."

He tucked the disk away under his hat and nodded at the tattoo in the hollow of her neck. "Bet that hurt like a bitch."

"Well, I felt it, if that's what you mean."

He clinked the ice in his glass. "Tell me about your tat."

"Nothing to tell." Sometimes she wished she hadn't gotten it. Or gotten it in a less visible place.

"Half a heart?"

"Drunk."

He nodded. "We'll go with that. I don't see you getting drunk too often." His eyes narrowed. "At least not in public. You might be a closet drinker, though, slamming it back behind your locked front door. You've got a heaviness of soul that just reeks drinker. Plus, you don't seem to dig people too much. Can't figure out why the hell you would have gotten into law enforcement."

"I don't drink much and I do like people, I just don't—just don't connect very well sometimes. Not much with the whole social skills thing."

"You're doing fine with me."

The music switched again, this time to a funk thing. The crowd, what there was of it, had thinned out, leaving only them and a drunk or two at the bar, another lonely in a booth nodding his head to the music.

"See that guy?"

He looked over his shoulder. "Yeah."

"Pretty sad, don't you think?"

"Maybe he likes it that way."

"Yeah, and the homeless are homeless because they want to be." For a moment, she let the funk play through her head. She thought it might ease her mood a little, but it seemed heavy and obvious. What she wouldn't give right now for Chet Baker's easy voice or Wynton's quiet trumpet.

"We're supposed to be the good guys," she said. "You told me that yourself. We're supposed to be the ones people come to when they're scared. Now I'm scared and I've got no one to—"

She snapped her mouth closed. Embarrassed, she stood suddenly and tossed a five on the table. "For the beer."

The TV was on, but the sound was turned down. Gramma liked to watch it that way sometimes. She made up her own conversations and believed hers were more interesting. In her lap was a knitted blanket she'd been working on for years. She'd been unraveling part of it when Jace knocked and came in.

"I miscounted way back at the beginning."

"I hate when that Alzheimer's kicks in."

"Funny girl. Miscounted because I was worried about you."

You and me both, she almost said. "You shouldn't be up this late, Gramma. And don't worry about me." She banged her chest, a barbarian threatening the enemy. "I'm tough."

Gramma said nothing. Jace sat on the floor near the couch

and watched the silent TV. Eventually, Gramma petted Jace's hair and sang, and Jace cried.

Chapter Seventeen

Her next shift on, she worked booking.

"I ain't done nothing," yelled a fat man.

Two street officers, chests rising and falling hard, glared at the guy. "You jumped us."

—434 to 405. Can you give me a 21—

—10-4 stand by—

The man was bloody. A red curtain fell from his Einstein-reminiscent hair, over his eyes, and across his nose. Blood was on his shirt down to his waist and he was cuffed to the metal bench, each hand on a side, leaving him mostly immobile. But every time he whipped his head around, blood spattered like post-modernist art over the industrial-beige jail walls.

"Better quit messing up my walls," a guard said.

The guard's words were tough, but his tone was bored. This isn't anything new, his tone said, and sure as hell not interesting. Jace couldn't imagine getting to a point where a bloody man screaming about police brutality was a standard day at work.

Somewhere in the distance came a deep boom, its reverberation hollow. It was followed by a second and then a third boom.

She didn't want to work booking. It was too scary and out of control. During her first week, working the pods when there were no transports, she'd become . . . not quite comfortable . . . but less anxious. She knew what to expect and what was unexpected, and if the unexpected became too much, the ERTs were only as far away as the War Doors. But booking was chaos. The newly arrested, still screaming their innocence, still willing to fight against the overwhelming anger of being cuffed and taken somewhere they didn't want to go.

Again, the booms sounded, mixed with the radio jabber that still set her teeth on edge.

—429 . . . 10-16 coming in twenty—

—415 . . . 407 is zebra 3 Wednesday a.m. . . . break a double?—

"Come on, man," the bloody man said. "That's the game. You arrest—"

—492 . . . 10-25 to Dillon—

"—me and I jump on you. 'S how we do it."

"Sorry, guess I didn't get that memo."

"This is bullshit."

"Let me outta here." It was a new voice, yet another layer to the din, muffled and coming from some hidden place.

Another man, further down the hallway, cuffed to the bench and awaiting a booking officer, turned toward the wall. Trying to hide, Jace understood. Trying to hide his shame or anger.

He turned and Jace's breath caught in her throat.

Trying to hide the heroin bugs. They covered his face, matching scabs and scars.

"The junkies," a young booking officer said from behind a booking computer while he entered a new prisoner's information. The new prisoner sat across the booking desk, picking at the seams of his jail-issued orange jumpsuit. "They all think they've got the bugs."

Lost in a chemical haze, users would dig until they tore their skin open. They were trying to get at bugs they believed had burrowed beneath their skin.

"They do," she said.

"What?"

"They have bugs. Under their skin."

"No, they don't."

"Metaphor," she said. "Trying to find something that's not there. Metaphor for life."

The inmate stopped picking and stared at her.

So did the booking officer. "Uh . . . okay. Whatever." His head turned toward the booms. "What the hell is going on back there?"

"Quit banging, you asshole," the bloody fat man shouted. "Or I'll cut your throat out."

"Let me outta here."

—ERTs from 459 . . . stand by—

The entire room went silent but the tension multiplied. Jace watched everyone's eyes close. Everyone working in booking right now—except her—was a member of the emergency response team. From the tension in the guard's voice over the radio, Jace understood that they all knew they might be barging through the War Doors in just a few seconds.

—459 from 405 . . . what do you have?—

—405 . . . it's Massie again. Being a little resistant—

—Bibb from 405 . . . what're they doing—

—405 . . . talking . . . talking—

The radio went silent for the better part of thirty seconds. Jace was certain no one breathed during that time. Two of the officers in booking began making their way toward a large closet with double metal doors. Behind those doors was the gear the ERTs would need to enter a pod.

—ERTs from 459 . . . disregard . . . situation under control—

—Bibb?—

—ditto that, 405. Situation under control . . . ERTs 10-22—

The tension evaporated. Someone cracked a few jokes and one of the booking officers banged a hand on the closet door, as though he were disappointed.

"Deputy Salome," Corporal Kleopping called to her. "You

down here tonight?"

"Yes, sir."

"I'm not a sir, I'm a cop." He nodded toward a woman at the far end of the line. "She's a keeper on a felony charge. You know how to search a prisoner? Get her searched and toss her—"

—419 from control—

He keyed his mic. "Go ahead."

—10-37 outside your main door—

Kleopping's head snapped to a double metal door in the middle of the hallway. "What? How the hell'd that happen?"

—I'm supposed to know, Kleopping?—

"You've got all the cameras, Bibb. Why didn't you see it?"

As soon as Kleopping closed his mic, one of the other booking officers shouted, " 'Cause he spends all his time watching chicks and pulling his pud."

"Easy," Kleopping said, though a smile sat easy on his face. "Jerry, got a noser outside the door. Got in when the sally port was open, I'm sure. Wanna escort him off the premises?"

A well-muscled deputy headed for the door and his voice came through Jace's radio.

—control gimme booking main—

A metallic click rocked the booking hallway and the man disappeared into the sally port. Kleopping turned back to her. "Get her searched and get her showered—"

—419—

His eyes closed. "Stand by," he said into his shoulder mic. "Two minutes in the shower and make sure she actually has a relationship with the soap, okay? There'll be a uniform ready for her. Get her dressed and dump her in Holding 1. There are a few other women in there. We'll move them all later. Got it?"

Jace nodded.

"Get to it." He keyed his mic. "Go ahead for 419."

—two more 10-95. Same 10-10 at Sinatra's—

"Damn, how many more?"

—last two, I think—

"Don't think," Kleopping said. "Know. I'm drowning down here. If we get anymore, we'll have to open up courthouse holding."

—you that busy?—

"Look at your damned cameras, Bibb. It look empty to you?"

—10-4—

With a tired sigh, Kleopping wiped his lips and looked at Jace. "I'm not that good-looking, Salome. Don't stare at me, get to the woman."

The boom sounded again, three, then four times. Louder and more insistent now.

"Joshua," Kleopping shouted. "Get that son of a bitch in Holding 3 quiet. Tell him if he beats on my door one more time, I'm gonna beat his ass." Kleopping eyed Jace. "You got a problem with that?"

"Uh . . . no . . . sir."

He sucked his teeth and his diamond-hard stare eventually crumbled. "I know, I do, too. But sometimes . . . ?" He shrugged. His words hanging, he disappeared down the hallway.

—453 . . . got a 10-88 when you're ready—

—stand by—

She swallowed as much of the fear as she could and steeled herself. Her boots clicked on the tiled floor as she headed for the woman.

"Ma'am, I need you to come in here with me." Jace indicated the showers but the woman refused to stand up. Carefully, Jace unlocked the handcuffs holding her to the bench, then stood back. The woman was maybe thirty-four . . . thirty-six years old, and no taller than five feet. Thin, with the scared look of someone who'd been beaten regularly. *I've seen that before,* Jace thought. Shaded eyes that wanted nothing so much as to be hidden completely. Furtive movements that were meant to be self-protective without being provocative. Choked gulps of fear and dignity that could never be allowed to bubble to the surface. "We have to get you a shower and a uniform and—"

—479—

"I don't want to go back there," the woman said in a pinched voice smaller than she was. "I really don't. I can't."

"Ma'am, there's nothing—"

—479—

"Please don't make me. Please."

"I'm sorry, ma'am, I really am."

Jace tentatively touched the woman's elbow to get her moving toward the showers. The woman stood, but rather than let Jace guide her, she clamped her arm tight to her side, trapping Jace's hand between her arm and torso.

—479! Listen up—

"I didn't do anything." The woman's voice spiraled up to the edge of something . . . hysteria or anger. Clenching her trapped hand into a fist, Jace yanked it free and put her other hand on her OC spray. She positioned herself so that the woman had no direction but the showers.

—Salome!—

Surprised, Jace stopped. "Yeah?" she said into her radio.

—479. That's you, Salome, listen for it. I don't have time to call you all damn day. What are you doing wrong right now—

She glanced at the woman, then at herself. "Uh . . . nothing. I've got good tactical position, I'm not too close to personal space, I—"

—yeah, yeah, whatever. What'd I tell you? Right now, you're taking her to the shower. No. I said search, then shower—

Jace blinked, ground her teeth. "Yes, sir."

—don't let her into those showers without a search—

"Yes, sir."

—don't give her a uniform without a strip search—

"Got it, sir."

—ain't a sir—

Jace signed, "Right," and turned to the woman, whose face was now as pale as the deepest days of winter.

"Please, don't make me do this."

"Ma'am, as I said, there's nothing I can do about this. We are where we are, this is what we have to deal with. Let's not make it any more difficult than it has to be."

"Yeah," the woman said. "Let's do."

Later, Jace would wonder when she'd lost control of the situation, or if she'd ever had control at all. But at that moment, when the woman's eyes narrowed to less than slits, when she went completely silent, when she lunged at Jace, Jace thought of nothing except Thomas.

I was wrong. This is *how it happened. Thomas grabbed Reynolds' throat, like this woman is doing to me. Thomas tried to knee Reynolds, tried to get his knee up where this woman's is. Could Reynolds breathe? Because I can't. I just never saw Thomas throw his punches. I never saw that right cross to my eye or that left hook to my breast.*

—10-78—

Then the woman's foot was behind Jace's legs, planted on the tile. Her arm swept hard against Jace's chest and shoved her backward. Jace tripped over the woman's foot and hit the ground. Her teeth clacked together.

—419 10-78—

—where the hell is it—

10-78, Jace heard. Officer needs assistance. *I'm right here.* The pain began to do its work. It was dull and far away, but coming at her fast.

—at the showers . . . it's the new one . . . what the hell's her name—

My name, as the pain sharpened, *is Jace Salome.* The hurt blossomed as hot as a high summer afternoon. It burned from behind her eyes and from the muscles in her guts. She rolled to her stomach, tried to shove herself away from the madwoman clinging to her from above.

"I'm innocent, you bitch," the woman yelled. "I didn't do anything wrong. I shouldn't be here."

She jammed an arm around Jace's throat and pulled up as though Jace were a horse needing to be stopped.

Jace's air was gone. As easy as the snap of a finger.

And almost as quickly, it was back and the terrible weight was gone from Jace's back. Replaced by louder and more authoritative yelling. Replaced, too, by seemingly hundreds of booted feet and by the forest green and black-seamed stripe of county uniform pants, by a hand firmly pressing her against the floor.

Just like in A Pod. Just like the night Thomas died. Jammed down to the floor as though she had done something wrong, as though she was the criminal.

But I'm not pissing myself. I'm not the criminal and I'm not pissing on myself.

—10-22 booking—

—it's over—

She howled and when she tried to stand, the hand kept her in place. "Get the hell off'a me."

She elbowed whoever was above her, spun, and shoved them off her. The man, one of the computer techs she'd seen earlier, grinned and let her get up.

"The hell was that for?"

"Didn't want you to get stampeded while they were dragging that woman out." He vaguely shrugged. "Might'a gotten hurt."

"I'm fine." Her voice was knife-edge sharp. "Damn it, I'm not some first day rookie. I can take care of myself."

The officer chuckled. “Good for you, then.” As he turned to get back to the computer, he shook his head. “No big deal, deputy, happens to all of us one time or another.”

“Can’t count how often it’s happened to me.” It was a deputy she didn’t know and he said it as he headed back to the inmates from whom he’d been getting info. A bright red scratch stood out on his arm.

Grinning like a little kid, another officer clapped her on the back. “Welcome to the job.”

Swallowing heavily, a bit of embarrassment sliding down her throat, Jace nodded. “Uh . . . yeah, thanks, I appreciate it.” She sucked her teeth until her heart slowed. “Next one’s on me.”

A low chuckle ran through the room as Kleopping came out of a holding cell. Grinning, he said, “That was a little extreme to get out of searching her, wasn’t it?”

Jace felt the color rise in her cheeks. “I didn’t—I mean, wasn’t like that.”

“A joke, Salome. Don’t sweat it. It happens to all of us. That’s why we get the big bucks.”

—big bucks? They pay you? I do it ’cause I looooooove it—

Kleopping laughed, keyed his mic. “Back to work, slackers.”

—booking from 405 . . . 10-30—

Biting his grin back, Kleopping keyed his mic. “Yes, sir.” To Jace’s confused look, he said, “405 is Dillon. Ten-thirty is too much radio traffic.”

As quickly as it had all gone south, it all came back. Back to inmates cuffed to the bench, back to officers striding the hallway. The booking officers were back behind their computers, their fingers banging keys hard and fast. Somewhere, showers popped on. Somewhere else, inmate and guard laughed.

“I still ain’t done nothing to you guys,” the bloody man said. But his voice was much calmer. “Ain’t no reason to thump me like that.”

"Chill out, buddy," Kleopping said. "Let's get you booked and in front of a judge, see if he'll let you out tonight."

"Tonight?"

Kleopping shrugged. "Never know."

"Rock and roll, baby," the man said, suddenly impatient to get through the process. "Let's get it done."

—419—

"Go ahead."

—got one coming—

Kleopping took a deep breath. "I really don't have the room. Don't have the manpower, either."

—zebra 1, 419, zebra 1—

There was a long pause as Kleopping keyed his mic but said nothing, his eyes on his officers. Finally he released the mic. "Son of a bitch." Another pause, more keying and releasing, as though he couldn't decide what to say.

That's a bad sign, Jace thought. *Man's got about a million years experience and he's not sure what to do. Bad, bad sign.*

Finally, he seemed to recover a bit. "Who is it?"

—I don't know but you got—

The doors at the end of the hallway slammed open, banging against the walls behind them.

—a pile of Rangers coming in—

Six men, all in perfectly creased jeans and straw Stetsons, their chests each heavy with a circled five-pointed star, hustled through. One came to the booking computers, one stopped at Kleopping and Jace's side. The others spread out along the hallway.

"The hell is this?" the fat, bloody man asked. He grinned. "Y'all gotta get extra help to deal with me?"

"Shut it down," a Ranger told Kleopping. "And clear it out."

"I'm still gonna get out tonight?" the fat man asked.

"Shut it down."

"Who do you have?" Kleopping asked.

"Shut. It. Down. Now."

Kleopping went beet red. "Don't come in here, ordering me around, asshole. This is my jail."

"It's mine now, Deputy," the Ranger said. "Shut it down or I'll arrest you for obstruction."

Kleopping spluttered.

"Paul," a man said from the doorway. "Calm down. There's no reason to be an ass."

Captain Ezrin. He nodded to Kleopping as he removed his hat. "Paul's right, though. Gotta shut it down. Clear the floor."

"The room or the floor?"

"It's a pain in the butt, Deputy, I know, but . . ."

"Son of a bitch," Kleopping said.

Ezrin nodded. "Yeah. Zebra 1 . . . clear the entire floor."

Everyone else—inmate and guard—had gone silent, their eyes dancing between Kleopping and Ezrin.

"Sure." With a sigh, Kleopping glanced at Jace. "This is when the job sucks, Salome."

"What's going on?" Jace's stomach tightened another notch, as though someone controlled an Inquisition rack and just kept turning the big handle.

Ignoring her, Kleopping keyed his mic and spoke slowly. "Listen up. Zebra 1. Zebra 1. Clear the floor . . . the entire floor." He tossed a questioning look at Ezrin, who held up a single finger. "One stays and since I'm senior, you know it won't be me. Volunteers? No? Fine, Jerry, you're the lucky winner tonight. You stay."

Ezrin shook his head, dropped his single finger down until it pointed at Jace.

"10-22 that, Jerry. Our worm, Jace Salome, takes home the Christmas turkey."

Panic rose in Jace's throat. "Uh . . . no, that's okay. Jerry can have the turkey."

"That's an order, Deputy," Ezrin said.

"Control," Kleopping said. "Announce Zebra 1, wait ten minutes, and then give me a full lockdown."

—entire facility?—

"Full lock," Kleopping said.

Ezrin shook his head, tapped his watch.

"Correction control. Announce and wait . . . five minutes? . . . three minutes, then give me a full lock. Nobody gets in or out—and I mean nobody on any floor or through any door—without my permission. I'll let you know when we're green again. Double check each and every exterior door. Funnel those of us in booking into the temp pod upstairs. Don't wait for requests, get those doors opened now. No arrestees at the jail until further notice. Agencies will have to hold in their own stations. Then turn those booking cameras off."

"On, corporal," Ezrin said.

"Correction. Booking cameras on, in full record."

—phones?—

Kleopping raised an eyebrow at Ezrin, who thought for a moment and then shrugged. "Phones can stay on for now," Kleopping said. "As soon as I see our prisoner, I might change that."

—you got it—

"All right, slackers, get to work."

The hallway exploded to life. Officers moving, clanking cuffs and leg shackles, feet tramping the concrete floor, quiet questions from anxious inmates. The officers answered a few questions but mostly kept their mouths closed except for directions and commands.

"What do I do?" Jace asked. "I don't even know what Zebra 1 is."

"VIP arrest. Someone of note. Politician. Celebrity."

Something deep inside Jace froze. Instinctively, she knew.

This wasn't any local Republican or Democrat, no teacher or local TV news celeb. "A cop?"

Kleopping nodded. "Could be."

"Why me?" she asked Ezrin.

He said nothing while they watched the floor clear. Less than three minutes later, what had been a nightmare of activity when she arrived was dead silent. She had never seen any part of the jail this quiet, even after nighttime lockdown, and it unnerved her. Every inmate in the booking hallway, all of them in the holding cells, all of them in the release cell, everyone in the sally port, was gone. Every deputy was gone. Every door closed.

Captain Ezrin leaned close to Jace so only the two of them could hear. "Because this is your thing, Deputy Salome, this is where you brought us."

"I didn't do anything."

"Welcome to the bigs, Salome. You're in law enforcement now. This isn't the playground at recess. You can't just point the road out. You point it, you gotta travel it."

Into that suddenly serene environment came the Zebra 1, escorted by four Rangers.

"You fucking bitch."

Deputy Reynolds. Cuffed. Shackled.

"You did this. This is your fault."

Chapter Eighteen

Her head buzzed. In her ears and behind her eyes. White noise that quickly—inexorably—darkened through reds and blues, through purples, to jet black.

"Ain't gonna forget this, worm." Reynolds' voice was a growl. "Ain't gonna forget."

That growl was the calling card of a West Texas coyote. Yeah, he was in cuffs and obviously he was going into administrative segregation, then trial and then whatever after that, but this animal was lethal and somewhere down the line, there would be some price to pay for his standing here in cuffs.

Reynolds leaned in as the Rangers guided him past her. The stink of his sweat was pungent and yet it failed to hide the sweet odor of too much aftershave. "And I got a looooonnnngg reach."

"Reynolds," Ezrin said. "I got no problem shooting you here and now. Shut the fuck up."

Reynolds' head snapped toward Ezrin. "Shoot me here and now? But that would be illegal, Ranger, sir. Plus, they don't allow weapons in the jail, certainly not in booking."

Ezrin grinned and it was as though someone had pasted a different face over his skull. There was none of his warmth or good-old-boy openness. "Test that assumption whenever you want."

His tone scared her and she knew it scared Reynolds, too. Reynolds' mouth opened and closed a couple of times. He glared at Ezrin while letting a Ranger move him toward the metal bench, though he didn't sit without some resistance.

"Don't make this worse," Ezrin said.

"Sure thing, sir. Yes, sir," Reynolds sneered. "Fuck you, Ranger. You ain't no real cop. Pretty boy with a pretty hat and pretty jeans and a nice, shiny badge. But you ain't nothing at all."

The Ranger shrugged. "Tonight, some beautiful woman I haven't even met yet will take off my pretty jeans. You? You'll get stripped down by men and then we'll look down your throat and up your ass. But you might be right."

Jace, hands shaking, turned away and willed her stomach to stay down. Her arms went firmly across her chest. "I'm not booking this man."

Ezrin's voice was quiet, almost soothing. "You're either in or you're out, Deputy."

"I don't imagine anything's that simple."

Ezrin rested one hand on the wall, crossed his feet as though he were drinking a beer with his buddies over a grill loaded with chicken and sausage. "You're right. This business isn't that simple, but this is where we are. Reynolds murdered a man." In her ear, he whispered, "We both knew it. That's why you kept looking."

"I didn't know anything."

"Knew enough to bring me some video."

That had been the mistake. She had watched the footage and had tried to get Rory to watch. Ultimately that didn't matter because they were just correctional officers. But Ezrin putting some eyes on that footage sure as hell mattered. Had Jace not taken that step, this nightmare never would have sprouted.

"Salome, listen to me, this is the job. You either do it or you don't and it is that simple. Either you're a cop—with everything that means: integrity and honesty and truthfulness and all the rest of the sentimental cornpone—or you're not." He removed his hat and toyed with the brim. "I'm not saying this very well. It's too heroic, even for me and I like this kind of maudlin bullcrap. But being a cop is a good *thing* . . . and it's a *good* thing. It has to be. If it's not, if we're what so many people think we are—fat and lazy and stupid and more likely than not to snag a dealer's stash before shooting him in the head—then what's the point? If we are that kind of police officer, then everything we humans have falls apart. We have to be above reproach." He blinked. "What?"

"You're right, that's pretty corny."

"You two figuring out when and where to do the sheet dance?" Reynolds called. "Salome, either blow him or get over here and get me processed." The Ranger had cuffed Reynolds' left wrist to the bench, but the right one was free so he'd be able to sign the booking forms. Now that fist banged his thigh while his cuffed hand banged against the bench.

"Another word," Ezrin said.

"And what, Ranger? You're already going to frame me on a bogus murder, what else can you do?" Loudly, he snapped his fingers. "Oh, right, I remember a wildly inappropriate and unprofessional threat to kill me with a smuggled weapon."

Ezrin ignored him. "Look, Deputy, we have to do what's right, we have to be held to a higher standard. Why? Because we have the only job in America where we are legally sanctioned to kill people. If we let him get away with this just because he's a cop, then we are no better than those we arrest."

"More corn," she said.

"King Corn."

But weren't his words pretty much those of Gramma and Preacher? Wasn't that line of reasoning pretty much what had driven her to take Ezrin the video in the first place? But believing a thing was one thing, having the guts to follow through was something else again.

Ezrin yanked a thumb toward Reynolds. "This guy is what you say you aren't. You should be proud to book him."

"Maybe, but I'll be a pariah in the department. Not only the deputy who dropped a dime on him, but the one who booked him for murder."

"No one knows you dimed him. I went to Bibb and got my own copy of the video. And you can't help what you've been ordered to do."

Reynolds wore the same face he had that first night: smug, arrogant, contemptuous. This guy had killed someone and righteous justification ran deep in his veins.

Eventually, Jace took a breath and started.

"Name."

"That's a joke, right?"

"Name. Address. Phone number."

"I ain't giving it."

With a shrug she hoped was more casual than she actually felt, she punched a bunch of commands into the computer. The screen went black, then came back.

"Let's see," Jace said, forcing a lightness into her voice. "Jeffery K. Reynolds for arrestee's name. 314 Comanche Road for arrestee's address. Arrestee's phone number? 915-694-1151."

Ezrin leaned over for a better view of the screen. With a chuckle, he said, "Pretty good, Deputy."

A simple cruise through the Sheriff's Office internal network, where daily memos were posted, gave her everything she needed. Work schedules, car maintenance schedules, weapons qualifying schedules, and various internal bookkeeping, along with employee addresses and phone numbers. A deputy never knew when they might need to call another deputy to split an overtime shift or borrow a piece of equipment or send a birthday card.

She grabbed the info, copied and pasted it into the various blanks on the booking form.

Reynolds sneered. “Ain’t you the smart one?”

“Any medical conditions, arrestee?”

When she looked at him, his eyes had filled with stark calculation. “Asthma. I want the drugs my doctor prescribed, not any of that bullshit jail medical. I want an actual doctor.”

“Yeah, I’ll forward that up the line, arrestee. We’ll see how it plays.”

“Ain’t you the bitch all of a sudden? Where’d you find that backbone? Maybe that Ranger jammed it up ya’ when I wasn’t looking.”

“You know, if this murder thing doesn’t work out for you,” Jace said. “You should get into movies, with that incredible imagination. A woman’s working you over so she has to be sleeping up the food chain, right?”

As Reynolds, jaws grinding visibly, stared down the empty hallway, Captain Ezrin gave a tiny laugh. “You’re fine. I’m going to have a quickie with my guys and figure out the rest of the night.” He pointed toward the holding cells. “Right there, if you need anything, okay?”

She nodded and turned back to Reynolds. “Emergency contact name and number.”

“My mother, Sheila. 687-4408. She loves me, you know?”

Jace licked her lips. “Well, I guess even a broken clock is right twice a day, arrestee.”

“Why the hell you keep calling me that? I’m a certified correctional officer in the state of Texas.” His face had splotched angry red.

“You were a certified correctional officer in the state of Texas,” Jace said. “Now you’re inmate number 10-15348.” She looked right at him. “I’m sure your mother does love you.”

He softened his voice. “Probably like your mother does you,

Jace. No, that wasn't it, was it? What'd she call you? What was the special name?" He thought for a minute. "I'd lay money on Jacer."

She bit the inside of her mouth.

"How many nights you think they spent worrying about us? We getting enough to eat? Getting our shots so we don't get sick? Make sure we get educated, get a good job."

"Scars, marks, tattoos, arrestee?"

"Wanted a tattoo once. Mom wouldn't let me, said it would demean me, Jacer. She said people wouldn't respect me if I had tattoos all over me. Cheap man's fine art. But you got one, didn't you?"

Jace stopped typing. "Where we going with all this?"

Anger flashed. "Just talking about family, Jacer. She told you all the rules, right? Don't talk to strangers, don't get in cars, don't follow a man who wants to show you his puppy. All that good stuff, all that mom stuff. They all say it. 'Cause they want us to grow up strong and happy and complete."

"What the hell are you talking about?"

"They want us complete, Jacer. They don't want some stranger to steal a part of us. You know they steal our soul, don't you, Jacer? Ours and our children's and our children's children's." He shrugged and the cuffs rattled.

"Shut up, arrestee."

"It keeps going, Jacer. Steal it once and every generation that comes along, every next parent's new kid, feels that theft. Theft of the father, isn't that the saying?"

"Sins of the father."

"You think?"

"Shut up, okay? Just shut up." After saving the booking file, she sent it to the fingerprint server.

"It rolls downhill for the victim, maybe it does for the doer, too. Maybe, when you do something like that, you carry so much guilt it touches your kid and their kid and their kid, too. So maybe they hurt just as much as we do. Damn straight they're burning in hell. But maybe before they get there, they get a little taste."

"Jesus already, shut up. You yap like a damned Chihuahua."

"*Yo quiero* Taco Bell. It's not yapping, Jacer, it's the truth. One day you'll figure it out and then you'll never sleep again. I promise you'll worry about it and be ashamed at what you're doing right now."

"Oh, my God, shut the hell up." Her hands clenched to angry fists. "And quit calling me Jacer, you understand that? My name doesn't fit in your mouth, asshole."

"I'm sorry, Jacer, I'm just trying to explain—"

"Don't call me that." Her voice bounced angrily off the walls as she stepped forward and then just as quickly backed up, getting out of the reach of his free hand.

But the man's hands never moved while his mouth never stopped. "Jacer, listen to me, please, all I'm saying is—"

"Shut up." She held up a finger. "One more time with my name on your lips and we won't even bother with Captain Ezrin."

His eyes sparkled. He wanted her angry and burning red-hot so he could grab the advantage. Yet even as she understood it, she was powerless to stop it.

It *was* Mama's name. Jacer. It was the *hidden* name, the code name that reassured Jace. Even Gramma didn't know the name and now this bit of flotsam tossed it at her like they were the best of old friends.

"The slippage of morality. That's what it is. You listening? 'Cause I've got the truth if you wanna hear me, Jacer. I've got—"

She was on top of him before she realized it. Her right hand grabbed his wrist and jerked him toward her. She had thoughts of spinning him around, getting at his back, using his cuffed left hand as a fulcrum point. But really, all the training in control tactics and suspect management was stomped down beneath a need to hurt this son of a bitch who had stolen Mama's name.

As she grabbed and pulled at him, his face lit up. Even as he tightened up, he showed teeth. "We playing now, Jacer?"

"Shut up, just shut the fuck up."

With her left hand, she grabbed him tight at the right elbow. She tried to twist his arm behind him, tried to bend it at the elbow and to turn the hand until the knife blade of his outer hand was pointed at the ground. *Wrap your hand around his. Torque it up, higher than the elbow. Pressure-counter pressure. That's where the pain compliance begins.*

"Go, Jacer, you got it," Reynolds said, his voice filled with surprise and maybe a slice of admiration but also a measure of contempt. "Get that wrist lock on me. Get it tight. I might jump out of it. Might kick your ass. Get that wrist lock, Deputy, do it like they trained you."

But all she heard was "Jacer," over and over.

"Get some," Reynolds said. "Get some, bitch."

She wrenched his fingers toward his wrist, yanked his wrist up, and shoved his elbow more tightly into his body.

Then his hand slipped, slicked down by her sweat, and it was all he needed. With a triumphant yelp, he snapped his arm dead straight and locked it. The force with which he moved it surprised her and dragged her around in front of him. She tripped over his feet and fell to the ground.

"Now what, Jacer. Don't you remember the training? I've got you on the ground. Cuffed or not, I'll kill you. What'choo gonna do?"

His face loomed and he slid as far off the bench as he could, put his knees on either side of her legs. His free hand grabbed her neck. "You gonna die tonight, Jacer? You get in my way and maybe you should." He lowered his head toward her. "God's work, Jacer. Keeping all of them complete."

"Let go, fuckstick."

Panic ripped through her as he began to cut her air. *Think! Damn it, they taught you how to survive.*

But at the Academy, when she knew she was going to be okay, it was different. She didn't know that now, while his hand squeezed tighter and her chest heaved for lack of air. She didn't know she was going to be okay here. Maybe Reynolds *was* going to kill her.

"Let go."

—479?—

"The hell's he doing?" one of the Rangers said.

"Damn it." Ezrin's voice exploded from the holding cells, the lead in a chorus of angry Rangers.

Don't let him do this to you, Jace thought.

She grabbed his choking hand, jammed her fingers beneath his, pried them backward. His grip loosened, but didn't come free.

She wasn't going to roll him off her, not with his right hand cuffed above them both, the leverage was wrong. *So, if you can't roll him, grab his left leg instead. Grab and twist it, up over your head and slip out from beneath.*

"Reynolds," one of the Rangers yelled. "Get the hell offa her."

She heard them coming to her rescue but they moved so slowly. *They won't get here in time, you have to save yourself.*

Jace yanked his calf out from his body, until she was rewarded with a yelp. When she jammed it hard and fast toward his head, she got another howl. Then she rolled right and held his left leg at his head while squeezing his extended right leg between hers and dragging it with her while she rolled from beneath him.

He didn't howl this time. He yelled. Hard and angry and from the very bottom of himself.

"Enough of this bullcrap."

As Ezrin slammed a knee into Reynolds' back and pinned him to the floor, she gave one last yank on his leg, jerking him away from the bench until the cuffs bit into his wrist and she was rewarded with a touch of his blood.

"Too late, Ranger-Bob," Reynolds said. "I got to her."

When a second Ranger grabbed both of Reynolds' feet and pinned them backward, Jace let go. A third Ranger snapped Reynolds' free hand into another bench cuff while a fourth slammed the shackles back around his ankles.

All breathing heavily, the Rangers carefully stepped back, their bodies tense. *They're ready,* she realized, *for battle. He surprised us, but it won't happen again.*

"Damn it." Jace stormed the hallway. Her fist banged against the concrete wall. "Goddamn it."

An inmate had gotten beneath her skin. Not only that, she realized, but he'd gotten under her skin so deeply that she'd jumped first. She had thrown the first punch.

"Deputy?" Ezrin asked.

"He got to me." She tried to speak softly through the adrenaline dumped in her blood.

"Yep."

"Got right to me."

"Yep."

A grin slid over Ezrin's face. "But you took his ass, didn't you?"

"Good job," one of the Rangers said. "I get in a scrape, I want you with me, all right?"

The Rangers gave her a round of applause, small and quick and more embarrassing than empowering. Except a little scary, too. *You're basking in the glow of having beaten a man, Jace, of having bloodied a man.* She wanted them to stop. Yet when they did, she realized Reynolds had been clapping with them. Cuffed to the bench, the cuffs making an awful metallic racket, his hands banging against the bench seat.

"Helluva fight, Jacer. You got me, Jacer. Damn straight. Tore me up. Beat me down. Put the boots to me. Yeah, me all cuffed up but you done good, old girl. Don't sweat it, chick, you'll do okay someday. Not as good as me 'cause you ain't trained like me."

"Won't get much training in prison," she said.

"Prison?" He laughed. "You don't think I'm actually going to prison, do you? Hell, I won't even go to trial."

"You'll go," Ezrin said.

Reynolds' face was absolutely calm. "What if I do? Ain't no jury gonna convict me. And what if they do? I'll get a few months, maybe a few years, but it'll be an easy slice of time, Jacer. And ain't none'a that matters anyway. I'll take the time. We know who we are and what we are and you don't have a fucking clue, Ms. Deputy Sheriff. You and Ranger-Bob there haven't stopped anything."

"Stopped you, didn't we, arrestee?"

He laughed. "Just like we did you, bitch."

"Meaning?"

"You're as dead as Thomas." He winked. "They'll put you down as easily as I did him."

His laugh continued to boom out through booking.

Chapter Nineteen

After her shift, she cried.

Not for Reynolds and honestly not that much for Thomas. Mama's song played repeatedly in the emptiness of her sparse living room while the last of the night's black gave way to early morning's pink and purple. Listening to the tune, the velvet voice, Jace cried for Rory.

At Kleopping's urging, Dillon had ordered Jace to go home rather than work the last few hours of her shift. As she'd left booking, she passed Rory, who'd been shifted over from medical to take her place. They'd exchanged no words or sounds or even a simple wave.

It was the missing wave that hurt the most. Every time they saw each other, for the last week and a half or so, there was a wave. Or the flash of a peace sign. It was something Jace had tossed her few friends for as long as she could remember and Rory had picked it up. On duty, they handed it back and forth frequently. So the absence of it hit Jace harder than she'd realized until she saw Rory's face. And what had Rory's face said?

As the song started over, the ninth or tenth time it played, Jace didn't have an answer. But she thought Rory's face might have been equal parts anger and heartbreak.

Chapter Twenty

The air in the Sea Spray's front office was insistently lavender, the aroma of Gramma's beloved candles. The light scent mostly countered the stale summer air, though occasionally Jace caught a gamey whiff of cattle or the bitterness of oil refineries better than twenty miles away.

As the day rounded the corner on three o'clock, the sunlight had already begun its run up to oppressive. Zach City summertimes were harsh, with the harshest hours coming late in the day when the sun bleached everything. Colors lost vitality while heat mirages sat heavily on streets and the tops of buildings. In those splashes of heat-silver, the Denny's across the highway disappeared and reappeared. When Jace was a little girl, she'd spent quite a few hours watching cars sink an inch or two into the melted asphalt on Zach City's streets.

"You okay?" Gramma's adding machine stopped clicking. "A little quiet today."

Jace shrugged. "Got a head full."

Click-click. "Always did, little girl, always did."

Grapa had always believed Jace's head was too full. "Too young to be that full," he'd said countless times. "It'll weigh you down . . . like swimming with a belly full of rocks."

He'd always said it with a laugh. But inside that joke lived a blade of reality from which Grapa had wanted to protect her. At least once a day, he'd snatched her around the shoulders and hugged her as hard as his brittle bones allowed. And even as he died, he reminded her that everyone—Jace's mother included—loved her.

"Got a visitor," Gramma said, nodding toward the front parking lot. A boat of a car—a Buick Electra 225 circa mid-'70's, and how did Jace happen to know that bizarre bit of trivia—with a few spots of dull gray primer layered against a green skin shuddered to a stop. A large black woman emerged from the car and walked slowly across the cracked asphalt parking lot.

"Afternoon," Gramma said as the woman strode into the lobby. "Looking for a room?"

"Looking for a cop." The woman's eyes, a thick, molasses brown, landed on Jace. "You're a cop."

Jace stood, hands in front of her as they'd taught her at the Academy.

"I'm Delilah." A gap in her front teeth, slightly off-center, made her face look lopsided. "I'm not here to do any harm, Officer."

"Jace?" Gramma asked.

"I think we're fine." Jace's throat was heavy. "Who are you?"

"I already told you who I was. Better question is who my son was."

"Fine. Who was your son?"

"Lemuel Stimson."

The name hung in the air, though Jace couldn't attach anything to it. The woman stared at her as though it should.

"We lived in Odessa most of our lives."

"Lived? You don't anymore?"

"I do. He's living six feet under; killed one year, two months, and four days ago."

Jace let a deep breath roll through her. She consciously tried to stand confident, but an itch had started deep in her gut. "I'm sorry to hear that."

"Okay."

"How does your son's death concern me?"

An ill-fitting grimace stumbled onto Delilah's face. "You were there."

"What? Where?"

"Zach County Jail. When that man Thomas was murdered."

The two women stood, a step between them, their eyes locked. The black woman's eyes were sunk deeply into her face and sat low above full, loose lips.

"Died," Jace said.

"You say tomato."

"Jace?" Gramma's voice filled the chasm. "Should I call someone?"

"No. Ms. Stimson, Mr. Thomas died while in custody. End of story."

The far corner of Delilah's mouth upticked. "Don't drink the Kool-Aid, Officer. He was killed and you know it. Otherwise Reynolds wouldn't have been arrested." Moving her hands slowly, she reached into her oversized bag and drew out some pictures. "Thomas wasn't the first."

Mostly, the pictures were old and faded, some torn. All of them showed a man—"That's Lemuel"—and most showed Stimson with various kids. "Some are his kids. All are my grandkids."

Lemuel Stimson. Jace tried to understand why a bell rang deep in her skull. She turned her attention back to the pictures. "Good with kids, was he?"

Delilah's laugh was as dry as the cotton fields that laid siege all the way around the city. "Yes, ma'am. My son had a few bad edges, there is no doubt about that." She shook her head sadly, then mimed drinking from a bottle. "Get himself too far down in his cups sometimes. He loved his tequila. Don't get me wrong, he tried to stay away from it, but every once in a while, he had to have a little taste. But he was a good man. He didn't deserve to be murdered."

"Let's not be so casual with a word like that."

But Delilah Stimson stood solidly in the Sea Spray's lobby while sweat stains darkened her armpits. "I like that tattoo, little girl. Who's got the other half?"

Jace bit hard on her tongue.

"Jace?"

"Gramma, could you give us a minute? Just a few minutes, Gramma. Please."

"You should have known him."

Where Delilah had been full-throated before, now her voice was a church whisper. Without an invitation, Delilah sat in one of the chairs, an overstuffed monstrosity Grapa had found at a trading post in Lubbock and inexplicably brought home.

Lemuel, Delilah said, had been a man of fantastic appetites. For fun, for jokes and riddles, for picnics with tamales, for summer nights on a front porch with Sly and the Family Stone on the CD player.

"He got picked up by an Ector County deputy and was dead nineteen days later. Cop said he'd been speeding. Said he stopped Lemuel along the frontage road coming out of Odessa. Do you know where I mean?"

It was a beat-up road running just a bit north of the highway. "County Road 124."

Delilah nodded. "When I was growing up, we called it Frontage Road, fronted on Highway 80. They call it Interstate 20 now, but it's the old Highway 80. Used to be the only road between here and Odessa.

"Lemuel's father, that son of a bitch, used that road all the time. When he and I were kids, and that's been a few years ago, he'd come over and we'd . . . well . . . spend some time together."

Her black face, long since washed out by age, colored a deep red and her eyes avoided Jace. "Anyway, there was a place in Odessa, Billy Dykes' Zodiac Club. Black lights behind the bar and velvet posters on the walls and funk on the jukebox. Cheap drinks and lots of dark corners. I'm pretty sure one of those dark corners is where Lemuel started life."

The woman sighed, a big sound that matched her broad shoulders and wide hips. "Lemuel was fighting the black the night he got pulled over."

"The black?"

"His depression. That's what he called it. It wasn't too bad. He'd eat a few meds and that kept it mostly under control. But sometimes it hit a little harder. That was when he went swimming in his tequila bottle."

"A drunk."

She shook her head emphatically. "His drinking never got that bad. But it was a little . . . sloppy. Nothing I couldn't handle."

"You? No wife in the picture?"

"Long gone, Officer. She gave him three kids and then decided she didn't want to be a mother. Took Highway 80 west. But Lemuel had some good friends. They knew when the black had him. They wouldn't stop him from drinking, but they'd get him home safe." Her chest puffed. "I can say that until that night, my son never drove drunk, never got arrested for DWI, and never hurt anybody."

"Until that night?"

Defeat was full and ripe in her nod. "I don't know. Maybe. Probably. It was his birthday, his twenty-seventh, and somehow he'd managed to convince himself his daddy would send a card. He was too old for that sort of nonsense, especially over some guy who was probably already dead."

On the highway, a semi-rig's horn blasted the air. Jace jumped but Delilah never moved.

"He'd never been to the Zodiac before. Said he never wanted to take a chance on stumbling over his daddy."

"Daddy was gone when?"

Delilah snorted. "Damn near as soon as he squirted. Certainly before I got done delivering." She offered a tired smile and Jace braced herself for the gut punch, the part of the story where a drunk-driving Lemuel killed four people, or took the leg off an elderly woman, or left a six-year-old boy permanently in a wheelchair.

But Delilah shook her head. "It should have been speeding, that's all. But . . . I don't know. Then there was a name check . . . and . . ."

"He was drunk."

Delilah's eyes were full of sadness. "Twice the limit."

"So simple speeding became a DWI."

"Straight to jail," Delilah said.

"Plus the failure to appear."

Delilah's eyes flashed.

"The name check," Jace said. "It was a check for outstanding warrants. Standard part of a traffic stop. Happens to everyone."

"It was a failure to pay, actually. He got ticketed a few years ago for riding an ATV on the road. He and his oldest were taking the thing to a friend's acreage and had to cross 1787.

"He just wanted to take the kid riding. It wasn't a big deal but a deputy saw him and ticketed him. He forgot a pay date or ignored it. I don't know, but they issued a warrant and it came up on the name check."

"Two separate bond charges," Jace said. "One for the DWI, one for the warrant."

Delilah nodded. "I was getting it, but . . . I don't have a ton of money."

"So Lemuel went to jail and never came home."

Ector County had probably left him in a holding cell for the better part of a day but eventually, when he couldn't make bail, the deputies would have had to move him from holding to general population.

"That's when it all went bad," Delilah said. Her mouth opened, but a wariness had enveloped her face and no words came out.

"Delilah?"

The woman shook her head, her face a road map of distrust. "I shouldn't be—shit. I should get on home."

Jace folded her hands in front of her, relaxed and casual, as nonthreatening as she could manage. "You're already here, Mrs. Stimson, go ahead and finish your story."

The woman flashed a bitter smile. " 'Mrs. Stimson' is it now? Now that you want something from me, I'm not just some old nigger woman."

"I apologize, Mrs.—Delilah, I shouldn't have been so condescending. I was trying to make you feel comfortable. But know this: I don't care what color you are. Second, if you'd been some piece of crap off the road, I would have booted you out twenty minutes ago. Please, you brought me this far, tell me the rest of the story."

Delilah shook her head. "You're just another police officer. You're just like the rest of them, right? Doesn't matter what she said about you, does it?"

"She who?"

Delilah shrugged. "Doesn't matter, you all stick together . . . one for all and all for one."

"That was the Three Musketeers."

"Maybe so, but don't think they weren't a bunch of kill-happy cops, too."

With a shrug, Jace leaned back in the chair. "Fine. Then I guess we're done." She narrowed her gaze on the woman. "You came here to see me, maybe someone told you to, maybe they didn't. But you came to tell me something so now, I guess, the choice is to climb back in that big old Buick or tell me what you're not telling me."

Jace's words hung in the air long enough for a nearby dog's heat-enraged howl to fill the space, then disappear as though it had never been there.

"Easy, Jace." Preacher's West Texas drawl slid easily over the stifling air. "She's here because she needs to trust someone."

He'd come in through the office's employee-only door, which meant he'd taken a moment or two to eat some of Gramma's orange muffins. He shrugged an apology. "I shouldn't have listened, but I did, so . . . well . . . there it is."

Delilah said nothing.

"This is Roland Newman," Jace said. "He's a preacher."

"Really?"

"Used to have a church," he said, wrapping his hand around the large silver crucifix he always wore around his neck.

"You still a man of God or is the cross for show?"

"Hmmm. Maybe a little of both."

She indicated Jace. "You might be right, Mr. Newman, I might need someone to trust. Do you trust her?"

"Life, heart, and soul."

"Don't put that ratty old thing in my care," Jace said. The joke fell flat. Heat flamed into her cheeks.

In spite of Preacher's appearance, Delilah hesitated. Eventually, after wiping the sweat from her face and staring at the car, she nodded. "I've seen that deputy before."

"What deputy?"

"The night he arrested Lemuel, that wasn't the first time I'd seen him. I went to the jail to see if they'd give him a signature bond or something. I didn't have the money, all I could do was ask. The arresting officer talked to me, but that wasn't the first time I'd seen him."

"You'd seen him before?"

Preacher sat on the arm of Grapa's chair, put his arm gently around the woman's shoulders. She leaned into him. "Maybe ten times."

"What? Ten times? What are you talking about?"

Dillon's words came back to her. Don't believe them, they'll tell you anything and everything. It's not always a lie, but it's rarely true. Except this wasn't some locked-up inmate, bent on extra privileges or a free phone call. This was a mother wearing the sadness of her son's death like a shawl.

"I saw him up and down the block, usually when Lemuel was out with my grandkids. A few times I saw him at Lemuel's work."

"What were you doing at his work?" Jace asked.

Hot eyes flashed. "I can't go to my son's job? Can't go have lunch with him or give him a ride when his car is broken?"

Jace played with her fingers. "Of course you can. Sorry." But she shook her head. "You didn't see the same deputy, ma'am. Ector County has how many deputies? Maybe a hundred on the road? You got confused."

"Please. It was the exact same deputy."

"How do you know that?" Preacher asked, giving voice to Jace's question.

"Car number 18-D."

The deputy wouldn't be the only one using that car. Ector County didn't have take-home cars for their deputies. Each car had two or three different deputies driving it during a twenty-four-hour shift.

In response to that, Delilah ran a finger down the length of her left cheek. "They all drive the same car? Maybe, but you ain't gonna tell me they all gots the same scar on the same cheek."

Lemuel had been murdered, Delilah said, by an Ector County correctional officer. "At least twice a day, every day, they inspected his cell. He went from general population to segregation and back again five times. They'd inspect the cell he was leaving and the new cell as he got there, every single time."

Shakedowns? Hadn't that been what Captain Ezrin mentioned to Inmate Bobby? And hadn't Bobby's response been about multiple inspections?

"They didn't give him any visits, either, but didn't tell him beforehand, so he'd sit in visitation waiting for someone to show up." A single tear, fat as a summertime raindrop, left a streak on her skin. "I'm sure he thought we'd all forgotten about him."

Thomas had dealt with just about the same thing. Different in the details but the same situation. "What happened to Lemuel?"

The woman took a deep breath. "They say he attacked a CO. CO fought back, Lemuel ended up dead."

Jace trod carefully. "If he attacked an officer, they have the right to defend themselves."

The woman nodded. "I have no problem with that, but I also know that this is law and order Texas. How often does somebody get arrested on something the cops can prove because them same cops are mad they couldn't prove something else?"

"I don't think that—"

"Bullshit," Delilah said. "Happens all the time and we both know it. Can we talk like adults? They didn't get Al Capone for killing."

She nodded at the pictures. Stimson was in all of them, surrounded by children, and everyone smiled and hammed it up for the camera.

"What do you want from me?"

"You proved a cop murdered Thomas. I want you to prove a

cop killed my Lemuel."

Jace let a beat pass. "How do you know anything about Reynolds?"

"I ain't saying nothing about that."

"Well, I didn't prove anything, a Texas Ranger found the videotape."

"Go do the same thing in Ector County."

She shook her head. "I couldn't prove it even if I believed it."

"You do believe it, I can see it in your eyes." Delilah leaned in close. "You can prove it because you're a good person who happens to be a cop."

"I'm a jailer, ma'am, there is a difference. There are things I can't do. I can't go waltzing over to Ector County and demand to see anything. And who even knows if they've got video from that night?"

"I hope you ain't built a wall between yourself and your humanity." Her gaze went to Preacher, then back to Jace. "Mr. Thomas and my Lemuel aren't the only ones."

"Meaning?"

"Eight in the last two years."

Preacher sucked in a lungful of air. "Eight dead inmates?"

"Eight murdered inmates," Delilah corrected. The heavy accusation sat nestled between the gap in her front teeth. Why, her entire face asked, are inmates being killed? "Street justice. Except it's happening inside the jails."

Jace shook her head. "No, ma'am."

"I wonder why Deputy Reynolds had Mr. Thomas up on disciplinary charges so often."

"You seem to know a lot, Delilah."

Stone-faced, the woman nodded. "A deputy called Sneed had my boy up on a mess of disciplinary charges, too."

"So don't those charges prove the action?" Jace asked. "Thomas had a history of discipline problems. Seems logical he'd eventually attack a guard."

Delilah stared at her for a long while, her eyes heavy and disappointed. "Closed-minded, refusing to see the truth right in front of you. What flavor Kool-Aid do you like?"

"Enough with the Kool-Aid, Mrs. Stimson."

A last time, Delilah held the pictures out for Jace and Preacher's inspection. "You see anything in those pictures?"

"A man and his family."

Delilah snorted loudly. "Fine. I'll get you a lifetime supply of Koo—of punch." She headed for the door. "I shouldn't have come here, you're the same as all the rest."

Preacher never moved. Jace stood in the doorway and watched the woman go to her car, her shoulders full and her back straight, dignified in spite of walking out empty-handed. Then, with one foot in the car, she turned back to Jace and said, "You're going to make a great cop."

"I'm sorry you think so," Jace said. "And I am sorry about your son."

"Shut up about my son, woman, you don't know anything about it. You have no idea about death."

Jace didn't correct her, she just let the woman go in a gentle spray of exhaust. Not with a streak of tires against asphalt, not with a scream of a high-revving engine. There was nothing to race to, her exit said, no reason to get excited because it's just another day for the cops.

"What?" Jace felt herself withering beneath Preacher's stony gaze. "She can't honestly expect me to do anything about her son. Even if it were in my county I couldn't do anything."

She stormed to the far side of the counter, but even with it as a shield, Preacher's disappointment was hot and obvious. "Damn it, Preacher, what? I can't do anything."

He shook his head. "I don't believe that. But that's not the thing."

"Then what's the thing?"

"The pictures."

"A man with his family. So what?"

"Not a man with his family. A man with children. In every picture."

Jace breathed. "Son of a bitch." A man with kids all around him.

In every single picture.

Chapter Twenty-One

Sixteen hours ago she had booked a fellow officer for murder under the color of authority. Four hours ago, Delilah Stimson had visited the Sea Spray and left with a tang of bitter disappointment on her tongue. Now Jace stood under a sky that was an early evening copper. It shone like a polished tourist market bracelet. But clouds dotted the expanse, leaking the intense cobalt blue of a recent storm into that copper.

As she had journeyed out to find Robinson—without Preacher—the skies had opened. By the time she left the string of bodegas and pool halls, she was soaking wet, her hair gone flat and stringy and her toes squeaking in wet shoes. It had been a hard storm, and Jace had found herself walking the streets with her face turned up to the rain more often than she was comfortable with.

She was looking at the clouds, she knew, because her mother was in them. The woman's thin body swelled and became the rainwater-pregnant clouds while her laugh became the metallic thunder. Eventually, daughter saw mother entire in the clouds: a gaunt woman wrapped in too-tight jeans and too-expensive cowboy boots and a knockoff Stetson hat.

The day Mama left wasn't even a speck in Jace's memory. Jace had been eight years old and she believed a trace of the memory was there, though it resisted her efforts to find it. But she knew Grapa and Gramma's stories well enough. There had been a job offer in Lubbock, seventy-five miles north. It was a good job that would pay well enough to get her and Jace off the public dole and into a decent apartment that wasn't Section 8 housing with the junkies and whores and mental meltdowns.

"I'll just be a few hours, Mama." Gramma said it the same way every time, her voice light as though that had actually been how Mama spoke.

What Jace remembered was a voice deepened and made husky by cigarettes and coughing fits. She believed Gramma's imitation was something from a distant past when Mama had been young and blameless.

Jace walked the back alleys and strolled in and out of the markets and cafés and wondered again if Mama had ever shopped here. Jace believed these places were Mama's places: gone sour with violence, dark, dangerous at the edges. But what if the woman *had* shopped here? Was Jace going to soothe her own soul by searching for Mama like she did for Robinson? And what if someone did remember her? Did she want someone else's memories in her head?

The drunk driver had been nabbed after his car went through the front wall of a post office. He'd told the responding cops he'd hit a deer or something back up the road at better than eighty miles an hour. The driver said he was pretty sure he'd knocked the animal into the creek. When the cops checked, there was no deer, but there had been Mama's purse. They'd never found Mama. She had probably curled up under some vegetation near the creek and died. Grapa and Gramma and Jace had a ceremony and Jace knew it to be the last thing Grapa and Gramma believed they could give a daughter they'd lost long before.

A breeze blew against Jace, almost like a whisper, and it could have been a mournful note from jazzman Clifford Brown's trumpet. The storm had tossed itself on the city and then slipped away, leaving only these last few breezes.

"I just want you to be proud of me, Mama."

That was the reason behind everything, she supposed. It was a cheap and easy cliché, but didn't things become clichés because so often humanity proved them true? Jace wanted Mama to stand next to St. Peter and say, "That's my daughter, Pete. Came out okay, didn't she?" And he'd nod and say, "Yeah, she did."

Jace had to be at work in a few hours, and she hadn't slept much today. She hadn't slept much in the last ten days, in fact. The time had crawled past, as though Zeus himself had put a finger to the spinning world and slowed it down. And as it slowed, she was able to think of nothing except Thomas and Reynolds. And now a man named Lemuel Stimson.

"Damn," Jace said.

An old lady, standing next to her waiting to cross the street, crossed herself, shook her head, and trundled across the street.

When she got back to her apartment, just about nine o'clock that night and under a deepening blanket of dark blue, her apartment door stood open. Sometimes Gramma cleaned the place to her own standards—higher than Jace's—or stocked up Jace's fridge and then acted as though Santa had paid a visit.

But this wasn't Gramma. This was, Jace knew with dead certainty, a violation. Someone was in her apartment.

Reynolds. Maybe he'd sprouted some bail cash. Or maybe someone had gone the bail for him. Either way, would he be that terrifically stupid? To threaten her publicly twice and then actually break into her apartment and wait for her?

"That son of a bitch."

She kept her footsteps quiet on the stairs. Her left hand gripped the thin, metal banister while her right clenched into a tight ball. At her open door, Rory's voice—recorded—stopped her.

"ERT call." From the night of Thomas' death. "Probably a fight." Then the loud pop that had become deathly familiar.

Reynolds had found the DVD. He'd probably ransacked the place, looking for God only knew what, found the DVD, and popped it in. More than likely, he would have recognized Bibb's sloppy handwriting on the DVD. Only a few minutes of watching would have told him Jace had dimed him.

Her jaw tight, she blasted into her apartment. "Get the hell outta here, you son of—"

Rory sat on the floor in front of the TV, her face completely remade as she watched the DVD. She squeezed the remote until her fingers bled white. Shadows and light from the DVD played on her face. Three times, she watched it, without ever acknowledging Jace. Then she snapped it off. Her eyes were flat, her breath shallow, pinpoints of sweat on her forehead. "He did it."

Jace nodded.

"I'm not sure—damn. I don't—" She took a deep breath. "Your grandmother let me in."

"Gramma."

"Yeah. I brought you those." On the edge of the coffee table was a manila folder. Jace thumbed through them. Page after page of disciplinary reports, all filed by Reynolds against Thomas and one other man, an inmate Jace didn't know.

"Why does Massie's name sound familiar?"

Rory looked at her, blank and confused. "Who?"

"Massie." Jace pointed at the discipline reports.

"Some mope in ad-seg. Sexual assault. I don't know him."

Jace chewed the corner of her mouth. "In ad-seg? I think he was in A Pod a few nights ago. I think I moved him from upper to lower." Reynolds had listed twelve different charges against Thomas. "Too many packages of cupcakes?"

"Can only have two."

"Thirty-seven seconds too long on the phone?"

"Three minutes, that's it."

They were petty charges because he was pushing Thomas. Reynolds was poking him, like a kid with a stick would a wounded animal. Reynolds was using the small things Thomas wanted to get the one big thing Reynolds wanted. Chronologically, the disciplinary charges got larger and larger. The small bits were weeks ago, the larger charges the days before—and the day of—his death.

"Thomas frustrated him because he never threw the first punch."

Rory pointed at the black TV screen. "So Reynolds had to."

"Why are you here?"

Rory shrugged. "Wanted to watch you walk funny."

"What?"

"With your newly acquired jail balls." Another shrug and Rory's embarrassed gaze slipped out the window. "I ran out of Skittles."

Something had picked at her, Rory said. The itching began when the Zebra 1 busted through the doors. They had cleared the entire floor for the zebra, though usually they just cleared the booking room. Then Jace had been sent home while Rory covered for her, and it all came on the heels of Captain Ezrin, Company E of the Texas Rangers, investigating Deputy Reynolds.

"Wasn't that hard to put together . . . even for me." Standing, Rory's fingers trailed along Jace's CDs. "I'm a lot like this guy."

"What guy?"

"Marcus Roberts. I checked him out online."

Jace snickered. "Yeah, a white chick with zero musical ability is very much like a genius black pianist."

"We're both blind."

"Rory, I'm not really following. Jail balls. Skittles. Blind piano players. You're going to have to road sign for me a little more."

Rory opened and closed the Roberts disk. Over and over, the tiny click soft but insistent. She shuffled through all of Jace's Marcus Roberts CDs and eventually, Jace realized she was alphabetizing them. Then she paced the apartment. "What did you dream about when you were little? What did you want to do? Teacher? Or nurse? Do you remember that picture of Governor Richards, when she was wearing all that white leather, sitting on that big bike Harley-Davidson gave her? I loved that picture."

She stopped in front of the Wonder Woman poster and stared at it. From the TV stand, she took Jace's Golden Lasso and twined it through her fingers. "This thing really work?"

"You wanted to be Ann Richards?"

"Hell, no, I want to be who she gave that bike to."

Richards had donated the bike to the Department of Public Safety. The state troopers.

"I've always wanted to be a cop, Jace. From day one. There was a week or so I wanted to be a ballerina but mostly copping is all I ever wanted to do. It'll probably be all I ever want to do." She took a deep breath and sat with the lasso in her lap. "I've been in the jail for three years and I love it. Not the jail particularly, but being a cop. I love it now and I'll love it when I get to the road and I'll love it when I get to investigations and whatever else is after that."

"You're that certain?"

"That I'll get there or that I'll love it?"

"Both."

Rory cocked her head toward the TV. "More certain of that than that Reynolds killed Thomas." She put a tight fist on her chest. "This is me. I am the police."

"And you think cops should get issued a fresh bag of Skittles at every shift."

"Listen to me." Her harsh voice descended like a hammer blow.

"Okay, Rory. I'm sorry."

"Sometimes, because of what I want, I get blind. Sometimes I am Marcus Roberts."

This time, Jace let the jokes pass. Tentatively, she reached out and held Rory's hand. Rory didn't pull away.

"I get so caught up in the camaraderie of being a cop that I can't see. I love being with those guys so much, I love wearing that badge so much, that I get stupid sometimes. My love of community overcomes my brain."

"Rory, what are you talking about?"

Rory bit her lip, then shook her head. "We knew, Jace. We all knew Reynolds was bad news. You can't be human and not see that. But kill a guy? I don't think any of us thought he was capable of that. I mean, we're all capable of that; cops have to be capable of killing, it's part of the job. Self-defense or defense of a life. Not . . ." She pointed at the TV. "Not that."

She looked away and her breathing grew ragged. "How was I supposed to tell a cop from some other agency what I couldn't even tell myself?"

Jace opened her mouth but Rory held up a hand. "Don't. Don't say I have to do the right thing. I know that, but I don't have the guts, okay? There it is. I don't have the courage to do the right thing." Her breath hitched deep in her chest and a tear traced a thin line down her cheek.

"Why?" Jace asked.

"The car."

"What car?"

"The patrol car. I'm ashamed to say I'd stay quiet about something like this because that's how bad I want to go to the road."

Jace tasted sweat, wiped it away, and realized that in spite of the heat on her skin, a heart-deadening chill had filled her.

Rory squirmed. "Don't stare at me like that." She wiped away some tears, sniffed loudly, and smoothed her uniform shirt. "Okay, show's over. Quit staring or I'll beat your ass."

"I don't think you would stay quiet about something like that, and probably everyone is Marcus Roberts at some point in their life. Rory, you are a good woman."

"Pure as the snow."

"Yeah, it doesn't snow in Zack City and I never said pure." Jace gave her a squeeze of the shoulder. "I said good, and I believe it."

"Well, I'm not the one who saw the footage and went to Ezrin. You did. You showed him, he got a warrant, and arrested Reynolds." A cracked smile slipped over her lips. "But I gotta tell you, it's freakin' hysterical he made you do the booking."

"Oh, yeah, that's funny stuff." Jace snorted. "Ezrin said I had to. Said I'd taken him to the brink and he wanted me there when we all jumped over."

"It was funny."

"Funnier to you than me. I was scared to death."

"I know. It was all over your face when you left."

Jace put the reports back in the folder and changed tack. "You sent her, didn't you?"

Standing at the window now, Rory said, "Delilah cleaned rooms with my mom. Mom spent a lot of years bent over someone else's toilet and washing someone else's clothes."

"I had to learn to do my own laundry," Jace said.

"Me, too."

"But—"

A tiny laugh bubbled up. "You think she wanted to do laundry when she got home? After spending all day doing it? Anything she did at work became my chore when she got home." Rory pressed a hand against the glass, as though if she could touch the heat, it would dispel the coldness of her declaration about the patrol car. "She could fix a mean car, though."

"What?"

"That's what she did to relax . . . repaired cars at my uncle's garage. Banging engines and whatever with wrenches and hammers and screwdrivers. It was hilarious, actually." Her tone dropped. "She used to strip bolts all the time. I think she was seeing her clients' faces on those bolts. I think she was wringing their necks because she was pissed at having to be their maid."

A not-quite-full silence fell over them. The chronic hum of the highway, flavored with the occasional airplane or dog barking or car horn from the surface streets filled the space between them.

"Delilah's pissed," Rory said.

"Why'd you send her to me?"

"Who else could I send her to?"

"Captain Ezrin."

Rory shook her head. "Cops killed her son and our friend Captain Ezrin was the lead Ranger investigator. Nothing happened. Self-defense. She doesn't trust him or most other cops."

"I got that impression," Jace said.

"A few months ago she asked me to look into it. I absolutely didn't believe it but I sniffed around a little. What could I do, really? No one in Ector County was going to tell me anything and I even know Sneed's sergeant. He taught me to shoot at the Academy and we're decent friends. But after I saw Thomas' disciplinary charges, I thought . . . I don't know . . . thought you might be able to at least talk to her. It was the same thing that happened to Lemuel."

"But you didn't want to sniff much because of the car."

Rory stood as straight and tall as she could. "Yeah. That make you feel better? To snark me like that? Yeah, Jace, I got scared. Guess I'm not as good a person as you. This shit scared me right outta my white cotton granny panties."

"You don't think this scares me, too?"

Rory worried the lasso, twisting it until her fingers were knotted with it. "Yeah, well, you probably don't wear granny panties. You've probably got some kind of thong thing going on."

This woman, pacing Jace's living room and desperate for some Skittles, had thrown Jace for a twist. In spite of the smart, quick mouth, in spite of never backing down from the boys at the jail—inmates or deputies—in spite of the brass and sharps vest and shiny black boots, Rory was a terrified little girl. Rory wanted to do the right thing but didn't want to lose her dream and the battle between those two things was pressing her down like the ERT shield against Jace's face that first night.

"So what do you think?" Rory asked. "What do we do for Delilah?"

Jace frowned. "Delilah mentioned the disciplinary reports. You gave them to her."

Rory pressed her lips between her teeth and set the lasso on Jace's bookshelf.

"Those are internal documents, Rory, you could get fired for that."

"Well, ain't I courageous, then?"

"You can't just hand out—"

"I couldn't do nothing. Not after what happened to Reynolds. And that was before I watched the tape. I didn't know Lemuel, but I know Delilah and she was hurting. Still is. I thought this might help her not hurt so much. Didn't work that way."

"I'd say not. She's convinced it's some sort of conspiracy."

"She's grieving. It's not a conspiracy, it's a couple of bad deputies." She glared out the window. "As if that isn't bad enough."

"More than a couple."

"What?"

"Delilah's list is eight names long." Quickly, Jace filled her in on the details Delilah had given her.

"Holy crap. She didn't tell me that."

"Thomas told me if I didn't let him out, he'd be dead. Actually, he said he'd be murdered."

"He knew it was coming."

"He told me that 'he' had told everyone. That 'he' wanted them to kill him."

" 'He' being Reynolds, 'them' being the inmates."

Jace nodded. "And Reynolds kept yelling at Thomas. 'Tell us the truth.' Louder and louder. 'Tell us what you did.' "

Rory frowned. "What he did? I don't understand."

"Delilah has a ton of pictures of Lemuel with kids. I wonder if there are pictures of Thomas with kids. Or any of the other dead men. Plus, when I booked Reynolds, he kept talking about how I couldn't stop 'them.' Basically said 'they' were doing God's work. And he kept talking about being a kid and parents wanting them to be healthy and whole and complete."

"What? Why does that—oh, no. Kids?"

Jace nodded.

On the couch, Rory sagged and leaned forward with her head in her hands. "Oh, man, that's bad. Jace, what's going on?"

"I wish I knew." She tapped her wrist watch. "I've got to get dressed for work." Leaving Rory to herself, Jace went to her bedroom and put on her uniform. Even with everything going on, snapping those buttons on her sleeves and zipping the shirt and tying the laces on her boots put something in her throat. She hesitated to call it pride or the confidence of community. She'd only been in the job a few weeks, after all, and right now it was a disaster. But there was something that coursed through her when she looked at herself in the mirror.

It was the same thing Rory was talking about. *Rory focuses on a squad car and I focus on my uniform but it's the same thing.*

"Hey," Rory called from the front room. "If Reynolds told Thomas to tell everyone what he did, then he knew Thomas had molested kids. But that's not what Thomas was in for. There wasn't anything like that in his file and I'd dealt with him before on minor stuff. Failure to appears and misdemeanoring."

"Well," Jace said as she came back into the living room, "Reynolds knew it and I think he picked Thomas because of it. Delilah said maybe Lemuel was punished on the thing we could prove—driving suspended or whatever it was—for the thing we couldn't prove—molesting kids."

From outside, a semi's air horn, explosion loud, split the air. Tires and brakes screamed and Jace knew, from years of living next door to a highway, that some car had just cut the truck driver off.

"Lemuel wasn't like that," Rory said.

"You said you didn't know him."

"He wasn't like that."

"Thomas wasn't like that, either, except he was and we didn't know it. Maybe Lemuel was, too." Jace popped the DVD out of the player and slid it between two jazz CDs. "But it doesn't matter, Rory, because we can't fix any of this. This is way above our pay grade."

"The hell we can't. Look what you already did. You got a murderer off the streets . . . outta the jails, same thing."

"But I just stumbled across that information, Rory. It's not like I launched some big investigation. Hell, I don't even know *how* to launch a big investigation, I'm just a worm."

"Jace, enough with the rookie stuff, okay?"

"But what would you have us do? We need to go to Captain Ezrin."

"You think he doesn't already know what's going on? He doesn't care. Good ol' boys and all that."

Jace shook her head slowly. "I don't think so. If that were the case, he would have ignored anything I showed him. He didn't do that. He moved on it."

And then it was there, right in front of her eyes like a melody Thelonious Monk had hidden in a cascade of improvisation. "When Delilah told me her son's name, it felt familiar but I couldn't figure out why. Ezrin mentioned Lemuel when he was interviewing me. Lemuel and a bunch of other names. Ezrin asked me all about how I would have fought off Thomas and then asked about my instructors. I didn't recognize any of the names. He asked about jails, too; if my class had been to other jails to see how they did things. Gaines County, Sterling County."

"Ector County?"

"Yes."

"He knew about Lemuel."

"Maybe."

"Jace," Rory said. "If he mentioned the man's name and the county, he knew."

Ezrin had thought Jace was involved in Thomas' killing, or had known about it, and their entire conversation that night had been to include or exclude her from that death. So the other names and counties had to be connected, and more than likely connected to Delilah's list of eight. "He said to me he could only prove what he could prove."

"Smart man."

"You just now swore about him and now he's smart. You're going to give me whiplash changing directions that fast."

Rory said, "He arrested Reynolds because of proof you gave him. Now he's playing you to dig up something else. Something about Lemuel or one of the other guys. I'm sure he can't get anywhere because no one will talk to him."

"They think he's out to hang cops, is what he told me."

"He wants you to do what he can't . . . prove Lemuel was murdered." Rory pointed at the Wonder Woman poster. "You and her, sister. You and her and the Golden Truth-telling Lasso thing."

Chapter Twenty-Two

Captain Ezrin met Jace at Dennis the Menace Park the next afternoon. When she was little, it was her and Gramma's favorite park. Today, she needed to be at this park again with its collection of monkey bars and slides and wading pools and open grass.

"Thanks for coming," she said.

His hat was tucked firmly on his head, his jeans pressed to knife edges, and his boots were as shiny as the department's patrol cars. "Sleep any better the last couple of nights?"

"I'm not really here to talk about my sleeping habits."

"Fair enough. What's up?"

"I remembered the instructor you asked me about."

He looked sideways at her. "What instructor?"

"Stimson."

The name hung between them.

Ezrin looked at the swing sets, at the kids. "Stimson."

"Lemuel Stimson. He's no instructor."

"No."

"No, he's a dead man. Killed in the Ector County Jail." She nodded toward the pile of kids splayed across the playground. "It's the kids, isn't it?"

He brushed his pant leg. "I'm not sure what we're talking about, Jace."

"Deputy Salome, Ranger."

"What gives you cause to talk to me like that?"

"You're playing me."

"Really."

"You knew it was the kids the first time you interrogated me. Those guys are molesting kids."

"Interviewed, not interrogated."

"Semantics."

"Whoa, hang on." He tried a weak laugh. "I don't know all those big words. I'm just a cop."

"Stop it, Captain, just stop it. I'm not an idiot . . . although I was stupid enough to think that when you said Stimson was an instructor, you meant he was an instructor. When I was in the fifth grade I was in the school spelling bee. I worked pretty hard, learning all those words. I practiced for hours while Mama was at work. She'd take me with her and every once in a while, I'd look up and she'd be working and I'd go back to my words."

"I bet you did pretty well." Ezrin waved at a young kid who was goggle-eyed at the gun on Ezrin's hip and the badge opposite the weapon.

"I made it to the final round. With a kid named Jason Schertz. Back then, he was just a geek. I guess we all were in fifth grade. In high school, though, he turned into this monster athlete. Ran track and broke all kinds of school records.

"He died in Afghanistan. An explosion took his legs off. His mother told me he called her and said he couldn't feel his legs anymore. Pretty hard to run when you have no legs. He decided he didn't want to not feel his legs anymore. Blew his head off with a .45."

"I don't know what to say to that."

"He beat me in that spelling bee, Captain. I went bust on an easy word and Jason spelled his word just fine. He won and until you came along and lied to me, I never felt more stupid than when I choked on that word."

Ezrin played with the drink sword from his hatband.

"You lied to me, Captain Ezrin. I wanted to help. I told you everything I knew and you lied to me." She sighed. "Should have known you'd play me to get what you needed."

"And what is it you think I need?"

She paused. "Are you investigating all of them?"

Biting the corners of his mouth, his eyes stayed well away from hers.

"Were all those names dead inmates?"

"Deputy Salome, you obviously misheard me."

"That's crap, Captain, there is something going on."

He smiled but his eyes never warmed. "No, there isn't."

"I can hear it in your tone, Captain."

"My tone, huh? Let me ask you this, then: what if there is? What if there is some statewide conspiracy?"

Surprised, Jace said, "You have to stop it."

"Nothing to stop." With a brush of his shirt, he stood and re-centered his hat. "This little conversation has been nice, Deputy Salome, but I'm busy."

"You have to stop the murders."

"Let me be clear, Deputy: there are no murders except for your jail." In his gaze, she felt his accusation. "That's the only place I've proved there was a murder, Deputy. You're the only one who's brought me proof of a homicide . . . Deputy."

"You're an asshole."

He grinned but his eyes seemed surprisingly somber. "I get that a lot."

"So if there's nothing going on, why did you mention a statewide conspiracy? Why was that the first thing out of your mouth?"

Ezrin's face was as obvious as a morning sunrise. Her words had hit him sideways. "What?"

"Statewide."

He recovered quickly. "Doesn't mean anything."

"Are we going to talk like adults, Captain?"

Somewhere in the distance, Jace heard the thump of a stereo. It played while he took her full measure. Eventually, with a curt nod, he pulled a folded-up sheet of paper from his shirt pocket and handed it to her.

On it were rows and rows of names. A name, another name, a county. The counties touched every geographic part of Texas; most of the big cities and many of the rural jails.

"Which ones are the cops?"

"Inmate, officer, county."

"Are they all dead?"

Ezrin nodded. "Yeah, going back more than five years. When an officer's involved, it's always a correctional officer. It's about fifty-fifty between jailhouse suicides and jailhouse attacks."

Jesus God, she thought, reading the list. Houston, Dallas, Austin, San Antonio, Beaumont, Abilene, the death in Zachary County, Stimson in Ector, Potter County, El Paso.

"There are more," Ezrin said. His voice was low and tired and his shoulders had slumped. "But proof is tough to come by. We have proof on an officer in Bexar County who simply walked into a cell and beat the inmate to death with his baton. And we have proof on an officer in Memphis . . . Hall County. He's on tape stringing up the unconscious inmate from the light fixture. Said later it was a suicidal hanging."

"Damn that videotape," Jace said. But neither laughed.

Jace tried to hand the paper back. "This . . . I'm sorry but I'm out." When Ezrin wouldn't take the sheet, she let it fall to the ground. "This is the honorable profession of law enforcement? Bullshit. This is criminals wearing blue instead of jailhouse orange." Her voice rose in the same kind of anger she heard in Preacher's voice when someone told him his son Robinson would never come home. "This is not me."

A handful of the kids looked over, anxious.

"No, Jace, this is not you." Ezrin lowered his voice. "But this is exactly what you should be doing."

He picked up the sheet, refolded it, and gently slid it into her shirt pocket. The move should have offended her. He shouldn't be that close to her personal space. He shouldn't have his hands or fingers that close to her breasts. But there was no lewdness. There was sadness and exhaustion and a plea for help.

"I can't do anything about the whole state, Jace, but I can do something about West Texas if you help me."

Biting the inside of her lip—and knowing she had bitten it bloody because of the warmth in her mouth—she said, "So it's not about the kids?"

"It is about the kids. No one says so but that's the common denominator. Most of these inmates have some kind of sex charge in their history."

"Most."

"Only a couple don't. Lemuel Stimson, a guy from Davis County, couple others down along the border."

Jace shook her head. "That's not the only common denominator or you wouldn't have mentioned control tactics instructors. You have a line on Will Badgett."

This time, Ezrin didn't let any surprise show, but Jace felt like her stab in the dark had drawn blood.

The man shrugged. "Suspicions, nothing more."

They fell silent and the air between them grew uncomfortable and awkward. Eventually, Ezrin walked away. Halfway out of the park, he said, "You remember your word? From the spelling bee."

"Timorousness, if you can dig that."

After spitting into the dry grass, he went to his car. A moment later, that car disappeared down South Garfield Street.

Chapter Twenty-Three

Ector County Sergeant James Evans sat on a picnic table and took a can of snuff from the pocket of his pants. His thick fingers shoved some into his mouth. After spitting, he wiped his bottom lip and put the can back in his pocket. During the entire thing, he never looked at Jace.

"Who's this?" he asked Rory.

"Friend of mine."

"Yeah, huh."

"She's a good gal. Rookie. Just started in the jail."

"Yeah, huh. What's she doing here?"

Jace opened her mouth but Rory jumped in quick. "Just introducing her around a little. Plus, she shoots pretty well."

"Yeah?" His eyes flickered, showing a vague interest.

"Passed state qualification with a nearly perfect score."

"Nearly."

Jace felt warm blood rush into her cheeks. "Ninety-five percent."

"Nearly."

"Ease up, Jimbalaya," Rory said.

Looking at his watch, he stood. "Break time's over, I guess, so long as I'm being called that shit-ass name."

"Hey, man, you picked it."

"I was drunk."

"You picked it, you wear it."

His face sat granite hard on his skull, but after a few seconds, there was the barest touch of a grin. On the twenty-five mile drive from Zack City, Rory told her she and Evans had known each other since he'd showed up at the Academy shooting range as adjunct instructor and yelled at her about how she shot right-handed but sighted with her left eye.

"You're leaning your damn head down to your ass," he'd yelled. "Open the other eye and straighten that head."

Rory, with no previous gun experience, had followed his instructions and promptly shot a perfect fifty. She'd kept shooting that well, too, and had recently gotten her certification to be an adjunct range instructor.

"Sure thing, Whorey-Rory." Evans shifted his weight on the table, let his head roll around to stretch his neck, but Jace saw his eyes catch the camera hanging about fifty feet behind them. It panned side to side on a timed circuit, seeing the entire outdoor break area. "So you had one cash it in, huh?"

Rory nodded toward Jace. "She was there, saw the whole thing."

For the first time since they'd arrived, Evans cast a look toward Jace. "How many rounds you put in your clip?"

Jace answered carefully. "In my 'clip'? There is no such thing, Sergeant, but I do load thirteen in each of my magazines."

"And?"

She paused thoughtfully, though she knew the answer immediately. "And one in the pipe."

He turned back to Rory. "Heard there were a couple coppers in there. Thought it might be you, looking for a reason to shoot that gun. I'll get you next time. Would've won the last shoot." He looked at Jace. "Had a cold. Sneezed while I was shooting, threw my aim off."

"Yeah, it was the sneeze that hosed you," Rory said. "That and your crappy shooting. Look, I brought her to see you because she's a little freaked out. She thinks maybe she didn't do things as well as she could have. Maybe she could have done this or that. I told her it was fine, but . . . you know . . . rookies."

Evans spat. "Yeah."

Jace shrugged. "Thought I'd see how you guys handled things and maybe I could learn something to do it better next time."

"Think there'll be a next time?" He regarded her. "What'd you learn about the safeties on those shitty Glock 21s you guys carry?"

Jace ground her teeth, tired of the testing. "The only safety, you of all people should know, is that useless trigger safety. Sarge, if you don't know that, you probably shouldn't be a range instructor."

Her words sat in the air for a long while. Eventually, Evans gave Jace a shallow nod. "Our guy died."

"Yes," Jace said.

"Your guy died."

"Yes."

"Nothing else to learn, I'd say."

Rory sighed. "Come on, Jimba—sorry. Jim. Help us out here. Jace saw her first dead guy and she's a little bothered."

"The dead don't bother me."

Whether he'd meant to or not, Evans had frozen her completely. The utter indifference made her uneasy. He might have been describing the color of dirt.

Around them, Odessa sounded much like Zack City. It had all the same cars and trucks, the same motorcycles and pedestrians. But the sound was also deeper and rougher, as though the soundman couldn't quite get a decent polish on the recording. Odessa had always been the flip side of Zack City. Where Zack City twisted itself into ulcers over its status as the white collar center of sophistication, Odessa didn't worry much about anything. Odessa drank and fought and reveled in its blue collar roots.

"Stimson, his name was," Evans said, pulling his can of snuff out again. "Came in . . . I don't know . . . year and a half ago, something like that." Evans opened and closed the can repeatedly, sometimes tapped the top or thumped the bottom. His eyes roamed the break area, stopped momentarily on the handful of deputies sucking down a soda or cigarette. Two women ate from the same giant plate of sweet and sour chicken planted between them. Steam rose up from their dinner. "In on traffic or something."

"Driving While Intoxicated," Jace said.

"Yeah, huh?" Evans spun the snuff can between his fingers. "Anyway, he came in and had a couple of outstanding warrants, probably FTA. Couldn't make bail so he was a keeper."

"Failure to pay," Jace said to Rory. "He'd gotten a ticket for riding an ATV out in the country."

An irritated look flashed across Rory's face.

"He was on a twenty-three and one schedule," Evans said. "That's tough on a man."

"Twenty-three and one?" asked Jace.

"Twenty-three-hour lockdown, one hour liberty. You'll see it when you work discipline pod." Rory urged Evans to continue.

"They kept moving him, too," Evans said. "General population to administrative segregation, gen pop to ad-seg, gen pop to ad-seg. And shaking the hell outta him. Every time they moved him, they'd shake the cell he was leaving, then shake the cell he was going to. Make him stand there and watch, too. Damn well should have."

"Why?" Jace asked.

A sour look ran over Evans' face. "Major league diddler."

Rory held herself tight, zero expression.

Evans nodded. "Who knows how many kids."

Rory whistled and though Jace knew her disgust was genuine,

the whistle and the shiver that followed seemed exaggerated. "God, that just . . . Uuugghhh."

"How do you know?" Jace asked. "Was it in his file?"

"Didn't catch him on it this time, but I can spot a pedophile a mile away, rookie. I could have told you, by the way, that your dead guy was, too."

"Have a chance to spot Mr. Thomas, huh?" Jace asked.

"Don't believe me? Then why was he in the process of pleading out on it? He's just as guilty of it as the guy in Sterling County."

Pleading to it? Jace wasn't sure she believed that, but nodded thoughtfully. "Did Stimson attack your officer?"

"Thomas went off his rocker and busted up one of our guys," Rory said.

"Reynolds. I heard he got booked on a murder bang a few days ago. Couldn't pay me enough to book a fellow officer." Evans visually challenged Jace and then kept going. "Stimson attacked Deputy Sneed. Didn't want to be where he was, I guess. Or maybe didn't like jail. Probably didn't like the prospect of staying for a while."

"Or maybe he just didn't like how he was treated," Jace said.

Evans, who'd been leaning back with his hands planted firmly on the table, leaned forward, a deep furrow between his eyes. "Maybe. Or maybe he just got stupid. Maybe he just jumped on a guard and got his ass beat."

"Maybe," Jace said. "Or maybe the guard was pushing him. Maybe the guard wanted him to take a swing. Maybe the guard wanted to test his skills."

Evans snorted. "Lemme tell you something. Deputy Dave Sneed didn't need to test anything." His hard gaze knocked her around. "No one in our jail knows more about ground fighting. He knew what he was able to do."

"Kill, apparently."

Evans stood. His bulk—a tight 200 pounds on a 5'9″ frame—crowded her. "You building up an implication?"

"Come on, Sarge," Rory said. "That's not what she meant."

Evans sucked at his teeth and spit. The wad landed just about on the toe of Jace's boot. "So what's up? You guys are here in service of the great Texas fucking Rangers . . . Captain Ezekiel."

"Captain Ezrin," Jace said, her mouth snare-drum tight.

"Ezrin, huh? You bagged your guy so now you're looking to take another one?"

"First of all, I didn't bag Reynolds. Ezrin saw the entire thing on the videotape."

A tight grin slipped over Evans' face and his body language sat back, satisfied. The ground under Jace shifted. Ten seconds ago he had to prove his department had done nothing wrong and now he was the fat cat.

"I heard someone sent him toward that video."

Jace shrugged. "I have no idea."

"Yeah, huh." Still crowding her, the way Reynolds had done both Thomas and her, Evans stuffed his snuff can back into his pocket. "Break time's about over, I guess. Catch you later, Whorey-Rory."

"Sarge, wait."

"No, I'm good, Rory. You guys better get to work. Got a shift in a couple hours, don't you? Don't ever bring that bitch here again."

He planted a meaty fist on the door and a half-heartbeat later it popped open. When it slammed closed, Jace looked around. The break area was empty. But on the table, the plate of chicken was only about half-finished. The steam still rose.

Chapter Twenty-Four

In the moment between when the lights go down in a concert hall and the first notes splash from the trumpet or piano, the world is dead silent. The audience is hushed and expectant. The musicians take a last breath before their lips or fingers lay down the groove. That moment had always been Jace's favorite because it was only an instant but also endless. There was no deeper silence.

Driving back to Zack City reminded her of that silence. Stretched. Elongated. Pulled tightly between the two women. Rory drove with her face set and hard. Her jaws ground together so violently that every few miles, when the engine or some other part on the car popped, Jace was unsure if it was the car or Rory's teeth.

"You didn't play that so well, sister."

Jace pressed her lips. "I got what I needed."

"You did, huh?"

Jace hadn't and she knew it, but rather than admit it, she sat up straight. "Evans said Deputy Sneed killed Stimson."

"Really? What I heard is that they pushed Stimson pretty hard and Sneed defended himself. Didn't hear about murder."

Rory was right. Jace had walked out of that conversation without any evidence that Sneed had done anything other than defend himself.

She banged a fist against the door. "Damn it, I didn't get anything."

"You got dick." Rory sighed. "But Evans got stuff he didn't even know he wanted."

"Meaning?"

"Did you guys do interviews at all? In the Academy? I'll take the silence as a yes. Did you pay any attention?"

Jace clamped her tongue between her teeth. She *had* been in that class and she *had* learned how to interview. But tonight, when faced with doing it, she had lost herself. She hadn't known how to ask and hadn't known *what* to ask. All she'd done was react to what he said.

"You gave it all away, Jace, and you can bet, sure as shit, he knows you dropped Reynolds."

"No, he doesn't."

"Really. He screwed up Ezrin's name and you gave it to him. Think that was an honest mistake?"

"He did it on purpose?"

"You betcha. He wanted to know you knew Ezrin's name."

"Everyone knows Ezrin's name."

Rory's head bobbled. "Maybe. But then he said someone handed Ezrin the tape and the first thing out of your mouth was a denial. Those two things and he knew exactly what was going on. He didn't say a word about you and you immediately denied it. From then on, sister, he had you. Couldn't you feel it? Everything after that was him pumping you for information . . . what you were supposed to be doing to him."

"So I'm one of the bad guys now," Jace said. "For him, I'm one of the bad guys . . . going to the Rangers and diming cops."

"Maybe. I don't know. But Jimbalaya is a good cop and a good man. It's probably freaking him out that his guy did this terrible thing, but deep down, he's a good cop."

Mile markers passed them with a Dave Brubeck rhythmic steadiness that Jace found comforting. If Evans was a good cop and a good man, then he could not stand idly by while a man was murdered.

"Was Lemuel fucking children?" Rory asked at the outskirts of Zack City.

Jace took a deep breath. "I don't know." Mama had always believed that no one was exactly what they showed the world. Everyone had shades and shadows inside their skin and a darkness they kept hidden from the world; subsurface like a cancerous cell quietly spreading infection. "It's possible . . . with both of them. Maybe that's what ties all of them together. Reynolds believed it about Thomas and Evans believes it about Lemuel and whoever the guy was in Sterling County."

"I'll call the DA," Rory said. "See if Thomas was actually in the process of pleading."

"They were shaking and moving Lemuel just like Thomas," Jace said. "And I'd bet you a case of Skittles it was exactly the same in Gaines and Sterling County and God knows where else."

The Sea Spray was quiet as most of its inhabitants were down for the night. A light burned in one or two apartments but predominantly the tenants were daytime workers or long hour workers at factories or construction sites or drilling rigs.

"I gotta be honest with you, Jace. If those guys were diddlers, my sympathy meter goes way down. Anyone who could do that to a kid."

"If they were. We don't know. We aren't the judge and jury, Rory."

"Spare me the lecture, I know exactly what we are and aren't. I'm just saying if this is about men who raped kids . . ."

"But they shouldn't be killing innocent men."

When she faced Jace, headlights traveling left to right on the highway lit her face intermittently. "None of these guys are innocent, Jace."

Jace let Rory's anger sit. Eventually, in a soft voice, she said,

"Which guys? The cops or the inmates?"

Rory bit her lips. "Both. Now go get dressed so we can get to my place. Don't have much time before shift."

"You want to come up and wait?"

"No, I'm fine here."

"Give me ten minutes."

"Yeah, yeah."

Two minutes later, Jace was hustling around her apartment, putting her uniform on, eating a banana, grabbing a leftover sub sandwich for dinner, and getting her iPod in case she was on clerical duty tonight. And all the while, Wonder Woman stared down at her.

Chapter Twenty-Five

Saturday night and the jailhouse walls were bursting with Zachary County arrestees.

—booking from control: we got another winner coming. Beat his grandfather into the hospital—

—10-4—

—two more off the domestic—

—10-4—

—415 . . . uh . . . 10-1 . . . try again—

—control, gimme a 10-29 on a late-night visitor at the south door—

Drunks and junkies, late-night burglars, God and Wonder Woman alone knew how many car thieves and domestic abusers. On her way to the sally port during a break, Jace wandered through booking and was stunned at the sheer number of arrestees. Kleopping generously asked if she was there to help but, with a batting of her eyes, she apologized and kept moving, ignoring the two armed robbers and the pile of men picked up for disorderly conduct who'd gotten into a fight at a tranny bar.

Welcome to the job, she thought. Yet in spite of the madness of booking and the minor skirmish in B Pod just before lights out and the 93-year-old man's seizure in E Pod, it had been a good night. There had even been times when she realized she hadn't been thinking about Thomas or Lemuel.

Those realizations were always followed by guilt. She should feel more for the dead men. She shouldn't be able to dismiss them and it bothered her that she had. For Rory, it was exactly the opposite. Jace felt as though something had lifted from her in the last day or so but Rory seemed to be getting smothered by the blackness. They'd worked different assignments but during roll call and dinner and a break or two, Rory was quiet and reserved in spite of the hurricane in her eyes.

The yellow and blue stripe broke left while the green and black rolled out in front of her and red broke right. Picking up red, Jace headed for medical. She'd been all over the jail most of the shift, but now Dillon wanted her in medical.

Somewhere down the line, doors opened and closed, voices called and answered, some argued and others yelled. The occasional clang let her know a trusty or two was in the hallways. Another pop and a deputy stepped through a secured door and headed toward her.

A blast of cleaning-chemical tang hit her and she sneezed.

"Gesundheit." Bibb's voice came from the speakers lining the hallway.

Without stopping, Jace glared at one of the cameras.

"Uh . . . sorry," Bibb said. "No big deal, just taking care of my deputies."

—479 from 476—

A woman whose name Jace was unsure of. Jace keyed her radio. "476 go ahead."

—what time you doing lunch?—

"Uh . . . hadn't thought about it yet."

—well, we've got some Brooks coming . . . ribs, links, and some brisket . . . interested?—

Surprise rolled through her. "Uh . . . yeah . . . absolutely. Uh—" She paused. "Thanks for asking. I . . . I'll have to get some cash, I'm a little dry."

—yeah, don't sweat it, we've got it covered—

"Uh . . . sure, thanks."

—anytime—

Aside from a single lunch break with Dillon a few days after Thomas died, she'd only ever eaten with Rory or by herself. Yet was this anything more than a temporary defrost? It would last only as long as the correctional staff didn't know about her part in Reynolds' arrest.

Rounding the last corner, she keyed up. "Control from 479. Medical outer."

The door popped and when the door closed behind her, the inner door popped unprompted. She entered and yanked the door closed behind her.

" 'Bout damned time," Royce said. He sat at the nurse's desk, his black duty boots propped on the desk blotter.

"What are you doing here?"

"If it's any of your business, I'm getting some overtime. That a problem?"

Jace frowned. "How's the bad hooch going?"

"Dumbasses. Massie brewed it but everyone else drank it. He's the only one ain't sick off it."

"Massie brewed it?"

"I just said that, didn't I? He's getting charged with it. Anyway, the idiots who drank it are all pissed at Dr. Cruz. He won't give them anything for it, just wants them to ride it out. Wouldn't even come in to talk to them. Just let his assistant . . . what's his name . . . Dr. Wrubel . . . do it."

"Seems pretty harsh," Jace said.

Royce snorted. "Hell, the best part of these morons ran down their mama's thighs." He jerked a thumb toward the beds in the back.

"Nurse not here?"

"You don't see her, do you?"

Jace blinked. "Uh . . . no."

Rolling his eyes, he craned his head toward the cells. "Big

Carol's on tonight."

Royce made no move to fill her in on anything, nor to get up from the desk. He sat in a pile of smugness and stared at her.

"Busy night, huh?" She tried again. "So what's up?"

"I have to do everything?" he said, his impatience full-on. "It's in the pass-on book."

She reached for the log but his boots remained atop it. "Boots, please."

He didn't move.

"Ditch the game and tell me what's what."

"So you can go running to Captain America?"

A beat passed. "What?"

"Gotta make sure everybody—except the cops—gets their rights."

He picked his teeth and for a moment, she thought it was with a frayed toothpick. But when he opened his hand, she clearly saw a plastic drink sword.

She tried to swallow down the heavy-grit sandpaper that suddenly scourged her throat.

"What's the matter, worm?" Royce said. "Did I say something wrong? Or did you?"

Touching her tattoo, hoping for some kind of talismanic strength, she faced Royce. "Clever, playing with the sword. Who thought it up for you?" She pointed at his uniform shirt. "They should have thought up how to keep you from stabbing yourself."

Two tiny drops of blood dotted his chest and when he looked up from it, anger had replaced the smugness. He jumped up. "You think you're funny, bitch?"

"Ah . . . bitch. Couldn't think of any other words?"

"Aren't any other words for it."

In spite of her fear and anger, she laughed. "Oh, yeah, buddy, all kinds of other words. If you can find a seventh grader at

Alamo Junior High to teach you how to use a dictionary, maybe you can discover a few."

He came around the desk. One forearm crossed her at the shoulders and ground into her throat. With his free hand, he grabbed her ponytail and yanked her head painfully sideways. "You listen to me, *bitch.* I know what you did. You pimped out Reynolds and you'll cough up for it."

Her eyes bulged and her knees, suddenly limp, would have dropped her had his arm not pinned her against the wall. A painful white noise crashed through her head. He jabbed her gut with a quick strike and her breath blew out. She gasped but got nothing back as his forearm worked its way deeper into her throat.

"Why'd you rat him out?" A light slap across her face and she bit back her humiliation. "He didn't do anything the rest of us wouldn't have done."

"Don't speak . . . for me, asshole."

She worked her arms up and got them beneath his. She wanted to pry him off as she'd been shown at the Academy, but he had better leverage. She was back on her heels, pinned against the wall. He leaned forward, his entire body weight into his forearm, his grin huge in her face. The sleeve of his free arm rode up over his bicep enough to bare his tattoo.

A "T." And an "F."

It took a moment, long past when her eyes had swept to the camera hanging in the corner, before she realized she'd seen it before.

Royce's face lit up when he caught her eyes. "You think that asshole Bibb's watching? Too busy pounding his pud or feeding his fat face. Wouldn't save a piece of crap like you, anyway."

The edges of her vision darkened and still her hands bumbled against his arms. So she tried to turn her body. Her left shoulder bit painfully backward into the wall as she forced her axis to reorient.

He shook his head. "You ain't no police."

"Yeah. I am."

"Watch your ass. Reynolds and Sneed are my friends. You wanna go out like Thomas? We know everything. We know where you live and what you drive and what your grandmother looks like."

With a grunt, Jace feigned a turn to the right. When he stopped the move, and leaned in to laugh at her, she head-butted him. Hard and fast and focusing exclusively on his teeth.

There was a loud snap and Jace was free. She fell sideways as he staggered backward, sat hard on the nurse's desk, and filled the medical pod with his howl. His hand flew to the spreading red stain over his lips and she used the moment to rush him. She punched him in the head and stomped his toes. He howled again as she backed away with her fists up.

"You know dick. Stay away from me and my family or I'll kill you myself."

He tried to laugh through the blood and broken teeth and for a second, she thought he might lunge at her.

Part of her wanted it. Some part she hadn't known was there wanted him with his fists flying because she wanted to taste the violence again. It hadn't been the bitter, sour taste she'd expected. It had been elegant and sweet, and had slid easily down her throat. "You want to beat on me, then get to the beating."

Now nothing came through his red-smeared face, no grin, no nod or shake, nothing, and she realized he hadn't expected her to fight back.

Just as she keyed up to call for help, the outer door popped open and then closed. A second later, the inner door popped and Dillon strode in. He stopped. "Salome? Do we have a problem? Deputy Royce?"

Royce breathed through the blood. "Got nothing here, Sarge."

"And the blood?" He looked at Jace. "Yours or his?"

"Mine," Royce said. "Tripped coming out from behind the desk."

A long silence fell between them. "Uh-huh. Gonna stick with that, or you want to come up with something better?"

His gaze on Jace, Royce took his time answering. "No, I'm good with that."

Dillon pointedly looked at his watch. "Overtime's finished."

"Yeah." With a dismissive shrug, Royce went to the inner door. It didn't open.

"Control," he said into his radio. "M-medical inner."

The door popped and closed behind him.

—come on, Control, m-medical outer for cripe's sake—

Jace heard it over her radio. *Nicely done, Bibb,* she thought.

"What in the hell was that, Deputy?"

In that moment, Jace saw it all. Everyone knew she had given Reynolds to Ezrin.

"Salome?"

"Don't bother writing up that he attacked me."

"He what?"

"Doesn't matter. He's just like the rest of them. They all know and it's going to be like this every damned shift. So don't worry about it." She pulled the badge off her shirt and held it out. "I'm done."

Dillon blinked. "Hang on. I'm confused."

"And this was a good night, too. You know they're having Brooks delivered late and they let me know?"

"You like Brooks?"

"What? Yeah. Well, it's okay. Look, the point is they included me, Sergeant. I ate once with you and I usually eat with Rory. No one—not a single person on my shift—has ever asked me to eat with them."

He shook his head. "Man, you've gotten all worked up for all the wrong reasons. You bet some of them know what you did. I'd lay good money most of them know. That's why the invite came. Some are proud of you."

"Well, some aren't."

"Damn straight some aren't and they never will be. That's how it is." Dillon shook his head. "This job is no different than any other. We've got nearly three hundred people working here. Damn straight some of them are going to be idiots. Simple percentages."

She shook her head. "I got jumped on and I'm done. I'll be there to testify against Reynolds but I'm done with this job. I got attacked, Sergeant. Don't you understand that? I came to work and did the right thing and got attacked."

He licked his lips. "So that's that."

"That's that."

He made no move to take her badge.

"Is there anything I can say?"

"No."

"You're a quitter."

"Nice try but you better get your money back on your college psych courses because you're not very good."

Red flamed his face. "How about this, then? I don't take resignations in the medical pod. You want to do this, then do it right." He pointed at the computer. "Write up a letter." His voice was ragged and angry. "Bring it to my office in ten minutes."

She nodded.

"498 from 405," he barked into his radio.

—405 go ahead—

"You're in medical. Get down here. Now."

—uh . . . yes, sir—

Dillon stormed out. The doors slammed behind him and she imagined the bang was harsher than it had been before. Her stomach fluttering, she sat down at Big Carol's computer and started her resignation letter.

Chapter Twenty-Six

When she walked into Sergeant Dillon's office, Jace's breath caught.

"Just the effect I want to have on people," said Sheriff Bukowski. He smoked down the last bit of a cigar.

Jace stood as tall as she could. "I didn't expect you, sir."

"Yeah, that's probably true." With a mostly empty smile, he motioned to a chair. "Sit down, Salome, and relax. It's just me."

"Just me" was Caleb Bukowski, sheriff of Zachary County through the last four election cycles.

"Is there something I can help you with, sir?"

"First of all, drop the 'sir.' Sheriff is just fine. Or James, if you prefer."

"Uh . . . yeah, I don't think it'll be James."

The sheriff laughed and toyed with the smoking stub of his cigar. Then he touched a finger to a manila folder that lay facedown on the desk. "You know there is no smoking in this facility, right?"

"You want me to write you up?"

A smile slipped across his face and his dark eyes flashed with glee. "You should . . . technically I'm violating a city ordinance, though the county jail is county property. That would be one helluva story for the halls, wouldn't it? 'Sergeant Dillon, I went in to accept her resignation and she wrote me a ticket.' Christ, that'd be funny."

Jace set her letter on the desk. "Speaking of resignation, I—"

"I don't care," he said. "I care about budgeting." He rubbed his temples. "I hate this time of year. Commissioners want a smaller budget. Cut training or uniform allowances. Or fleet maintenance." He shrugged. "Taxes are too high but don't think every taxpayer in the county doesn't want the best in law enforcement. Rolls-Royce for the cost of a VW."

Jace arched her eyebrows in what she hoped was a show of support.

"Yeah, it's tough at the top." Bukowski flexed his shoulders, as though getting down to business. "Dillon's pretty high on you. He thinks you're a damned good officer for someone who's been here two weeks."

"Sir, excuse me, but I've been here almost two months."

He shook his head. "Orientation . . . the Academy. You've been on the job—the *job*—two weeks. What's this crap with a resignation?"

His abruptness surprised Jace. "I—well . . . Sergeant Dillon's opinion notwithstanding, I don't think I can do this job, Sheriff." His face gave her nothing back so she filled the silence. "I've had a few problems."

"Had one fifteen minutes ago from what I heard."

What are you doing here? Why isn't Dillon here? It pissed her off. She didn't need the intimidation of the sheriff sitting across from her.

"Why are you a cop, Salome?"

Before she could fend off his question, he flipped the manila folder over. The Lubbock County Sheriff's Office logo was splashed across the cover. Jace knew what it was.

"Zack City looked at it, too," he said. "Local girl. Not much in either file. Lotta questions. Not a lotta answers."

"And?"

"We're law enforcement, Salome. Means we live in the real world. Sometimes cops don't ask enough questions."

As if to punctuate his point, a pod door somewhere down the hall popped and then slammed closed.

"What pod was that? I'll bet all the money in my pocket against all the money in your pocket you can tell me."

"A."

"And you've only been in those pods two weeks."

"Smoking in a public place and now gambling, Sheriff? Maybe I should cuff you up."

"Be the most fun I had in months." When he leaned across the desk, he pushed the file toward her but kept his finger on it. "This woman—this dead woman who no one gives a shit about except you—is why you became a cop. The badges who investigated didn't ask enough questions and the search teams didn't look long enough. Now you've got yourself a job where you can ask all the questions you want."

"Sir, I don't know what you're talking about."

"Pull your head out, Salome. This isn't literal, this is metaphor and symbolism."

"And here I thought you were just another politician."

"Hard to believe I was a real human being once, isn't it?"

Taking his finger from the file, he leaned back in Dillon's chair. "This is a bad precedent, Salome, but I'm going to be honest for a minute." The joke fell flat. "I know you popped Reynolds with Captain Ezrin."

"Sir? How do you—"

"There is damned little that goes on in this office without my knowledge. More so when it comes to one of my deputies being arrested for murder."

She felt as caught as when Gramma'd seen her snatching Gramma's pocket change for beer or when the conductor caught her slipping onto the zoo train without a ticket.

"Reynolds was something I didn't know was happening and I'll live with that." His face clouded. "You're asking the questions, right?"

"I haven't really thought about it."

"Again with the cowshit."

"Sheriff, honestly, I haven't given it much thought."

"Well, think about it."

"I won't be here long enough to worry about it."

"Yeah, you will because I don't accept your resignation, Deputy Jace Salome."

She moved to the edge of the seat. "You have to, sir. After this shift ends, I don't work here anymore."

His laugh knocked holes in the wall. "I don't have to do dick, Salome, I'm the big guy. A whole lotta deputies know exactly what you did, and they have no problem with it. And let me tell you this: a whole pile out of that bunch are embarrassed."

"At?"

"Their hesitation. Some of your fellow jailers knew Reynolds was bad news, or so they say now. Yet none of them did anything. None of them voiced their concern to Ezrin. You did."

"So I get attacked in medical for my trouble."

The sheriff's face darkened. Lightning flashed in his eyes while thunder rolled deep in his chest. "Sergeant Dillon and I will deal with that situation. But don't let that bullcrap make you forget about Brooks."

"Brooks who?"

"Barbeque. I hear you're quite the expert. Didn't they order Brooks for tonight?"

"That's what they said."

"Didn't they invite you?"

"That's what they said."

"Ain't that interesting? Co-workers who haven't said ten words to you just happen to order up something you like and then reach out to you. There are people here who are proud of what you did, Salome."

"Then they should have done it."

"How many people do you think saw that videotape?"

"I don't know. What about the detectives?"

His head shook slowly. "I don't want my people anywhere near this investigation. Conflict of interest. But you either blew that off or didn't know—"

"I'm sorry, sir, I didn't—"

He waved a hand. "Get your ass back to work. And always—absolutely always—do the right thing, no matter how hard it is. The only thing you have in this job is your word. Nobody can take it away but you sure as hell can give it away. And if you decide to give it away, make certain it's for a good reason."

"Sir, I am not going back to work. Regardless of those you say approve of what I did, there are those who don't approve and they are not going to give me a break. They will make this job impossible for me."

"Only if you give them the power. Plus, you don't have to please them. You have to please Dillon." He held up a single finger and then added a second. "And you have to please me."

Standing, stretching his legs until his knees popped, he said, "We're good to go, Deputy Salome. One last thing: don't plan on not showing up for work after your two days off. If you go that route, I'll send a roadie out to cuff you and drag you back here."

In spite of herself, she grinned. "Cuff me? Can you legally do that, Sheriff?"

"I could give a shit about legally this or legally that. You will work here because you want to and because I want you to. We both know you can be good police, you proved that in how quickly you wrapped up this little investigation of yours." He giggled like a schoolboy. "God, I love showing the Rangers up."

He went to the door and left the file on Dillon's desk. "I don't guess Lubbock County or Zack City PD needs another copy of their own file, do they." It was a question meant to hang heavy in the air. "I'll ask Dillon to hold on to it." A last time, he grinned and shoved open Dillon's door. "Leave those citations in my mailbox."

Ten minutes later, Dillon came back in and dropped into his chair. "Have a nice chat?" He put the manila file in his desk. "You're in the kitchen rest of the shift."

She stood. "Uh . . . yes, sir."

Chapter Twenty-Seven

"He did not." Rory stood with one arm draped over the roof of her purple Monte Carlo SS.

One hand over her heart and the other aloft, Jace said, "Sure did."

"To put them in his basket." Mischievously, Rory lowered her head and looked through the tops of her eyes. "And you did, right?"

Jace snorted. "I think I'll pass on that particular brand of career destruction."

"Career destruction?" Rory said with a laugh. "You were trying to resign."

Her laugh became a somber sound that filled the early morning air. "I've been trying like hell for three years to get on his radar screen and you pop along and boom! He's having a meeting with you."

"I didn't—"

Rory held up a hand. "Ain't nothing but a thing, Jace. Don't sweat it. Just makes me a little crazy. I'll go have a breakfast sundae and I'll be over it. Don't get your panties in a bunch."

All across the parking lot, other jailers trudged out of the facility and hit their cars with a nod or wave or muttered a word or two. One, an older woman who'd worked the jail since long before Sheriff Bukowski won his first election, went to the bus stop and sat heavily on the concrete bench. In ten minutes or so, Jace knew, a wheezing city bus would pull up, disgorge a few downtown workers, and she'd climb aboard.

"They're charging Massie," Jace said.

"With?"

"Brewing the hooch."

Rory's head cocked. "Massie? That's crap. Gotta be a setup."

"His name just keeps coming up, doesn't it?"

"What?"

"I moved him one of the first nights I was here. The jailer—I can't remember who it was—told me Massie wanted off second tier because of heights. Massie hadn't even packed."

Rory frowned. "Fear of heights? He used to be a telephone lineman."

"Up on the poles?"

"Thirty or forty feet up. Sometimes worked the big towers. Hundred feet high."

"How do you know this?"

"Talked to him once. Decent old man. Walks kind of like my grandfather did, all crooked over."

Rory stared into the rising sun and closed her eyes. *She's trying to cleanse the dirt away,* Jace thought. Rory had said she'd felt nothing but dirty since they'd spoken with Evans. Eventually she opened her eyes. "What's up?"

"Huh?"

Rory tapped her temple. "What's going on in the brain?"

Jace sucked a deep breath through her nose. A whistling sound highlighted the sorry state of her sinuses. "Nothing."

"Jace, please, this is me. We've had a pretty full two weeks. I think we're kinda getting to be friends. I mean, it's either you or the retards and I choose you, so spill."

Jace licked her lips. "We have to go to Sterling County."

A pained look crawled across Rory's face, filling the comfortable space the sun had filled moments earlier. "Why?"

"Sheriff Bukowski told me to."

Two hours later, headed north in Rory's Monte Carlo and listening to Los Lonely Boys, Rory leaned back, splayed her hands out along her thighs, and said, "I think you ought to write him."

"Why?"

"As long as you're nailing cops, nail the sheriff, too. Smoking in a public facility and illegal gambling."

"Nailing cops? Is that what we're doing? I thought we were nailing murderers."

"Doesn't seem to be much difference this time around." Snapping off the CD player, Rory rolled her window down. A rush of wind and the dry tang of the desert filled the car. "Sterling County, too, huh? What's that get us?"

Jace concentrated on driving, keeping the nose of the car dead center in the lane as it quick-stepped at about eighty. "I don't know. Maybe this is just so we can sleep at night."

"I have no problems sleeping, sister."

"I don't believe that."

"Yeah?"

"I know you, Rory."

"Two weeks and you know me inside and out, huh?"

A sun about halfway up toward noon laid the question bare, daring either woman to answer. To their right, a jackrabbit darted from the shoulder into the anonymity of the desert.

"I can't sleep. I don't think you can, either."

"Because there are bad things going on in the world?" Rory rolled her eyes. "Bad things have been going on since Cain left Abel bloody and dead in the dirt. And I can tell you this: bad things will happen long after we're in that same dirt." She nuzzled close to the car's door and her left leg rose until the knee covered her right thigh.

"If you believed that, you'd have quit this job long ago and you know it."

"I don't know any such crap," Rory said.

The Monte Carlo chewed the miles reliably. It smelled of Rory's slightly musky yet sweet aroma she always wore. Jace had thought it odd that she'd put on perfume to work in the jail and she'd assumed it was for the boys. After a few shifts, she'd realized that the jail air, stale and chemical-laced, was deep in her skin and nose and would be there while she slept.

"Hey." Jace pulled a few Tootsie Pops from her pocket. She'd grabbed them on her way out the door. Preacher kept her well supplied from the stash he kept for the children at his church. "Wanna sucker?"

"What?"

"Tootsie Pops."

"No."

"They're probably fresh."

"Probably always fresh," Rory said. "Processed sugar."

Jace smacked her lips. "My favorite kind."

With a shake of her head, Rory grabbed one. "I want to be pissed about what's going on and you want some candy."

"What I want is to not forget I'm a decent human."

"Don't you worry. With you? It's encoded in your damned DNA." With a flourish, Rory yanked the wrapper off a grape Tootsie Pop and jammed the thing in her mouth. After a few hard sucks, she handed it to Jace.

Jace hesitated, then stuffed it into her own mouth.

"So . . . you going to write him those tickets?"

Jace handed the Tootsie Pop back. It promptly disappeared in Rory's mouth. "He's the sheriff."

"Sounds like a direct order." The sucker clicked on Rory's teeth. "Can't disobey orders."

"Watch me."

"You think?"

"If they're illegal or really stupid, and I'm pretty sure writing my boss two citations would be pretty stupid."

Handing the sucker over again, Rory laughed, but it was a strained sound that played a counterpoint to the beautiful day through which they traveled. "Yeah, it might be."

Chapter Twenty-Eight

At first, it was the sharp snap of someone only feet away hitting a long pipe with a metal hammer. Then a secondary reverberation of someone a great distance away hitting that same pipe with a rubber hammer. Jace's eyes fluttered and her heart stepped up a bit. Her skin grew warm.

"Take it easy." Rory winked. "Not our jail, not our inmates. Don't get all Rambo on me."

Jace laughed nervously. "I'm fine, I just—"

Behind them, a shape stood in the doorway, momentarily frozen by the harsh sunlight that backlit him. The piercing yellow-white daylight burned the figure to a deep midnight black. There were no colors in the man's face, nor any shading in its crevices and hollows. There was only the shape of his head, and in outline it seemed impossibly large. Tufts of hair stood at attention on either side, close-cropped and each curved ever so slightly inward. Meaty arms slithered out from the man's large upper body, while a thick, powerfully shaped hand grabbed at the door handles and yanked the door open until it banged against the brick wall behind it.

When he stepped into the hallway, he became human. The sunlight faded beneath the glow of blue-white fluorescent bulbs. The light gave him life beyond the blackness and his face and clothing, and he became real.

With a surprised nod, he smiled. "Salome? Bogan? The hell are you doing here? Awfully far from home."

"Had a day off, sir," Rory said.

Will Badgett. Plastic ID card around his neck on a lanyard, leather binder tucked under his arm, Total Force knit shirt tucked neatly into his Dockers. Jace took a deep breath and nodded.

"Get a day off and go poking around cop shops." He grinned conspiratorially. "We can't get enough of it, can we? The best officers don't just work it, ladies, the best officers *are* it."

Rory shrugged. "Well, I thought we'd come see an old friend of mine."

Badgett's face shifted slightly and became something closer to the face Ezrin had used while questioning the inmates. "Yeah? Who's that?"

"Eddie."

"Eduardo Vasquez? He's a helluva officer."

"You know him?"

"He was one of my guys at the Academy."

Something dark and quick flicked across Rory's face.

"Got a class today?" Jace asked.

"Setting one up. Gotta meet with the big cheese. The chief deputy."

"Not the sheriff?"

Badgett leaned in close. "Always go to the chief deputy. That's the person in charge, ladies. Like David Cornutt at Zachary County. He's a good man. The sheriff is a politician. The chief deputy—or deputy chief at police departments—is the law enforcement. You want something done, get the big cheese on it."

Badgett pulled a card from his shirt pocket, handed each of the ladies one. Total Force, it said. Jace's stomach hitched as she stared at the logo. It was nothing more than black ink on a white background. Except for the stylized TF, laid out in a powerful font.

"Deputy?" Badgett asked. "You okay?"

"Yeah . . . uh, yes, sir," Jace said. "Just a little hungry."

He nodded, but didn't look away. "Gotta eat breakfast. Most important meal of the day."

"What my grandmother says."

He smiled but it was an empty thing, sitting on his face like an abandoned structure. "I wanted to ask: have you guys heard anything about Sonny Brook? I know your daily hotsheet had him listed a few days ago."

Jace had no answer and glanced at Rory. "As far as I know," her friend said, "he's still out there."

Badgett shook his head sadly. "God, I hope they catch him. He'll kill a kid this time, you wait and see." His lips pulled back and he bared his teeth. He had the look of a wolf. "Damned guy shouldn't have gotten out of jail at all. Life sentence, as far as I'm concerned."

"Didn't he finish his sentence?" Jace asked.

"Life's the only thing that works for those guys. Rehabilitation, living and working restrictions, GPS anklets. None of that crap works. They slip through the holes in the system and snatch a kid anyway. It's hours—at best and usually days—before anyone realizes it and usually, by then, the kid is dead."

"What about civil commitments?" Rory said.

"Now you're talking. Finish that jail sentence and put 'em somewhere else for life. We know they're going to offend again. What's the recidivism rate, like 95 percent or something, even if you castrate them?"

"Castration doesn't have anything to do with it," Jace said. "It's not the penis, it's the urge. It's mental. Besides, we can't just lock them away forever, Mr. Badgett, it's not legal."

When he looked at her, his tongue played on his lips. "The government's main job is to protect its citizens."

"Yeah, but—"

"If we can't protect the least able among us, how can we insure the survival of our civilization? Kids are the only future we have. And those who prey on them are a slow bleed, Deputy. They get on our undersides and suck us dry."

Jace found herself nodding. That much of what he said was at least true. The kids, as much as she didn't have the patience for them, were all society had. In many ways, the past didn't matter if the future couldn't be protected.

"And they're fucking everywhere," Badgett said. "MySpace just booted what . . . nearly 30,000 pages because they belonged to registered sex offenders? They're trolling MySpace looking for victims."

"Well, at least Brook didn't take a kid this time," Rory said. "It was a lady."

"Small miracles, I guess," Badgett said.

The next few seconds were awkward. The red that had worked up into Badgett's face drained and the sweat that had broken on Jace's back dried.

"It was good to see you guys. Call me anytime. I've got a few guys in Zachary County I've trained. I could do you, too."

Shoving the business card into her pocket, Jace followed Rory deeper into the jail.

"I did something about it, Rory," Vasquez said.

His fingers knotted together on the blue tablecloth. A heaping bowl of French fries sat between them, surrounded by sodas and ketchup packets squished flat like bugs against a windshield.

His brazenness surprised Jace. "You're telling me you killed that guy?"

Vasquez's face was a mixture of horror and satisfaction at her suggestion. "*Homicidio?* No, your Honor, I did not murder him." He stuffed a handful of fries in his mouth. Ketchup bled down his chin.

"But you did kill him."

Vasquez's eyes were a fluid green. They rested on Jace. "That's how it worked out."

Rory whistled. "Man, I bet that's got some synapses working overtime."

"Pardon?"

"In your brain?" Rory pointed to her head. "Got you a little mixed up."

"Nothing to be mixed up about. Joe Paul Hewson came at me, I defended myself. He died as a result. No different than if we'd been on the street and he came at me with a deadly weapon. Just like we learned at the Academy."

"You guys were at the Academy together?" Jace asked.

"Sí." Vasquez leaned back and spread his arms along the back of the booth. "It's not what I expected when I strapped up that day, but this is the job. It happens that way sometimes." Finger out like a blade, he jabbed the table once or twice. "But I did not kill him unprovoked. Ask the Ranger, even. I was on suspension forever because of him. He got himself all lathered up over this thing but couldn't make his case."

"Ezrin?"

With a slurp of his Coke, Vasquez nodded. "First he tried murder; straight-up attempted capital murder. That didn't go so he started talking about violations of the civil rights of a person in custody."

"Second degree felony," Rory said.

"No crap. Scared me to death. Tried a couple other things after that but the judge and the district attorney wouldn't bite. I'll tell you this, though: Joe Paul Hewson was a kiddie-diddler. No question. He fucked little kids."

"How do you know?" Jace tried to keep her voice neutral, just an interested third-party.

His face hardened. "The guy pleaded to it, that's how. Just

waiting on sentencing. Plus, he'd been charged with this crap before. Five or six times and all the victims—the ones we know about, anyway—were getting younger."

A waitress came over carrying a pitcher of soda. "Refills?"

Without an answer, she poured and kept turning an interested eye toward Vasquez. Vasquez was in uniform, crisp and authoritative with his badge and nameplate. "Ain't you the guy who—" Her voice faded as her hip cocked and she dug up the memory. "Yeah, you the one he attacked, ain't you? The child raper."

Vasquez cracked just enough smile to encourage her but not enough to revel in the attention. "Yeah, that was me."

She gave him a warm wink. "You done good."

"Or even well," Jace said.

The waitress glowered at Jace. "You got something to say? I'm glad somebody took care of him. I got three little girls I don't want nobody getting in their pants. The officer hadn't done it, I would'a."

Taken aback, Jace could only nod.

"We're fine," Vasquez said. "*Gracias* . . . and *gracias*."

Her glare lingering on Jace, the woman stormed away. Behind the counter, they could hear her huffing and muttering.

"Can't say she's wrong," Vasquez said. "Nobody wants their kids hurt. And this guy, he was the real deal. His first victim was twenty-two. Then a nineteen-year-old girl and then seventeen. Then he did a sixteen year old but pleaded that out to consensual sex. It was a white-trash kid and I'd bet Daddy sold her for some smack. Then, boom, he bags a ten year old. Snatched her out of a grocery store while Mom was somewhere else, takes her to a rest area up on the highway, rapes her, sodomizes her, kills her."

"God." Rory leaned forward on the table, resting her head on her extended arms.

Along with the waitress and cook, there were only a handful of other people in the place. The joint was covered in neon beer signs and years-old framed ads for different tobaccos. The air was heavy with the bitter odor of fried foods and the floor slick with a fine layer of grease.

Ten years old. Jace could hardly remember when she was ten. The age was lost in a haze of endless tourists and traveling salesmen calling the Sea Spray home, and Grapa and Gramma and the industrial cleaning smell that always seemed to walk with them. What would they have done if she'd been abused?

Vasquez lit a cigarette from a pack in his uniform shirt pocket, and inhaled deeply. "Trying to cut down. We had Hewson in max. It's just a regular cell, only four beds, but it's all we have, as small as we are. We had a guy who killed his best buddy in a fight. They both got coked up and beat each other's brains out. Two others on adult sexual assault charges. And Hewson."

"The kiddie-diddler."

Vasquez nodded. "Those guys are all over the place. Even with Thomas dead, you guys still have a couple. Ector's got a couple right now. Howard County's got one."

"Zachary County has two?" Jace asked. She tried to remember back over the names but with so many prisoners, it was hard to dredge up a particular name or two.

Vasquez nodded. "Lars Massie and somebody name of Butterworth."

"I haven't heard anything like that about those two," Jace said.

"Hadn't heard it about Thomas, either," Rory said.

"Give it time." Vasquez finished off the cigarette and stubbed out its remains. "They always crack once they get inside. The pressure gets to them. They 'fess it up, wait and see. You should watch Massie, too, he's going to be a problem for you. Son of a bitch gets all cranked up, throwing his weight around, demanding special favors."

"You've had him in Sterling County?" Rory asked.

"Two or three times. Had to face him down every time."

"Nothing like facing down an old man," Jace said.

Vasquez half-smiled. "That a joke? Some of my worst fights have been with old people."

Jace twirled the ice in her glass. "So you managed to save the state some money."

"Hey, he attacked me and I defended myself. The fact that we don't have to pay to jail that son of a bitch is just . . . you know . . . a little bonus."

Jace frowned. "But it's not our decision. We're not the judge or jury. We're just the jailers."

Vasquez glanced sharply at her. "Yeah, but ain't we human? Those monsters kill our children. It's a disease and there is no cure. It's not like you can lock them up for ten years and when they get released they're fine. They will rape children over and over and over. They won't stop. So society has to stop them." Confused, he glanced from Jace to Rory repeatedly. "Am I missing something here? Isn't that why we became cops? To protect society?" His eyes tightened. "Tell me again why you came to see me."

Rory shook her head. "It ain't no thing, Eddie, don't sweat it. Jace was there the night Thomas attacked Reynolds. Your dead guy might not be bothering you, but ours is screwing with Jace something fierce. You can tell just by listening to her. She's a little confused and—" Rory shrugged. "And I think she's probably a little scared. You've been there. I thought you could help her."

He said nothing and in a silence filled only with the hiss of cooking burgers, Jace knew he wanted to leave. He wanted to get back on the block and at least twice almost got up. "I know Reynolds. He and I took some advanced CT classes together."

"With Badgett?" Jace asked. "We saw him in the hallway today. He said he was putting together a class or two."

For the first time since she'd met him nearly an hour ago, Vasquez seemed to lighten up. "He's here? Great, I need to talk to him. He's a great guy. Hell of an instructor. Man has probably forgotten more about ground fighting and self-defense than I'll ever know. You know he spent ten years working the hardblock in Huntsville? Man's got a million stories of riots and gang fights and inmates attacking guards. And he always managed to be in the middle of the shit." Vasquez chuckled. "At least in his own stories."

"Huntsville? I thought he was San Antonio PD."

"Nah. He was a prison screw. Might'a worked outta Dallas PD for a few years, I think."

Rory slurped down the last of her soda. "Too bad I had the other guy when we were at the Academy, Eddie. I'd have loved to get some floor time with Badgett."

Vasquez frowned. "He wasn't at the Academy. We had Beers, remember? Big boy, always making sure his hair was perfect? I met Mr. Badgett at an advanced class I took."

"Right, right. Now I remember."

"You know," Jace said, "this has me so muddy-brained, I went to Ector County, too. Talked to Sergeant Evans about Deputy Sneed. Just trying to get a handle on this whole thing. I mean, I've never seen a dead body before."

"Deputy Sneed. He's getting a shitty hand to play. Not as bad as Reynolds but close. Ezrin is all over this stuff. Can't get Rutherford so come on over and screw with me. Can't get me so head straight over to Ector and mess with Sneed. Now he's got Reynolds in his sights." His eyes popped to theirs. "Did I hear Reynolds got arrested?"

They nodded.

"Man, that's tough. Didn't get that far with the rest of us."

He nodded and played with his hands. "It'll be okay. He'll get out of this okay. He defended himself."

"Like you did," Rory said.

"Like all of us did, exactly like we were taught to do." He lit up again and took a long drag.

"In the advanced classes," Jace said.

"Exactly right and I'll tell you what: Mr. Badgett's building a brand-new facility and it's going to rock. He said he's gonna let me be an adjunct instructor. Listen, I gotta get back, guys."

"Here," the waitress said. She set down a check for Rory and Jace but not for Vasquez. "Yours is on the house, 'cause'a what you done."

Vasquez laughed. "Thanks, sweetheart, I appreciate it."

"My little girls appreciate you," the waitress said. "Perverts. Ought to just round 'em up and shoot 'em, like a rattlesnake kill."

Outside, Vasquez sucked down the last of the smoke, nodded, and walked across the street to the jail.

Jace caught Rory's eye and held it for a long, uncomfortable moment. "He's dirty."

"Jace—"

"Reynolds is dirty, too. This whole thing is dirty and Badgett is the one spreading the dirt."

Blowing hot breath through her puffed cheeks, Rory nodded. "Yeah."

"They said he was resisting," Jace said. They were in the parking lot of the jail, staring at each other.

"Old people fight, Jace, I've seen it. Hell, I've fought with old people."

"Massie a fighter?"

Rory shrugged. "I don't know, maybe."

"Maybe."

"You remember the reports?" Rory asked. "The disciplinary reports I brought you? On paper anyway, Massie was escalating."

"Or they are pushing him."

"You think Massie is on their list?"

Jace nodded toward the jail and Vasquez. "The name rolled right off his tongue, didn't it?"

Chapter Twenty-Nine

An uncompromising sun blasted off the glass front of the store and pierced Jace's eyes. The air smelled of the sunlight: dry and hot. They'd stopped at a roadside gas station. Rory had demanded it and then stormed inside.

Jace stared at a road upon which nothing moved. It was a hardly used, dusty, two-lane county road. Weeds grew tall along the edges even as some had the guts to sprout through the cracks in the blacktop. The yellow line, a constant presence from one county to another to another, was faded and blistered. They hadn't seen a single car since they left Sterling City. The road out of the county seat had been theirs alone, as though no one else wanted to travel the road they drove.

Returning, Rory sat heavily in the car, two bags of candy in each hand. She tore one open, dumped the contents into her palm, and started sorting out the greens. Everything else went over her shoulder to the back seat. One by one, the green candies disappeared between her lips. She chewed slowly.

"Just lime?" Jace asked.

"I . . . just . . . I don't know . . . that's what I want, I guess." She bit another one in half and chewed slowly. "Let's go."

With a nod, Jace got them back on the road. When they were well away from town, Jace noticed an SUV a few miles behind them. "Somebody else does use this road, I guess."

"Can there be that many bad cops? It's like they're everywhere. Every time we turn around, there's another cop killing off another child molester. Makes me sad. Doesn't it make you sad? That waitress isn't so different from me. Pedophiles make me crazy." She crushed the empty bag of Skittles. "Just as soon beat them senseless. What? I'm not the monster. Or, if I am then we all are."

Jace eyed her friend. "When did it happen to you?"

Rory shook her head. "Uh-uh, not me."

The wind kicked up a dust devil in a cotton field next to them. It spun for a moment before falling apart beneath the force of its spin.

"Her name was Jennifer Alton," Rory said. "She was my best friend when I was little. She used to come over and we'd play—don't laugh at this—we'd play cops and robbers."

"And you were . . . ?"

"I remember stopping her on her tricycle and writing her speeding tickets."

"Hmmm, impersonating a police officer. Maybe I'll write you when I finish with the sheriff."

"It was her father's best friend. I met him a few times. Nice enough guy. Laughed too loud, though. She didn't tell me until we were in high school."

"And Daddy's friend?"

"Dead by then. Jennifer said some other little girl's father shot him in the balls; took care of the boogeyman for her." Her face hard, Rory looked into the back seat. "Crap, there's candy everywhere. Jace, I think she took care of her own boogeyman. Everybody's got to do their own thing."

"Why did you tell Vasquez you wished you'd had Badgett for CT? You knew Badgett wasn't there."

"Didn't know any such thing."

She tore the second bag of Skittles open and spilled it on the dash. Then she switched colors and picked every orange candy and jammed most of them in her mouth at once. "He's right,

Jace, they will kill the children. And if they don't kill them, they will ruin them. Alive, maybe, but as dead on the inside as if they'd been shot in the head. The judges just let them go. All the time, those guys serve a few years and walk right back out again."

"We may not like it but that's the law. Get it changed."

"Bullshit answer."

"Only one I've got."

"Too bad. Murder can be righteous, Jace, and you'd know that if someone did to your Gramma what they do to those kids."

"Whoa, Rory, hang on—"

"Maybe those deputies came up with a better answer."

Rory leaned over the back seat and began picking orange Skittles from the seat and floorboard. She ate seven or eight in a single mouthful. Chewing, blowing bits of the shell out with every angry breath, she nodded. "Yeah, that's exactly how it is." She slammed a fist against the dash. Skittles bounced and scattered. "It's not supposed to be like this."

Behind them, Jace watched the SUV move up and for a moment, she thought she could see one of those cartoon smears behind it, the kind of color blur that lets the viewer know something is MOVING FAST.

It was black, tricked out with miles of chrome and a V-shaped antenna, but it had been driven hard. Mud spattered the sides, flaring up from the front wheel wells. The hood and the windshield were both dirty with dried mud that reminded Jace of the blood drops on the second tier after Thomas and Reynolds' fight. Across the top of the windshield, in letters maybe eight inches tall, it said, "My name is Mud."

Jace chuckled.

" 'S up?"

Jace nodded backward. "Mudder behind us. 'My name is

Mud,' he calls the truck."

Rory looked behind them and her eyes went wide. "What the hell? Go, Jace. Go. Go."

"What?" Jace looked in the rearview mirror. The truck was huge. It had gone from a mile away to barely a handful of yards behind them.

It hadn't slowed at all. It kept coming as if the driver had no idea they were there. Jace goosed the Monte Carlo but even as they gained speed, the truck never slowed.

"Shit." Jace pulled the car to the right, running it halfway on the shoulder so the SUV could get around before he smacked them off the road.

"Hey," Rory yelled as the truck went around them. "What's your problem?"

"Think they can hear you?"

"Put that window down, he'll hear me." She tossed a couple of red Skittles at the truck. They bounced off Jace's window and dropped down between her thighs.

"Great, just what I always wanted between my legs."

"He's not passing."

Her tone caused Jace to look first at Rory. Then Jace looked at the truck. Her gut tightened and her hands clenched around the steering wheel. She gently raised her foot from the accelerator and felt the car ease back.

The SUV stayed with them.

"Son of a bitch," Rory said. She sat up straight, the Skittles forgotten, and drew her purse closer to her.

"Rory?"

"Don't panic. Probably just some mutt having fun." She tried on a nervous laugh. "Sees two hot chicks out for an afternoon drive, what else is he gonna do except try to make some time with us."

"Yeah," Jace said, an icy finger touching her spine. "That's what it is, he's hitting on us. Happens all the time."

"Does to me, anyway."

But her tone belied her attempt at humor. Rory was scared. Jace kept her head on the driving. She let off the gas even more and bit the inside of her mouth when the SUV matched her move.

"Speed up," Rory commanded. "Not a lot."

Jace did and again the SUV stayed with her. Its muddy nose came right a few inches before moving back to the center of the road.

"Maybe drunk?" Jace asked.

"No."

Then he came over again. Much further this time, well into their lane. Jace yelped and pointed Rory's Monte Carlo car off the road onto the shoulder. The passenger side tires hit the soft dirt and sank.

"Shit," Jace said. "Hang on."

"Ain't going anywhere."

The SUV moved away from them, hesitated, then came back their way fast. Jace yanked the wheel right and expected a violent collision, but at the last moment, the SUV went back hard left. Jace touched the brakes and slowed them down enough that the SUV seemed to jump out in front. It slid into their lane and the brake lights flashed. But a second later, the truck kept going. It grew smaller and though they waited, breath held hot in their lungs and hands clenched, the thing never came back.

"Damn it," Rory said, still staring hard at the truck. "Mud all over the plate."

"So?"

"Get the plate we can run it, see who we're dealing with."

Licking her lips, Jace said, "Wow, that was a little disconcerting."

"Disconcerting? I'd call it freaking weird. Dumbass driving 101. Disconcerting. Give up those three dollar words, sister, I'm a fifty cent kind of girl."

"I've heard that." Jace paused. "I find it quite disconcerting."

Chapter Thirty

Two days later, when she was back on, Bibb stopped her in the main hallway. Inmate Bobby mopped nearby.

"Getting used to it?" Bibb asked.

The stomach-churning tang of bean burrito assaulted her. Jace ran a hand across her nostrils. "Evening, Sarge." She waved the juvenile fingerprint cards. "Gotta get moving. Corporal Kleopping's waiting."

"You getting used to it?"

"To what?"

He touched the radio mic clipped at his shoulder. "That first night you were on, your ear was glued to this thing. You didn't miss a word."

Annoying or not, Bibb was right. She hadn't let a single syllable slip past because she'd been worried she'd miss something important. Yet tonight, just a couple weeks after she went solo, she couldn't say for sure there'd been any radio traffic.

She panicked and keyed her mic. "Traffic for 479?"

Bibb chuckled. "Nobody called you, Deputy. I'm just saying you aren't as hooked to the thing as you used to be."

"I guess I'm learning to hear what I need to. I'm pretty much ignoring everything else." She held up the fingerprint cards. "Well, I guess I need to get going."

"Booking'll wait. You remember the footage of you in the go-between?"

She ground her teeth. "Yeah."

His body language eased. His shoulders slumped and he offered a weak shrug. "I'm sorry about your ass and—your . . . uh . . . rear and chest. Yes, I taped them and yeah, I watched them. I think you're attractive and I'm probably a pervert and yeah, you could sue me and the department and probably the county for enough to buy your own island. I'm sorry about that. I did it and I can't change it, but this is no bullshit, okay?"

Under the weight of his apology, she twisted the fingerprint cards.

He handed her a dulled disc and licked his dry lips. "The fight. In medical."

"With Royce. You were watching."

"Dial down the shock, you knew I was watching. I won't apologize. You know there are some deputies who ain't any too happy about what you did, right? Don't think for a second they won't take a shot if they can. Don't forget Royce."

"I was there, Sergeant. I won't forget."

He tapped the disc. "Not if I can help it. Those guys are the minority. There are a helluva lot more officers around here who have raised a drink to what you did."

Jace stuck a defiant chin. "Yeah? I haven't heard from any of them. Where is this groundswell of support? Where the hell are they?"

He grinned. "One of them is right in front of you, dummy."

She looked away.

"Watch this. Repeatedly." He turned them away from Inmate Bobby. "I've seen a lot of things, Salome. I've seen everybody screwing: guards, civilians, visitors, inmates. Even solo sex a few times. I've seen contraband smuggled in and out; on-duty drinking, on-duty sleeping. But more than anything, I've seen violence. Blood. Bruises. Teeth on the floor and bones in pieces. The point is that I've already seen what I saw in you during the fight."

"Which was?"

"You wanted that fight."

"I don't think so." But hadn't she? Hadn't she wanted to stake out her own ground? Stand up against the ERTs who'd embarrassed her and against the cops who'd killed inmates and against Reynolds for dumping her in the middle of this jackpot?

"Yeah. You enjoyed it."

"Sarge, you are absolutely wrong, and I have to get these cards to—"

"Deputy . . . Jace . . . I've been wrong about lotsa things. Not this. I've seen it too many times." He pointed at the disc. "Don't fall in love with the violence."

She spluttered. "What? Fall in love with—I hate the violence."

"Well, I think it might love you."

She spun away from him.

"One last thing, Deputy." It was the Sergeant tone, full of command and authority.

"Yes, sir?"

"Dillon give you the speech?" He cleared his throat and tried to imitate Dillon's thin voice. " 'This is the gig, your career starts now.' "

She nodded.

"And he probably also told you that your fellow jailers would be there for you when the shit hit the fan."

"Yes, sir."

"When you bagged Reynolds, that changed. From now on, a couple of cops will be a step slower when it comes to you. Or when they ask me for the door."

He towered over her. "I am not one of those officers. Neither is Dillon or Bogan. We, and a whole lot of others, are there when you need us."

"If I need you."

He laughed. "*When* you need us."

—479 from 419—

She keyed her mic. "479 . . . go ahead."

—take a break in Cancun? Where are you?—

"On the way." She hesitated. "Sarge?"

"Yeah?" Bibb said.

"You know anything about Massie?"

"Know he got busted for brewing bathtub gin a few days ago."

"Did he do it?"

"I don't understand your question."

"He doesn't strike me as a troublemaker."

"Well," Bibb said. "I've seen him get mouthy a few times. Was uncooperative when they brought him in. Took two deputies to get him calmed down in booking."

Jace nodded. "Well, I was just wondering what you think. You see these guys all night every night."

For a long while, Bibb said nothing. Then he shrugged and headed down the hallway. "Mostly I watch the deputies."

—479 . . . what's the deal—

"On the way."

—good, 'cause I gotta piss—

A beat later, Dillon's voice cracked over the airwaves.

—watch the traffic, Corporal Kleopping—

—ditto that—

She recognized the exhausted voice. Adam 1. Sheriff Bukowski. In the split second his voice was on the air and his mic was open, she clearly heard the lonely click of his boots on the concrete floor.

"Hey," Smit said. "How's it going?" He took a seat next to her and played idly on the booking computer.

"Fine. More overtime?"

"Yeah. Can't ever put enough bank away."

Jace sat behind a booking computer and read newly arrived inmates' files. It was her way of familiarizing herself with those she warehoused.

"Been pretty tough for you," Smit said.

She closed her eyes and wondered again how her role in Reynolds' arrest had gotten around the jail. "Nothing I can't handle."

"Yeah. You know, I told Warner you had some tough."

"Right, your Neanderthal partner."

Smit laughed. "That'd be him. He's a decent guy." Smit leaned in close. "Get him drunk enough and he'll probably admit you're tougher than he is."

"Don't really want to see him drunk, but thanks for the advice."

Grinning, Smit said, "Call me when you need something."

During slow nights, booking personnel had little to do. Some tried to look busy but others didn't bother. They stood in ever-evolving clumps, conversations started and interrupted and gotten back to later.

—control from 405, booking sally port—

Jace craned her head. Near the middle of the hallway, the sally port door popped open. Dillon had an easy smile.

"Smit," Jace called. "Cover me for a minute, would you?"

Jace left the computers and stopped a respectful distance from Dillon and Kleopping. When the corporal nodded and left, she stepped up. "Sarge?"

"Salome."

"It's pretty slow here tonight. Can I run down and check on Massie?"

He frowned. "Lars Massie?"

"Yeah. He's in ad-seg."

Dillon looked at his clipboard but Jace knew he wasn't seeing anything. He asked, "What's his charge?"

Jace fumbled for a moment. "I can't really remember, but being in ad-seg, it's probably something sexual, isn't it? With kids, maybe?"

"Why do you need to see Massie?"

"Uh . . . he's . . . uh . . . a family friend. I told his wife I'd check on him."

—control from 456, D-David War Door—

The heavy door between booking and the discipline pod snapped open. Rory came through, her face a heavy mask, and came straight to Jace. "It ever happen—" She eyed Dillon. "Excuse me. Sorry. This can wait."

Dillon turned away.

"What?" Jace said.

Rory lowered her voice. "It ever happen to you?"

"Not like that. Some guys felt me up a little, that's all."

"How old?"

"Nine or ten." Jace bit her bottom lip. "I figured it was part of growing up female in America."

"Probably." Rory spun and walked hard back to the pod doors. "D-david War Door." The door popped and she was gone.

"Anything I need to know?" Dillon asked.

Jace tried to keep her face empty. "Massie? I promised his wife."

"You really want to spend your time doing favors for inmates?"

Heat blossomed in her face. "Family friend."

Dillon surveyed the hallway. There was a single inmate near the computers, handcuffed to the bench. The deputy who'd arrested him hadn't yet finished the citations, but the guy had bail money with him. Once the citations were finished, the guy would be in and out in less than a half hour. Waiting for that process to start, the guy slept.

"Got someone covering booking?" Dillon asked.

"Smit's here. I won't be long, just a few minutes."

"Massie's probably asleep."

"I just want to be able to tell his wife I saw him."

"Five minutes, Salome."

"Thanks." She headed for the door.

"By the way, he's not in ad-seg. He's in E Pod. And it's bad checks."

"What?"

"And I'm pretty sure he's not married."

He held eye contact with her just a sliver longer than needed. *I don't know what's going on,* his gaze said, *but get me a better story next time.*

In the hallway, Jace picked up the orange stripe. This short hallway would dump her into the main hallway, which would curl around the outside edges of the pie-shaped pods. E Pod was halfway around the facility.

But the trip gave her time to think. Why had Lars Massie caught the attention of those who notice sexual prisoners? Was he one of those men for whom, if he died, it was hard to have sympathy? Bad checks weren't sexual, but Vasquez said he'd been in Sterling County on sex charges. Maybe it was another case of proving what could be proved in lieu of what couldn't.

Regardless, Massie had cropped up on Badgett's radar and they were doing to him what they'd done to the others. He'd been moved repeatedly, shaken down constantly, and brought up on charges, and now Jace remembered who'd asked her to move Massie.

Royce.

Who had jumped on her in the medical pod and who had a Total Force tattoo on his bicep.

A team effort. Someone identifies the men who they believe are predators, word goes out, the members of Total Force make sure that person ends up dead, and they've been covering themselves in thinly veiled legalities.

At the E Pod door, she glanced at a camera and the door popped.

Jace gave Sergeant Bibb a wave and disappeared into the pod.

Chapter Thirty-One

A warm, early morning breeze touched Jace's skin as she watched the clouds push and jostle for position in the sky. By late afternoon, when the temperature had reached up into the 90s, those clouds would be towers over the earth. Hopefully, they'd deliver on the faint scent of rain in the air already.

"Babygirl," Preacher said. He sat and lit his pipe. The spicy-orange aroma circled around his head. "You lookin' like you got a problem."

"How many problems, let me count."

"Tell me one."

"The water."

"Ain't following."

"The wind," Jace said. "It's coming from the wrong direction again."

"Guess you love that uniform so much you had to stay in it?"

Instead of changing, Jace had sat at the side of the Sea Spray's pool and dipped her hand. Her uniform was wet to her elbow.

"How was work last night?"

Jace's hand traced endless figure eights. "I went to see a prisoner last night. A guy named Lars Massie. The deputy in Sterling County mentioned him."

"Sterling County. That was where that boy tried to run you down, right?"

"The officer said Massie was a child molester."

"That's a bad person, do something like that to a kid."

As Jace had stared through the window at a sleeping Massie, she understood the need to see a molester. Did the man have the marks of Preacher's Beast? Or scarlet letters branded into his forehead? She wanted to see an obvious sign of the kind of vileness that allowed men to rape and kill children, to empty them of everything they might ever be. Because if she could see something that terrible, she might understand someone's need to kill.

But she wasn't sure Massie was one of those awful people.

"Would you have killed Hitler?" Jace asked.

"I don't know. Would'a stopped all that suffering, though, wouldn't it?"

"What about Pontius Pilate?"

After a long puff on the pipe, Preacher said, "Can't say I would, little girl."

"But that would have saved Jesus."

"Now, little girl, you and I both be knowing Jesus had to die."

"Do these men—these predators—need to die?"

"Ain't for you and me to say."

The traced eights continued to disappear. "He was just an old man, Preacher, sleeping in a ten by ten cell. The way he twitched, he was probably having the same bad dreams I have. He probably wakes up three or four times a night to pee like Grapa did and maybe he's confused about where he is until his feet hit that cold concrete floor."

Preacher slipped a heavy paw over Jace's shoulder. "I'm pretty sure he ain't having your bad dreams. I been in jail a few times in my life, babydoll, and I weren't ever confused about where I was. You went looking for some kind of swamp boogie monster and all you found was a skinny old man. Evil ain't always obvious. Mostly, I think it looks like you and me. There's folks say the Devil's best trick was making like he wasn't even here. You can't smoke evil out just by looking."

Jace told Preacher everything. When she'd gone to Massie's cell in E Pod, she'd found instead an old black man with a single arm. The jailer on duty had told her Massie was in a cell on the far side of the pod. The second jailer casually mentioned it was Massie's fifth E Pod cell in three days. The cell had been absolutely clean, too. When she'd asked about it, the jailer said, "Oughta be, as much as they're shaking him down."

"Twice a day," Jace told Preacher. "Every day, always on the day shift and five disciplinary charges in the last month."

Those charges were as petty as Thomas' had been.

"Sounds like all them jailers reading from the same book, don't it?"

"They are."

"And what they reading up on?"

"They've decided to rid the world of predators."

"And you gonna stop them."

She shook her head. "I can't. I know what's going on, but I have no proof."

He chuckled and when she looked at him, he said, "You like Zipporah. Jethro's daughter."

"Jethro? That's a Biblical name?"

"Yeah. His name is Reuel, too, but to my old, Southern ear, Jethro sounds better. See, Zipporah was one of Jethro's seven daughters. They were little girls with lots'a chores. One thing they had to do every day was water Jethro's flocks. But they'd go to the well and these punks would laugh at 'em and make 'em wait. See, them girls was trying to circle 'round that well, trying to get that water, and these mutts wouldn't let 'em do it."

Jace nodded thoughtfully. "Badgett's deputies are keeping me away from the well. The proof is in the well and they don't want me to see it."

Preacher shrugged. "Probably ain't thought it out that much, but yeah. Guess what you gotta answer is who's down in that well, giving water to everybody. Why come these other deputies won't talk to Captain Ezrin?"

"The Rangers scare them to death. More so since Ezrin arrested Reynolds."

Deep in her pocket, her cell phone vibrated. A second later, Thelonious Monk's "Straight, No Chaser" hit the air. It was her ring tone.

"Captain Ezrin looking for the truth?" Preacher asked.

"Hello?" She held it out to Preacher. "Ask him yourself." She brought the phone back to her ear and asked, "You looking for the truth? Or are you just looking to hang cops?"

"Yeah," he said, his voice thin in the phone. "Because I get an extra special award at the end of the year if I arrest at least ten officers. You're smarter than that, Deputy Salome."

"What do you want?"

"I heard you were running around the Flat, asking people about a dead kid. Name of Robinson."

Jace's eyes popped up to Preacher, but the man was staring at the pool, his pipe resting comfortably between his teeth.

"Are you running a missing persons investigation I don't know about?" he asked.

"If I am," she said, "it's none of your business. You can't have all of me, Captain."

He laughed. "I heard one other thing, too. I heard you were out at Sterling County, asking about Joe Paul Hewson."

"Did you hear we nearly got run off the road on the way back? Did your network of spies tell you that part?"

He said nothing but she could hear him breathing. "No, Deputy, I hadn't heard that part. I'm guessing you don't think it was random."

"After getting attacked in my own jail and having one of

those fuckers threaten my Gramma? No, it's not random."

"So help me prove it."

Jace took her hand from the water and shook it dry. Preacher watched her but said nothing. Blue smoke from his pipe circled around his head. Finally, she said, "You're not going to find it in the obvious records."

"Commissary, phone logs, visitation."

"Right. There's nothing there."

"I've found a few things in the disciplinary records."

"Petty charges. Those'll escalate eventually, but you're looking in the wrong place."

"Well, where *should* I be looking, *Detective* Salome?"

Jace ignored the sarcasm. "Day to day. Cell assignments. Shakedowns. Take those records and correlate them with training records, see who trained with who."

"That doesn't sound like enough to get any indictments."

"It's all I have."

"Then we have to get more."

"And when you say 'we,' you mean—"

"You."

Without another word, Jace snapped her phone closed.

"Man got you all kinds of mad," Preacher said.

"Sergeant Dillon ran a criminal history for me, Preacher."

His eyes flicked an interest. "You checkin' on me?"

"No, but that's funny, maybe I will. I checked on Massie. Vasquez told me he'd been in Sterling County two or three times for sex. He's never been there."

"Maybe his child molesting all happened here."

"Lars Massie's not a child molester. He wrote bad checks but he hasn't touched a child."

"How you know that?"

"Criminal history is all financial crime. Never a crime against a person . . . or a child."

"Don't mean nothing."

"Employment history does. He's never had a job where he'd have access to kids. If all the dead men were unquestionably child molesters, killing them would be wrong but somehow understandable. At least two dead men weren't molesters and now a third's in their sights. There's something else going on."

"And it's keeping you awake at night, ain't it?"

He wants me to be able to sleep again. Gramma had told him about Jace's sleep-talking and Jace knew it worried him. *Why else would he be waiting for me this early in the morning? For him to see I was at the pool, he had to be watching.*

She reached up and hugged him. "I love you, Preacher."

"I love you, too, babygirl."

Twenty minutes later, Jace was deep asleep.

CHAPTER THIRTY-TWO

Most of Thursday's shift passed in a fog of indecision. Jace had checked Massie's disciplinary records from previous jail stays and there were just enough charges to believe he could be a problem. But if he weren't, the only other conclusion was that he'd been targeted by Badgett's boys. She was absolutely certain now, however, that he was not a sex offender.

So what in hell was going on?

After her shift, she gave Rory a quick goodbye and headed home. After a quick change, she left again, this time in Preacher's beat-up pickup because of the bad brakes on her own car.

For breakfast, she grabbed a Tootsie Pop from Preacher's glove box. As she upwrapped it, her eyes fell on Preacher's .38 pistol. He'd bolted a small holster to the side of the wheel well, easily within reach of the driver. He had done that because in his life, Preacher had two hopes. One was that he'd eventually find his son Robinson. The other was that he'd come across Satan during his travels. "I'll drill him right in the ass," Preacher had said once. "Drill his ass, then put a cap between his sneaky, lying eyes. Ain't no jury in Texas gonna convict me of that."

Jace chuckled. The man might make sure Jesus got killed, but he'd make damn sure the Devil got it, too.

Heading to Seminole, which was northwest of Zachary County, the skies were purple and scarlet and streaked with blue and yellow, but she didn't think it was going to rain at all.

The land was, like so much of the Permian Basin—though she supposed Gaines County was too far north to still be part of the basin—scrubbed brown and left with cactus-green scars. On the final stretch of Lamesa Highway, which would take her to the Gaines County Law Enforcement Center, the earth seemed to crackle beneath the weight of Preacher's pickup.

"Can I help you?" a pleasant-voiced woman behind the counter in the complex asked.

Jace didn't know anyone here and now the decision to come seemed like hollow bravado. "Uh . . . yeah . . . I'm a deputy from Zachary County."

The woman's smile grew. "Well, hiya." She offered a hand. "I'm Deb. Off duty today?"

"Yeah. Call it personal discovery." Jace hadn't worn her uniform, but she had brought her badge.

A frown of curiosity slipped across Deb's face. "Well, however I can help."

"Civilian?" Jace asked.

Deb nodded. "Used to be law enforcement. I dispatched here, but the hours were terrible, the pay was terrible, the benefits were terrible. Other than that, it was great. When the front desk job opened, I snatched it up." She shrugged. "They took my badge away but I've got a better schedule and more money."

"I'm with you there. I could always use more money."

Deb nodded as though money was the universally understood truth for the day. "And what about that schedule?"

Jace bemoaned her shift and the two women fell into an easy conversation that left Jace, twenty minutes later, face to face with Deputy Bentley Devereaux, only recently back from nearly six months of administrative leave after the death of inmate #4359, a man by the name of John Rosely.

Devereaux was in the sally port, a ring of blue smoke around his head like a bruised halo. "I knew you'd get to me eventually."

The stink in their oversized garage was nearly unbearable. So much worse than the Zachary County Jail, with its coating of forest- and spring-scented cleaning products slathered on by the trusties. Here, the air was stale and thick, peppered with urine and sweat and moldering dark corners and men stored away. It burned her nose and made her eyes water.

"I know, smells like shit." He exhaled a deep, smoke-laced breath. "I hate this place."

"Then why work here?"

"All I ever wanted to do. Family business, too. Had a few farmers in the family, but mostly, since we got American, we've grown cops."

He tapped a toe against the concrete floor. "This place isn't so bad. Most of our bad guys are pretty soft. They're not really terrible people. Most are just idiots who can't seem to not get caught with a couple of blunts or drinking and driving or whatever. One or two are lost forever but most are just guys who made a mistake and are trying to get their time done. It's not like we're Lubbock or Dallas or, God forbid, Houston."

"Sounds too good to hate."

His answer was a long time coming. "I think I do, though. We had a bad guy. A real bad guy."

"The man you killed?"

His stony gaze sent a bullet through her spine. "Don't kid yourself, Deputy, I did a good thing. John Rosely was a piece of shit." Absently, Devereaux brushed hair from in front of his face. "All I did was fight back. Just like I'd been trained in the Academy."

"Where'd you academy?" She kept her tone easy.

"Lubbock Law Enforcement. I loved it. Loved the law classes and the gun range and control tactics."

"Yeah, who'd you have on the range?"

"Molloch. Great guy."

She shook her head. "I had Stevens. What about CT? I had Badgett."

He nodded. "Yeah, me, too. Son of a bitch worked my ass off and taught me things I had no clue about. Did you join?"

"Total Force?" She shook her head. "No . . . didn't think much about it. What's the story there?"

"Just a group. Control tactics. We're pretty much all over the state so we don't have monthly meetings or anything. But we have a newsletter and members-only stuff online."

"Sounds cool."

He shrugged. "Yeah."

At the bottom of Zipporah's well was Will Badgett, Jace was certain now. Badgett doled out the water for those who would drink.

Devereaux sucked on the cigarette. Half of it disappeared into ash. "Her name was Katrina."

"Who?"

"The girl he stole."

Jace had been preparing to manage a graceful exit from Gaines County. She had what she needed and hadn't expected to talk about Rosely's victim.

"I knew Katrina, Deputy. This whole county only has about fourteen thousand people and everybody pretty much knows everyone else. Plus, you get cop's eyes . . . watching out for everyone."

"I'm brand new. I only work the jail."

"Doesn't matter, jail or road, you learn to watch. You'll realize you're paying attention to everything. Definitely the kids. The kids and the old folks. You generally know where the mopes are most of the time."

He stubbed the butt and blew out a last bit of smoke.

"Katrina was a beautiful kid. Six years old. She had this thick blonde hair with all kinds of curls. And big ol' green eyes. She was runner-up for Little Miss Gaines twice. She was probably gonna win in the next year or two and then she'd probably keep winning right on up through Miss Gaines and maybe the Texas state pageant. She loved puppies, too. Not so much the big dogs, they scared her a little, but puppies and those little yappie mutts. Saturday mornings she'd walk up and down her street, petting just about every dog." He laughed. "She'd walk straight down the sidewalk until she got to Termite's place and then she'd cross the street. When she was past his shack, she'd cross back over."

"Termite have a big dog, did he?"

"Damned pit bull. Scared the crap outta me, too. I told Termite once if that monster ever got loose when I was around, I'd shoot it."

"How that go over?"

"He said he understood and if I had to, there'd be no hard feelings. Tell you what, though, he made sure that dog never got out."

The man's voice was quiet, surprisingly soft given his size. At times, Jace had to lean forward to hear him. At other times, the words simply disappeared into the sultry midday air.

"John James Rosely. Forty-two years old. Big guy, maybe six-three? Six-four? I remember thinking, the first time I saw him, he must be sick. Had that look, you know?

"The first time I saw him was maybe a week before Katr—" He stopped, his eyes hard but wet. "I noticed him right off but didn't pay any particular attention. Like I said, this is a small place and strangers are pretty obvious but we do get a good share of people running 62 west to Carlsbad Caverns or to hit the slopes over in New Mexico. Stop and get gas and maybe some lunch or something. But they don't stay long, you know?

So the law around here usually sees them but they don't stick in the brain unless they're obvious problems." He tapped his temple. "This guy should have stuck. He didn't look the part. Had decent clothes and shaved and smiled for everyone. Thought he was a goddamned tourist."

Jace shook her head. "You can't know everything all the time."

He almost growled at her. Instead, he lit another cigarette. "Two days later he's still in town. So I notice him and then some of the other deputies notice and then the two city guys notice and pretty soon everyone wants to know who this guy is.

"Saturday morning, Katrina was making her dog rounds. Walked across the street to avoid Termite's beast, then crossed back to pet Mrs. Johnson's old Yorkie who can't hardly walk anymore and is half-blind and then . . . poof . . . she's gone."

Jace swallowed. She'd come here convinced the dead man was another mistake, killed by sadist guards who just wanted to get over on people. Now she stood in the Gaines County Sheriff's Office sally port, heat wrapping around her while the stench fingered her nose, and hated how her gut had already tightened though Devereaux had told her precious little yet.

"Rosely use a dog?"

Devereaux shook his head. "You'd think, right? So many pedophiles do that. But he didn't. He just saw her. Said he watched her walk halfway down the block and was seduced." His jaw bulging with anger, Devereaux tapped an impatient toe on the concrete again. "His word, not mine. He said she seduced him. He walked one block over and stole a car and came back and snatched her. Opened the driver's side window and dragged her into the car. One punch, he said, and she was out cold. Five minutes later, he was out of town."

It was a half hour, he said, before anyone realized Katrina was gone, and even then, that knowledge came only when the car owner realized her car was gone. Dispatch had gotten a report of a stolen car and sent a town cop to take the information. While he was taking care of that, he heard Katrina's mom calling for her.

"It snowballed from there."

Within fifteen minutes of the cop hearing Katrina's mother, there was an alert countywide. A few minutes after that, someone asked innocently if the car and missing kid were connected.

Devereaux's face paled. "God, if we'd only realized that quicker."

Missing that connection meant Rosely had nearly an hour's head start. He could have been in another state by then. Or damn near in Mexico.

"He should have stuck in my head."

Let me out of here, Jace wanted to shout. *I don't want Rosely in my life. If he shoves his way through the same door Thomas and Reynolds and Stimson did, he'll be in my head for the rest of my life.*

Devereaux paced the sally port and tapped a fist on top of a giant grill. "We got a night guy, goes out and gets at least one DUI every damned shift, and then comes back and cooks brats and hot dogs." The man laughed but it was inappropriate and he knew it. "Nothing like two or three brats at two in the morning."

"I'll bet."

"Salome, right? Jace Salome?" He offered a hand. "Sorry, I should have introduced myself."

"How'd you know who I was?"

"Heard you might come see me."

"Yeah?"

He sat on a worn lawn chair. "Law enforcement is a pretty small community. I'll bet there isn't a single cop in this state who is more than five or six people away from you. We've all been to the same academies and classes and conventions and seminars. We all know each other. I heard there was a newbie there the night Zachary County's guy died. I heard you were having a hard time and went and talked to some people. Figured you'd come see me eventually to talk about what you did."

"I didn't do anything."

A single eyebrow rose and Devereaux let the silence hang. Jace wasn't sure she liked the implication held in the fist of that silence.

"What you seen, then," Devereaux said. "So what is this? Personal curiosity? Or professional?"

Jace frowned. "I don't understand the question, Deputy, and I'm not sure I like your tone."

"Like I give a shit. You came to see me, remember? You came to get into my head and find out what to do after you've killed a man."

"I haven't killed a man."

"You're trying to pry me open like that Ranger did and you tell me you don't like my tone? I. Don't. Care. I spent months with that asshole chasing me. Every decision I made in the jail was up for grabs. Every disciplinary report I filed, every prisoner transport I took, every prisoner I questioned. Everything I did, he put under a microscope."

Devereaux stood and flexed his arms before slamming them across his chest. "Let me tell you how it happened: Rosely stole a child. He raped a child. Then he killed a child. He got caught. Then he went to jail. Then he came at me and I defended myself. Anything else? Oh, yeah, he died."

Jace put great care into her voice. "Deputy Devereaux, I'm not here on anyone's mission." The lie slid out so easily it was almost embarrassing. "I'm here because I saw something I'd never seen before. I've been to some of the other jails for the same reason. I don't know . . . I need to know how to handle this."

"There's nothing to handle."

"Yes, there is. At least for me, there is. I saw a man die, Deputy. That was the first time I ever saw a dead body and it wasn't a neat one. It hadn't been cleaned up and laid out for viewing. It was bent and broken and bloody and I—I cried, okay? It's gotten stuck in my brain and I still cry sometimes."

And that was true, maybe truer than Jace had realized until this moment. Yes, she might be on a mission for Ezrin, trying to help him prove good men had done something acceptable to bad men. Except not all the good men were good and not all the bad men were bad and the deaths were colored with a shifting tint of gray.

"Rosely threw the first punch, didn't he?"

"Yeah."

She trod carefully. "And he was a pain in the butt, wasn't he? Had to constantly move him around? Getting into disciplinary trouble? That's the way it happened with Thomas. Hell, we had to move him five or six times."

With a snort and a nod, Devereaux lit up again. This time, he held the smoke deeply in his lungs until Jace thought his face might turn blue. Then he slowly blew out a series of concentric rings.

"I was on the search team. The sheriff had it organized within an hour or so. Got the Amber Alert going and told the county newspaper and the radio stations, but we had to get the horses out."

"The horses? Didn't you think he had fled the county?"

Before he answered, Devereaux let a long plume of slow, blue smoke slip from him. It hovered around him before slipping up into the metal beams of the exposed roof.

"I think the sheriff believed Katrina was already dead. He came from Dallas PD and he had spent a career working those cases. I think he knew she was dead the second she got snatched.

But he also knew we had to do something. So he sent our county guys up and down every single road and alley and field entrance in this county. He put the rest of us on horses and told us to look at every weed and cactus and tree and fishing hole and whatever else in our world."

Jace nodded. "Keeping you busy."

Devereaux nodded. "But the whole time I was out there, I couldn't get my head on the search. I was so angry. If I had stopped him the first time I saw him . . . If I had run his name outta every state in the country, I'd have discovered the Florida warrant for child abduction and the Pennsylvania conviction for aggravated sexual assault of an eight-year-old girl."

Violently, he wiped away a tear and sucked hard on the cigarette.

This is going to kill him. He'll die of the cancer he's so furiously courting with those smokes. But long before he gets there, he'll end up a bitter shell of a man living by himself and sitting in the middle of his trailer in a dirty recliner. He'll wear torn boxers and a stained bathrobe and surround himself with pictures of little girls and headlines about predators, and he'll drink until he can't feel anything.

But maybe before any of that happens, he'll put a bullet in his brain.

"I didn't find Katrina. But I was third on the scene. It was two days later and I was still out looking."

His eyes, empty, came to her. "I saw what was left."

It wasn't gory, he said. There was almost no blood at all. In fact, wipe away the tiny spill from her nose, put some makeup over the bruising around her neck, and she'd simply be asleep. It was the gentleness that made it so terrible.

Rosely had found himself a nearly forgotten trail in the northern part of the county. A local rancher, checking the fence around his acreage, had noticed the car way back in the scrub that passed for timberland in West Texas. It was near an old bunkhouse that had once been filled with cowboys and ranch hands and then oil rig tool pushers and drillers and then no one except rodents and the wind. The rancher thought the car probably belonged to some teenagers.

"But I knew," Devereaux said. "Before I even heard the plate on the car, I knew."

Two deputies had been barely a mile away from the place. He'd been just about two. All three had spurred their horses mercilessly.

"The first two deputies arrived. I heard them over the radio. A few minutes later—" He eyed her. "I felt it." He put his hand over his heart. "I felt her light get blown out."

Then he turned away, embarrassed. He coughed, then lit up another cigarette but just as quickly stomped it out.

Later, when Rosely was so matter-of-factly telling the deputies what had happened, he would say that he'd heard the deputies clatter up on their horses. He would say he'd looked out through a crack in the boarded up window and had seen law enforcement converging on him and the girl. He would say he feared the girl would cry out to be rescued, or cry from the pain of his love, or simply cry for Mommy and Daddy.

He would say to the detectives while the crime scene techs processed the bunkhouse and Katrina's body that he'd strangled her with a leather bootlace he'd found on the floor. When the deputies opened the door, he said, they found Rosely sitting Indian style and Katrina in his lap, her head at his crotch, her skin still warm.

"Here's the thing," the jailer said. "She wore a perfectly clean, white dress. Like a communion dress or confirmation dress or something. Her Mama said she'd never owned a dress like that." Devereaux turned his gaze to Jace. "He had that dress, Deputy. He came to town with that dress. And he carried it with him when he was walking around."

The man wiped his lips, the way Jace had seen a million drunks do and she knew she'd been correct. Booze, along with the cigarettes and nightmares, was already eating him alive. He'd never be an old man. "He's why you hate the job now."

"I hate that a man could claim to put a child on a pedestal yet leave her bleeding from the rectum. I hate that he attacked me and I had to defend myself. But I do not hate that he's dead."

"Do you hate that you killed him?"

"I don't think I do, Deputy. But I'm getting out of here."

"Got something in mind?"

He nodded and for the first time since they'd started talking, his eyes twinkled. "Mr. Badgett's building a training academy. I'm going to hire on there."

"Doing what?"

"Training officers in protecting themselves. I'll be able to stay connected to law enforcement but I won't have to see anything like that again."

A moment later, he keyed his radio. "Susie, can you open the north door, please?" He looked at Jace. "You can go out that door. The lot you parked in is just around the corner." He toyed with his pack of cigarettes. "Look, I hope you find whatever kind of peace you're looking for." He made a sound that might have been a sad laugh. "If you do, drop some in a package and send it to me."

Ten minutes later, Jace sat in Preacher's truck, staring at Preacher's old, scarred .38 Saturday Night Special. If she had seen Rosely, if she had known what he had done, could she have drilled him as easily as Preacher wanted to drill the Devil?

Without answering, she cranked the truck to life and pulled away from the parking lot.

Chapter Thirty-Three

Jace opened a window in Preacher's old truck and sucked down a deep breath of dust and dirt. As she passed a herd of Texas longhorns, she was thankful to get a snoot full of their shit. That the overpowering stench of their feces comforted her she found disturbing. *Because as long as you smell those steers you won't smell Devereaux and his jail. You might be able to pretend you were never there.*

She stopped. In the middle of the road, the truck poised over a yellow line. Then she climbed out and breathed deeply.

The metaphor didn't escape her. She knew she was sucking down shit because that was easier to deal with than what she'd learned about Rosely or Badgett's men. Rosely believed deeply in what he defined as love but Badgett's men believed just as deeply in their kind of social justice.

The sickening realization was not that there were victims who had raped children, but that there were victims—at least Lemuel—who hadn't touched anyone. And what about Massie? Why had those two made the list?

Eyeing the steers, she said, "I have no idea."

The animals stared back while one of them issued a deep-throated bellow and an impressive stream of urine.

She laughed and fired up the truck.

But rather than getting on the road, she thought about Katrina. Dressed in a stranger's white dress, her eyes closed and neck bruised. That there was just a trace of blood made it worse.

If Katrina had been more obviously violated, the picture would be more recognizable and easier to digest.

"A more identifiable monster."

It was the same thing that drove her to seek out Massie's alleged monstrousness. For Katrina, that monster hadn't made itself known with a roar. Instead, it hid in the background with just a whisper. But if the monster whispered, how was Jace ever to know when it was near? If it didn't announce itself, how would she recognize it?

Across the cotton fields, the spires of downtown Zack City were visible. She was twelve or fifteen miles from home and that seemed both too close and too far.

Wiping the standing tears from her eyes, Jace put the truck back on the road.

Two miles down the road, she saw it.

The black SUV was behind her, coming up fast.

Stunned, Jace jammed the gas pedal and grabbed for her cell phone. The engine screamed and the truck barely moved forward.

"Damn it, let's go." She willed the truck faster.

Her throat dried but her palms were suddenly sweaty and her hands slipped over the wheel. She managed to dial Rory's phone but it only rang.

The SUV gained quickly.

Still Rory's phone rang.

The SUV rode huge in her mirror. The driver, his face illuminated now by the late afternoon sun, glared at her. It was a Hispanic kid, maybe mid-twenties, curly black hair falling in a sloppy heap over a sharp, angled face.

"What are you doing?" Jace yelled at the kid as Rory's phone came alive.

"Yeah, this is Rory, do whatever you want." Then a buzz tone.

"Rory. He's behind me again. Goddamn it, where are you?" She looked again in the rearview mirror and tried to keep the front of the SUV in her vision. "Uh . . . 3-6-Nora. Charles . . . damn it . . . Charles-John-5. Rory, damn it, where are you? I need—"

Then the truck was at her side, tearing her outside mirror off. Chunks of aluminum and shards of glass exploded. The SUV straddled the broken yellow line and she looked around hoping a trooper might happen to be nearby. But the road was empty in both directions.

Jace fumbled the phone to the floorboard and clamped both hands on the wheel as the SUV started weaving back and forth into her lane.

"Stop. What're you doing?"

The truck feinted toward her, then faded away, then came back toward her. Jace nosed Preacher's truck toward the road's shoulder. The passenger tires hit the ragged edge of the road. A loud, arrhythmic thump echoed through the cab.

"Stop it, stop it."

But the kid crowded her until her right-side wheels were into the dirt. Plumes of brown erupted behind her. The steering wheel wobbled in her hands.

When the SUV came over again, she refused to move. The SUV tried again, and again she held her ground.

As they hit seventy miles an hour, the SUV decided to simply move her.

The vehicles made contact. With a metallic crunch, the front left of Preacher's truck crumpled. Wide-eyed, Jace yanked the wheel hard right. Preacher's truck went completely off the road and careened toward a cattle fence.

The SUV kept crowding her. The truck nosed over further and further, not letting her get back to the road.

Her wheels bounced over ruts, knocking her around. She

slammed into the driver's side door. Pain blossomed bright and pink in her vision.

At better than sixty miles an hour, she was in the fence. Posts exploded beneath the bumper and snapped over the hood. One piece glanced off the windshield while barbed wire strung itself around the hood and cab. Dirt flew up around them. To Jace, it was like being in the middle of a summer sandstorm. She was lost in a sea of dirt and dust.

Her teeth banged together and caught her tongue between them. Warm blood filled her mouth and she spit it out as more holes and ruts and fence posts slammed the truck side to side.

A post came through the windshield, spidering the glass and sending shards of safety glass through the cab. She screamed, yanked the wheel hard right, and slammed on the brakes. The truck locked up and drifted left.

"Shit shit."

The two trucks drifted toward each other, the SUV a hulking smear of black. Jace raised a hand to shield herself, but rather than colliding, the SUV shot past in a blur of black, dented metal.

Barbed wire followed the fence post through the giant hole and slashed at Jace's face. Her hand got wound up by the wire. Her neck and chest and hands all felt the tiny bites.

Preacher's truck stopped as the SUV's brake lights twinkled red and the monster came around. It sat for a moment, its tricked-out front end staring at her.

She heard the SUV revving its engine.

"Son of a bitch."

From the holster, she grabbed the .38.

"Let's go, then."

The motor revved again and when the SUV moved, she fired twice. One shot went wild but the second plinked a hole in the SUV's windshield. The kid driving threw himself down over the seat before popping back up and slamming the truck into drive.

It jumped out of the dirt on the shoulder and hit the pavement. It spun away from Jace and finally the tires grabbed.

"Bullshit."

She jammed the gun out the broken windshield and fired while the truck sped away. Most of her shots went wild but one punched a hole in the back windshield while another shot off a piece of the V-shaped antenna.

Bleeding anger, Jace yanked the trigger over and over until the gun clicked empty.

"Try to kill me?"

She rummaged in the glove box, looking for extra rounds. Past old maps and napkins with pieces of sermons and Bible quotes. Through the pile of dried-up pens and broken tire-pressure gauges.

Stop it, Jace.

It was Bibb's voice and she ignored it. She wanted those shells. She wanted to loose more rounds against that motherfucker who'd tried to kill her. In fact, she wanted that son of a bitch dead.

Don't let the violence win. That's not who you are.

It was as though Bibb was in the truck with her, sitting next to her, lecturing her.

He was wrong. She was violence. She loved violence and how it coated her mouth and throat. Right now, all she wanted was more of it while she blasted that SUV until it exploded.

But there were no more rounds.

She stopped, leaning against the back of the bench seat, breathing hard and fast. Her hands shook and the pit of her stomach was on fire.

She'd felt this way the night Thomas died. And when the female attacked her in booking. And when Royce jumped on her in medical.

And when she'd let Reynolds win.

But this was the first time she'd welcomed the feeling. This was the first time she'd wanted more of the feeling.

Slowly, as carefully as she could, Jace unwrapped herself from the barbed wire. The pain began almost immediately.

"Oh, holy hell."

Blood streaked her hands and arms, though not as much as she would have thought from the amount of wire or the pain. She put the wire aside and looked back at the damage. Maybe a half-mile worth of smashed fence, more than enough for the herd to get out, though they seemed to have disappeared during the commotion. As soon as she could, she'd dig up the rancher's name and call him.

She tossed Preacher's gun into the cab.

"Damn it."

She had a message from Bibb. It had come during the shooting. His voice was strained. "Been watching the tape. He didn't brew anything, at least not that I could see. But a few deputies're pretty interested in him. Coming and going at all hours. Talking to him through the door. I'm guessing he ain't sleeping much."

CHAPTER THIRTY-FOUR

With Wonder Woman dead on the living room floor, the water hit Jace cold and hard.

It was fist-sized and it pummeled her until her blood ran cold in the drain. Yet it wasn't painful enough to erase the memory of an SUV trying to kill her or of Katrina and Rosely.

Or of her wanting to kill a man.

No, she thought, crying so hard her chest hurt. *Go further back. Erase everything since I started this job.*

But even that wouldn't be far enough. If she had a magical eraser, she'd go back to when Mama was still alive and they would curl up in bed together at the end of a hard night's work and back to when the Hot Five were actually still a quintet rather than a trio. And maybe, just maybe, she'd go back to the spelling bee and get that word right.

But leave me the one memory. Let me remember how good it felt to shoot at that man. Let me celebrate the power I had in that .38 and how that power made even the painful cuts on my arms and face seem petty. Let me get annoyed that I didn't have more bullets or that I didn't have a bigger gun.

Leave me that single, beautiful memory.

Except she didn't want to want that memory. She didn't want to think about how she grinned when she pulled the trigger or about how the only time during the entire incident that her hands didn't shake was when she was shooting.

She turned away from the pulsing water, overcome again

with sobs. She'd been crying since she climbed back into Preacher's truck less than an hour ago. She had come straight home, peeled her clothes off, tossed them out her bedroom window, and headed for the shower.

But before she'd found the water, Wonder Woman yelled at her. Towering over the living room, her very silence lectured Jace. *You're supposed to be the good guy,* Wonder Woman said. *You* are *the good guy.*

"Shut up," Jace had said, standing naked in the middle of the room.

The good guys don't shoot at people, Wonder Woman said. *They don't try to kill people.*

"Yes, they do." Jace's voice bounced off the walls.

Angrily, Jace ripped the poster from the wall and stomped it into the carpet.

She cried, she knew, as emotional release. She'd been horrified at the Gaines jail and then scared to death when the SUV appeared. But the tears were also an overflow valve. *Could I have killed the SUV driver? Not through accident or a lucky shot, but through deliberation and forethought? Could I have taken aim and shot him in the head?*

Yes.

She sagged against the tiles. Her arm hurt where she'd hit it against the pickup's door. Her face hurt where the barbed wire had cut her. Her finger hurt where she'd continued to yank the trigger even after she heard the hammer fall on an empty cylinder.

How can you judge those deputies when you tried to kill, too?

When she heard the bathroom door open, Jace's breath stopped. But when she heard the hum, floating tenderly in the steamy air, she laughed a tear-filled, sloppy laugh as she slumped to the shower floor. She sat heavily on her butt, her knees drawn up to her chest, her head tilted and resting on her knees while her hands encircled her legs.

"I'm losing her, Gramma," Jace whispered.

"No, you're not."

"I can't remember the way her face moves."

"Just like yours. Your face is hers."

"I can't remember."

After a while, Gramma said, "Jace, I'm worried about you. Your friends are worried, too. You need to stop—"

"Gramma, please, don't. Okay? Just don't. Not today."

"What happened to you? I found your clothes outside. I picked them up, but Jace, they're going to have to be laundered. Maybe in an acid bath. They smell like . . . like . . ."

"Throw them out. Don't wash them, don't give them away. Just throw them out. Or burn them."

"Jace, that's wasteful, I can't—"

"Gramma, please."

"Hey, how about I call Preacher? We'll go eat. Luigi's, maybe."

Jace cried silently and Gramma filled the silence with her humming. Finally the woman began to sing, softly, "Embrace me . . . my sweet, embrace me."

It was Mama's song and Mama had given it to Jace when Jace was just a little girl. Mama sang it slow, the way Sarah Vaughan had on her 1954 version. Mama had never been much of a jazz fan, at least as Jace remembered, but this song had spoken to the woman.

"Embrace me . . . you irreplaceable you," Gramma sang.

"I miss her, Gramma."

"Just one look at you and my heart grows tipsy." Gramma's soft voice floated through the shower steam and through the Rosely stench and the sore trigger finger and into Jace's heart.

And still Jace cried.

Chapter Thirty-Five

The door just opened.

Jace was buried beneath a pile of pillows on her couch while Chet Baker sang about the touch of lips and two bayberry candles burned against the dry embrace of the summer heat coming through an open widow.

The door simply opened and the Hot Five crowded into her apartment. "Sure, come on in. Don't worry I'm naked or something."

"Hush up, little girl," Preacher said. "We worried about you."

"That naked thing might be okay, though, you wanna go ahead and do it up." Hassan cocked his old hips and stared at her.

Gramma smacked him in the back of the head.

"What are you guys doing here? Really, I'd rather just spend some time with Mr. Baker, no offense."

Preacher stepped forward. His voice lowered into what she thought of as his serious voice. "The Jew has something to tell you."

"The Jew?" Hassan said. "That's how you talk about me . . . when I'm right here? The Jew?"

Jace stood. Her robe flapped and they got a flash of upper thigh. She cinched the robe tighter. "Out. I really don't need any—" She stopped, the tears and anger and fear locked just behind her teeth.

"Hassan," Preacher said. "Tell it. Now."

After a deep breath, Hassan said, "You know I play poker."

"And?"

"Well, I play with a lot of different people. Bankers and county commissioners and store clerks and a stripper or two. There's one guy, an appraiser. Office is in Zack City but his company's in Dallas. They do appraisals all over the country. He's the West Texas guy." His eyes darted to Gramma, then back to Jace. "He told me . . ."

"What, Hassan? What did he tell you?"

"This guy is a nosy dude. Last time he and I were playing, my mouth got to running and I maybe talked about Thomas and Reynolds and Badgett and I don't know what all."

Jace panicked. "Tell me you didn't."

"I did, Jace, and I'm sorry. You know me, sometimes I just talk and don't know what I'm saying."

Jace paced the apartment like a fresh inmate in holding.

"Jace," Gramma said. "Calm down. We'll deal with Hassan being an idiot, but you need to hear the rest of this."

"One of those names stuck with him but he wasn't sure why. Said he does so much business for so many people that eventually everybody's name just sort of runs together. So a few days ago he was at the office alone and he punched that guy's name up on the computer. Sure as shit came up."

"Whose name?"

"Like eight or nine contacts," Hassan said, excited now. "Ten or twelve times, Jace, that guy hired an appraisal. The land is all over West Texas."

"Hassan, take a breath. Whose name?"

"Badgett. Will Badgett. He's listed as the contact agent on all this land."

Jace frowned. "Okay. I don't know what that means."

Hassan said, "It means he's buying land all over the damned state. But the thing is, the land is crap. None of the parcels are very big and none are worth shit. My guy said it's nothing but scrub in the middle of nowhere. Cain't even run much cattle because all the parcels border one state route or another."

"Maybe he wants to build vacation cabins," Gramma said.

Jace dug back to the first time she'd met him. "No, he told me he's building a training facility. The jailer at Gaines County told me the same thing." She frowned. "They've all told me that, now that I think about it; all the Total Force guys and most of them say they're hiring on at the facility."

Was Badgett bumping off predators and buying their deaths with positions at this new academy?

Hassan produced a sheet of paper and slammed it down on the coffee table. It was a printed map of West Texas, extending from El Paso to Abilene and Lamesa down to Mexico.

"My guy printed this up for me. The red is the land Badgett's had appraised."

Five small, red blotches covered portions of the map beginning near Lamesa and ending along the Mexico border. Just a few miles south of Lamesa, on Texas Highway 349, was one tiny red smear. It was matched further south on 349 near Patricia. On the southern edge of Ector County, near a tiny burg called Pleasant Farms, was another bit of red, this time at the interchange of Highway 385 and Farm-to-Market 1787. A good distance further south, just outside of Fort Stockton on U.S. 67, was another. Then a few miles further south again, just outside the border town of Presidio, was another, again off U.S. 67.

"What're these?" Jace asked, pointing to various parcels that had only been outlined.

"My guy says this is land the company has been asked about appraising but hasn't done. And guess what?"

"Hassan, please," Jace said.

"Oh . . . uh . . . sorry. Look, Badgett is always the contact person listed, but my guy's only talked to him like three times, maybe four. All the other times, calls come in from this company, Total something—"

"Force. Total Force."

"His company bought them but he wasn't the one to call my guy about appraisals."

"Who did?"

Hassan shrugged. "No name on it. Calls came in, gave the locations, and said it was part of the Total Force contract."

Preacher pulled out his pipe, loaded it with tobacco, but didn't light up. "Sounds like that ol' right hand ain't met the left."

Was there dissent inside Total Force? Or was this just how business was done? Open a standing contract and then anyone can make a request. Jace had zero experience in business and so had no clue if Hassan's information was standard procedure or something odd.

The largest of all the parcels, appraised and not, sat where Highway 385 and U.S. 67 crossed paths near McCamey, Texas.

"That's where he's building it, I think," Jace said. "Look, guys, I have to think about getting to work. I appreciate everything you've done, but this doesn't have anything to do with anything. Whatever his landowner tendencies, that doesn't figure in to him teaching men how to kill."

"Drugs," Hassan said, a hopeful note in his voice. "Maybe he's gonna grow drugs."

"And maybe you can be his consultant," Gramma said.

"I have no idea what you're talking about," Hassan said. "We of the Jewish faith don't do drugs."

"Luckily, you're lapsed Catholic masquerading as Jewish."

With a sheepish grin, Hassan nodded. "Well, yeah, there is that."

"You know, you keep claiming Judea, they gonna make you cut it off."

"Cut what—" Hassan's eyes narrowed. "I don't think so, old woman. I'll fight to the death anybody wants to cut Ol' Willie."

"You didn't actually name it Ol' Willie?" Jace asked.

Hassan mimed taking a hit from a joint. "In honor of Willie Nelson, patron saint of dope smokers."

"Thanks for checking on me, but I'm fine. I had a hard afternoon but someone I dearly love sang me a lullaby and some friends came over and now I'm better." She lowered her head. "But . . . uh . . . Preacher? We have to talk."

Hassan laughed as he left her apartment. "I told you that piece of crap had a few new dings on it. And that whole missing windshield thing, I'll bet that's a story."

When Hassan was gone, Preacher took a deep breath. "Girl, you know I don't care about that truck. I'm glad you okay, but that truck's just a truck, it can be fixed." His eyes bored in on hers. "I guess I'm questioning why that gun is empty."

"What gun?" Gramma asked.

"Gramma, Rosely wasn't the only thing that happened this afternoon."

Twenty minutes later, Jace was alone again. Neither Gramma nor Preacher was happy with what she told them, but they didn't press her.

Once they were gone, Jace opened her computer and did some research on those roads from Mexico to Lamesa. Badgett didn't strike Jace as the type to buy random bits of land, and a training facility didn't need ground strung from one end of the state to the other. At the same time, this obviously wasn't just about Badgett and his deputies, at least not the land part of it. There were, probably, other people involved. Ultimately, she believed the company's land had nothing to do with anything, but it was another question, wasn't it? It was another question that needed to be answered, even if the answer was completely banal.

Ask the next question, Jace.

And when she did, she found an answer.

"Imports? What the hell . . ."

Chapter Thirty-Six

On shift that night, Rory roared.

"Just listen to it." Her words boomed in the go-between during a break.

"I was there, I know what—"

"*Listen* to this."

Hesitantly, angry at Rory's anger, Jace listened.

"Rory." Jace's voice. Loud and scared. "He's behind me again. He's here." Her words rushed out like she was trying to make them all a single word, though she remembered the incident as an excruciating slowness.

"Goddamn it, where are you?"

She heard the truck's engine screaming and the screech of tires on pavement.

"3-6-Nora. Rory, damn it, where are you? Charles . . . damn it . . . Charles-John . . . uh . . . John-5. Rory, I need—"

And then nothing. The phone connection was still active but she had dropped the phone to keep both hands on the wheel. Then the bone-jarring slam of truck against truck.

—434 to medical ASAP—

—10-4—

"Are you fucking crazy?" the recorded Jace yelled. "You're going to kill us."

Jace knew what came next. More panic, then bravado.

"Let's go then."

And, "Bullshit."

—434 expedite—

"Rory, they're having a problem in medical, we should go help."

Before she could answer, the shots came. Loud and jarring, bone rattling even through the phone's tiny speaker. Two shots. POW. POW.

Then four more.

Rory snapped the phone shut. "Are *you* fucking crazy? You're shooting now?" She yanked Jace's uniform shirt. "What if you'd killed him?" She shoved Jace backward and clenched her fists. "You manage to not get your ass kicked in a single fight so now you're Wonder Woman? Wearing your big girl panties? All Ramboed up and ready to do battle? What if you'd killed him?"

Jace licked her lips. "I wanted to."

Rory stepped back. "You wanted to."

Jace told her everything, from Rosely to the SUV. Rory's jaw muscles bulged as she ground her teeth.

"Get as pissed as you want . . . sister . . . but I had to go. Then. Right then, I had to go. I had to talk to him, Rory, I had to know if Gaines County was the same as Zachary and Ector."

"Why? You knew he was going to tell you the same thing they've all told you. You knew it was no different. Why then and why alone?"

Jace chose her words carefully. "Because I had to do it by myself."

"I don't understand that."

"Everything has been with you. And that's fine. You're a great woman, Rory, and I'll never be able to explain how much you've meant to me just in the few weeks I've known you. But I needed to do it myself."

"Well, that bid for independence almost got you killed."

"I had to see if I could be the cop you think I'm going to be."

Rory's head shook. "Don't pin this on me. I never told you to go poking around by yourself."

"Not pinning anything on you. I just, I don't know, I just wanted to be—"

For the first time, a sly look slipped across Rory's face. "You wanted to be me."

"Maybe I should get a new psych eval?"

Rory's anger stayed in place, but diffused some. "You're lucky you didn't get killed. I mean, I'd hate to have to bury you, or worse, come across you half-dead, flopping like a deer with a broken leg. I'd hate to have to put you down."

"Yeah, I'm glad you didn't have to shoot me."

"You think Gramma would've paid for the bullets?"

"Bullets? Plural? Are you that bad a shot?"

"Touché." Rory shook her head. "I can't believe that's how you spent your afternoon. Hell, all I did was wash and wax my ride, and drink some beer."

Jace glanced up at the camera and nodded. She assumed Bibb was watching and she wanted to tell him thanks for his information. "Speaking of. Massie didn't brew the hooch. At least Bibb doesn't think so. He's been watching the tape."

"So how'd it get there?" Rory asked. "And why? You think they're pushing Massie, too? He a diddler?"

Jace shrugged. "Who knows. If I had some idea of what Badgett is doing, then maybe I could answer that question."

Rory shook her head. "You're getting too bogged down, sister. Look, one thing you're gonna learn in this job is that evil is completely banal. There is no giant conspiracy going on. There is no grand plan. Most 'plans' that come through our doors are planned only after the killing has started. I don't think we've got anything other than vigilante deputies taking out molesters."

"And those they think are molesters."

"Yeah."

"Maybe," Jace said.

Rory said, "You understand how inmates sometimes transfer their need for home to a cell, right? Those cells become home. It's why they're so angry when we do shakedowns. They don't have much, but they do have those cells. When we go in, we're invading their home."

Jace nodded. "Maybe that's why the deputies keep moving those inmates . . . keep them from settling in. Then they take away the little privileges, phones and extra soap and whatever."

The little things, soap and shampoo and extra toilet paper, were what made a jail run smoothly; either always having them or never having them. The Zachary County Jail allowed inmates to have those things so Reynolds had used them to get under Thomas' skin. But rather than wait for Thomas to lash out, Reynolds jumped the gun.

"You should have seen Devereaux's face, Rory. He was absolutely convinced he'd done the right thing. It was almost like he expected a medal."

"A patriotic duty. Keeping society clean of its trash." Rory sighed. "I agreed with them all the way down the line."

"Sure you did," Jace said. "That's the brilliant stroke. Not very many people are going to question the death of someone who rapes and kills kids. We all believe those men deserve worse than what they dole out. Rosely, who we know without a doubt raped and killed a child. Joe Paul Hewson who we know stole two kids and molested them. Our guy, Thomas, who apparently touched a kid or two and was pleading out."

"Then why Lemuel?" Rory asked. "I'm telling you, he did not touch a child."

"Well, they thought he did. Remember the picture Delilah showed me. Full of kids. God knows how they could screw it up so badly. They have perfect knowledge about one guy but don't about a different guy? And it's not a couple of punches during booking or taking away some phone privileges, we're talking about killing men. That's not something you just do as a matter of course after breakfast."

"You wanted to kill a man. You said it pretty easily."

"Sure, but that man was trying to kill me."

"Self-defense, is what you're saying."

A hot, bright blast of anger shot through Jace. "So I'm one of them?" She went to the outer door and keyed her mic. "C-charles outer." The door popped and Jace opened it.

"That's not what I'm saying, Jace, and you know it. But you see how easy it is to justify something? You just said the same thing they say."

Jace stood a moment longer, the door held between them, each woman seeing the other through the slim window.

—479 from control . . . you're letting out all the cold air . . . in or out—

Jace swallowed and stepped back into the go-between.

Rory said, "So they got it wrong with Lemuel?"

"You tell me, you knew him. The question is: are they getting it wrong with Massie, too?"

"Yeah, but Reynolds is gone. He can't do the deed."

"Royce isn't."

Rory cocked her head. "He studied with Badgett, I'm pretty sure."

"He's the one who jumped on me in medical. Plus, he asked me to move Massie once. And he's got the Total Force tattoo."

"Total Force just keeps popping up," Rory said.

"Now, just to muddy the water a little more: have you ever heard of something called La Entrada al Pacifico Corridor?"

"No."

"Will Badgett has. He's buying land from the border all the way to Lamesa. It's a trade highway. When George W. was governor, he signed a bill that created a route from Mexico to Lamesa."

Rory laughed. "Lamesa?"

"Yeah, doesn't seem like the greatest end point for a transcontinental highway. If it ever gets built—and the Internet stuff I read didn't make that seem likely—it'll come across the border at Presidio and run north and east on 67 before hitting 385 past Pleasant Farms and into Odessa to Midland, then 349 to Lamesa. It was supposed to take advantage of NAFTA. Supposedly the ports in California are too busy and Chinese goods could get to market faster with this highway."

"And so Badgett's . . . what? Hoping the government'll buy it at a higher price or something?"

Jace shrugged. "He's building the Total Force compound, we know that for sure. Maybe he's building a few places. Lamesa, which would put him closer to Lubbock. One here, close to Midland and Odessa. One closer to the border, maybe he thinks he can get a gig training Border Patrol and ICE."

Rory shook her head. "No. Three that close together is a waste. Why pay three times the staff and insurance and land taxes and all the rest when the next facility would only be a hundred miles away."

"Well," Jace said, "Maybe he's going to sell it to some developers. Maybe he thinks they'll put up strip malls or a McDonald's or gas stations. In theory, there'll be a ton of Mexican trucks coming right across the border. Lots of people to buy lots of stuff."

Rory sat heavily in one of the chairs, crossed her legs, stared into space. "Which has exactly what to do with child molesters?"

"Nothing that I can tell."

Rory licked her lips. "Pleasant Farms?"

"You know it?"

"Heard of it. Never been there." She sighed. "Damn it. But I know someone who has."

"Yeah?"

"Delilah Stimson."

A hard, heavy ball dropped straight into Jace's gut.

—456 from 419 . . . you coming back or are we on our own—

Rory keyed her mic. "On my way." When she released the mic, she said, "Working for Kleopping tonight." She pulled out her cell phone and punched a number. "Delilah? Yeah, it's Rory. I know, I know, it's like two in the morning and I'm sorry but I have a question. What happened to Lemuel's land after he died? That go to you or the kids?"

The go-between went silent except for the crackle of occasional radio traffic. The radio had been going all night, and most of it had run in one ear and out the other. Yet the four or five times someone had called her, Jace had heard it instantly. *Maybe you're getting the hang of this stuff,* she thought. *A small victory in the midst of this crap.*

"Hang on," Rory said. She lowered her phone and pressed the speaker button. "Say that again."

"Damn, girl, I need my sleep." Delilah's voice came through loud and clear. "Okay, one more time, then I'm going to sleep. Lemuel owned an acre or so and left it to me. It wasn't worth a whole lot, just a piece of scrub a little ways off the highway. He was building a retirement house but he wasn't building it any too good. The roof leaked and most of the doors hung crooked. Guy had made an offer on it about a month before Lemuel died and Lemuel turned him down flat. For ten thousand dollars. After my boy died, his land came to me but I sold it to help pay for his funeral."

"Delilah, who'd you sell it to?"

"The guy who made the original offer. But he paid a whole lot less after Lemuel died. I only got five grand. Company was called Total Force. They do self-protection services or some crap. Guy said he wanted to build a facility out there, train corporate executives or something. I don't give a shit what he builds, long as his check clears."

The ball that had dropped into Jace's gut exploded into hundreds of pinpricks, like the cluster bombs she saw on the news, drop one bomb that becomes hundreds of others. "What was the guy's name?"

"William Badgett."

"Thanks, Delilah."

"This mean something, Rory? What'choo got going on?"

"Go back to bed, Delilah. I'll call you in a couple of days. And don't go getting mouthy to all your crazy friends."

Delilah laughed and to Jace's ears, it sounded almost giddy. The woman understood it wasn't a random phone call. "You don't call me and I'm gonna get mouthy."

"See ya', sister." Rory snapped her phone closed.

Jace said, "It's not about land for a facility. I mean, some of it is, but not all of it. The rest of it is about Badgett getting what he wants, even if it's something he doesn't need."

"Wrong, Jace. This is about nothing more than power."

"There were a number of parcels that Badgett wants to get appraised, but doesn't yet own. Something else, too. Badgett's only contacted the appraisal company three times, but there have been more appraisals than that. Someone just calls, basically says put it on the Total Force tab, and off they go."

"So there's someone else dealing on the land stuff while Badgett kills predators."

"Does Massie own any land?"

"Bet he does and I'll bet you a bag of Skittles Badgett's made an offer like he did with Lemuel's land." Rory keyed her mic. "C-charles outer." The door popped almost immediately. She held it open for a few seconds.

—456 from control . . . again with the open door, you're letting out all the air—

"You're not paying for it, Sarge, calm down."

Jace cracked a smile but a second later, Dillon was on the radio.

—do you people have an ounce of professionalism in you—

Rory acted as though she was going to key up again, but Bibb beat her to the punch.

—between us all? Maybe an ounce—

Dillon didn't respond. The silence stretched to forever.

—sorry, sarge—

"Listen," Rory said. "When we get off, let's go rattle a chain or two."

"What?"

"Enrique Salazar."

"And he is?"

With a smirk, Rory said, "3-6-Nora-Charles-John-5. 36N, CJ5. Registered to Enrique Salazar." She winked at Jace. "Good job getting the plate."

Jace felt a rush of heat to her face. "Well, you screwed up so badly the first time we saw him, I guess I just knew I needed to save your ass."

"Yeah, thanks for that. Another twenty or thirty times and we'll be even."

The door closed loudly behind her.

"C-charles inner," Jace radioed.

When the door popped, she took a deep breath. The next four hours would be a normal night on shift. She had to put everything out of her head. For now, she'd have to check tomorrow's docket and see who got to walk over for a judge and who got to walk home and who got to walk into their new home.

Chapter Thirty-Seven

Enrique Salazar lived in the Flat.

The area straddled the railroad tracks, spreading both north and south before going east to the massive oil tank farm that sidled up only yards from the county's poorest residents. The Flat was a place of possibility, where the depth of the kink didn't matter, only the depth of the wallet. Leather or lace, rubber, a little tie-up or tie-down, eight balls or skank, maybe a hundred tabs of E or a trailer of untaxed cigarettes. It had always been a place where someone lonely could find someone else lonely and between them, they could find a price that would alleviate their desolation. In the winter, when the cold air trapped the city deep beneath a thermal blanket, the deeper back alleys carried the stench of glass heated red-hot to cook five-dollar rocks.

In the electrically hot summer of 1974, a white policeman had chased a young black man into this area but the man had slipped away. Zack City PD used his disappearance as reason to put the area—called the Flat since the 1920's—under a vague sort of martial law. They checked homes and businesses, stopped drivers, and rounded up nearly a hundred people on warrants. They never found the kid but they did find a man wanted for killing two prostitutes in Dallas. The arrest became a shootout that left one officer dead and another paralyzed. The bad guy got shot twelve times by the only other witness to the shooting of the officers: a third white officer.

That third officer also notched the death of an older Hispanic man that night. The cop said the man was killed by stray bullets. But the local community—black, white, and Hispanic, all poor—said the cop shot him for a raft of other reasons. Rumor was that the dead Hispanic supplied heroin to the officer in quantities enough to supply any co-workers who had a taste.

Later, during the internal investigation into officers' drug usage, seventeen officers refused to submit to any sort of drug testing. The roster spots that opened when they were summarily fired were filled with a mix of black and Hispanic recruits.

Jace swallowed heavily when they parked half a block down from Salazar's address. The incident with the dead Hispanic had been better than thirty years ago and now something like 15 percent of the PD and 12 or 13 percent of the Sheriff's Office was Hispanic, but memories of a dead man themselves die with difficulty.

"Don't sweat it, sister, we'll be fine." Rory sounded confident, but her face was a mask of worry lines and constantly shifting eyes.

The residence was a ranch-style place, painted in an adobe red that had faded beneath the harsh sun. Two small Virgin Mary statutes sat on either side of the doorway while a large cross hung on the door. The yard was mostly green, with flower beds along the house that were full of summer color.

At this hour of the morning, the neighborhood was quiet. Rory's hard knock resounded up and down the street. Eventually, an older woman, wrapped in a housecoat and with her hair pinned up, answered. *"Sí?"*

"Mrs. Salazar?" Rory said. "We'd like to talk with Enrique."

She eyed them a moment, then nodded slowly. "I'll get him. Wait, please." She closed the door. Clearly, both women heard: *"Policia."*

Rory said, "He's running."

"What?"

Rory ran around the side of the house and Jace followed. They hopped the low chain-link fence and got to the back door just as it opened. A young man—the driver, Jace knew immediately—spilled from the house. He tripped over a small planter and hit the ground hard.

Rory stopped but made no attempt to forcibly detain him. "Where you going, Pancho?"

The young man glared at her. "Enrique." When his gaze slid over to Jace, his eyes went wide. "Son of a bitch. I didn't know." His hands hit the ground but still he made no attempt to flee. "Goddamn it, I knew this was bullshit." His voice was shrill in the early morning air.

"Rico?" His mother stood at the door, her hands at her chest, worry high in her face.

Enrique waved at her and forced a smile. With an angry glare, the woman closed the door. Her face immediately popped up in the kitchen window.

Jace said, "What didn't you know?"

He nodded toward his mother. "She knew you were the cops."

"Smart lady," Rory said.

"I didn't."

Rory helped him stand. "Smarter than you, I guess."

He turned to Jace. "I'm real sorry, Officer, really I am. I had no idea."

"It's deputy and what are you sorry for?"

For a moment, he looked startled. "What for? For trying to run your ass over." He pointed to his ride. The black SUV—plate number 36N-CJ5—sat far back in the long driveway, nearly hidden from sight. "But look what you did."

There were nearly identical holes in the front and back windshield and a piece was missing from the antennae. But also, there was one hole in the hood and one in the driver's side door. With a disturbing sense of satisfaction, she realized she'd shot better than she'd thought.

"You hafta do that?"

Jace shrugged as though it meant nothing. "That's what happens when people try to kill me."

"Try to kill a cop." Rory shook her head like the entire weight of a sad, desperate world was now solely on Enrique's shoulders. "That's some heavy, heavy time, Enrique." She turned to Jace. "Actually, isn't that death penalty?"

"Could be."

"And this is Texas, where we have the Death Needle Express." She glanced at her watch. "Enrique, you could be dead by . . . I don't know . . . next Thursday."

His eyes grew huge. "Wait . . . whoa . . . I ain't up for no death penalty. And she shot at me. I didn't know she was a cop, I've been saying that."

"Say it and say it and say it," Rory said. "But you followed her twice, tried to run her off the road twice." She held up two fingers. "Two separate incidents, Enrique."

Jace held up a finger on her left hand, then a finger on her right hand. "Two separate counts of attempted murder of a law enforcement officer."

Enrique's head rattled back and forth like a bobblehead doll riding heavy on PCP. "Nononononono, it ain't like that. This ain't me. This ain't 'cause'a me."

Whoever had hired Salazar, and Jace's money was on Badgett, was pushing him just as hard as the guards did the inmates. *But are we doing anything any different from Reynolds and Sneed and Devereaux and the rest? We're hoping we can push him into telling us what is going on.*

"It's not you?" Rory asked. "What's that mean, Enrique?"

His mouth clamped closed in a hurry.

"And while you think about that, answer me this." Jace turned toward him, her finger in the bullet hole in the door. "How'd you know I was in those two jails? In Sterling County and Gaines County? Or did you just happen to be in the area and so thought you'd run a nice lady off the road?"

His eyes constantly darted back to the house. "I can't, he'll kill me."

"The state will if you don't," Rory said. She sat lightly, as though she hadn't a care in the world, on the redwood patio bench.

Jace crowded him. "Who hired you?" Exactly opposite of what they'd taught her at the Academy. *Stay back, give them personal distance, don't get within arm's length.* "Tell me, Enrique. What's going on?" *In reality, if you want to crowd them mentally, crowd them physically. Just be prepared for the punch.*

Without touching him, she pushed him backward, until the backs of his legs bumped up against the bench where Rory sat. She forced him to sit. He looked up into Jace's eyes and there was still a spark, still a sliver of fire and independence.

Do it, she thought. *Jam a hand against his throat. Or grab his shoulder. Squeeze a little, Jace, just enough to get his attention. Don't hurt him, don't become one of them, but use their tools if you need to.* She stood taller and let the sun play around her shoulders and into his eyes. *I'm in front of him, but it's more than just me. It's me and the sun. When he looks at me, he has to blink, he has to turn away to keep his eyes from being completely burned out.*

Use their tools.

He stared at her, his brown eyes narrowed and intent on her. His breath came shallowly and his body shook the slightest bit.

But whispering in her head, loudly, was Preacher. He didn't tell her to do the right thing. He didn't tell her to avoid the looming chasm. He just said her name, over and over while Gramma sang. Jace blinked away a hot tear.

"Jace?" Rory's voice was quiet. "You okay?"

Enrique's spark was dying. Then he slumped and propped himself up on his knees with his elbows, his face resting in his hands. "Yeah, he hired me. He didn't say kill you, but that's what he wanted. He suggested I run you off the road. I think he hoped you'd crash and maybe die and it would look like you dodged a coyote or something."

"Who?"

There was a long pause.

"Listen, Enrique, you cough up the right answer and you walk away from all this. We were never here and you go back in with your mother. Those two murder attempts?" She snapped her fingers. "Poof. Never happened. Deputy Salome ran off the road. Wasn't paying attention, probably calling her boyfriend."

"You want me to snitch him up and then you're going to leave me on the streets? He'll kill me."

"So whoever hired you is capable of murder?" Jace turned back to them.

Enrique stared at her, open-mouthed. "Capable of—hell, yeah, everybody's capable of killing."

"Everybody?" Jace shook her head.

"Yes. Everybody." He smirked. "You, too, Deputy."

"I don't think so, Enrique, I don't play in your sandbox."

"Play in my sandbox? When you was standing over me just then you looked like you thought you owned the sandbox. Everybody is capable . . . especially this guy. And you want to turn me out and then dump me."

"Enrique, let's be adults, shall we?" Rory asked. "You've got contacts all over the country. You and I both know it. You hop on one of the thousands of long-haul trucks you run and you're in L.A. in a few days. Or Miami. Hide yourself in one of those hidden compartments designed right into the floor of the trailers and no one will ever find you. That's what you've been down for, right? Production and distribution?"

He shook his head. "No production. Just the distribution."

"Ah, my mistake." Rory leaned back on the redwood table. "Time to take a vacation. Take Mama home to Chiapas for a while. We leave you out and you've got a chance to get gone."

His eyes narrowed. "You seem to know a lot about me."

"How often do you think I talk to people and not know who I'm talking to? You've been busted all over the damned southwest, *hombre.*"

"Sounds like he's not that good a drug dealer," Jace said. "Maybe he wants to think about a new line of work."

"You label me? I'll label you. *Policia.*" He spat near her shoe. *"Asesino."*

"That's right." Jace nodded. "And as the police, I am going to give you a choice. Make your decision right now."

"Damn it." He sucked his teeth. "I knew this was going to crash. Look, it was Badgett, okay? He called me both times and told me the town and what you were driving."

"Why?"

He snorted. "I asked why and all he said was that I shouldn't be Salome, that's what he said." Enrique nodded toward Jace. "That's you. Salome."

"Yeah. So Badgett hired you."

"Blackmailed. Snatched me up a year ago riding heavy."

"How much?"

"Ten keys."

Rory whistled.

"Put that weight in his back pocket, said he'd keep it there forever, pull it out whenever he needed it. Said I play his game and the weight disappears." Enrique laughed bitterly. "Asshole actually said he'd give me back my product and send me on my way."

Jace frowned. "You know he's not a cop, right?"

"She's right, Enrique. All he does now is train cops."

Enrique slumped. "And hustle drug dealers."

Rory stood to go. "We're good here. You don't have to worry about us again." She winked. "Not on this stuff. But if I see you, I'll pull your ass over for anything I can find so don't carry in Zachary County, dig?"

He snorted. "I dig, *chica.*"

Then Rory softened. "And listen, I'm sorry I made the crack with Pancho. It was stupid. All a man has is his name."

"Thanks." He looked at Jace. "Speaking of names, what's up with yours? You know she's in the Bible, right? Chopping off heads or some shit."

"Yeah, I heard that somewhere."

Chapter Thirty-Eight

Just after noon, Preacher surprised her when he put his hands on her shoulders. "You find him?"

"Not yet."

"I appreciate what you doing, babydoll, but you don't have to do this. Robinson is my burden, not yours."

The wizened old black man in the bodega she'd just left, whose deep purple skin had long since gone a gray shade of tanned leather, had shaken his head sadly when she presented Robinson's picture. He had wanted to help and it obviously hurt that he couldn't.

"I'm sorry," he had said. "But if I see him—" He pointed to the slip of paper with Jace's number pinned to the wall behind the register. "I'll call you."

After getting a few hours' troubled sleep, she had gone looking for Robinson by herself. Preacher had found her after the fourth store. "I saw you walking with that Robinson look on your face."

She tried a grin but knew it fit badly. "I had a feeling about today. Today might be the day."

Preacher nodded. "Might be. Speaking of them nasty ol' burdens, how yours doing?"

"Not a one."

He chuckled. "You are a terrible liar, babygirl. You're gonna hafta do better than that if you want to make it as a cop."

With a second's hesitation, she said, "If I want to, I guess."

There was no breeze and the sweat ran between Jace's breasts and down the backs of her legs. It was hot and the sun tore them down like a wrecking ball against old brick.

"One time," Preacher said. "I was preaching up a storm out in East Texas. Man called Verbal showed up. Had the spirit like I ain't seen before or since." Preacher lowered his voice. "He was crazy, you wanna know the truth. Him wishing his dead wife back to life." Preacher rolled his eyes around like marbles. "Crazy as a piss-house mouse."

He said it so earnestly and so unselfconsciously that Jace thought she might get misty. Robinson had been dead for years but still she and Preacher—usually just Preacher—searched. Preacher shuffled endless papers around in his briefcase, calling it Robinson's homework, and trying to keep it up to date so his son could graduate. Robinson had died when he was thirteen but Preacher still believed in his life.

"After the revivaling was done for the night all I wanted to do was get some shut-eye and start fresh the next morning. But he came to my tent and asked could he have a word."

"Yeah? What was his word?"

"Killing. Said the next sunrise would be his last. Said he couldn't control his head. Had no idea what was going on in it most of the time. Black out and come to and ever'body—family and whatnot—would be scared to death. Crying and carrying on and telling him about dark things he just didn't remember."

"What did you do?"

"What I'm best at, babygirl? Talking. I wanted to take me a bath and eat and sleep, but I talked to that boy all night long. We talked about God and Satan and love and hate. We talked about what man's supposed to be in the eyes of God and what man thinks he's supposed to be and what man actually is. We talked about sanity and consciousness and the like. He knew his mind was leaving and I think the knowing was tough on him.

"But the worst was his family. They were so scared of him they asked him to leave, and that tore him up, Jace. It was killing him as surely as the cancer took your Grapa.

"I talked and talked and worked myself right up into a sweat. My clothes were dripping. My socks were even wet. I knew that man had a gun in his pocket and I knew he had a bullet in that gun with his own name on it and damned if I wanted that man's blood on my heart. I was going to convince him that life would be okay and he ought to see it through to God's conclusion.

"I thought I made it, too. That sun came up and when he saw it, he grinned and shook my hand and gave me a hug like what Robinson used to give me.

" 'That's a beautiful sunrise, ain't it?' " he asked me.

"I told him it was and we looked at it for a few minutes.

"Then he walked himself into the middle of that river and used that gun. His body just floated away."

"Preacher," Jace said. "That's—"

"But before he did it." Preacher steamrolled her like she hadn't said a word. "He looked at me and smiled and yelled out a thanks." His gray eyes came to Jace. "That was the best I was going to do for that man, Jace. He made up his mind to die but I gave him something to hold while he did it. I gave him back the world, let him know his family was going to be okay and that they were going to miss him, sure, but at least they wouldn't be scared no more."

Jace was horrified. "That's what you told him?"

"That's what he got from our talking. He got what he needed but I couldn't save him. You understand what I'm saying?"

Jace wasn't sure she did.

"I couldn't save him and I knew it and that made me want to be anywhere but in that tent with him. But I stayed there and did it because I am a minister. You think I wanted to be sitting there, working on a lost cause?"

"You?" Jace said. "You are all about lost causes, Preacher."

He shook his head. "That ain't my point, little girl. My point is that you ain't gonna save everybody but you try anyway. And in that trying, you gonna save more than you lose."

"What if, while I'm trying to save some people, other people are trying to kill me?"

"Well . . . better make sure you got more bullets than them."

"I'm not sure I'm interested in saving everybody."

"Ever'body? Hell, no. You only got one person you got to save."

"Who? And don't say myself because not only is that too melodramatic, it's bullshit."

"I'm the Preacher of Lost Causes when it comes to you, but that ain't who I'm talking about." He turned her toward him and gently touched the tattoo at the base of her neck. "Her."

Then he turned them both home toward the Sea Spray.

Chapter Thirty-Nine

That afternoon, a few hours before her shift, Jace talked to the monkeys.

Salazar's revelation that Badgett was trying to kill her made her cry all the way home. Without a word, Rory had put her to bed. In spite of the summer heat, she'd crammed Jace beneath the comforter and turned the air conditioning down as far as it would go.

She's cocooning me. This veteran of the jail, who desperately wants to be out on the road in a shiny marked car and has put in part-time applications at every small-town police department in the county, is making certain I'm safe and secure and that I know I'm safe and secure.

Rory had also saved Wonder Woman. With some clear tape she'd dug out of a drawer, she had repaired and rehung the poster.

"So I can feel someone standing over me protecting me?"

Embarrassed, Rory said, "Chick who whips out a .38 to blast the shit out of a truck and goes toe-to-toe with Royce in medical don't need protecting."

"No, that's not—"

"And that's just the physical stuff, Jace. Don't forget how many cops to whom you've said: 'This is what's right. Love me or hate me, this is what's right.' " She shook her head. "I think you've found your jail *huevos*. When I grow up I want to be you." Rory sat heavily on the bed and wiped a tear from Jace's face.

"You remember what you said my first night? That if I needed help you were there for me? And that if you didn't come, it was because you were already dead?"

"I say that to all the girls. I didn't really mean it."

"Shut up a second. I just wanted to tell you how much that meant to me."

Rory had stood and swallowed visibly. "I'm getting a little nervous with all this squishy girlie stuff, okay? I'm a cop, you're a cop, we have to be tough."

Jace grabbed Rory's hand and said, in a falsetto, "But, honey, can't we be tough while we have our nails done? Please?"

Rory shook her head. "These attempts at humor are just sad."

Then she was gone and after a nap, Jace had come to the zoo. Now, leaving the animals behind and nearing her car, she saw a man sitting on the hood. "Chafee."

"Yeah." Standing, he offered a hand.

"I've seen you around." She shook his hand. "Salome."

He chuckled. "Like I didn't know that."

Chafee was a dead-shift road deputy. Big and blond with a face so sharp she could have chipped diamonds with it. She'd never spoken to him before.

"What can I do for you?" She looked around but they were alone.

"Don't worry, I'm not Royce."

"I guess word's gotten around."

He handed her a manila envelope. "I belong to Badgett's CT group."

"Total Force." She backed up, balled her hands, and set her feet.

"Whoa." Chafee raised his hands, palms out. "I misspoke. I

used to belong."

She kept herself ready for battle. "Give it up for Lent?"

"Salome, I know what you've found . . . at least, I think I know."

Jace opened the envelope and pulled out a Total Force newsletter. Reynolds had been reading one the night Thomas died.

"Comes out every month," Chafee said, his hands wrapped around his thick upper arms.

Jace flipped through it and stopped on a page stuck in the middle. It said "Members Only" at the top. "Lots of names." She recognized some of them. Thomas, Stimson, Hewson, Rosely, the others Delilah had mentioned.

Massie.

"What is this?"

Chafee shrugged. "Just names, Salome, nothing more. At least as far as is explained to us. It's just a page we can access. But run those names and see how many are no longer with us."

"Dead."

"Yeah."

Some of those names would match those on the list Ezrin had given her at the park. "It tells you guys who to watch for. These guys get arrested in the wrong jail and they'll end up dead."

"They're bad people, Salome." But his voice was strained. "Predators and perverts."

"Not all of them."

"Yeah." The word leaked out of him. "I know. Stimson and a guy in Davis County. Everybody else has some kind of sex crime attached to them."

"How do you know that?"

"Because I ran them, okay? I bribed Rosalie in records to do some work for me."

"Why?"

Eventually, his gaze settled on her. His hands dropped to his sides and he stood before her, symbolically open to her questions. "Because this is wrong. Whatever it was at the beginning, it's garbage now. Look, no one ever told us to target child molesters, okay? No one ever said that."

"Subtext, then."

"The students are all taught how to irritate an inmate, but it's all done in the context of a jail investigation. If you need to make someone uncomfortable—for whatever legit reason—Badgett shows you how to do it."

"But at the same time, he keeps talking about predators. Drain on society and all the rest." Her phone rang, Thelonious Monk's "Straight, No Chaser." She ignored it.

Chafee nodded. "He constantly yapped about rapists. Now, I don't have a problem screwing with molesters, Salome, understand that; and I have no problem with the state killing them officially. But I do have a problem with us killing them extra-judicially and then blaming them for the killing. That's not—" His face suffused with anger.

"That's not what we are," Jace said.

"It's not what I am, anyway."

"Explain the land to me."

"What land?"

"All the land Badgett's buying."

"I have no idea what you're talking about."

"Stimson owned some. Badgett bought it from Stimson's mom after Stimson was killed."

He shook his head. "I'm sorry, Salome, I have no idea. He never talked about land, just about fighting and predators, that's his main thing."

"But not his only thing."

Chafee shook his head. "No, he wants to be Blackwater . . .

DynCorp, maybe. Training cops all over the world, but also providing security and terrorism consulting and counterinsurgency solutions and I don't know what all."

"Why?"

Chafee shrugged. "Maybe because he got tossed off the force. Maybe he's pissed at the industry."

"Wants to prove he's better than those who threw him out."

"That's all psychology above my pay grade. But he's got an entire advisory board feeding the dream. Chiefs and sheriffs and a Ranger or two and some FBI and some military."

If Total Force had ideas beyond ground fighting, then perhaps they believed they needed multiple compounds. Maybe that explained the odd locations of the land better than some trade highway that was never going to be built. And maybe it was someone else on his board calling the appraisal company. "So why did you come to me?"

"Your investigation."

She shook her head. "Captain Ezrin's, not mine."

"And he's getting a copy of this, but—" He shrugged. "You before him, far as I'm concerned."

"Why?"

He sucked his lip. "He's a Ranger."

She smiled. "I've no problems with the Rangers."

" 'Cause you're a worm, you don't know any better yet. Take all that to Dillon or Sheriff Bukowski or Captain Ezrin or whoever. Make sure you put my name in your report. I don't care about the glory or the credit, but if it goes bad, you shouldn't be the only one taking the weight."

"Whoa," she said, trying to exaggerate her look of horror. "No one said anything about writing a report."

"Worm." But he said it with a grin.

★ ★ ★ ★ ★

It was another message from Bibb.

"A copper brought it. A gallon jug. When he was in medical. Sacco. Another of Badgett's guys. He brews for fun in his garage or something."

Chapter Forty

Headed home, her phone rang. She answered and Rory's voice mocked her.

"Since you were doing things on your own, so could I. But since I'm attentive to my friends' concerns—"

"You have friends?"

"Since I'm attentive, I chose to spend the day contacting a few people and getting some dusty records pulled."

Now Jace was interested. "Queen again?"

"I don't have time for sex right now. First of all, do you know about Badgett's Board of Advisors?"

"Yeah."

"Oh." Rory sounded deflated. "Well, how about this: Badgett doesn't actually own majority stock in Total Force. On the original incorporation papers, he has only a quarter of the company. Various board members have the difference up to 49 percent, and someone else owns the rest."

"Someone else owns majority stock?"

"But I don't know who. I'm sure it's someone on his board."

"You've been talking to people about this?"

"Yes, Jace, I've talked to people."

"Who?" Jace tightened her grip on the phone.

"Well, I started with James Evans at Ector County."

"Your sergeant friend . . . the shooting expert."

"Yep. He was in Total Force way back at the beginning. Hasn't been a member for a few years. He thought Badgett was the only guy. I had Delilah call her uncle. He lives in Austin and knows his way around the state offices."

Jace signaled, turned along the old Highway 80 frontage road. Downtown rose to her right. "Okay, interesting but ultimately useless."

"Maybe. But I also know that the largest bit of land on that marked map you got from your Jewish-Arab drug dealer buddy is owned by a guy named Het. And Het's last name is?" Rory waited.

Jace thought for a moment. "Massie."

"Give the copper the Christmas turkey. Lars Massie's father."

Jace blew a breath as she passed a Zack City PD squad car. The officers inside looked bored. "That's why they're pushing him. Badgett wants that land. I'd bet Badgett has made an offer or two and been rebuffed."

Rory laughed. " 'Rebuffed'? Well, even if ol' Het wanted to sell, maybe take in a few topless cuties in Cancun, he couldn't."

"Too old for sex?"

"Okay, two reasons. There are liens on the land."

Jace's mouth dried. "Total Force?"

"Wow, you ought to be a cop. Seems ol' Het is in the beginning stages of Alzheimer's, but if he ever took the lienholders to court, he'd probably win. The liens are completely bogus, sister."

Jace took a deep breath. Every few years, Texans who believed any and all governments—except those they set up themselves—were illegal authorities placed illegal liens on various elected officials' residences or bank accounts. The elected officials were always able to get out from under the liens, but sometimes it was tough. If Hetfield senior was suffering from Alzhiemer's, he might be beyond helping himself.

"Bibb's voyeurism has come in handy," Jace said. Quickly, she explained the false alcohol charge.

"Man, oh, man," Rory said. "They're framing him neat and

tidy, aren't they?"

"According to Deputy Chafee, that's what they do."

"Big, beautiful Ronny?"

"He was waiting for me when I left the zoo." Jace filled her in on the details. "I'm looking at the list right now, Rory. The first eight names are all dead guys. I think Badgett is going down the list, checking them off name by name. Lars Massie's name is next up."

"We gotta get this stopped."

"It's not just here, Rory, it's happening all over the state. Ezrin gave me a list. It's got names going back five years and they're all over the place."

Through the phone, Jace heard Rory breathing heavily. "We can't do anything about that, Jace, we can only deal with here and now. Did you ask beautiful Ronny about Stimson's land?"

"Yeah. He looked honestly confused."

Jace's watch gave her two hours before going on duty. "Okay, when we get on tonight, we go straight to Dillon. They're not going after Massie tonight and—"

"You don't think?"

Jace shook her head as downtown fell behind her. "They haven't pushed him hard enough yet and as near as I can tell, he hasn't done anything like lashing out."

"Yeah, but Reynolds made the first move, remember?"

"It'll be fine, Rory. But it's our first thing, okay? We can't do this by ourselves anymore. If Dillon doesn't believe us, we'll go to Sheriff Bukowski."

"Yeah. That's good. Okay, sister, I'll see you in a couple."

Jace snapped her phone closed and within ten minutes, she spotted the blue and white Sea Spray sign. After parking, she glanced at the pool. This time, the slight breeze was coming from the right direction. The water moved right to left as it had all her life.

"It's about damned time," she said.

Chapter Forty-One

Her door was open.

This time not the friendly face of Rory, but the forced smile of Will Badgett.

He leaned against her window with the last of the falling sun behind him.

"What are you doing here?" She stopped with the narrow expanse of the living room between them.

"You've got that look on your face, Deputy."

"What look is that?"

He smirked. "Your skin's clammy. Your heart's pounding. Your mouth is dry. You're scared to death."

"Of big, bad you?" She forced a laugh and tried to look casual while moving through her living room and cutting the distance between them by half.

"Good. Push me back, don't let me have any of this space. Nice tactical move. Establish primacy."

"Shut up with the Academy bullshit and get out of here."

Badgett held up a small box. One corner was darker than the rest.

She knew it was blood. "What's left of Mr. Salazar?"

For an instant, surprise flashed across Badgett's face. "Very good. Sadly, he died in a car crash. Ran off the road near Stanton. The car rolled and crushed him."

"Ran off the road or got run off the road?"

Badgett shrugged. "Doesn't matter." He set the box on the

coffee table. "Take a look . . . if you don't believe me."

She snorted. "Don't believe you? About death? You're all about death."

Badgett pulled a cigarette from his shirt pocket.

"Don't smoke in here, asshole."

Watching her closely, he pulled a lighter and snapped a flame to life.

Jace stepped forward. "Apparently you didn't hear me. Don't smoke in here." In one quick move, she snatched the cigarette and hit his wrist hard enough that he dropped the lighter to the floor.

"Those feel like jail balls."

"We're not in the jail, we're in my apartment. That means, when I kill you, I'm legal and square."

His booming laugh iced her heart. The sound alone nearly made her flee, but the look in his eyes—along with powerful hands that came up to his chest in an aggressive posture—nearly made her throw up. *This is wrong. You can't deal with this guy alone, he will eat you alive. He has killed people.*

Badgett, his stance somehow both bored and alert, opened the box. He pulled out a brown-skinned ear. Holding it so she could see it perfectly, he circled through the apartment, his back contemptuously to her, until he came to a picture of Jace and Gramma. He pressed his finger against Gramma's face.

Jumping over the coffee table, Jace grabbed Badgett from behind with her right arm, taking him around the neck. She planted her right foot forward, her left back, and tried to toss him over her hip to the floor.

Instead, he twisted and slipped his left hand over Jace's head. Then he jabbed two fingers into her nose. When he pulled backward, a sharp pain rocketed through her. She released him and stumbled to the floor.

"Decent try," he said. "Maybe, if you'd taken some of my

classes, you'd have known what was coming."

"You keep your hands off my Gramma, you understand me?"

"Is that who that is? I had no idea."

Crawling, Jace backed away until there was enough room to stand. "Are you kidding me? You're about as subtle as a two-by-four to the head."

"Subtlety is not one of my strong points."

"Your recruits use that same two-by-four. Make the inmates crazy. Make them strike first. Then an officer can defend himself and not have those pesky legal problems. I wouldn't have singled out child molesters but maybe you thought there was a nobility there that I'm just too stupid to see."

"There are so many things you are too stupid to see, Deputy."

"Enlighten me."

"Enlighten you, Deputy?" He spat the last word. "You have no idea the war we're fighting. All of us—all of us in law enforcement—have been emasculated. The police chiefs and the sheriffs and prosecutors and judges and everyone else who is scared to death of lawsuits and who'd rather plead something down to an easy win than fight the harder battle. They've stolen our soul, woman, and no one will let us take it back."

"Oh, my God. You're a walking cliché-fest. How about something a bit more original or more nuanced. No one has taken your soul. If anything, you gave it away."

"Believe what you want. But remember: I did nothing wrong."

"Zachary County and Thomas. Dead by a jailer who took your class. Ector County and Stimson. Ditto. Sterling County and Hewson. Gaines County and Rosely. Lubbock County and Howard County and Davis County."

He grinned again but she thought she saw a hairline crack in it. "You know dick. All I've done is train cops. Those cops have used that training to save themselves. You have squat."

"Maybe. But what happens if I compare the Texas Rangers'

list of the dead to your list?"

"What list?"

"The online list."

His eyes narrowed.

"One of your acolytes provided it to me."

"That's—that's not for public—you shouldn't have that."

"And yet, I do." She took a step and felt a wave of glee when he backed up. "They weren't all kiddie-diddlers. Don't give me the bullshit face. Some were innocent and you know it."

"I don't know anything like that."

"Yeah? That's a pretty good coincidence, then, Total Force buying so much land from so many recently dead inmates."

This time, he was actually surprised. "What?"

"You left a trail, Badgett. Every time you hired the appraisal company or filed a new deed. You've got paper everywhere." She swallowed, remembered Rory's lesson about not giving too much away in an interview, but plunged ahead. "Nine parcels?"

He stared at her, smug. "Bad information, Deputy. Better check your sources. Total Force has bought three parcels. We're building for the future. Too bad you don't have one."

In spite of her fear, she laughed. "Three? Check *your* sources, Badgett. Nine and counting." She frowned, theatrically puzzled. "But it's someone else from Total Force who's been making the phone calls."

Badgett frowned. His jaw ground furiously during his silence. He blinked repeatedly and had to work at keeping his gaze on her. "Fuck off."

"That the best you can do?" Jace laughed. "The last refuge of those who have nothing else to say. What's the matter? You suddenly realize someone else is calling the shots? The majority shareholder? The man who owns your company but lets you run around playing law enforcement trainer?"

"It's a lie."

She shrugged and held her phone out. "Let's call the appraisal company. They're in Dallas but they have a man in Zack City. Plays poker. Likes his Jack Daniel's in Dr Pepper. He'll bring the records. Who's in charge, Badgett? Who owns your company?"

"I own my company. *I* say what's what in my company. *I* am the director."

"Whatever you say. Whatever it takes for you to sleep." Sneering, she put her cell phone away. "Thought you were smarter than that. Didn't you realize hiring those appraisals would leave a trail?" Then she understood. "You didn't think anyone would check. You thought you were free and clear. Your Total Force disciples would keep their mouths shut, if they even knew, which most didn't."

"That's crap. I'm a good man, Deputy."

"Maybe, once, a long time ago. I heard there were some commendations back in San Antonio. Four or five. But then you start tossing suspects around, get a few excessive force complaints, and suddenly you're unemployed."

"I quit that force. Administration wouldn't let us do what we needed to do."

"You got fired. Then there was that ill-fated three years with the Texas Department of Criminal Justice. Hell, you never even made it to the big joints. Never got to the glory of Huntsville." She shook her head sadly but kept her eyes moving around the apartment looking for something to use against him. His anger kept his eyes on her.

"And then no one else—in the entire state—would hire you. Pretty big state to be unemployed in. So you had to reinvent yourself as a control tactics instructor and now it's even better than copping because you train the cops. How does it work that you guys started killing pedophiles—"

"I've never killed anyone."

"That's bullshit and we both know it. You're just good at covering the bodies. You go from killing pedophiles to training people to kill pedophiles to leaning on confused old men and then killing their sons to get worthless land?"

His head bobbed side to side while he backed up a step. "That's crap. I have no idea what—or who—you're talking about."

"Tell me about this control tactics empire. Gonna control the world with it? Terrorism and counterterrorism and God knows what. It'd be funny if it weren't so pathetic. Did they emasculate you that badly, Badgett? San Antonio PD and TDJC? Did the firings get that deep into your psyche?"

He spoke quietly as he set Salazar's ear back in the box. "You know shit, woman. Running around playing at being a deputy and you don't know shit. You're so unsure of yourself you haven't even told anyone else this, have you?"

Her hesitation, as quick as it was, gave him his answer. "I've talked to your majority stakeholder and they said—"

He shook his head dismissively. "You haven't talked to anybody. Too bad for you, I guess."

His move was instantaneous. With his right hand, he grabbed two of the fingers on her right hand, and snapped them like a teacher's stick of chalk. Pain bolted through Jace and tightened every nerve in her body.

When her legs crumpled, Badgett grabbed her. He kept her standing, his breath even and slow, by holding her by the neck.

"Snap snap. 'Your honor, I have no idea what happened. Must have been an inmate she pissed off. They got out and murdered her in her own apartment. Yes, sir, your Honor, it is a sad commentary on the state of this country.' Maybe that crazy old nigger boy will officiate at your funeral. You have no love for law enforcement, Deputy. You are not a cop. You are nothing."

She coughed as her pain grew. "I'm nothing . . . but . . . *I'm* employed. They wanted me . . . not you."

With a roar, he brought his knee hard into her gut, released her, and shoved her backward. She doubled over but somehow managed to stay upright while he yanked a cartridge from his pocket. When she tried to stand, white-hot spray hit her hard in the face.

Pepper spray.

She managed to turn her head and most of the blast hit her cheek. Some went into her mouth and burned like a blowtorch. She spat and tried to wipe the thick gel from her left eye.

His arm, tight as a band of steel, clamped around her neck. She tried to spin, as he had done, but he wedged her tightly against him. She felt his leg plant firmly in front of her and when he shoved and yanked at the same time, different directions, she fell.

There was so much in that fall. Not just gravity pulling her down against the coffee table, but Badgett slamming her against it. He gave her an extra shove, one of his hands hard around her throat squeezing the air from her while the other pressed against her nose and eyes to slam her into the tabletop. When she hit it headfirst, a thousand flashbulbs exploded in her head, leaving a black smear behind her eyes. Slashes of pain rocked her and she wondered, even as Badgett continued to push her to the ground, how much coffee table glass she had sticking from her. She hit the floor, his hands still on her, and felt her nose break.

He spit and the gob landed on her cheek and dripped into her open mouth along with her own blood.

She heard him kick something. A moment later, she heard the sound of her books and CDs sliding from the shelf.

She could do nothing to stop them from hitting her.

CHAPTER FORTY-TWO

Faxed pages spat out of Alley B's machine. They were copies of the articles of incorporation, filed in Austin, courtesy of Delilah's uncle. Rory stared and felt her eyes go wide. "Oh, man." She yanked her cell and dialed Jace. After the fifth ring, she left a message, assuming Jace was in the shower before work.

Chapter Forty-Three

Forty-five minutes later, when Jace was officially late for her shift, Gramma got a phone call. It wasn't from Sergeant Dillon or Rory. It was from a man who called himself Inmate Bobby.

"She's not here," the man said. "She didn't come to work and they're doing it." His voice was gravel, his words hurried and strained.

"Doing what? Who is this? What are you talking about?"

"Killing him," the man shouted. "They've moved him three times tonight and now they're shaking him down again. They're going to kill him before the night's over."

"How did you get this number?"

"Damn it, that doesn't matter. They're killing him. You've got to tell her."

Less than two minutes later, Gramma found Jace in a heap near her bookcase, covered in CDs and books and blood. A large bruise ran the width of her neck and blood had dried across her lips. Her nose was hidden beneath a blanket of dried blood and her left cheek was stained in orange.

"Jace? Jace!" Gramma knelt next to her granddaughter and her stomach clenched at the intense stench of chili peppers. Gently, but insistently, she helped Jace to sit before grabbing the phone.

"No," Jace said. "I'm fine." She said it easily and realized the pain, which had been like white-hot electricity dumped directly against her nerves, had subsided to a dull thud.

"Look at your face," Gramma said. "You're all cut up. I think your nose is broken."

"And my fingers." She held up a ruined hand.

"Oh God, Jace, you've got to call the police."

"I *am* the police," Jace said as she tried, one-handed, to scrub the orange pepper spray from her face as they'd shown her at the Academy. She trod gently around her nose. "I'll take care of it."

"You're *not* the police, you're a lost little girl who's playing at . . . I don't even know what . . . playing at something so you can have your Mama back. Jace, the woman is dead and nothing is going to bring her back. She is dead and your father is dead and Robinson is dead and Grapa is dead and nothing is going to bring them back. I mean, Jesus Christ, none of this ever happened until you started working there. Now you're beat up and bloody and criminals are calling here and—"

Jace froze. "What?"

Her tone icy, Gramma gave Jace the message. "He said his name was Inmate Bobby. Jace, I don't want inmates calling the hotel. Don't give out that number."

"I didn't," Jace said, already halfway out the door.

Chapter Forty-Four

It was nearly impossible to drive. Pain jacked through her hands and arms and joined the ache in her head and the chili pepper fire still on her tongue and in her eyes from the spray. She sped, she ran stop signs, and she blew through red lights, barely taking care to check for oncoming traffic. She tried to call the jail but found she couldn't drive and dial at the same time with only one useful hand.

Fishtailing into the parking lot, Jace screeched to a halt in front of the secured back door. She alternately jabbed the audio buzzer and hit the door and the only thing in her head was Massie. He was probably fighting for his life now, reeling from a series of blows or hanging over the edge of a railing.

Or he might already be dead.

She'd waited too long. She should have come directly to the jail, or called the sheriff. She should have done something. Again, it was like the first night. The problem was right in front of her and she'd done nothing.

"Damn it, Bibb, open the door."

Her voice boomed and the power she tried to put into it—the command presence—shredded her throat, as though someone slashed at her neck with razor blades.

"What the hell is going on out there? Salome?"

"Open the door."

Deep in the jail, Bibb pushed a button and Jace was rewarded with the click. She wrenched the door open and ran past the deputy on door duty, snatching his radio off the desk as she passed.

"Hey." He made a grab over the desk but missed. He immediately went to the phone.

"Salome." Bibb's voice came at her from both in front and behind, demanding attention every twenty feet where another speaker hung. "What's going on?"

"Lock it down," she screamed into the radio as she picked up the yellow line for Pod B. That was the last place she knew Massie to be. She rounded a corner and nearly crashed into a road deputy.

"Lock it down, Bibb." Jace held the radio between her torso and arm and keyed the mic with her left hand. She waved her battered right hand at the cameras.

—control from 401, what's going on—

—434 from 429, hey, you hearing all that noise? what's up—

"Lock what down?"

"Everything. The entire place."

The radio seemed to explode then. Voices from everywhere, all talking at once, turning the airwaves and the hallway through which she ran into a nightmare of gibberish and chaos.

—lock down? I didn't hear the alarm—

—control from medical, I've got an ambulance on the way, lock it down but keep my outside gate open—

—I'm by myself here—

—control from 459, roger the lock down in A Pod—

Why did that voice sound familiar? The radio was a din of voices. Why did that single one rise above the others? It stuck in her brain and she realized it was the only voice initiating her call for a lockdown.

—all call from control: there is no lockdown. Belay the lockdown—

"Salome, what are you talking about?" Bibb asked.

"They're killing him." She stared at the cameras as she ran, trying to give Bibb a reason to trust her. "Do it, Sergeant."

After a moment's hesitation, the world detonated. The alarm began shrieking and then Thomas was in her vision. He was at the stairs and against the wall and falling—endlessly—until he died over and over against the floor.

It didn't matter how quickly she ran, it wasn't fast enough. Her nose howled and she still couldn't breathe well through the remnants of the pepper spray. But she ran as hard as she could, the rhythm of her feet against the concrete like jazz drummer Art Blakey pushing his group, pushing and pushing until they were moving so fast the music became a blur of notes and colors.

—all call from control: the facility is in lockdown until further notice. Lockdown until further notice—

The radio went into lockdown silence as Jace rounded another corner and heard the confusion in Bibb's silence. He was on the phone, no doubt calling Dillon or jail administrator Lieutenant Traylor.

"Get Adam 1," Jace said. "And find Massie. What pod is he in?"

"Salome," Bibb said. "Stop. Stop running. That's an order."

She ignored it. Where was Massie? He had been in B Pod. But she knew they had moved him, Inmate Bobby had said so. Not to D without a disciplinary hearing, probably not back to E with the elderly. That would categorize him as less of a threat. No, they'd want him where he could be considered a serious threat. Not medical because it was recorded all the time. Obviously not female.

That meant A Pod.

As she ran, her teeth clenched. Of course it was A. This had all started in A Pod, with Thomas and Reynolds. There was no way it wouldn't end in A Pod, with another dead inmate.

"Where is Massie?" she screamed again.

When Bibb didn't answer, she changed her course, from the

yellow line to the blue. Another turn and a long hallway and she'd be at A Pod.

"Find Massie," she called. "Get him in lockdown. Don't let anyone near him except Dillon."

"Salome," Bibb said. "What happened to you? Tell me I didn't lock down because you're drunk. You're covered in puke."

"OC spray. Badgett did this. He tried to kill me in my apartment. He broke my nose. And my fingers."

Dillon's voice was measured over the speakers from the control room. "Salome, what are you doing? You stay out of any and all pods. Stop where you are and wait for me. Do you understand that?"

"Badgett is going to kill Massie."

"Badgett isn't even here, and Massie's in A Pod. He's in his cell and he's fine."

"Who's the jailer?"

"Royce."

The voice she'd recognized. Royce had been angry at her because she had gone to Ezrin with Reynolds. And when he'd jumped her in medical, she'd seen the tattoo that matched the Total Force logo. But Royce was a second shift grunt. What was he doing here on dead shift and how did he happen to be in the same pod as Massie?

Jace stopped running and stared into one of the cameras. "Sergeant, listen to me. Get someone else in there with Massie and Royce before Royce kills him. Sergeant Dillon, the blood in medical was mine. He attacked me."

"Salome, I know that. He's already been scheduled for a disciplinary hearing."

"Sergeant, please. I'm going to be fired anyway. If I'm wrong, no problem. But if I'm right, you'll have another dead inmate."

When she got no answer, Jace ran. Chances were good Massie was already dead, regardless of what Dillon said.

"A-adam outer," she said.

Bibb did not open it for her.

"Damn it, Sergeant, open the door."

—let her in—

Dillon's voice. On the radio and obviously on the move.

The pop snapped and the door swung open. After closing the door behind her, Jace ran to the inner door. It stayed closed.

—do not open that door—

Again, Dillon's voice.

"Damn it!" Jace banged against the inner door. Dillon had effectively locked her down. She keyed her radio. "Sergeant, please, I've got to get to Massie."

—Salome, no you don't. Massie is—

—dead, sir—

Everything stopped. Jace didn't even hear the lockdown alarm as she pressed her face against the glass in the inner door. Royce stood on the first tier, Massie's body slumped at his feet. Royce's face was bloody and he picked a loose tooth from his mouth before tossing it to the floor and keying up his mic.

—he refused lockdown. He came at me. Had to defend myself—

—control—

—I didn't hear a word about it, Dillon—

—no time to call in, Sergeant Dillon, it happened too fast. He shanked me before I realized it—

Massie was dead and Royce was covered in blood. His face and his arm, obviously cut with a blade. When Royce lifted his gaze, he found Jace and flashed her a slow grin. His eyes hard on hers, he keyed his radio.

—Deputy Salome is here, sir. She almost made it to help me. Can we get her a commendation for trying so hard?—

Jace pounded the inner door.

—I will obviously not touch anything else until the techs get here. No need to call the ERTs, this is over—

When a door behind her opened, Jace assumed it was Dillon coming in to fire her. She slumped and tore her gaze from Massie.

"Maybe not completely over."

Badgett closed the door. "Had to hustle in there when you busted your ass into the jail and called for a lockdown."

—how the fuck did that happen—

Badgett grinned at Bibb's wonder. "They really need to watch the outer doors better."

—405 from control . . . what's going on—

—405—Badgett is in the go-between with Salome. I don't know how he got into the facility, I never saw him—

—goddamn it, get someone in there. ERTs get to A Pod. Isolate everybody. Hang on, Salome, we're coming—

"The cavalry," Badgett said. He shook his head in admiration. "I thought you were dead. Guess I misjudged."

"Follow the subject all the way down. First thing they taught us in CT. Put him down. Make sure he stays down."

"I thought I did. Guess not well enough."

"You thought you could clean this up. You thought, with me dead, there'd be no one else who knew what was what. Change a few paper trails and erase a few others. Kill Massie, put the squeeze on his father, like you did Stimson's mother, get your land and cash out."

"You ruined it."

—B-boy Pod secure—

—D-david Pod secure—

Badgett's breath became a static charge as anger flashed across his face.

"It's done, Badgett." Jace took a deep, painful breath. "Can't you smell it? It's all gone bad and it stinks to the ends of the earth. And you were wrong."

"About?"

"The slow bleed isn't the molesters, Badgett. It's you. Cops like you and your guys. You're why no one trusts us, you stupid son of a bitch." Something sparked in his eyes and she tried to unobtrusively set her feet. She wasn't going to get surprised this time.

He laughed easily. "Getting ready, Deputy? Fight or flight?"

Her voice was a whisper. "Fight."

—control from medical, we're secure but my ambo—

—female Pod secure—

"We shouldn't be fighting at all. You should be dead."

"Follow the subject down, Badgett. Basic lesson."

"Yeah, well, I won't make that mistake again, will I?" With a dry chuckle, he glanced out the outer door window. There were no officers there yet but both knew they were coming. "You are right about one thing, though: this is all over." He took a deep breath. "So there's nothing left but you and me."

—Jace—

"And whoever owns your company, Badgett. Whoever's been pulling your strings. They've been feeding you the names, haven't they? You kill the inmates and they get the land. Who is it, Badgett? Who left the trail that led me to you?" She lowered her voice. "Who ruined you, Badgett?"

—Jace—

Rory was frantic and it surprised and touched Jace at the same time. Rory wanted to come for her but she was locked down just like everyone else. She would not come for Jace. This time, even though Jace was surrounded by cops, Jace was on her own.

I'm prepared for it. I will see him when he comes at me and I'll know what he's going to do and I'll see which direction he sets his feet to telegraph his intention and I'll be just fine.

"Who is it?"

"Kiss my butt, bitch."

In the end, Jace saw nothing. Badgett was on her as suddenly as Grapa, sick and dying, had winked and emptied his lungs. Badgett's left hand wrapped around her broken right fingers and squeezed. She screamed as he spun her around and slammed her against the wall.

—shit . . . 10-78 A-adam go-between—

Bibb's panic was thick as Badgett slipped an arm around her throat and bent her backward. Trying to counter it, she spun to his right side and tried to grab his nose over his head. She wasn't tall enough so she began hitting him on the back of the head, then tried to snake her hand around the side of his face.

Even as he turned away from her, she got two fingers inside his mouth. Curling them, she tried to rip a hole in his cheek but failed because her fingers were wet. He laughed.

Somewhere in the distance, exhaustion reared its head. It was small and bleak and she knew that from this moment, it would only get bigger.

They'll get here first.

Badgett tried to turn her back around to get at her airway. She fought that and instead turned more into him. Then she slammed her knee hard into his genitalia.

Grunting, he tightened his grip, which had the effect of pushing her closer to the floor and took away her ability to knee him again. He grabbed her broken fingers again, slammed her against the wall and drew her right arm high up behind her back. Biting back the pain, Jace stomped on his left instep. If she'd been wearing her work boots he might have faltered more. As it was, the soft-soled sneakers didn't do much damage.

But Badgett did lean to his left a little. With him off-balance, she pried them both away from the wall. A few inches, using her arm as a crowbar, then a few inches more. When there was enough room, she raised up, planted both feet on the wall, and shoved with everything she had.

When they stumbled backward, she drove her left elbow deep into his ribs. This time, Badgett did notice her strike. Her right arm and hand were suddenly free as he slumped left. She twisted and sank the fingers of her left hand deep into the flesh between his ribs. *Pull his ribs out, she thought. Pull them right the fuck through his skin.*

This time, sucking on the pain, Badgett fell right. Jace followed him down even as he clamped his arm onto her kneading fingers. When they hit the ground, she lost her hold and he twisted behind her. He wrapped a leg around her thighs and pulled her legs toward him. Then he put an arm around her neck and pulled her head backward, effectively bending her around his bulk like the wood of a bow, bent further and further by a taut string.

How long could she fight? At the Academy, they'd told her that if she were involved in a fight, it might go thirty or forty seconds. One instructor said it might go a minute or two or three. *How long has it been?* Long enough that her breath came in ragged gasps and her sides hurt from exertion.

The alarm shrieked and people yelled over the radio but now she couldn't hear anything except the blood pounding in her ears and Badgett's controlled, steady breath.

This was all he had left to him now, this measure of retaliation against her. He was, in this moment, nothing more than a mall shooter or a kid who walks into his chemistry class and takes out the teacher and half the students and realizes there is nothing left but death.

Don't let him kill you, Jace. Don't let this smear of a human kill you in this horrible place. If you're going to die, make it on your own terms. Not in this place, not at his hands.

With her broken hand, she reached backward until she felt his belt. Then she reached further down until she found his penis and testicles. She grabbed, barking at the blackness sliding into her vision, and squeezed until she heard her broken bones grinding together.

Badgett howled but kept pulling her backward. She jerked her arm up, taking his phallus with her as much as she could just as a loud metallic pop broke through the ceaseless alarm.

And then she could breathe.

And then she couldn't as an ERT shield pinned her to the floor.

"Again with this?" Jace asked as she slumped, sucked in huge gulps of air, and let the blackness take her down.

Chapter Forty-Five

At night, on the top floor of the Zachary City Memorial Hospital, it was possible to believe you could see into forever. At least, it was when you were full of pain medication and there was just enough moon to give the darkened sky some shadows in between the tall buildings.

Why in hell, Jace wondered, *would anyone name a hospital memorial? I don't want to think about anything "memorial" when some surgeon's working on me.*

Twenty-five hours ago, two paramedics and Rory's "big, beautiful Ronny" had loaded her aboard an ambulance. Then she was out and had slept through, apparently, everything. She woke up with a bandage on her nose, her fingers in heavy tape, and medicine as thick as sludge in her veins.

A bevy of doctors had come to see her—including the entire medical staff from the jail—and said she was going to be fine, though they were keeping her a day or so to monitor the concussion Badgett had given her against the coffee table and floor of her apartment. If she had no problems tonight, she'd go home first thing in the morning to begin an unknown number of weeks of enforced recuperation.

But before she passed out, while her face was jammed against the floor by an ERT shield, she laughed. A few feet from her, Badgett also had his face jammed against the floor by a shield. He was curled into a fetal position, cupping his balls and squeezing out a face full of tears.

Sheriff Bukowski strolled past the open outer door, stopped, and nodded. He held a cigar between two fingers but it was unlit. She returned the nod and then he was gone, lost in a blur of Sergeant Dillon and Big Carol.

Dillon's face was concerned and angry and maybe a little relieved. "Salome? Salome? Don't go out on me, kid. Don't go. Uh . . . okay, go on out."

Then Big Carol, the nurse with the oddest natural odor Jace had ever smelled, shoved him aside and got in Jace's face to ask wildly unimportant questions. Jace welcomed the pain and blackness as they slipped raggedly over her.

"Good drugs?" Rory asked. She'd been part of a rotation of butts keeping the chair warm. Gramma, Preacher, and Rory. Hassan had passed, unnerved by all the officers coming and going.

"Not as good as your Skittles, probably."

"Probably."

"They find him yet?"

Rory shook her head, her eyebrows furrowed. "No."

Deputy Chief David Cornutt was the majority stakeholder; Rory had discovered it in the incorporation papers. When Jace's phone had gone to voice mail, Rory hadn't worried about it. She'd assumed Jace was getting ready for work. When she'd arrived at the jail, she'd hadn't gone to anyone because she wanted to do it with Jace. When the nightmare started, Rory had run through the hallways until she found the sheriff. Together, they'd gone to Cornutt's office. A file cabinet drawer was open but empty. Four road deputies arrived at his house seventeen minutes later and he was gone. Thus far, no one had found him.

"Is he gone?" Jace asked.

"Yeah. Had a stash of cash. Passport to Mexico all ready to go."

"For his vacation."

In the silence that descended on them, her room door opened and closed. In the dim light emanating from the empty nurse's desk, Ezrin eyed her from beneath his cowboy hat. His plastic drink sword peeked out from the side of his hatband. "Deputy."

"Ranger."

"Uh . . . I think I hear my phone ringing," Rory said.

"I don't hear anything," Jace said.

"Uh . . . yeah, it's going to ring." Quickly, she left the room.

Ezrin chuckled, but the sound died lonely. "I brought you something." He sidled up to her bed but didn't sit in the visitor's chair. He held up a brown paper bag. "A Corona and a link sandwich from Brooks."

Hesitantly, she laughed. When she realized how well the painkillers were doing their job, she laughed a little harder. "Thanks."

"How'ya doing?"

"Well, I'm not dead."

"Good enough, I guess." He paused, obviously uncomfortable. "Deputy, I'm sorry about how this ended. To be honest, I thought it might."

"Funny, I don't remember you mentioning me getting hurt."

"No. I apologize for that."

The room fell silent. Jace watched him, feeling guilty for reveling in the man's discomfort. He rocked foot to foot and his eyes moved around the room.

"Pretty fancy room. County paying for it all?"

"Nobody's given me a bill yet so hope springs eternal. You badge the nurse to get in after visiting hours?"

"Hey, dial down the judgment. You badged the guy outside the club that night." He hesitated. "I wanted to say thank you, Deputy Salome. You did a helluva thing."

"Massie's dead."

Ezrin nodded. "Yeah, but word spread pretty quickly once Badgett was in custody. There were two—one in Deaf Smith County and one in Winkler County—who survived the night."

"But Cornutt got away."

Ezrin nodded. "We'll find him."

Aware that the sleeping meds were finally kicking in, Jace spoke carefully. Her lips felt thick as fat worms and just as slow. "You gave me a list of inmates in Texas. Is there another list? Maybe from around the country? Is there a list from Interpol?"

He shook his head. "No, Jace, there isn't. I don't believe this is going on around the country. I believe those kinds of cops are pretty rare." Then his face flushed. "But cops like you aren't. There are lots of them."

"I'm not sure I believe that."

"Ever been to Mexico? Or Venezuela? Nicaragua during the *Revolución*?"

"No."

"That's where we'd be if most cops weren't like you. Anyway, I just wanted to say thanks. And to tell you that you've got a pretty big IOU sitting on my back. Anything you need, you call." At the door, he turned back to her. "Oh, hey, I meant to tell you. I looked up your word. From the spelling bee. It doesn't fit you at all, worm."

Chapter Forty-Six

The next day, they released her. The Hot Five had been prepared to drive her home, but had been waved off at the last second. Now Jace sat, stiff and nervous, in Adam 1's car.

"Take a breath, Salome."

"Not going to happen, Sheriff."

He'd shown up a few minutes before her release. He'd asked, gently, if he could drive her home. Gramma had stared at him and in that stare, Jace had felt something pass between the two of them.

"How long have you known Gramma?" Jace asked.

He drove easily, well in control of the big county car. It had a police radio, which he kept tuned low, and a lights-and-siren package, and a shotgun secured above their heads. But none of the rest of the gear. No cage or extra cuffs. He didn't answer for two or three blocks. "For a while. Knew your grandfather, too. He was a good man. Never made as much playing with his oil as he should have."

"True."

Twenty minutes later, thick with silence, they arrived at the Sea Spray Inn. Sheriff Bukowski ushered her in and made sure she was comfortable on the couch. He lined up what seemed like thousands of pill bottles on a TV tray, along with a pitcher of water, and plugged her cell phone charger in next to the couch. He stood over her while she took a couple of pills to ease her pain and help her sleep, then fussed a bit more.

"I can do this myself, Sheriff, I'm not dead."

"Day's still young, I guess." He eyed her deeply. "You done good, Jace Salome. You're going to be good at this."

"Maybe someday."

"Someday."

Then he was gone, pulling her door absently shut behind him. It didn't quite latch and she debated getting up to close it. In the end, the pills kept her on the couch. She yawned, lay back, and was gone before she realized it.

Sometime later—it could have minutes or hours—he sat against the wall watching her. At first, climbing up from a deep sleep, she thought it was the sheriff. Then she thought it was Preacher. But when the man stood, she knew.

"Chief."

"I probably shouldn't be here."

"How long?"

"Early this morning."

She blinked. He'd been here when Gramma was cleaning the place up and when the sheriff brought her home. The man looked ragged. His clothes were rumpled and soiled, the creases long since gone. He had an odor to him and she wondered when he'd showered last. If he'd left immediately during her fight with Badgett, and she assumed he had, then he'd been running for two days now.

"So is this where you explain it all to me?" Jace asked. She tried to fight through the haze left by the pills. She had to get clear-headed enough to get some help.

"Like a movie? Wrap it all up at the end? No." He pulled his service weapon, but didn't aim it at her, just held it loosely; an idle threat.

"Kill me, then?"

"You fucked it up, Deputy. Everything was fine and then you jumped in the middle."

Jace tried to stand and even had he not warned her back down with the gun, she wouldn't have made it up. Her legs were too wobbly. She sat and realized her cell phone had slipped beneath her thigh. Shivering, she grabbed the comforter the sheriff had covered her with. "You mind? They've got me on blood thinners and I'm freezing all the time."

He grabbed the blanket and dragged it off the couch.

She brought a leg up to cover her hands, hoping she could get the phone open and dialed without him seeing. "They're never going to build that trade highway, Chief."

He chuckled but it was a tired sound. "No, they will at some point. American businesses are more than happy to give away their customers' jobs to people somewhere else. I have great faith in that, Salome. They'll build it and I'll have most of the land locked up."

Jace believed Chief Deputy David Cornutt had fed names to Badgett. In the hallway, on Jace's first night, he had talked to Badgett about an advanced CT class and had told the tactics instructor he had a list of possibles. Jace had assumed it was students, but maybe it had been victims, which Badgett then put on the members-only part of the website. Badgett hadn't known anything about the trade highway, but had been looking for land for the Total Force compound.

"But it's not just the trade highway. It's also about Enrique Salazar."

The man cracked a hint of a smile. "You're good, Deputy, I'll give you that. Dillon and Bukowski have been talking up a storm about you. I guess they were right."

"They're good men."

"Yeah, they are."

"Aren't you?" She ran her thumb along the buttons on her phone, searching for the 9. She punched it once.

A slow shrug rolled through his shoulders. "To some degree."

"Badgett, too?"

"Sure. Too zealous, probably, but doing good work."

Jace punched the 1 twice. "But that's not your bag."

"Molesters should be killed, sure, but—"

"But you wanted the land and you realized at some point that the owners of some of that land had some bad apples in their families." Jace hung up her phone, still buried beneath her thigh, and then redialed 911. She hung up again.

"Complete accident," he said. "But a useful one, once I figured it out."

"All boils down to drugs, though doesn't it?"

"Is that the limit of your imagination? Drugs aren't the only thing crossing that border, Deputy. In fact, there are more items going south than coming north."

She frowned.

"The Total Force board isn't the only board I sit on, Deputy. There's also Butler Arms."

"Which is?"

"We assemble weapons. Parts for military rifles. But Iraq and Afghanistan won't last forever."

"And just across the border is an endless war. Supply every cartel and profits just keep on trucking. Doesn't matter that Mexico is going to be a failed state right on the border and that those cartel wars have killed how many law enforcement officers."

"All right, time to be done with all this," Cornutt said.

Surreptitiously, Jace dialed again. "Why the land, if you're interested in the cartel wars?"

Cornutt said, "Because having that land as an end point for tunnels or barns full of easily accessible product is useful. It was a decent plan at one point."

"But now?"

"But now it's gone wrong, I don't know why. Maybe we all

got greedy for our thing. But we damn sure all got sloppy at covering our tracks."

"Damn it, David," the sheriff said. "I thought you were one of the good guys."

The sheriff had come back in, quietly, and something in his face told Jace he'd expected this. Waiting for his chief deputy was why he'd left the door ajar.

"Maybe . . . once," Cornutt said. "But it's been a long time. Maybe as long as your transition from actual cop to politician."

Neither man, Jace thought, seemed surprised at where they both found themselves. Their faces were haggard and tired, and even if they'd had the energy, Jace didn't believe they would have circled each other looking for the advantage. Neither gun came directly to the other man, but rather pointed at the floor, as though, if it came to shots, they'd rather tear up Jace's carpet than each other.

"I hear you," Bukowski said. "So now what?"

"Probably only one of us is leaving here."

"That's not what I want, David."

"Me either, but this has gotten out of control."

"Just put the gun down and let's go on in."

Cornutt shook his head. "I'm not going down for this, Sheriff. I'm too old and too long the cop to go to jail."

"Badgett's taking the hit, David. You don't have to, we can work this out."

Cornutt laughed. "Sheriff, he's a weasel, you know that. He's not talking now but that's only to get himself a decent deal. When it comes down to it, he'll sing like Sinatra."

Sheriff Bukowski nodded. "You knew about it. The dead men."

Cornutt nodded. "Sure. Some were on my orders. I wanted that land." He turned away and banged a hand against the window sill. A tiny breeze, full of late evening air, filled the apartment. "Not really sure what I was thinking, Sheriff. Just wanted to retire at first. Make a few bucks back and forth across the border, retire, and get my pale butt down to the Caribbean or somewhere and be done with this crap."

"It's done now," Sheriff Bukowski said.

Cornutt turned to them and Jace saw it in his eyes. "Yeah."

"David, don't—"

Cornutt raised the gun, but not at the sheriff. Instead, it came up pointed at Jace. The roar of Sheriff Bukowski's .45 was deafening and if Cornutt made any sound when he fell through the open window, Jace didn't hear it.

But she did hear him fall.

He fell and fell and for a second he might have been Thomas over a balcony railing or a puppy crashing through the trees. But when he hit the ground, the sound was exactly the same.

Chapter Forty-Seven

"I didn't piss myself." Jace grinned. She and Rory were at the Zack City Zoo. "With Badgett. I probably should have, I was scared to death."

"You and me both, sister."

"But I wasn't when the chief deputy was in my apartment."

"You're a better woman than I am," Rory said. "I would'a cried like some little sissy girl."

"Maybe."

The zoo was quiet. All the visitors were gone but they had been allowed to stay as long as the zookeepers were finishing up nightly rounds. From the far side of the zoo, the two women heard the elephants trumpet a goodnight to each other. A few responses filtered from out of the primate house but mostly, the place was quiet.

"Ezrin called me yesterday. He's reopening all his investigations. He talked with Chafee and he thinks more Total Force guys will talk to him now."

"Chafee did a good thing," Rory said.

"Quit getting all moony over him," Jace said. "He's not that good-looking."

Rory smacked her lips. "Better than those little donuts."

Jace whacked her on the shoulder and their melancholy laughs faded into the evening air.

"Cornutt always treated me good," Rory said. "I was surprised to see him involved with Badgett."

Badgett hadn't created the pedophile madness alone, Jace knew. There had been someone who showed him the play and someone who had shown that someone and someone before that and before that. And if they looked back far enough, Jace believed, there would be a group of three or four old school cops who'd gotten their bones back in the '40's or '50's and who believed a phone book to the head was pretty much the only way to police.

They walked for a while before Rory spoke up again. The night was getting softer and a sliver of moon had slipped from behind some thin clouds. Just beyond the zoo walls, the desert coyotes sang.

"You hear about Sonny Lee Brook?"

"No," Jace said. She'd been ordered to take at least three weeks off, then come back to light duty until her fingers healed.

"He killed her."

"The woman?"

"Wasn't about her. Turns out she had a four-year-old daughter. The kid is missing."

They stopped at the train. The conductor was waiting for them. With a nod, he indicated they should take a seat.

"Jace, I'm not really sure I wanna ride this train. Doesn't that seem a little . . . I don't know . . . childish?"

"Maybe. I just find it relaxing. After we're done, though, we'll go get a sundae, and then I'm going to need some help writing those tickets for the sheriff. You know, the smoking and gambling."

Rory laughed. "You going to do that?"

"Straight up, sister."

ABOUT THE AUTHOR

A working deputy sheriff, **Trey R. Barker** has published a bit of everything: crime to mystery, science fiction to nonfiction, plays to novels, short story collections to his blog ("Bullets and Whiskey," at www.treyrbarker.com). He spent seventeen years, off and on, as a journalist before moving into law enforcement. Currently, he is a sergeant with the Bureau County Sheriff's Office, the crises negotiator for the regional special response team, a member of the Illinois State Attorney General's Internet Crimes Against Children Task Force, and an adjunct instructor at the University of Illinois (Champaign) Police Training Institute. When he relaxes, it's usually behind his drums or with his camera. A Texas native, he currently lives in northern Illinois with three Canine-Americans.

31901055698403